COMES THE
WAR

COMES THE

WAR

BOOK TWO IN THE EDDIE HARKINS SERIES

ED RUGGERO

A TOM DOHERTY ASSOCIATES BOOK

NEW YORK

This is a work of fiction. All of the characters, organizations, and events portrayed in this novel are either products of the author's imagination or are used fictitiously.

COMES THE WAR

Copyright © 2021 by Ed Ruggero

All rights reserved.

Maps by Jon Lansberg

A Forge Book
Published by Tom Doherty Associates
120 Broadway
New York, NY 10271

www.tor-forge.com

Forge® is a registered trademark of Macmillan Publishing Group, LLC.

Library of Congress Cataloging-in-Publication Data

Names: Ruggero, Ed, author.
Title: Comes the war / Ed Ruggero.
Description: First Edition. | New York : Forge, Tom Doherty Associates
    Book, 2021. | Series: Victory in Europe series ; book 2 |
Identifiers: LCCN 2020042320 (print) | LCCN 2020042321 (ebook) |
    ISBN 9781250312877 (hardcover) | ISBN 9781250312860 (ebook)
Subjects: GSAFD: War stories.
Classification: LCC PS3568.U3638 C65 2021 (print) |
    LCC PS3568.U3638 (ebook) | DDC 813/.54—dc23
LC record available at https://lccn.loc.gov/2020042320
LC ebook record available at https://lccn.loc.gov/2020042321

Our books may be purchased in bulk for promotional, educational, or busi-ness use. Please contact your local bookseller or the Macmillan Corporate and Premium Sales Department at 1-800-221-7945, extension 5442, or by email at MacmillanSpecialMarkets@macmillan.com.

First Edition: February 2021

Printed in the United States of America

0 9 8 7 6 5 4 3 2 1

Dedicated to the American Soldiers and Sailors
Who Lost Their Lives at Slapton Sands, England
April 1944
While Training to Liberate a Continent

Facilis descensus Averno.
The descent into hell is easy.

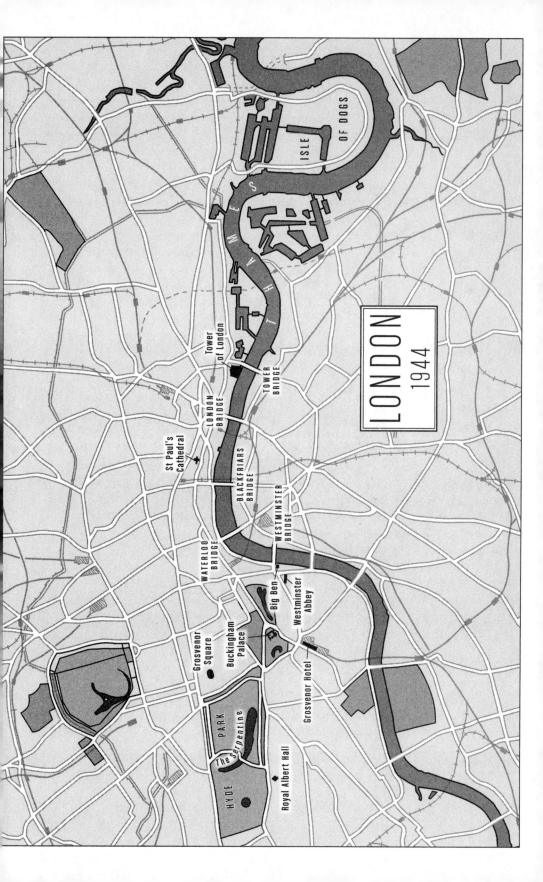

COMES THE
WAR

1

There was a white-helmeted American military policeman at the alley entrance when First Lieutenant Eddie Harkins got out of the staff car. He could see the body about thirty feet in, lying next to some rubbish cans; but there was no crowd, not a single curious onlooker, dead bodies having become all too common in bomb-smashed London. Inside the alley, a man in a dark raincoat squatted near the corpse, while another man stood writing in a pocket notebook.

The MP came to attention when Harkins approached, gave him a snappy salute.

"Who are those guys?" Harkins asked the soldier.

"Brits, sir. Detectives. They said the woman, the victim, is American, so they sent for us. Me and my corporal got here a few minutes ago and they told us to secure the alley. Corporal Quinn is down the other end."

Harkins looked up and down the street, blocks of two- and three-story buildings, the ground floors mostly shops, judging by the signs. Not one with all its windows intact. He wondered where the victim had been coming from or going to.

"They give you their names?" he asked the MP, nodding at the detectives.

"Yes, sir."

Harkins looked at the man, who said nothing.

"Care to share them with me?"

"Couldn't understand them, sir. I just can't get the hang of these accents. Sorry."

Harkins knew how the kid felt. He'd just spent two days in Scotland, waiting for orders, and he'd heard another GI ask, in all seriousness, what language the locals spoke.

He walked into the alley; the detective with the notebook looked up at him.

"You a copper?"

"Yeah. Eddie Harkins. And you are?"

"Just leaving," the man said. "This is one of yours, and happy to hand it over."

Harkins wasn't sure of the jurisdictional issues, but the detectives seemed to be.

The second detective stood up. He was taller than the first one, face sallow, cheeks sunken, like a man with a wasting disease.

"Pulled this card from her pocket," the tall man said. "She wasn't carrying a handbag, or at least we didn't find one. But she had a wallet, like a bloke's wallet."

Harkins took the proffered billfold, an identification booklet inside. Batcheller, Helen. American civilian. The tiny black-and-white photo stapled inside seemed to match the victim, though she looked considerably healthier in the picture. Her occupation was listed as "analyst." Her employer was the Office of Strategic Services, the OSS, which happened to be Eddie Harkins' new home in London.

"You a spook, too?" the detective with the notebook asked.

Harkins was looking down at the body, which lay faceup. The woman was missing her right shoe, the left one was worn at the heel.

"What's that?" Harkins asked, when he noticed the detectives looking at him.

"You with the OSS?" The one with the notebook was talkative, maybe a little pissed off. He wore an old-fashioned fedora, the brim pulled down at a jaunty angle.

"Yeah, but I'm a cop. I mean, I was a cop. Then I was an MP."

"But you're not an MP now?"

"I don't know yet," Harkins said. "I just got here this morning."

"First day on the job?"

"Yep."

"Aren't you the lucky bastard."

Harkins squatted next to the body, examined the wound, one clean slice across the throat. The wide spray pattern of blood on the ground meant the cut most likely sliced both carotids; the killer knew what he—or she—was doing. The victim's hands and sleeves were bloody; she had probably made a futile attempt to staunch the flow and save herself in the few seconds before she lost consciousness. Probably bled out in a minute or two.

"Any theories about where she was coming from or going to?" Harkins asked as he stood.

The man with the notebook said, "That's your problem now, mate."

"Don't be an arse," the tall one said to his partner. Then, to Harkins, "It's just that we've had a lot of back-and-forth over jurisdiction with you Yanks. Tommy here is a little bit tired, that's all."

The tall man held his hand out, and the one named Tommy handed over his notebook.

"Why don't you take a walk, Tommy? I'll catch up in a bit."

Tommy gave Harkins one more sour look, then walked toward the end of the alley.

"Name's Hoyle," the tall detective said, offering his hand. "Detective Sergeant."

"Harkins." The men shook.

"The way it started, this was back in '42, any crime where both the victim and perpetrator were American was handled by your military authorities. If a British civvy was involved, either as victim or perpetrator, we investigated alongside your provost marshal. After a while it got so the American investigators were cutting us out altogether if a Yank was involved. Naturally, some of the fellas resented this. Tommy, for instance."

"I see," Harkins said. And he did. During his time as a Philadelphia cop he'd seen arguments over jurisdiction break into actual fistfights among detectives.

"Well, this victim is definitely yours, so you'll take charge of the remains. Tommy and I will do a sweep of the neighborhood, see if we can scare up any witnesses."

Hoyle wrote something in his notebook, then tore out the page and handed it to Harkins.

"Here's my number. We're at the station at Somers Town. Phone me at this number later today, sooner if you find something."

As Hoyle walked away, Harkins saw the MP at the end of the alley talking to two American officers. A major stepped around the soldier and walked quickly toward Harkins, a captain and a civilian trailing. The civilian was dressed in a rumpled suit and carried a camera. The captain was very tall.

"You Harkins?" the major yelled when he was still twenty feet away.

"Yes, sir," Harkins said, saluting.

"Glad you got my message to get your ass over here. I'm Sinnott; this is Wickman."

Major Sinnott did not offer his hand. Wickman reached forward as if to shake with Harkins, then thought better of it.

That explained the first part of Harkins' morning. He had reported to the reception desk inside OSS headquarters on Grosvenor Street, duffel bag on his shoulder and exhausted from an all-night train ride from Scotland, only to have the duty NCO hand him a barely legible note with an address he read as, "Cramer's Pancreas."

Fortunately the duty driver, a young British woman in the drab uniform of the Auxiliary Territorial Service, deciphered the note and delivered Harkins to Cromer Street in Saint Pancras.

Sinnott was about five ten, same as Harkins, bigger through the shoulders and chest. His uniform, Harkins noted, looked tailor-made, definitely not from some musty quartermaster's bin. When he removed his service cap to wipe his brow, Harkins noted the jet-black hair, slicked back like Clark Gable's. Seemed a little fussy for a crime scene first thing in the morning.

"We have an ID," Harkins said, stepping away from the body as the photographer went to work documenting the scene. "Name's Helen Batcheller."

Sinnott stepped past Harkins and bent over the body, cutting the photographer's line of sight.

"Christ," Sinnott said. "That's a mess right there."

He stepped away, checked the bottoms of his shoes for blood; Wickman did not approach the corpse.

"Know what the *maquis* call that?" Sinnott asked. He made a slashing move across his throat with one thumb. "A Gestapo collar. The Krauts use piano-wire garrotes; tighten 'em up real slow to get the poor bastards to talk."

Harkins wanted to ask what a *maquis* was, but Sinnott never paused to take a breath. A real talker, this one.

"We're going to run this investigation," Sinnott said as he moved farther away from the bloody mess that had been Helen Batcheller. The photographer went back to work.

"What about the provost marshal, sir?" Wickman asked. He was easily six or seven inches over six feet, rail thin with narrow shoulders and long arms. He spoke softly, as if worried about interrupting someone's nap.

"They've got that new branch," Wickman continued. "Criminal investigators."

"Criminal Investigation Division," Harkins said. "CID."

The new office—only constituted in January—was allegedly staffed by trained investigators and responsible for policing the vast numbers of crimes committed by GIs crammed into Britain.

"To hell with them," Sinnott said. "We're going to run our own show, no matter what those CID clowns do. Wild Bill is going to go ape-shit crazy when he hears about this."

Harkins knew "Wild Bill" was Brigadier General William Donovan, legendary head of the OSS, the Office of Strategic Services, America's blandly named spy agency.

Harkins had already held a number of jobs in his twenty-seven months in the Army, but he'd never been, never trained as, and certainly had never volunteered to become a spy or a spy-catcher. Yet here he was, and the folded set of orders stashed in his duffel bag clearly directed him to report to OSS, London Base. Major Richard Sinnott was his new boss.

"You're going to have to survey the area," Sinnott said to Harkins. "Look for witnesses who saw or heard something."

The response that popped into Harkins' mind—because he'd been up for twenty-eight hours—was something like, "No fucking kidding." But he just nodded.

"I can talk to her coworkers and her boss," Wickman said. Eager. He leaned forward, and Harkins wondered if he had a hard time hearing people who weren't also freakishly tall.

"Harkins is going to take the lead on this," Sinnott said. He watched Harkins' face, gauging his reaction to this news.

Wickman looked surprised. After a few uncomfortable seconds, he said to Harkins, "Lieutenant, can you give us a moment, please?"

Harkins walked to the end of the alley near where the same patient MP stood. It was full daylight now, and the soldier was stifling a yawn as Harkins approached. As he expected, the brick walls on either side of the alley carried the conversation between Wickman and Sinnott nearly perfectly. You learned some things growing up in a city.

"Sir," Wickman said, "I'd really like to get a shot at this investigation. Besides, Lieutenant Harkins was supposed to start training right away for his assignment."

"That was before one of our people wound up in an alley with her throat laid open," Sinnott responded. "Besides, Harkins has experience investigating murders."

"I have three years in the Los Angeles Police Department," Wickman said.

"Gold shield?" Sinnott asked. He didn't sound curious, more like he already knew the answer.

"No, sir."

"You drove a desk, right?"

Wickman didn't answer. Sinnott called, "Harkins, come here."

As Harkins approached, the camera's flash turned the lake of Batcheller's blood from deep crimson to black.

"Sir?"

"You conducted a murder investigation last summer, right? In Sicily."

"Yes, sir. But I'm not a trained investigator." Harkins almost said, "I wasn't a detective, either," but it would have been clear he'd been eavesdropping.

"I was a beat cop."

"I heard you have good instincts," Sinnott continued. "Got that straight from Colonel Wilbur Meigs, who was provost over there for General Patton."

Harkins remembered Meigs, a World War One vet who'd come back in the service to lead the provost marshal's efforts to maintain law and order amid the chaos of a combat zone. Back in Sicily, Harkins had spent an unpleasant morning with Meigs pointedly reminding him that supposition, guesswork, and half-baked theories were not the hallmarks of a good investigator.

"He's the one who recommended you," Sinnott said.

"Recommended me for what, exactly, Major?"

Sinnott smiled at him. Probably, Harkins thought, the same way the Romans smiled at a doomed gladiator.

"Don't worry about that yet. For now, I want you working on this murder. The CID guys will probably show up at some point, but I want you to keep after it, too. Don't get in their way, but keep after it."

The three men looked down at the body. Lying on her back, one arm flung to the side and the other across her stomach, Helen Batcheller, late of the Office of Strategic Services, looked small and lonely. But she wasn't inconsequential. She was someone's daughter, maybe a wife, a sister. She was a volunteer, perhaps a critical contributor at OSS, certainly part of the vast footprint of American might come to help save the Old World. And at the end of her too-short life, she was a victim. Now it was up to Harkins to find some justice for her.

Harkins got word that it would be at least an hour before the U.S. Army hospital morgue could send a team for the body. He started pacing the length of alley, looking for clues, pieces of clothing, a handbag, the victim's missing shoe—anything that might give him some idea of how and why she ended up here.

Sinnott grew bored quickly and left, Wickman and the photographer in tow. The MPs stood at their posts, one at either end of the alley, and after a few minutes the duty driver called out to him.

"May I approach, sir?"

Harkins could not remember her name; she was simply the driver who'd been up next on rotation from the motor pool that supported the American Embassy and OSS staff.

"Sure. Can't hurt to have another set of eyes help me."

When the woman drew closer, Harkins saw that she was young, about the same age as his sister Aileen, who would turn twenty-one in September. She wore a loose wool jacket and baggy pants, the bottoms of her trouser legs tucked into canvas leggings. Her face was thin. Like a lot of Brits, she'd probably lost weight since rationing started. Fifty-five months, meat scarce, cheese doled out in tiny bits not much bigger than a sugar cube, endless root vegetables grown in household gardens that might, during peacetime, have been rose beds. The Dig for Victory posters hanging everywhere always showed a colorful bounty that was hard to replicate.

"What's your name?" Harkins asked.

She gave him a British salute, palm out, snapping her heels together.

"Private Lowell, sir."

Harkins returned the salute, then stuck out his hand.

"Harkins."

She hadn't anticipated a handshake and fumbled to remove her leather driving gloves, which made Harkins wonder if British officers ever shook hands with troops. Lowell had blue eyes and fair skin, a spray of freckles across her cheeks and nose. What hair Harkins could see peeking out from under her flat cap was curly, strawberry blond. She could pass for his sister.

"We're going to walk the length of the alley again, see if anything looks out of place, anything doesn't belong here."

"Right. Very good, sir."

The alley was no wider than ten feet, so Harkins and Lowell were practically shoulder-to-shoulder as they walked.

"You know the area around here?" Harkins asked.

"Saint Pancras? Just from driving, sir. I'm from Holloway."

When they reached the body, Harkins half expected Lowell to look away. Helen Batcheller's throat was sliced open, neck muscles and tendons gleaming wet in the dull dawn light. Instead, the young woman squatted down, much like Detective Sergeant Hoyle had done. She kept her knees pressed together demurely, though she wore pants.

"What do you see?" Harkins asked.

"Well, she's missing one shoe," Lowell said. She looked around. "I don't suppose you've found it."

"Nope."

"So maybe she was dragged in here. Bit of a scuffle with the murderer. Lost her shoe that way."

"Could be," Harkins said.

"On the other hand, her clothes are blood soaked, but not disheveled. If there'd been a struggle her blouse would have come untucked."

Harkins squatted next to the body to confirm Lowell's observations.

"You look a little young to have been a cop," Harkins said, standing again. "You an aspiring detective?"

"No, sir," Lowell said, looking up at him. "I just read a lot of Sherlock Holmes when I was young."

Harkins chuckled, but Lowell didn't crack a smile. She hadn't meant it as a joke.

"Yeah, of course," Harkins said.

"You want me to walk the alley?"

"Yes, but if you find anything, don't touch it, okay?"

"Certainly, Lieutenant."

Lowell stood and walked slowly toward the next street, head down, taking her time.

Harkins walked in the opposite direction. The MP—GIs called them snowdrops because of the white helmets—was asleep on his feet. He flinched when he heard Harkins.

"Sorry, sir."

"It's okay. I'm only awake because I'm walking."

Lowell called when the detail from the hospital showed up to retrieve the body. When they met by the corpse, Harkins asked, "Find the shoe?"

"No, sir. Can't imagine where it could be, unless she came here in a car and left it behind."

Harkins thought about a guy he'd helped apprehend in Philadelphia, a serial rapist. When they searched his room they found a stash of women's personal items: shoes, underwear, a few dime-store necklaces. The detective on the case called them trophies, something the bad guy had kept to help him remember—and probably fantasize about—his crimes. Harkins did not share this memory with young Lowell.

There were two GIs with a stretcher, a bored staff sergeant overseeing the detail.

"You seen anybody from CID?" Harkins asked the sergeant.

"What's that?"

"Investigators," Harkins said. "Like detectives."

"No, sir. Nobody here but us chickens."

Harkins scanned both ends of the alley, wondered if anyone had notified CID, wondered how Sinnott had learned about the murder seemingly ahead of everyone else.

"Ask a doc to take a look at the victim for me," Harkins said to the sergeant. He lowered his voice, trying to make it harder for Lowell to hear. "I want to know if she's been raped, assaulted."

The sergeant looked at Harkins, then at the body. He walked over to where the stretcher lay on the ground and unceremoniously hiked up Helen Batcheller's bloody skirt.

"It ain't brain surgery, Lieutenant. Look, her knickers are intact, still pulled up to her waist."

Lowell stepped closer, looked at the corpse, then at Harkins. She nodded her head slightly.

Helen Batcheller was beyond caring about her dignity, of course, but the open-air exam bothered Harkins.

"Okay," he said. He motioned with one hand and the sergeant pulled the skirt back down. One of the GIs produced a wool blanket and covered the body.

After Batcheller had been carried away, Harkins thanked and dismissed the MPs after writing their names in his notebook, then he and Lowell started back to the staff car a half block away. The vehicle, olive drab with a white star on each of the front doors, was the same shade as every other piece of equipment shipped from factories in the States, all of which were running two or three shifts.

"Here we are, sir," she said, looking at him over the roof. "Where to next?"

"Why don't we walk around the neighborhood and see what's nearby, see where she might have been coming from. Pubs, hotels, restaurants, that kind of thing."

"Right," Lowell said. She reached into the car and pulled out a folded map.

"One moment, sir," she said. She crossed the street to where a man in shirtsleeves was sweeping glass off the sidewalk below a faded sign that said GREENGROCER.

The businesses on either side were boarded up. A few doors down Harkins saw a shop where the front door had been torn off. A paper sign fluttering in its place read *More open than usual.*

"They got you last night, I see," Lowell said to the man. He stopped sweeping and leaned on his broom.

"It was the only shop window left on the whole block," the man said, surveying the street. "Don't know how it lasted, but it did. I thought about breaking it meself, just to end the suspense, but the Jerries took me worries away last night."

"Was there a bomb?" Lowell asked.

Although he was no expert, Harkins thought her accent had changed. She sounded more like the shop owner and less like the BBC.

"Couple of blocks over. Six or seven of them, I think. Must have been a lone plane who missed the docks and just dumped his load wherever he could." The Brits were calling these latest indignities the "Baby Blitz," which was smaller than the Luftwaffe's attacks in 1940 and '41, but just as deadly if you happened to be where one of the bombs fell.

A woman came out of the shop wearing an apron, a kerchief covering salt-and-pepper hair.

"Good morning," Lowell said politely.

"We're not open yet," the woman said, none too friendly. "And you need your ration coupons."

She glanced at Harkins, who leaned on the staff car a few yards away.

"I'm sure your Yank could get you a lot more than we have in here."

"Now, Margaret," the man with the broom said. He sounded a little apologetic, although Harkins wasn't sure if he was apologizing to Lowell or his wife.

"I just wanted to ask a few questions about the area," Lowell said. "I'm helping the investigator here and we haven't the petrol to be driving around in circles."

Margaret folded her arms across her chest and gave Lowell the once over, as if inspecting her uniform. Then she turned on her heel and went back into the shop, muttering something about petrol rationing.

"What do you need to know, my dear?" the shopkeeper asked Lowell.

"I'm afraid there's been a woman murdered not too far from here. An American woman. We're trying to figure out where she was coming from, or perhaps where she was going to. Public places, most likely."

Lowell spread out her map on an empty fruit stand and offered the greengrocer a pencil. He ticked off some public places that Batcheller might have visited on her last night: two pubs, a hotel, a concert hall, and a church, all within a half-mile radius.

"Thank you, sir, thank you very much. This has been most helpful," Lowell said.

Lowell showed Harkins the map, and they spent the next hour walking to the various points. Only the church and hotel were open at this hour of the day. The rector hadn't seen anyone fitting Batcheller's description, and the hotel turned out to be a tiny place, a dozen rooms with a sleepy desk clerk.

"I've been on all night," the clerk said when Harkins asked. "Quite a few Yanks coming and going, but all with British girls."

The clerk gave Lowell an oily smile.

"You two need a room?" the clerk asked. "Rates by the hour."

"No," Harkins said. "So you didn't see any American women?"

"Like I said, Yank. All British girls. War-bride candidates, I'm sure."

Harkins looked at Lowell, whose poker-face expression hadn't changed.

"Come on," he said.

They stepped outside into the gray dawn. It wasn't raining, but it wasn't dry, either. The air was filled with mist, a fog shot through with the smell of pulverized masonry.

"Let's come back later when the other places are open," Harkins said. "Maybe we'll find more people out and about, too."

They walked back toward the car.

"So what was that back there, with Margaret? At the greengrocer," Harkins asked.

"Not everyone thinks that women should be in uniform. My mother told me that back in the Great War they had the Women's Auxiliary Army Corps. Some of the men called it 'the Army's groundcloth.'"

"Oh," Harkins said. Soldiers stretched out atop a waterproof ground-cloth when they slept outdoors.

"You've been on a crime scene before?" Harkins asked when they were in the car.

"You could say that, sir. My father was an air raid warden in the Blitz. I helped him pull neighbors from the rubble." She reported this matter-of-factly.

"How old were you?"

"Sixteen when it started, autumn of 1940, turned seventeen on Boxing Day."

When Harkins didn't respond, she added, "That's what we call the day after Christmas."

Harkins thought about his three sisters, whose adolescent years were about dances and boys and schoolwork.

"We used to listen to Edward R. Murrow's reports from London. During the Blitz, I mean," Harkins said.

Lowell kept her eyes on the road, her hands at ten and two on the wheel. She hadn't flinched at the sight of Batcheller's slaughtered corpse, hadn't complained when the greengrocer's wife insulted her, or when the hotel clerk made suggestive comments.

"Must have been bad over here," Harkins said.

Lowell looked at him in the mirror. "Nothing to do but soldier on, I suppose."

Harkins, who'd been feeling a bit sorry for himself for catching this investigation, for his exhaustion, for the basic fact that he wanted to be at home instead of driving around London's gray, battered streets, had to agree.

"I suppose," he said.

2

Lowell maneuvered the Dodge onto a narrow street, stopping in front of an unremarkable building: brick front, four stories, rows of identical windows. Some of the glass was taped—to reduce the prospects of dangerous shards—and some windows were covered with planks. The boards were streaked with rust where the nails holding them had been exposed to the rain, maybe for years.

"Your new home," Lowell said.

There was nothing on the front of the building, of course, to identify it as the headquarters of the Office of Strategic Services, the center for American espionage and counterespionage. There were, however, scores, if not hundreds of Americans in uniform crowding the sidewalks and pouring in and out of buildings up and down the street. Dawn had brought no bright sunlight, and everyone walked head down into the mist that wasn't quite rain.

"I bet I'm the foreigner on this street," Lowell said. "With my accent, I mean."

"Are you on duty the rest of the day?" Harkins asked.

"Yes, sir."

"Good. I'll want you to go back to that neighborhood with me, ask some questions at the pubs the greengrocer identified."

"Well, that's fine with me, Lieutenant, but it's possible I'll get pulled onto other duties. If I'm sitting around and they need a driver for something else, I mean."

"Tell the dispatcher that Major Richard Sinnott of the OSS detailed you for a special investigation, that you're just waiting for me to finish here before our next trip to the crime scene."

"Did he?" Lowell asked. "Detail me, I mean?"

"I just did," Harkins said. "Easier to beg forgiveness than ask permission."

"That's an Americanism I haven't heard before," Lowell said.

"I got a million of 'em."

Harkins got out of the car on the curb side and stepped around the front of the vehicle to cross the street. Like most Americans, he looked to his left for oncoming traffic and nearly stepped out in front of a speeding jeep. The GI at the wheel yelled at him.

"Watch out, ya dumb bastard!"

Lowell rolled down the driver-side window.

"We drive on the left here, sir."

"Right," Harkins said. When Lowell smiled, he corrected himself. "I mean, okay."

Harkins entered the lobby, duffel bag on his shoulder, and presented himself to the duty sergeant, who sat at an ornate wooden desk. The man who'd dispatched him to the murder scene that morning had gone off shift.

"I'm looking for Major Sinnott or Captain Wickman," he said.

"Upstairs, Lieutenant," the sergeant said. "Third floor. Number three-twenty."

Harkins found the room, knocked twice, opened the door. Wickman's office would have made a roomy telephone booth.

"Come on in," Wickman said.

Harkins dropped his bag in the hallway, then squeezed into the space in front of the desk, which was clean except for a stack of ledgers and an adding machine dangling a long roll of paper tape.

"That was a joke, actually," Wickman said. "No one can come into this ridiculous excuse for an office. Let's go to the conference room."

Wickman sat on the desk and swung his long legs around to the front— there was no room to walk around the one piece of furniture—forcing Harkins back into the hallway.

Two doors down they entered a bigger room with a long table and eight or so chairs. The room reeked of cigarettes and sweat, the windows were painted black, the chairs did not match.

Harkins handed over his orders; Wickman read them while Harkins studied his new colleague. He took the captain for late twenties, though his blond hair was already pulling back from an unlined forehead. Wickman had removed his dress coat, and his shirtsleeves came only within three inches of his wrists. He seemed made entirely of elbows and knees.

"Well, you're in the right place, but I'm not sure you're what Major Sinnott requested from personnel." He looked up. "No offense."

"None taken. What did he ask for?"

"An experienced counterintelligence officer, someone who'll be able to track down German agents."

"Is that what I'm going to do?" Harkins asked.

"That's the plan, for now, anyway. You'll train here in England, then go over to the continent at some point. They expect the Abwehr will leave behind spies, locals or people who can pass for locals, to watch our troop movements. Section X-2's job is to catch them."

"Section X-2?"

"Spy-catchers," Wickman said. "But you said you were just a beat cop."

"Pretty sure I didn't say 'just.'"

"Right. Sorry," Wickman said, smiling. "I was a beat cop for a while, too. In L.A. Working toward a gold shield, but got sidetracked."

"The war, huh?" Harkins said.

Wickman shrugged, made a face that Harkins took to mean he didn't want to answer.

"So, any experience with counterintelligence?" Wickman asked.

"I did run across a spy in Sicily. A German spy."

"How do you 'run across' a spy?"

"Almost by accident, to tell you the truth. And he wasn't a very clever spy, either."

"And you think that qualifies you for this job?"

"Absolutely not," Harkins said.

Wickman laughed, showing a gap between his front teeth. "So why did they send you here? Seems like you'd be a better fit for this new Criminal Division."

"Criminal Investigation Division," Harkins said. "CID. Anyway, you heard Major Sinnott say that the Seventh Army provost, Colonel Meigs, recommended me. I guess Meigs thinks an investigation is an investigation, whether you're chasing a spy or a murderer."

Wickman handed Harkins his orders. He shook his head, another GI marveling at the mysterious ways of the United States Army.

"I cannot figure this place out," Wickman said.

"How long have you been here?"

"Not quite two months. I've been promoted, which was good. Just pinned on captain's bars last week, but I'll tell you, this outfit's got me stumped. Nobody seems to know what anyone else is doing. Everyone is just making stuff up as they go along. SNAFU."

"If it makes you feel any better, Captain, I didn't want this job. Never volunteered for it. Would be happy to go back to an MP company."

Harkins was just about telling the truth. The months he'd spent with his military police platoon were a little dull after the murder investigation in Sicily, after he tangled with the German spy. He'd been at least open to the idea of a new job, but Wickman was hardly painting a rosy picture.

"Well, I did volunteer, so I've got no one to blame but myself," Wickman said. He leaned back in his chair, crossed one ankle over the opposite knee, exposing a good six inches of calf that was pale as snowfall. "Anyway, Major Sinnott thinks you're just the right guy for this murder investigation."

"Sorry if I rained on your parade there. Sounds like you wanted to take the lead."

"I did, but it's not your fault. I volunteered for OSS because I thought the work would be interesting, but so far, it's pretty much like what I did at home."

"You were on patrol?"

"Started out on patrol, but they switched me over to administration after I got hurt."

"Line of duty?"

Wickman smiled. "Nothing quite so dashing. I was cleaning the gutters at my mother's house and fell off the ladder. Broke my ankle. Anyway, one of the assistant chiefs found out I'd studied accounting. Turns out I was pretty good with budgets."

"Will you go to the continent to chase spies?"

Wickman started to speak, but before he could say anything the door opened and a colonel walked in. Harkins and Wickman stood.

"Men," the colonel said in greeting. "You going to be in here long?"

"We can clear out if you need the room, sir," Wickman said.

The man was young to be a full colonel. Maybe early thirties, with a long, handsome face and dark hair, uncombed. The circles under the colonel's eyes made Harkins think he wasn't the only one short on sleep.

"Who are you?" the colonel asked.

"First Lieutenant Eddie Harkins, sir."

"You new here?"

"Lieutenant Harkins just arrived, sir," Wickman said. "He's headed for X-2."

"Oh, you're the guy Major Sinnott picked for this murder investigation, right?" the colonel asked.

"Yes, sir," Harkins said.

"I'm Haskell, head of this circus. For now, at least, until I get fired or drop over from a heart attack. What do you know about Batcheller?"

"Not much, sir," Wickman said. "I thought we'd start by talking to her boss."

Haskell looked at Wickman, then back at Harkins, then raised his eyebrows in a "Well?" gesture.

"Looks like there was no struggle," Harkins said. "The killer was quick, knew what he was doing."

Haskell nodded. "Go on."

"I got a list of pubs and other public places in the area and am going back this afternoon, when everything is open again, to see if anyone remembers seeing her. And it doesn't look like she was assaulted. Sexually, I mean."

"You examined her?" Haskell asked.

"Her drawers were in place, sir," Harkins said. "Doesn't mean it wasn't sexual, though, in some way."

Haskell leaned against the conference room table and crossed his arms. Harkins noticed a ring on his left hand. West Point.

"What makes you say that?" Haskell asked.

"She was missing a shoe. We couldn't find it anywhere around. It could be that she came in a car and it fell off there."

"Or?"

"Sometimes perverts like to keep souvenirs of their victims. Jewelry, pieces of clothing. A shoe would do the trick."

Haskell shook his head.

"Jesus H. Christ," he said. "The things people do."

"Yes, sir," Wickman said.

"You've learned a lot in a short time," Haskell said to Harkins.

The comment didn't seem to need an answer, so Harkins kept quiet.

"Seems like Major Sinnott made the right choice for an investigator."

"The CID will get involved at some point, sir," Harkins said. "They're supposed to be trained and they have jurisdiction."

"I guess Major Sinnott wants you to conduct a parallel investigation," Haskell said. "Keep our best interests in mind. Tell him to keep me posted."

"Yes, sir," Harkins said.

Haskell looked around the meeting room.

"Smells like a goddamn locker room in here." Then, turning to Wickman, "Be out in fifteen minutes."

"Certainly, sir," Wickman chirped.

When the colonel left, Wickman said, "You're already making pretty impressive progress."

"I don't know how impressive it is, but I'm asking questions. By the way, I'm keeping that driver I had this morning," Harkins said. "She's sharp."

"She's a motor pool asset, so I think that'll be up to the dispatcher."

"Nah, I already told her to use Major Sinnott's name, tell the dispatcher she's on special duty."

"I just mean that they probably have procedures we should follow," Wickman said. "I mean, if we want cooperation from other agencies."

"Didn't you just say that this is a seat-of-the-pants operation?"

"Well, yeah."

"So maybe the best way to get things done is to be even more seat-of-the-pants than everyone else," Harkins said.

"Hmmm," Wickman said, unconvinced.

"In the meantime, how about you help me get a picture of who Helen Batcheller is. Was."

Wickman stood. Harkins had to lean back to keep eye contact.

"You play basketball?" Harkins asked.

"No. I was a jockey."

Harkins almost said, "Really?" before he saw Wickman's smile.

"Come with me. Leave your duffel bag; we'll get you a place to stay later."

Harkins put his bag in Wickman's tiny office, then they took the stairs down to a second-floor corridor. Harkins could see inside another big conference room, where some long tables held what looked to be various small pieces of machinery or office equipment, everything marked with little cards, like a museum display.

"What's all this?" he asked.

"Oh, stuff the elves make. Bunch of brass coming through today to see a display."

"Elves?"

"That's what we call the guys who work in the basement," Wickman said. "Research and development. Like Santa's workshop, always hammering away at something new. Things we use in the field. I'll show you."

Wickman stepped into the room, where two women in civilian clothes were tidying the displays.

"Okay if we have a quick look, ladies?" Wickman asked, flashing them a big grin.

"Just don't move anything," one of the women said. "We've finally got the labels straight."

Harkins looked down at a large pile of animal feces on one table. The hand-written card next to it said, "Camel dung."

"Strange, huh?" Wickman said. "It's an explosive. Supposedly, you could scatter a bunch on the road, even from the air, and it would look natural. Then a heavy vehicle rolls over it, like an enemy tank, and it blows the wheels off."

"Interesting," Harkins said.

"Major Sinnott loves all this stuff. He always drops in when they're training new people, tells them war stories. Here's another explosive."

He held something that looked like a large piece of high-quality coal.

"You put it in the coal bunker of a train and when it goes into the fire—boom!"

There were tiny radios, palm-sized cameras, a lamp to signal aircraft. Another table held a line of glass vials in racks, like in a high-school chemistry lab. Wickman walked alongside, sweeping his hand over the collection.

"You've got your invisible inks, your various kinds of makeup, your poisons that kill people, other stuff to just make 'em sick. Stuff to dump into a vehicle's fuel tank so the engine seizes up."

"It's like a toy store for spies," Harkins said.

"Exactly. Hence—Santa's elves."

When he reached the door, Wickman stepped out into the hallway, where the same two women stood as if waiting for someone else to arrive.

"Thank you, ladies," Wickman said, same big smile. Neither woman smiled back.

"They can't keep their hands off me," Wickman whispered from the corner of his mouth as the two men made their way to the stairs. When they were outside, Wickman turned toward Grosvenor Square. The big captain was not only long-legged, he also walked fast. Harkins had to step it out to keep up as they waded into the sea of American uniforms.

"Looks like every GI in England is right here," Harkins said.

"Yeah. It'll be better for all of us when we finally do jump across to the continent," Wickman said. "Too many Americans jammed onto this island. About a million, million and a half GIs crowded into a space about the size of Georgia that already had a sizable population. I think we're wearing out our welcome."

Harkins' brother Patrick was a chaplain and paratrooper with the U.S. Eighty-Second Airborne Division and would probably jump into France in the first hours of the invasion that everyone knew was coming. Right now, he was at a training site somewhere in England. Harkins hoped to track him down if he got a few hours to himself.

"So what's the story on that colonel?" Harkins asked.

"Haskell is a West Point Class guy. His dad was a general, and he has a brother who also works for Donovan. He's a good guy, and he has connections that can get us air assets, so we can parachute agents into France. He's sharp. Can't say that about everybody I've run across here."

Harkins had heard stories about the original OSS being a social club for Ivy League dilettantes.

"The first boss was right out of the society pages," Wickman said. "Millionaire banker, Hollywood wife, champagne tastes. He was great at throwing cocktail parties for the toffs in British intelligence. Now, with the rationing, anytime a few Brits get together, seems like all they talk about is food."

"Speaking of food, I haven't had anything to eat since lunch yesterday," Harkins said. "Is there a canteen or officers' mess?"

"Headed there now," Wickman said.

Wickman led Harkins along Grosvenor Street, dodging foot traffic on sidewalks packed with GIs.

"Looks like Market Street two days before Christmas," Harkins said. He'd spent the Christmas of 1943 dreaming of his Philadelphia home while transporting German and Italian prisoners of war from Sicily to North Africa for shipment to the States. On Christmas Eve the dispirited Germans had sung "Stille Nacht" until some blowhard American captain yelled at Harkins to "tell those goddamned Krauts to shut the fuck up."

They were leaving Grosvenor Square at the southwest corner when Harkins remembered something he'd read in *Stars and Stripes,* the GI newspaper.

"Which one of these houses is where John Adams lived?"

"John Adams the president?" Wickman asked. "Why would he have lived here?"

"He was the first American ambassador to England. After the Revolution."

Wickman didn't slow down, but he gave Harkins a sideways glance.

"You and Sinnott will get along great," Wickman said.

"Why's that?"

"He's always dropping little facts like that. You watch; I'll bet it takes him less than five minutes in your first conversation before he mentions that he was a Rhodes scholar."

Just short of a bigger park—Harkins thought it might be Hyde Park—they came to an elegant building wrapped in a ten-foot stack of sandbags layered three deep. Inside, Wickman joined a queue; Harkins joined him and got a glimpse of the largest dining room he had ever seen. The floor, which might have been a dance floor at one time, was swept but badly scuffed. Where there had once been table service, there were now hundreds of tables and four lines of American officers holding cafeteria trays.

In the serving line a civilian woman in a hairnet and stained apron spooned out reconstituted eggs, orange with streaks of green. Harkins followed Wickman down a narrow aisle between tables until they found two chairs. Harkins sat down and immediately started shoveling eggs into his mouth. He hadn't realized how hungry he'd been until they stepped inside the mess, which smelled of bacon and cigarette smoke.

They ate in silence for a while, then Harkins asked, "So what's Sinnott's story?"

"He was on the continent already. France," Wickman said.

Harkins had heard stories of Allied agents parachuting into occupied France to help organize the Resistance.

"So he came back here to do what? Train other people to do the same?"

"Yeah," Wickman said. "But there are rumors, you know? That he got sent back."

"Demoted?"

Wickman shrugged. "I heard he was working with the Resistance down in southwestern France. Moving downed fliers into neutral Spain. He found out that two of his people were feeding information to the Gestapo, exposing other cells."

"That's pretty low," Harkins said.

"Story is, Sinnott killed them both," Wickman said. "Completely unauthorized. People in the OSS love that story."

"Is that what got him pulled out of the field?"

"I don't know," Wickman said. "I figured that working for him would put me in line for something exciting, but it's not panning out so far."

"What does he have you doing?"

"Budgeting. He was pretty happy when I managed to get some money set aside for a special project he's cooking up. In fact, that's what got me promoted. But he won't tell me—or he doesn't know—what will happen to me after the invasion."

"I always ask for the jobs I want," Harkins said. "You don't know until you try."

"How's that working out for you?"

"Hasn't worked at all," Harkins said, smiling. "Not even one time."

Harkins downed his coffee, and when Wickman finished, the two men carried their trays to a window. A GI, sweating through his white T-shirt and apron, took the dirty dishes. Harkins wondered what stories the kid would share if he made it home to some American Legion bar. Most of war, at least as Harkins had experienced it, was a colossal waste of time interspersed with a few minutes of sheer terror.

Harkins followed Wickman out of Grosvenor House, then south and east, away from Hyde Park and generally back in the direction of OSS headquarters.

"How long were you a cop in Philadelphia?" Wickman asked.

"Just over three years."

"You join right after Pearl Harbor?"

"Yeah, but don't make me out as too big a patriot. It was a good time for me to do something different. How about you?"

"I wasn't sure they were ever going to put me back on patrol, so I joined the California National Guard in the summer of '41," Wickman said. "Pearl Harbor comes along and we all went into federal service. My family was dead set against me joining, especially my mother. Pretty sure she was counting on me getting a draft exemption since I was with the PD."

Harkins had a complicated relationship with his own parents—especially with his mother, once she found out that Harkins had helped his sixteen-year-old brother forge a birth certificate, making him old enough to join the navy. Michael was lost at sea when his ship was torpedoed in the spring of 1943. He had just turned eighteen.

Harkins got mail regularly from his three sisters, occasionally from his father and from Patrick, the paratrooper. His mother did not write.

Wickman stopped in front of a two-story building that was, like Grosvenor House, wrapped in a triple wall of sandbags. "This is it."

"This is what?" Harkins asked.

"Where Batcheller worked."

"So I can get background here?"

"You can try," Wickman said. "Maybe talk to her boss."

"Who was her boss?"

"I don't know," Wickman said.

"I thought you were going to tell me about her."

"I just shared everything I know," Wickman said. "This is where she worked."

"You ever been inside?"

"No, but I'm happy to come in with you."

Harkins thought the captain looked hopeful, like teaming up with Harkins might be more interesting than going back to his adding machine. But Wickman's boredom wasn't Harkins' problem.

"Thanks," Harkins said. "But I think I'll go at this alone for now."

"Sure, sure," Wickman said, forcing a smile. "I'll head back to my spacious digs. If I have to go out on some important mission, like escorting some USO showgirls around, I'll leave word with the duty sergeant about how to find your lodgings."

Harkins saluted and Wickman returned the gesture.

"They going to cooperate with the investigation?" Harkins asked as he faced the building.

"My experience?" Wickman said. "You're more likely to get Helen Batcheller to talk—from the other side—than you are to learn anything from the people in there."

"Well," Harkins said. "Nobody said winning the war was going to be easy."

3

Harkins found a reception desk just inside the cramped foyer of what had once been an office building. There were two stairways behind the duty officer's station, one of which was closed off with a hammered-together wooden barrier. That staircase was partially collapsed, the walls above it scorched by a fire that had licked upward to the second floor.

"Bomb came right through the roof," someone said.

Harkins turned to where an American staff sergeant stood, hands on his hips.

"The bomb guys couldn't tell us why it didn't explode completely. Just enough to start a fire and drop the staircase. I heard it sat there for a whole day while they waited to see if it was going to blow up. Then somebody had to defuse it."

"Glad that's not my job," Harkins said.

"You and me both, Lieutenant. What can I do for you?"

"I'm doing an investigation and need some information about a woman, an analyst," Harkins said. "I believe she worked here."

The sergeant was taller than Harkins, and when he tilted his head back just a fraction of an inch, he was looking down his nose.

"Are you with the provost or something?"

"No. Actually, I just got here today, this morning. Assigned to OSS. My timing was poor, I guess."

"How's that?"

Harkins was supposed to be asking, not answering, questions.

"There was an incident last night, and I arrived just in time to be assigned to look into it for my boss."

"What kind of incident?" the sergeant asked.

"Look, Sergeant—what did you say your name was?"

"I didn't say."

Harkins ran his fingers through his hair; he wanted a shower, not a witty back-and-forth.

"There's a woman named Helen Batcheller," Harkins said. "I heard she worked here. I'd like to speak to her boss."

"You have some identification, Lieutenant?"

Harkins handed over his identification book, along with a single copy of the orders assigning him to OSS.

"Who's your boss?"

"Major Sinnott."

"Sorry, sir, I don't know him." The sergeant handed Harkins' papers back to him.

Harkins looked at his watch. It was approaching eleven. He'd slept fitfully on the train from Scotland and hadn't been out of his clothes in three days. His brother Patrick, the priest-paratrooper–Army chaplain, suggested he say a Hail Mary whenever he felt he was losing his temper. Harkins told his brother that the prayer he was most likely to come up with in a tense moment was more along the lines of "Dear Jesus, don't let me kill this guy." Patrick had not laughed.

"Look, Sergeant Whatever-Your-Name-Is, I didn't just wander in off the street to amuse myself. You afraid confirming that Helen Batcheller worked here is going to lose the war for the Allies?"

The sergeant smiled at him, a little power move that pushed Harkins a bit closer to doing something he knew he'd regret, though the sergeant would regret it more.

"What's going on here?"

A man in a shiny but well-tailored suit came down the remaining staircase and approached the security station.

"The lieutenant here says he's assigned to OSS," the sergeant said. "He wants information on someone he thinks works here."

"Helen Batcheller," the civilian said to Harkins. He was about forty, an American with a flat Midwest accent. The cuffs of his shirt were clean but frayed, his mustache neatly trimmed.

"I'm Lieutenant Harkins. Major Sinnott asked me to find out what I could about Batcheller."

"Major Sinnott your new boss?" the civilian asked.

"Yes, sir," Harkins said. "I think so. I've only been here a few hours."

"Sounds like you're having a helluva day." The man put out his hand. "I'm Doctor Reed. Come with me."

The sergeant looked disappointed, and Harkins was tempted to say good-bye with an obscene gesture; instead he just followed the civilian.

"Is it true they found her stabbed to death?" Reed asked.

"How much do you know already, sir?"

"Your Major Sinnott went to Helen's rooms, woke up her roommate, Annie Stowe, who also works here. I guess Sinnott was looking for some clue as to what happened. Anyway, Sinnott told Annie that Helen had been murdered. Stabbed, I think he said."

"Is Annie here now?" Harkins asked, scribbling the names in his pocket notebook.

"No, she's pretty distraught. I don't imagine she'll be around today; maybe tomorrow, either."

"You're Stowe's boss? And Helen Batcheller's boss?"

"Stowe works for someone else. Helen works for me," Reed said, then, "Worked, I guess."

A long hallway on the second floor was lined with office doors. There were no signs indicating what was inside the rooms. Reed pulled a keychain from his pocket and unlocked a door. Inside, six desks were lined up in neat rows. Three men and one woman were at work, bent over papers or typing. Only one of the men looked up.

Harkins followed Reed into a smaller, adjoining office with one desk, a coat rack, and a worn leather settee. When Reed turned on a desk lamp, Harkins saw that the single window was covered by a wooden case. The office might as well have been in the basement.

Reed moved a stack of papers from a straight-backed chair and, because his hands were full, kicked it in front of the desk.

"Have a seat," he said. "You understand there'll be things I can't talk about, right?"

"Okay," Harkins said. "Let's start with some easy stuff. The names I have so far are Helen Batcheller and Annie Stowe. Is that S-T-O-W-E?"

"Yes."

"And your first name?"

"Drew."

"Short for Andrew?"

"Well, my first name is actually Rutherford. Andrew is my middle name. You can imagine why I use a diminutive."

Ivy Leaguers and Rhodes scholars, Harkins thought. *I'll fit right in.*

"So what can you tell me about Batcheller's work?"

"Is it essential that you know all that?" Reed asked.

Harkins sighed. Back when he was a patrolman in Philadelphia, watching detectives work a crime scene, he admired the ones who turned an interrogation into something closer to a friendly conversation. That wasn't happening here.

"Well, first blush—she either got murdered because of her work, or because she was an American, or because she was a woman, or was just in the wrong place," Harkins said. "If I know what she did here, I might be able to rule out some theories, maybe figure who, if anyone, had a reason to hurt her."

"I can assure you that no one here would wish her any harm."

Harkins watched Reed for a moment, waiting for him to answer the direct question.

"Did you have daily contact with Batcheller?"

"Yes, unless I was away from London for something. Helen was one of my workhorses. She arrived in 1942. May, I think. Incredibly talented. Great imagination. She could always come up with a new way to look at a problem, one that no one else thought of."

"What was her field?" Harkins asked.

Reed looked distracted. "Sorry?" he said.

"Well, she wasn't a GI, and I doubt the OSS has Donut Dollies. Did she have some special expertise?"

"Each of us is here because of special expertise, Lieutenant," Reed said, a little proud of himself.

Harkins waited, looked at Reed without blinking.

"Helen was a first-rate economist," Reed said after Harkins stared at him for a long few seconds. "Doctorate from Stanford University."

"So, she worked with, what, budgets and things?"

"Heavens, no. She wasn't a bookkeeper."

Reed said "bookkeeper" like he might have said "streetwalker." Harkins felt the urge to work into the conversation that he'd been a "beat cop."

"She did high-level analysis of various trends," Reed said. When Harkins didn't write anything in his notebook, Reed continued. "She *counted* things."

"Like what?"

"Well, I can't comment on her work in particular, but in general terms—an economist might look at shipping numbers, for instance. It might be an economist who would figure out how many tons of food Britain had to import before the war, and how much those imports fell off once hostilities began. An economist might look at loans between nations or help draft plans for currency stabilization after an Allied invasion. Helen had an expertise in manufacturing. Raw materials, factory output, national productivity, things like that."

Harkins wrote some of the terms in his notebook.

"Look, Mr. Reed," Harkins said.

"It's Professor Reed. Doctor Reed, if you prefer."

I'd prefer to be headed to a nap somewhere, Harkins thought.

"Can you tell me anything else, anything at all about what she was doing?" Harkins said. "Was any of this work controversial? I mean, was she stepping on anybody's toes by looking at all these numbers, these measurements and things?"

Reed rested his elbows on the desk, steepled his fingers in front of his chin. Harkins noticed the frayed cuffs were held in place by gold cufflinks.

"No, no," Reed said. "I don't see how the *work* could have been controversial."

"Meaning?"

"Well, Helen could be a bit *prickly* at times."

"How so?"

"She had a very high opinion of her own products."

Harkins looked up from his notebook, waited for Reed to go on.

"She was also a woman of strong opinions. Opinions she didn't hesitate to express."

"Opinions about her work?"

"About anything," Reed said. "She could debate aspects of her work, or even the work of others. But she could also be very opinionated when it came to political discussions. About American policy vis-a-vis our allies. About postwar policies that are in the planning stages."

"She lock horns with anybody in particular?"

After a pause, Reed said, "No one springs immediately to mind."

Harkins held Reed's gaze, then smiled and said, "Well, perhaps something will come to you. I imagine we'll be talking again. Professor."

Harkins stood, looked at his notebook.

"What about the roommate, Annie Stowe? Is she an economist, too?"

"Well, as I said, Annie Stowe doesn't work for me," Reed said. "But I happen to know she's a mathematician."

"So she's probably really good at counting things, too," Harkins said. He meant it as a joke, but it had sounded better in his head. Reed's only reaction was to lift one eyebrow.

"What does Annie Stowe do?" Harkins asked.

"You'll have to ask her."

"Yes," Harkins said. "I guess I will."

Harkins found Lowell, his driver, waiting for him outside OSS headquarters. She'd parked her car a block away in a lot where a bombed building had been cleared, the rubble pushed to the back half of an open space now filling with weeds.

"Did you get some breakfast?" Harkins asked her.

"Yes, sir. Thank you, sir," she said. "Did you?"

"Got something to eat in the world's biggest mess hall," he answered.

"Grosvenor House," Lowell said. "It was quite the luxury hotel in its time."

"Well, leave it to the Americans to turn it into a feed lot," Harkins said. "Next we'll change the name to 'Lefty's' or something."

Lowell smiled. "What's next, sir?"

"Let's go back to where the body was dumped. See if we can find any witnesses."

Fifteen minutes later they parked the staff car at the end of the alley where Helen Batcheller had been found. There were a few more people out, most heading to work, along with a handful of mothers pushing prams. Harkins and Lowell stopped several passersby, with Harkins quizzing the GIs, Lowell asking questions of the Brits. No one remembered seeing an American woman in the area the previous evening.

The first pub the greengrocer had identified on the map was still locked up tight, but there were lights on in the second, where a sign above the door showed what looked to Harkins like a fat rabbit. The Resting Hare.

Harkins tried the door, which was locked, but he could see inside where a man in shirtsleeves was sweeping. Harkins knocked.

"You here for your mate?" the man asked when he opened the door. He looked somewhere north of sixty, with a thick shock of white hair.

"What's that?" Harkins asked.

"The major. He's sleeping off his night back in the storeroom. Not his first time, either. I don't mind, but the owner isn't thrilled."

Harkins stepped inside the pub, which was cheerful in spite of the fact that all but two of the windows were boarded up. Chairs sat upside down on the few tables, and the room smelled like disinfectant and beer.

"Who are you?" Harkins asked.

"Nelson," the man with the broom said.

"Any relation to Lord Nelson?" Lowell asked, grinning and making conversation.

"Not that I know of," he answered, smiling at the young woman. "Though my brother's middle name is Horatio. Parents had a sense of humor."

"You say there's an American?" Harkins asked. "Sleeping here?"

"Right down that hallway," Nelson said, pointing. "Mind your step. It gets a bit narrow. We used to have a shed out back, but there's an Anderson shelter out there now. Have to use every square inch indoors for storage."

Harkins motioned for Lowell to wait in the main room while he stepped into the hallway, squeezing past stacked crates of empty liquor bottles and a pile of what looked like rolled canvas. A door at the end of the hallway was propped open, showing a small, fenced-in dooryard, the cramped space completely filled by a half-submerged shelter of galvanized steel. Behind him, Harkins heard Lowell laugh at something the old man said.

A door on his left was marked WC. On his right another door was partly closed. Harkins pushed, and it opened just a little more before bumping into a pair of GI shoes. He leaned around to see inside.

An American officer sprawled on three seat cushions lined up haphazardly on the floor, his feet hanging off one end, head cradled on his bunched dress coat. On the jacket Harkins could see a major's gold oak leaves, the silver wings of a pilot, and a stain on one sleeve that reached from the cuff to above the elbow. The room was only a few feet wide, and the sleeping major—who looked to be a big man—was curled in the fetal position. Shelves on either side showed dusty glassware and some cleaning supplies. The space reeked of vomit, body odor, and liquor.

Harkins had rousted a lot of drunks during his time as a patrolman, and he knew they were unpredictable. Some woke up happy and cooperative; some woke up swinging. He leaned back into the hallway and kicked the bottom of the man's foot.

"Hey," Harkins said. The major did not stir; Harkins looked closely to confirm that he was breathing.

Lowell came down the hall and peered into the room. "Blimey," she said.

Harkins motioned her back into the pub's main room and followed her. Nelson had finished sweeping and was taking chairs off the tables, putting them back on the floor.

"Has he been here all night?" Harkins asked.

"Yes," Nelson said. "Came in around ten, ten thirty, and was still here when I started closing up around midnight."

"Was he by himself?"

"At the end of the evening, yeah. But he'd been in here earlier with a woman. An American woman."

Harkins felt a little jolt of adrenaline. Nelson seemed to come into sharper focus.

"Can you describe her?"

Nelson stepped behind the bar, pulled an apron from a hook and tied it around his waist.

"She was about as tall as your friend here," Nelson said, indicating Lowell. "Older though. In her thirties, maybe. A bit heavier."

"What was she wearing? Do you remember?"

"Looked like she was dressed for work. Office work, or a bank."

Harkins produced his notebook, penciled in the times Nelson had given him, then pulled Batcheller's identification book from his pocket and showed Nelson the tiny photo stapled inside.

"This her?"

"Looks like her," Nelson said. "Yes."

"Were they drinking together?"

"He was; she wasn't. Drinking, that is."

"So she left earlier than he did?"

"No," Nelson said. "I mean, yes. I mean they left together the first time; then he came back by himself. He was drinking faster on the second go-around. Alone, too."

"What time did the two of them leave?"

"I'm not sure. I try not to look at the clock too often. Makes the evening go too slowly if I'm always checking the hour."

Harkins looked at the timeline he'd drawn on a notebook page. "So they came in together, the first time? When was that?"

"Half eight, I'd say."

Harkins looked up, and Lowell said, "Eight thirty."

"You're the interpreter, then?" Nelson asked her. Again with the smile. The old guy was flirting with her.

"And then they left together and he came back alone around ten, ten thirty," Harkins said.

"Sounds about right."

"Any idea how long he was gone the first time?"

"Doesn't seem that long," Nelson said. "I remember thinking that if he walked her home, she must live close by. Maybe fifteen, twenty minutes."

Harkins wrote "2130" in his notebook, the best guess so far as to when the major and Batcheller left together.

"He's been in here before last night, you said."

"Yeah, and he's slept it off here a few times, too. Bad habit, but a nice fella. Name's Fred. Don't know his last name. I do think he's got a bit of a problem, though. Drinks until he passes out. A lot of the pilots, RAF and American, are hard drinkers."

Harkins looked around the room, which might hold forty people if they stood close to one another. He rolled his head on his neck, felt an ache creeping up to the base of his skull, a throbbing from lack of sleep.

"Any other Americans in here during that time?" Harkins asked.

"A few, at different times of the evening, I would think," Nelson said. "The major and his friend didn't talk to any of them, at least that I saw."

Harkins paused, but no other question came to mind immediately.

"May I?" Lowell asked, looking at Harkins. He motioned with an open palm.

Lowell turned to Nelson. "Were they friendly with each other? The major and the woman, I mean."

"Seemed like they knew one another, like they were on friendly terms," Nelson said. "But I don't think they were a couple, if that's what you mean."

Harkins walked back down the narrow hallway. The major—first name Fred—had not stirred. Harkins tried kicking him on the bottom of his foot, then again, a little harder. Nothing.

"Get me a pitcher of water," Harkins directed Lowell, who watched from the main room.

When she returned with a small carafe, Harkins emptied it on the major's face. The drunk scrambled to get upright, pushing off the floor with both hands and banging his head on one of the storage shelves.

"Whatcha do that for?" he complained, rubbing the top of his skull. He seemed to have trouble focusing. Harkins saw a flask partially hidden by the major's rolled-up uniform coat. There was a chance the pilot was still drunk.

"I need to ask you a few questions," Harkins said.

"Who are you?"

"Lieutenant Harkins. I'm investigating a crime and I need to ask you a few questions. Come on, get up and come into the other room."

Harkins held out his hand; the major reached for it and missed.

"Jay-sus," Harkins said. "How much did you have to drink?"

The major blinked his eyes once, twice, then showed a satisfied smile. "I can't drink all they make," he said. "But I got 'em working nights."

Behind him, Harkins heard Lowell chuckle.

Harkins turned, said to his driver, "Give me a hand here, would you?"

The two of them squeezed in, shoulder-to-shoulder—and each took one of the major's hands, pulled him to his feet. He wobbled, caught himself on the doorjamb, then took a step forward.

Harkins had been right; the major was a big man. At least a few inches over six feet, and probably handsome before his night of excess. This morning his hair was matted, his uniform dirty and disheveled, his breath like exhaust from a dying engine.

Lowell pulled a chair out onto the floor of the main room and the major fell backward into the seat, nearly toppling it.

"What's your name, sir?" Harkins asked.

The man's head drooped onto his chest and he leaned forward, threatening to fall again. Harkins put one hand on each of the big man's shoulders and nudged him to the seatback.

"Your name?" Harkins asked again.

Lowell came out from the back room with the major's uniform coat, holding it so Harkins could see the row of ribbons below the pilot's wings. One of the awards was a Purple Heart; the major had been wounded in combat.

Harkins took the coat and rifled the inside pockets. There was a folded sheaf of typewritten pages on one side. Harkins flipped it open, hoping to find a clue as to the man's name, but the top sheet was just a list of what looked like German names with some dates and a few columns of long numbers. There were no headings on the columns, and the other pages— there were ten in all—looked mainly the same. At the bottom, a handwritten note said, "Copy 1 of 2."

Harkins rolled the stack like a newspaper and stuck it in his back pocket.

In the major's other pocket Harkins found a paybook. He held up the picture stapled inside, then tipped the drunk up by the chin to compare. The man in the photograph looked ten years younger than the wreck in the chair, though the date stamp on the picture said, MAY 1942.

"Our friend here has had an uphill paper route," Harkins said.

"Pardon?" Lowell asked.

"Cushing, Frederick James, U.S. Army Air Forces," Harkins read from the book. "Major Cushing had a rough night, maybe a few rough nights."

Harkins leaned forward and into the man's line of sight.

"You with me, Major Cushing?" Harkins asked. No response.

Cushing belched loudly.

"We're going to have to take him somewhere he can sober up," Harkins said. "I'm going to want to talk to him when he comes around."

Cushing lifted his head and mumbled something. Harkins leaned in far enough to hear Cushing say, "I don't feel so good." Then the major vomited on his own legs. Harkins jumped back, but not before his hands and feet were splashed with the contents of Cushing's stomach.

"Shit!" Harkins said.

Cushing slumped forward so that his chest was almost on his thighs. It didn't seem possible, but he didn't fall out of the chair.

"Can you please get him out of here before he makes a bigger mess?" Nelson asked, more sympathetic than angry.

"Bring the car around," Harkins told Lowell, who hurried out the door.

Nelson went to the back of the pub and returned with a bucket and mop. He pulled a rag out of the soapy water, wrung it out, and handed it to Harkins.

"Thanks," Harkins said. "Sorry about the mess."

"Oh, he's not the first one to get sick in here," Nelson said. "I feel sorry for the man. Those pilots deal with a lot. Dangerous work. One of the RAF blokes told me that on some raids they might lose a quarter of the bombers that go out."

Everything Harkins knew about the Allies' massive bombing campaign against Germany came from newsreels and air force press releases. If he believed what he heard and read—which he decidedly did not—everything was going swell and the Germans were being bombed back into the Stone Age and the war would be over by autumn. Yet the British hadn't given up during the Blitz. Why would the Germans be any different?

Harkins cleaned himself up as best he could. When Lowell came back after parking the car in front of the pub, Major Cushing was still defying gravity, still in the chair, his upper body bent forward and resting on his thighs.

Lowell rinsed another rag and tried to get the worst of the mess off Cushing's legs.

"I can't bring the car back to the motor pool with the seats covered in puke," she said.

Nelson went into the back and returned with a panel of cloth from a blackout curtain. He went outside and spread it on the backseat of the car, then he helped Harkins and Lowell carry Cushing out.

"Has anyone else been around asking questions?" Harkins asked Nelson. "American investigators?"

"I thought you were the investigator."

"So far," Harkins said. "There may be more."

Lowell was in the driver's seat, and when Harkins got in the front passenger side she asked, "Where to, sir?"

"It's going to take a while for him to sober up," Harkins said. "And I don't want him running off before I get a chance to talk to him again, since he was one of the last people to see Batcheller alive."

"There's a stockade, sir," Lowell said. "If that's appropriate."

"Maybe they have a drunk tank," Harkins said.

Eddie Harkins was only mildly surprised to learn that the American Military Police in London had established four drunk tanks, the largest of them capable of housing one hundred and fifty enlisted men, with a separate facility for up to twenty officers.

"This town is lousy with GIs on a weekend," the sergeant on duty told Harkins when he asked about holding a prisoner for questioning. "Last month we had a Friday payday and a full moon. *All* the crazies were out."

Fortunately for the still-intoxicated Major Frederick Cushing, it was a slow night and the officers' drunk tank, at least, was empty. Harkins buttonholed two big MP privates to help Cushing to his cell. He made sure the major was not in danger of choking on his own vomit, then had Lowell drive him back to OSS Headquarters on Grosvenor Street, where Major Sinnott was waiting for him.

"You look like shit," Sinnott said as Harkins climbed the stairs. He'd been hoping to grab his duffel bag, find his quarters and get a shower, maybe fit in an hour of sleep.

Sinnott, in contrast, had obviously changed into a fresh uniform since Harkins saw him at 0630. He did not look rested, but he was clean.

"You smell, too," Sinnott said when Harkins closed the distance.

"I was dealing with a drunk," Harkins said.

"I heard you briefed Colonel Haskell. I want all information to come through me."

"Yes, sir," Harkins said. "He asked me point blank what I knew, so I answered his question."

Sinnott waited for more, but Harkins kept his mouth shut. After a few seconds, Sinnott smiled, but it wasn't especially friendly.

"Sure, okay, I get it. Can't say 'no' to the man's face. Just, from now on, try to get the information to me first. Got it?"

Harkins nodded. "Right."

"Did anybody from CID ever show up at the scene?"

"No, sir."

"Figures," Sinnott said. "Guy named Blair called here. He heard we were at the scene, wanted to know what we learned. I told him I'd get back to him as soon as possible."

"You want me to brief them?"

"No. I don't want you to give them anything. They want us to do all the work, hand it to them on a platter. To hell with that. I want you to run with this as far as you can, as if you're the principal investigator."

Harkins figured that at some point this—stepping on CID jurisdiction—would come back to haunt them; it didn't seem to worry Sinnott.

"So, where have you been this morning?"

"Went back to the neighborhood where the body turned up," Harkins said. "Found a guy who was with Batcheller last night."

"Where?"

"A pub. The bartender saw this guy—his name's Cushing, a pilot—the bartender saw them together early in the evening. Then they left together and Cushing came back to the same pub a little later. The timeline works and the pub isn't far from where the body was."

"What did this Cushing say?"

"Nothing," Harkins said. "He was dead drunk when we found him, passed out in a tiny storeroom at the back of the pub. I tried questioning him, see how his story compared to the bartender's, but he only came around long enough to throw up on himself and on me. I took him to the drunk tank at Finsbury Park so I can question him when he sobers up."

"This bartender hear what they were talking about?"

"No. He said they appeared to know one another, but weren't a couple," Harkins said. "And I found this in Cushing's coat."

Harkins pulled out the rolled sheaf of papers he had taken from Cushing and offered it to Sinnott. The major studied the first page, then flipped through the rest.

"Any idea what we're looking at there, sir?" Harkins asked.

"This list on the first page—these are German cities," Sinnott said. "A bunch of them in the Ruhr, where their heavy industry is. Then there are some dates, or ranges of dates. I don't know about the numbers in these other columns."

Sinnott folded the papers, tapped them on his leg, then opened them again.

"You said Cushing is a pilot, right? These could be targets, in which case there's no way he should be carrying something like this around with him. It's most likely classified."

"I'll go back in a few hours, see if he can talk. I'll ask him then," Harkins said, holding out his hand.

"I'll hang on to these," Sinnott said. "Maybe Batcheller's boss will recognize this as her work. They might be classified, and you don't have a security clearance yet."

"Okay, sir," Harkins said.

"Wouldn't that beat all if you got your man in your first three hours on the job?" Sinnott said.

"Probably a little early to be celebrating yet," Harkins said.

"Well, just don't make this any more complicated than it has to be," Sinnott said. "This murder has already attracted attention from the big brass. We don't need this hanging over our heads while we're in the final stages of preparation for the big show."

"The big show?"

"The invasion, son," Sinnott said. "Jumping the channel. The adventure of our lives."

Sinnott's eyes were wide; he was genuinely excited.

"Think about it," Sinnott said, clapping Harkins on the shoulder. "A million men, maybe more, going into righteous battle to crush one of history's most evil regimes. And we get to be part of it."

Sinnott squeezed Harkins' upper arm. "It's a great time to be alive, son."

A remarkably easy time to get killed, too, Harkins thought.

"Yes, sir," he said. "But in the meantime, I'm going to change uniforms, maybe get a shower, before I go back to see Major Cushing."

"Yes, yes, of course," Sinnott said. "Captain Wickman got you all set up with a flat? Quarters somewhere?"

"I think so, yes, sir. I just have to find him."

"Don't expect too much. Probably a shared room in a cold-water flat."

Harkins hadn't been expecting the Ritz, but he had been hoping for hot water.

"You can't imagine how surprised I was to arrive at Oxford, one of the most prestigious universities in the world, and found out there were no hot-water showers. Just ancient, cold-water bathtubs."

Sinnott studied Harkins for a moment, and Harkins knew he was supposed to ask about the major's time as a Rhodes scholar.

"Anything else, sir?" Harkins asked.

"No," Sinnott said. "Come find me later if you learn anything interesting from this pilot."

"Right."

Sinnott still held the rolled sheaf of papers Harkins had taken from Cushing. He tapped Harkins on the chest with the roll.

"And get yourself cleaned up, Lieutenant. This is an elite outfit you've joined, so try to look the part."

4

Once she was back in the motor pool, Pamela Lowell cleaned the vomit from the staff car. Very little of the mess had gotten on the seat, thanks to the blackout curtain Nelson had given her. Lowell spread the panel on the rear end of the car, which the Americans called a trunk, to let it dry completely. She was pretty sure it would come clean with a good brushing. She had no idea what she might use the material for, but big pieces of cloth, even rough, cheaply made segments, had become quite valuable after five years of clothes rationing. Throughout the whole of the war so far, the only new clothing Lowell had managed to lay hold of, besides undergarments, were her uniforms.

"Where'd you get that?"

Lowell turned to see her team leader, Corporal Edith Moore.

"Used it to protect the seats. A Yank we transported had thrown up on himself and I didn't want the car getting dirty."

Moore, who liked to say she was a stickler for cleanliness, had more than once kept drivers long after their shift to clean vehicles. She rubbed the fabric between her fingers. "I asked where you got it."

"At the pub where we picked up the American," Lowell said.

Moore was only a few years older than Lowell, pretty, with a slight build and dark hair of which she was especially proud. When she was off duty she used red lipstick to give herself a Cupid's bow mouth, like a film star.

Moore looked up from the fabric and smiled. "Was it a detail for a Yank, too?"

Lowell nodded. All the drivers, most of whom in this pool were women, wanted to drive Americans, because they had access to the most fabulous food. A couple of times Moore had pulled drivers from choice details and inserted herself into the coveted spot. Lowell wanted to continue driving for Lieutenant Harkins, and he wanted her as his driver, too, but she couldn't overplay her hand.

"An investigator. Policeman. A Lieutenant Harkins."

"And what was he investigating?"

"A murder. Some poor American woman got her throat slashed."

"Sounds more interesting than anything else going on around here," Moore said. "Driving brass back and forth to Marble Arch so they can run down to the coast or out to East Anglia to count bloody airplanes all day."

Lowell doubted that Moore had driven anyone to the train station lately; she gave all the worst details to the youngest drivers. Or to the women she didn't like. Some drivers gave Moore gifts—trinkets they'd gotten from their American boyfriends—as a kind of tribute to avoid the worst details.

Lowell opened the back door of the staff car and brushed the seat with a dry rag. She had already cleaned the whole car and now was just trying to look busy. Moore leaned into the opposite door and sniffed loudly.

"Still stinks," she said. "Go over it again."

"Yes, Corporal."

Moore stood with her arms folded as Lowell retrieved a bucket and rags.

"Is he nice?" Moore asked when Lowell returned.

"Who?"

"Don't play daft with me," Moore said. "Did the Yank give you anything? Food? Chocolate? Fags?"

"No, Corporal," Lowell said.

"I bet he wanted to give you something," Moore said.

Lowell tried to keep from looking up but failed. Moore smiled and made an obscene gesture with her fist. When Lowell didn't react, Moore laughed.

"Oh, come on, Lowell. You're going to have to give it up someday. Might as well be to some rich Yank."

Lowell had gone out with exactly two GIs but had never gone beyond a chaste kiss good-night with either of them.

"You say 'yes, sir' enough all day eventually you're going to say 'yes, sir' at night, too," Moore said.

Lowell bent into the car so as to avoid Moore's glare and so didn't see their section sergeant, Wallace, come up behind her.

"What's so funny?" Wallace asked.

Lowell ducked out of the car; Moore dropped her arms to her sides.

"Oh, just having a bit of fun with young Lowell, here, Sergeant Wallace."

Wallace looked at Moore, then at Lowell. The sergeant wasn't much for fun.

"So now it takes two of you to clean out the back of a bloody staff car?" Wallace said in a tone that implied she did not want a response.

Wallace and her husband had owned a farm in East Anglia, but the husband lost his draft exemption and got called up after the Yanks paved over the farm to build one of their airstrips. He was killed in North Africa and Sarah Wallace, childless, joined the ATS to get away from her shrunken farm and vivid memories.

"Dispatch got a message that you're detailed to an American lieutenant," Wallace said to Lowell. "You drove for him this morning when he started investigating a murder. They want you back in an hour."

"Pardon, Sergeant," Moore said. "Shouldn't we use the regular rotation, the next driver on the duty roster?"

Wallace chewed the inside of her lip, which she did when she was annoyed.

"Look, Moore, if it turns out to be a plum and the Yanks don't care, we'll give your other girls a chance, too, all right? Right now, the Yanks want her."

"Some bloody Yank lieutenant gets to mess with our duty roster?"

Wallace exhaled. She'd been in Moore's company for three minutes and she already looked exhausted.

"It's a major, actually," Lowell ventured. "Major Sinnott."

"Who the hell is Major Sinnott, now?" Moore demanded.

"Lieutenant Harkins' boss," Lowell said. "I think Major Sinnott is in charge of the investigation."

"All right," Wallace said. "Whichever one it is, let him know that you're a dedicated driver now. When they release you, you're back on the regular duty roster. Keep Corporal Moore apprised of what you're doing."

"Yes, Sergeant," Lowell said.

Wallace walked away without saying anything else.

"Aren't you the clever one?" Moore said. "You didn't have any trouble remembering that major's name, now did you?"

Lowell had the assignment, should probably let it go at that, but Moore's pettiness was just so unnecessary.

"I didn't make it up, Corporal," Lowell said. "That lieutenant really did request me as a driver."

"Did you promise him something, Lowell? Maybe you're thinking he's the one who'll finally breach the walls of your precious, frigid little castle."

"It's not like that," Lowell said. "I—I . . . it's not like that."

She wanted to say she'd helped Lieutenant Harkins, but she wasn't sure that was true. Mostly, she *wanted* to help.

"I—I—I," Moore mocked. "Your motives are pure, right? Hard to imagine how you put up with the rest of us mere mortals."

When Lowell didn't respond, Moore huffed, "Clean this bleedin' car again before you go anywhere, you hear me?"

"Yes, Corporal."

When Moore walked away, Lowell plunged the rag back into the soapy water, then wrung it out, twisting and squeezing the cloth until her knuckles went white.

Harkins called the Somers Town precinct and left a message for Detective Sergeant Hoyle. He left Wickman's office number and said he'd call back.

Wickman had left an envelope for Harkins with the address of his rented flat, which was located about a half mile from OSS headquarters on a narrow alley off Wimpole Street. The skinny buildings reminded Harkins of the brick rowhouses in his Philadelphia neighborhood, except that five houses on one side of this street had been reduced to piles of shattered brick, charred wooden beams, and splintered furniture.

Harkins pressed the bell at number eleven, and when he didn't hear any ringing inside, he knocked. A moment later a woman in a blue dress opened the door.

"Good evening," she said.

"Mrs. Ludington?" Harkins asked, referring to Wickman's note. "I'm Lieutenant Harkins. I've been told I have a room here."

"Yes, yes, of course. The new Yank. Do come in."

Mrs. Ludington was in her early thirties, Harkins figured, dark hair pulled back tightly, bright eyes that picked up her smile, which looked genuine. If she was upset about playing landlord to an American, she hid it well.

"Tell me your name again," she said.

"Harkins."

"Got a first name, love?"

"Eddie. Eddie Harkins."

"An Irish American, then. The last fellow had a Greek name. So many nationalities in your American army. London has become quite colorful these last few years."

Harkins wasn't sure what she meant by colorful, since the gray weather and the piled-up rubble and even the ashen faces of Londoners all shared the same hue.

"Yes, ma'am," he said.

"Oh, please don't call me 'ma'am,'" Ludington said, smiling. "I'm not that much older than you and, besides, that's what one calls the Queen. Call me Beverly."

"Chat with the Queen a lot, do you?" Harkins asked. "Beverly."

"Aren't you the wit," she said, smiling.

They were in a tiny foyer, so narrow that Harkins had to hold his duffel behind, rather than beside his leg.

"This way, then," she said. When she turned Harkins saw that her left arm below the elbow was missing. The back of her dress had been mended, maybe taken in. A whole nation on a forced diet.

A door on the second-floor landing was open, and Harkins got a glimpse of bookshelves, stuffed beyond capacity with volumes and papers. There were piles of books and magazines on the floor, and a lone wingback chair, a floor lamp beside.

"You're a reader," Harkins said.

She turned on the stairway, right hand on the wall for balance.

"Yes, a librarian, too, though not all of those books are mine. I'm storing a number of them for a neighbor whose house was badly damaged."

"I saw where a few houses on your street got knocked down," Harkins said.

"All that happened in one night. September tenth, 1940."

Harkins didn't know what to say. Folks back in Philadelphia were upset about gasoline rationing, which meant no weekend drives to Atlantic City.

On the third floor, Beverly opened the door to a narrow room. The single window framed a view of rooftops and chimneys while a set of bunk beds took up most of the space. The bottom bunk was made with a GI blanket, the top rack held a mattress and a pile of his roommate's uniforms.

"You'll be in here with Lieutenant Wronecki," she said. "Polish fellow, with the RAF. Lovely manners. Not around all that much these last few weeks."

Harkins thought about Sinnott's comment about the upcoming Big Show. All these rented flats would be empty soon enough.

"Is there a shower?" Harkins asked, self-conscious of his odor.

"Oh, I'm afraid not, love. Shared bath on the first floor has a tub and running water."

"Okay, that'll be fine. Thank you."

She smiled at him and turned back down the stairs. Harkins wondered if there was a Mr. Ludington.

He stacked Lieutenant Wronecki's gear neatly on the bottom bunk, then emptied his duffel onto the mattress. The sheets at the foot of the bed were folded neatly, but were the color of weak coffee. One pillow had a bloodstain on the corner.

Harkins took a few minutes to arrange his uniforms, hanging a few on a hook on the back of the thin door. He stripped to his T-shirt, trousers, and socks, threw his small towel over his shoulder, and opened his shaving kit. There was a sliver of soap he'd been nursing for nearly a month.

Behind the stairs on the first floor he found a water closet just bigger than the toilet bowl. The next room was nearly filled by a small bathtub. Someone had painted a line on the inside. On the wall beside was a printed handbill that said THE EIGHTH ARMY CROSSED THE DESERT ON A PINT OF WATER A DAY PER MAN: DO YOUR BIT.

"Having a bit of a drought."

Harkins hadn't heard Beverly come up behind him.

"Is that what the line's for?" Harkins asked. "It's a fill line?"

"Exactly," she said. "They say the King gets by on one shallow bath a week."

"Well," Harkins said, "it hasn't been a week since my last bath, but I did have a guy vomit on me this morning, so I was hoping to get cleaned up."

"I'm sure we can make an exception," Beverly said. "In you go."

She went back down the hallway and Harkins closed the door and turned on the tap. The water wasn't as cold as it had been in his last shower, at a transit camp in Scotland, but it was cold. Probably no water heaters in these old houses. He stripped and stepped in, lowering himself like a baseball catcher. He had just scooped some water onto his face and hair when Beverly opened the door and came in with a bucket.

"Here you go, then. I'd been heating this up for my own bath, but I'll have time later on."

Harkins covered himself with his hands and watched as she lifted the heavy bucket with a strong right arm and expertly tipped it into the tub. Not a drop spilled on the floor.

"Be right back," she said. "Got another on the gas."

The water that sloshed around Harkins' feet wasn't hot, but it was warm. He sat on the edge of the tub and draped his towel over his midsection.

Beverly was back in less than a minute, hauling an even larger bucket. When she'd emptied it into the tub, she looked at Harkins.

"Sorry if I embarrassed you," she said.

"Uh, startled more than embarrassed," Harkins managed.

"I was married. Had three brothers. I'm probably not as bashful as your average English girl."

"I appreciate the hot water," Harkins said.

"Right. Enjoy your bath, Lieutenant."

5

Eddie Harkins managed just forty-five minutes of sleep between his luke-warm bath and Lowell reappearing at his new quarters, as he'd instructed. On the five-mile ride to the military police barracks he fell sound asleep in the back of the staff car.

"We're here, sir," Lowell said, waking him.

The jail was in a converted warehouse that squatted on an entire city block; the building did not have a single window. Inside, the duty sergeant sat at an ancient table, a small lamp beside him throwing a weak circle of light. He handed Harkins a clipboard with a visitors' sign-in sheet. One column was marked AGENCY, and all of the visitors that day had noted that they were from various military police commands, the Judge Advocate General, or CID. Harkins left the space blank next to his name.

The sergeant took Harkins to the cell block, which was somehow even darker and more depressing. They passed a small handwritten sign that said *Officer Country: Luxury Suites Available!* Only one cell was occupied, and in it, Major Frederick Cushing lay on a narrow cot, fully dressed, with one arm across his face, one foot on the floor.

The jailer on duty unlocked the cell and dragged in a wooden folding chair, the back stenciled with the crossed pistols of the Military Police Corps. Harkins dragged the seat closer to Cushing, who had not stirred. There was a bucket beside the bunk, no sign of vomit in it.

"Major Cushing," Harkins tried.

The man reeked of alcohol processed as sweat, a stench that took Harkins back to his parents' living room, Sunday mornings with his Uncle Jimmy passed out on the couch, sometimes on the floor. Mary Theresa, Harkins' mother, showed her displeasure with her youngest brother by refusing to speak to him, though she always made him breakfast and didn't kick him out.

Harkins reached over and shook the pilot's shoulder. Cushing let his arm fall away from his face and opened one eye.

"You bring me here?" he asked.

"This morning," Harkins said. "Do you remember what happened?"

Cushing squeezed his eye shut. "Nuh."

Still drunk, Harkins thought. He looked at his watch. It had been six and a half hours since he'd dragged Cushing from the pub.

"Do you remember who you were with last night?"

"Helen."

"Where did you leave Helen?" Harkins asked. "When did you see her last?"

"Dun remember," Cushing mumbled. "You'n MP?"

"Sort of," Harkins said. "Why were you meeting her?"

Cushing put his arm back over his face, which muffled what he said next.

"What was that?" Harkins asked.

"Could still lose this war."

That wasn't an answer Harkins was expecting, but he wrote it in his notebook.

"Did Helen Batcheller tell you that?" Harkins asked.

When Cushing didn't answer, Harkins asked, "What was the paper you had with you? That bunch of typewritten sheets with the names of German cities. Was that a target list?"

Cushing turned his head toward Harkins, a bit more alert. "Where is it?"

"Did you write that paper?" Harkins asked. "Did Batcheller write it?"

"D'you have it?" Cushing asked again, slurring. "Got to get that to Ike. To Ike's staff."

"Why do you have to get it to Ike's staff? Is that what you were trying to do?"

"Could still lose," Cushing said. "After all this bullshit, could still lose."

Harkins watched for a moment, and when he was pretty sure Cushing had passed out again, he stood and kicked the bottom of the drunk's foot.

"Why do you want that report to get to Ike?"

Cushing looked at him, as if trying to remember how Harkins had appeared.

"Isolate the beachhead," the pilot muttered. "Only way to get ashore. Got to have the assets. No use bombing deep. Damn production numbers are *going up.*"

The outburst seemed to exhaust the pilot. Harkins used the pause to scribble the jumble of phrases in his notebook.

Cushing had closed his eyes again.

"Did you kill Helen Batcheller?" Harkins asked.

It took him a good twenty seconds, but Cushing struggled to an upright sitting position. "What'd you say?"

"Did you kill Helen Batcheller?" Harkins repeated, watching Cushing's reaction. It was hard to tell, since the man was still drunk, but Harkins thought he looked surprised.

"Wait . . . Helen is dead?" Cushing asked. "Someone killed her?"

When Harkins didn't answer, Cushing leaned over the bucket and gagged up a string of clear bile.

Harkins sat quietly for a while, elbows on his knees. Finally, Cushing shook his head. "No," he said. "I didn't kill her."

"What was in that report, Major?" Harkins asked. "Is that what got her killed?"

Cushing said nothing, but shook his head. Harkins had just decided he'd have to return in another few hours, maybe the next day, when Cushing, his chin nearly on his chest, said, "Russians."

"What?" Harkins asked. "What about the Russians?"

Cushing fell back onto the cot, banging his head on the top rail.

"Ouch," he said, rubbing his scalp with one hand. Then, "It's where she got the information, the data."

The pilot drifted away again. Harkins wrote "source: Russians?" in his notebook, underlined the second word and the troublesome question mark. He needed to keep the investigation moving, needed details and evidence, but he was being stonewalled by a common drunk.

Harkins brought the chair out when he left the cell, asked the MP on duty to lock up behind him. As he walked, he looked at the nonsensical phrases scrawled in his notebook, plotting his next move, how he would spend his time while Cushing dried out a bit more.

"Probably not questioning Ike," he said.

Lowell was outside the gate waiting for him. She'd been leaning on the fender, but snapped to attention when Harkins came out of the building, gave him a sharp salute.

Harkins, whose salutes usually looked like a casual wave, tried to bring a bit more of the parade ground when he returned the gesture.

"Any luck, sir?" she asked.

"Not much," Harkins said. "He's still drunk, far as I can tell. Or a damn good actor. We're going to have to come back after he's sobered up some more."

"What were you reading in your notebook there, sir?" Lowell asked. She actually leaned forward to get a look.

"You mind, Lowell?" Harkins said, pressing the pages to his chest.

"Oh," she said, clearly embarrassed. "Oh, I'm so sorry, sir. I get excited sometimes and overstep my bounds. It's just that I'm eager to help any way I can. It won't happen again, sir. I promise."

She looked so clearly upset that Harkins felt bad about snapping at her.

"Never mind, I'm just an ornery SOB when I'm tired, that's all."

Harkins reached for the rear door handle but stopped when another staff car pulled up behind. Major Sinnott got out of one side, and a captain sporting the crushed-cap style of the Army Air Forces got out of the other. Harkins and Lowell saluted.

"Did you talk to our suspect?" Sinnott asked.

"Yes, sir," Harkins said. "He's still drunk, I think, so I was going to let him sit for a while, come back later."

"Did you learn anything new?" the captain asked. He wore the insignia of the Judge Advocate General Corps. A lawyer. No wings above his breast pocket, so he was not actually a pilot; he just wore his hat like one.

Harkins looked at the lawyer, then at Sinnott; he didn't respond to the question.

"This is Captain Gefner," Sinnott said. "He's from Eighth Air Force, where Cushing is assigned, and he'll be drawing up the charge sheet."

"Is that right?" Harkins said. He directed his comment at Gefner, but he was angry with Sinnott, who should be working to keep interference away until Harkins had a chance to conduct at least a cursory investigation.

"What are you planning to put on this charge sheet?" Harkins asked Gefner.

"I don't like your tone, Lieutenant," Gefner said.

Lowell was standing next to the car, listening. "Take a walk," Harkins told her.

When Lowell moved away, Harkins turned back to the lawyer. Sinnott wore a silly grin, which made Harkins think the major had already been celebrating happy hour someplace.

"Captain Gefner," Harkins said. "My name's Harkins, and until somebody from CID shows up—and they don't seem to be in any hurry—I'm the one investigating what looks like a murder. When it's time to call in the lawyers, I'll fucking let you know."

"All right, *gentlemen*," Sinnott said. Then, to Harkins, "What do you have so far?"

"Cushing said he was with Helen Batcheller last night, but he doesn't remember anything about the end of the night, doesn't remember leaving with her or how he got back to the pub."

"The guy is a lying sack of shit," Gefner said. "I wouldn't believe anything he has to say."

"Based on his reaction to the news, I believe he didn't know Batcheller was dead."

"I thought you said he was still drunk," Sinnott said.

"He's a little more coherent, but I wouldn't let him drive my car," Harkins said.

"What else did you learn?" Gefner asked.

Harkins looked at the lawyer. He was about thirty, Harkins guessed, with dark hair and a thick neck. A little spot of blood dotted his shirt collar, like he'd cut himself shaving.

"Who told you Cushing was here?" Harkins asked.

"When one of our officers winds up in the drunk tank, the command gets notified," Gefner said.

Harkins looked at Sinnott, who was still grinning but said nothing.

"Where did Cushing work?" Harkins asked the lawyer. "Is he on flight status?"

"Nobody is going to let that drunk touch the controls of an aircraft again," Gefner said. He stuck his index finger in the collar of his shirt, which was too tight.

"So this isn't the first time you've run across him?" Harkins asked. "He's been in trouble before?"

"He's attracted some attention from the command. Negative attention."

"So what were you planning on charging him with?" Harkins asked.

"He was the last one seen with the victim, right?" Gefner said. "And he admitted to you that he was with her in the pub. How much else do you need?"

"A motive would be nice," Harkins said. "A weapon. Some forensic evidence. A witness who saw them together outside the pub. Shall I go on?"

"Batcheller's boss said the report you found on Cushing looked like her work," Sinnott said, "though he didn't know she was working on it. It's classified, and Cushing should not have had it."

"What's the report about?" Harkins asked.

"Are you deaf, Lieutenant?" Gefner said. "He just said it was classified."

Harkins took a deep breath, counted backward from ten. Another calming technique suggested by his brother Patrick, the priest. This one didn't work, either.

"Let me rephrase the question, *counselor*," Harkins said. "So this report was enough to get somebody killed?"

"Sorry, Harkins," Sinnott said. "Can't tell you. Maybe after we upgrade your security clearance."

"I want to search his room," Harkins said. "Where was he staying?"

"I already have someone packing up his things," Gefner said. "His commander will take charge of his gear."

"Now you're the one who looks suspicious."

Gefner made a noise that sounded like *tsk-tsk,* then reached into a leather case he'd been holding at his side and pulled out a clutch of papers, three or four typewritten pages.

"We're going to charge him with the murder and with mishandling classified materials," Gefner said. He offered the papers to Harkins, who didn't look at them.

"Good luck with that," Harkins said.

"What's that supposed to mean?" Gefner said.

"Until I tell you what happened, all you have is some typed-up bullshit. You've got no case, no evidence."

"How about a confession?" Sinnott asked. He seemed amused by the tension between Harkins and Gefner.

"No confession, sir," Harkins said.

"Maybe he'll talk when he's sober," Sinnott offered.

"I'll be sure to keep you informed," Harkins said. He turned to Gefner. "Until then, how about you shove those papers up your ass."

Sinnott waited a few seconds, then said to Gefner, "Wait in the car for me, Captain. I'll be there directly."

Gefner shot Harkins a dirty look, then turned and walked back to Sinnott's staff car.

When he was gone, Sinnott smiled at Harkins. "I heard you were a pisser," he said. "Used to be a boxer, right?"

Harkins ignored the question.

"Why did you call that lawyer in so fast, sir?"

"I had to let Eighth Air Force know that one of their guys was in custody. The lawyer just came running."

"So it was his idea to come out of the gate with charge sheets already written up, before I even had a chance to question the guy? Or did you suggest that he come prepared?"

"Does it make a difference?" Sinnott asked. "If it was my idea or his?"

"You asked me to keep you informed about the status of the investigation," Harkins said. "I can certainly do that, sir, but I need something from you, too."

Sinnott looked slightly less amused. "I'm all ears," he said.

"I need you to give me a little room to maneuver here. Keep pains-in-the-ass like Gefner off my back for a while."

"I'm already doing that," Sinnott said. "The reason you haven't seen a CID agent is because I told them Cushing was at another drunk tank."

"Why did you do that?"

"Let's call it an honest mistake," Sinnott said. "If CID takes over the investigation, we're going to be cut out, and Colonel Haskell, not to mention General Donovan, they aren't going to like that."

Harkins didn't know the OSS well enough to know if that were true. Did the commanders really want to micromanage an investigation, or is that what Sinnott wanted?

"I need you to keep me updated."

"Yes, sir, though I won't waste your time giving you hourly reports," Harkins said.

Sinnott tilted his head back, arched one eyebrow.

"I don't like surprises, Lieutenant. Don't let me get blindsided by CID or anybody else."

"Okay, sir."

"There's already a lot of interest in this case, given Batcheller's status," Sinnott said. "It'll look better for all of us if we wrap this up pronto, with or without CID."

"Murder is a hanging crime, so I'm not as interested in how it looks as I am in getting it right."

"Sure, sure. I can't wait to hear what you learn from him when he's sober," Sinnott said, walking away.

"Kind of curious myself," Harkins said to himself.

When Sinnott had gone, Harkins turned and signaled Lowell, who'd been waiting by the car.

"What's next, sir?" she asked as she approached.

"Just a minute," Harkins said, adding to his notes.

After a few seconds of silence, Lowell said, "That lawyer got here quickly."

"How did you know he's a lawyer?" Harkins asked.

"Oh, I memorized the insignia American officers wear," she said. "I like to know who's in my car."

"You ever drive Major Sinnott before?"

"No, sir," Lowell said, with just a tiny bit of hesitation.

"But?"

"A few of the girls I know have driven for him." She pressed her lips together, a tight, pale line.

"Come on," Harkins said. "You've got something to say. Don't make me drag it out of you."

"It's just that he drinks a lot," Lowell said. "More than most Yanks. He's a mean drunk, is what I hear."

Harkins closed his notebook and tucked it in his shirt pocket; then he waited. He'd been down this road the previous summer in Sicily, trying to help women forced to deal with shitty men.

"He ever hurt any of your friends?" Harkins asked.

"More like he made them uncomfortable. Commented on their appearance, asked if they had husbands or boyfriends, if they dated Yanks, that sort of thing."

In her first job, Harkins' little sister, Aileen, had worked for a man—a married man named Dolan—who suggested that she could trade sex for a raise. Aileen had confided in the two other Harkins sisters, Mary and Saoirse, who told Patrick but tried to keep the secret from Eddie Harkins for fear of what their cop brother might do. Patrick had stopped by the man's office wearing his Roman collar. The boss had been polite—Patrick, a big man, had also been a boxer and had some authority in their Irish-Catholic neighborhood—but Dolan scoffed at Aileen's story, claiming that it had been a misunderstanding and that little Aileen, who was only sixteen at the time, was prone to drama.

Harkins waited a few days before he stopped by to see Dolan, who was in his office with invoices spread across his desk. Another, younger man—Harkins would learn later he was the assistant manager—sat in a straight-backed chair next to the desk. Harkins had changed out of his police blues but still wore his heavy black work shoes.

"Who are you?" the manager asked.

By way of an answer Harkins had slapped him, open-handed, on the side of the head, knocking him to the floor. Harkins then strolled around the desk, put one of his shiny cop shoes on the man's scrotum and applied pressure. The assistant manager scooted from the room like he was on fire.

Harkins leaned over, because the man's ears would be ringing and he might not hear the message.

"You met Aileen's nice brother the other day," Harkins said, a conversational tone. "Big priest? A sweet guy, really."

He leaned over, put more of his weight on Dolan's genitals.

"I'm the mean brother. If there are any more little chats like this, they'll be with me."

The following week Aileen opened her pay envelope to find a raise. Since she was too young to go to a taproom, she invited Patrick for an ice cream soda, sure that his talk with Dolan—the only one she knew about—had straightened things out.

"So Major Sinnott wants this investigation wrapped up quickly," Lowell said, snapping Harkins from his reverie.

"Looks that way."

"Where would you like to go next, sir?" Lowell asked.

"I want to take a look at Batcheller's rooms," he said. "See where she lived, maybe find her flatmate."

"Should be easy enough," Lowell said. "And after that?"

Harkins looked down at his notebook, at the underlined word "Russians," the most intriguing piece of information he'd kept from Sinnott.

"We'll see," Harkins said. "We'll see what develops."

6

Colonel Sergei Novikov and his personal secretary, Senior Lieutenant Vladimir Gorodetsky, stood on the sparse grass at the southern edge of Kensington Garden, studying the hatbox shape of Royal Albert Hall, another of London's famous landmarks.

"I wonder why the Germans did not destroy this in the Blitz," Gorodetsky said.

"Because they believed they would launch a successful invasion," Novikov said. "Probably wanted to use it for one of their big rallies."

"Do you think they were ever capable of crossing the channel?"

Novikov looked at the young man, a tanker, like himself. Gorodetsky had spent a year in combat and had put in a formal request—two, in fact—for transfer back to the front and the fight with the Germans. It was really the only place for a patriotic officer; Novikov would eventually have to let him go.

"The last successful cross-channel invasion was in 1066," Novikov said. "Back then, William did not have to worry about air cover. Now?"

"Now, no amphibious operation is possible without mastery of the air," Gorodetsky said. "The Americans and the British must be at that point by now, don't you think, Colonel?"

"Our allies have not shared everything with us, Vladimir; but I suspect you are right. I think they control the skies over France."

"So the invasion cannot be far off," Gorodetsky said. "Do you think they will tell us ahead of time?"

"Not a chance," Novikov said, smiling. "But you and I will see the movement to the coast. With all these men and all this equipment, it will look like someone tipped the entire island up on edge, and everything will slide down to the channel. We will know."

A voice boomed behind them. "What will you know?"

Novikov turned to see Colonel Yury Sechin approaching. Gorodetsky came to attention and saluted.

Novikov touched the brim of his cap with the fingers of his right hand. His left arm had been amputated and the shattered remains of his left eye removed at a field hospital near Kursk the previous summer. He wore an

eye patch, like a pirate in an American film. He'd once been handsome—
his wife used to tease him, claiming he'd have made a successful gigolo if
he'd been born in Paris—and now he was not; but he was alive, while tens
of thousands of his former comrades had been plowed into early graves,
like the remains of a failed crop.

"Colonel Sechin," Novikov said. "Thank you very much for meeting
us out here."

Novikov smiled; Sechin did not. The rumor among the younger embassy staff was that the new NKVD colonel only smiled when he was
torturing someone. Novikov wasn't sure it was an exaggeration.

"We were talking about the great fantasy," Novikov said. "The second
front."

"This spring," Sechin said. "Even the fucking British would not dare
delay it again. They are too eager to get all these whore-monger Americans off their precious little island."

"I am sure you are right," Novikov said.

It was all the Soviets could talk about, dream about, obsess over: When
would the Allies launch their invasion of the western end of occupied Europe, which would draw German strength away from the Eastern Front?
The great Soviet armies had the Germans on the run, but they had bled
millions of men and it was still a long way to Berlin and the ultimate destruction of the Third Reich.

"Give me a cigarette," Sechin said to Gorodetsky. The aide reached
into an inside pocket of his coat, pulled out a pack of Lucky Strikes. He
shook one loose and held it out to Sechin, who grabbed the whole pack.

"Decadent American cigarettes," Sechin said to Gorodetsky. "I will do
you a favor and take them off your hands. Do not spend too much time
with those butt-fuckers, Lieutenant. You will not be fit to return home."

Gorodetsky looked chastened.

"Wait for me over there," Novikov said to his secretary, pointing at the
path to the Serpentine, the long comma-shaped lake that split the park
in two.

Sechin watched Gorodetsky go, then said to Novikov, "Has he asked
to return to the front?"

"Twice," Novikov said. "I will have to let him go eventually."

"Best not to get too close to our young aides," Sechin said. "So many
of them wind up in shallow graves."

Novikov thought of the trenches the combat engineers dug for the dead
of his brigade. Many of his men, the ones who died instantly when the
German tank-killer rounds punched through their T-34s, did not leave
behind enough of a corpse to need a grave.

"You are in a cheerful mood, comrade," Novikov said.

"What the fuck do I have to be cheerful about?" Sechin said. "I spend
all day talking to British snobs or American amateurs playing at being
soldiers."

"How goes your work?" Novikov asked. He smiled when he said it, because he knew Sechin would never give him a straight answer.

Sechin glanced sideways at Novikov, grunted, then lit a Lucky with a wooden match. Novikov thought about offering him a light from his always-reliable American-made lighter, but didn't feel like being questioned about where he'd received the gift.

Sechin came by his paranoia and skepticism honestly. He was the senior officer of the Narodny komissariat vnutrennikh del—the head spymaster at the Soviet Embassy, recently arrived from Moscow to recruit disaffected government functionaries from among the Americans and British working in London. All of the senior officers at the Soviet Embassy, both civilian and military, had been thoroughly briefed on the importance of finding spies. Stalin anticipated that the collapse of Nazi Germany would be followed by a war with the West, perhaps not a shooting war, but a struggle nonetheless, for dominance of Europe. With millions of dead Soviet soldiers and citizens, it surprised no one that Stalin wanted a deep buffer zone between the USSR and the west, even if that meant taking over eastern Europe.

The time to plant moles in the British and American governments was now, while the three major powers were ostensibly allies. No U.S. embassy official, no British government employee was too inconsequential to be considered. Sechin's job was to orchestrate a vast recruiting effort, and Novikov did not envy him. Sechin's predecessor had not been successful enough to placate Moscow and had been abruptly recalled just a month earlier. That unlucky man was either at the front, in prison, or already dead.

"And how goes your job?" Sechin asked.

Novikov was a military liaison with the British and Americans. On paper, his role was to help the Allies share military techniques and ideas that had been successful against the Wehrmacht. In reality, he was supposed to take as much as possible and give very little in return.

"We are learning a great deal about our friends," Novikov said.

"I can get you a replacement for that aide," Sechin said. "I have a few very clever young men who could help you without being corrupted by contact with the westerners."

Novikov knew that anyone Sechin sent his way would be a spy, loyal only to Sechin. Novikov did not think of Sechin as an adversary, but he was certainly not an ally. Sechin was invested in his own success and, at a close second, that of the USSR. He might not want to see Novikov fail, but he would not hesitate to crush Novikov or any other Soviet officer if it meant advancing his own career and reputation.

"Thank you, Colonel," Novikov said. "I'll keep that kind offer in mind when the time comes to replace Gorodetsky."

The two men stood just a few feet apart. With these intelligence types, Novikov felt, one was always being sized up, measured.

Sechin was a big man, a true Russian bear stuffed into the uniform of an NKVD colonel. Famously foul-mouthed, bald, barrel-chested, with big arms and hands and an expanding waistline. He was a heavy smoker, even by Russian standards, and would probably be finished with the pack he'd taken from Gorodetsky in a few hours.

Novikov turned away, admired the dome of Prince Albert Hall once again.

"One of your American friends was killed this morning," Sechin said. "Murdered, is what I hear."

"Who?"

"A woman, an OSS analyst named Batcheller. I do not know her first name."

Sechin was perfectly still, and Novikov knew the spymaster was gauging his reaction to this news.

"You knew her, yes?"

"You know that I knew her, Colonel," Novikov said. "I have reported all my contacts with our allies, as required."

"Did you ever work with her?"

"No. We had some interesting discussions, that is all," Novikov said. "We met at a cocktail party the Americans held at their embassy."

"To show off their food," Sechin said.

"Perhaps. They do have excellent food, though one has to bring one's own vodka. But I think it was also to open up communications with us."

"What did you and this woman talk about while you were drinking shitty American whiskey?" Sechin wanted to know.

"She was an economist, like my father," Novikov said. "She had studied at a university in their California. Stanford."

"And?"

"We talked about how much she missed the weather in California."

"What was she doing for the Americans?"

"I have no idea," Novikov said.

"Some of the people now working in their embassy once belonged to the American Communist Party," Sechin went on.

"Some of them probably still do," Novikov said. "I cannot imagine you would want to recruit them. Party members in the United States will be the first ones suspected and investigated. Their FBI and its head, this man named Hoover, see Communists everywhere."

"Hoover was the former American president," Sechin said.

"Different Hoover," Novikov corrected. He wondered how good a spymaster Sechin could be if he didn't know the name of his principal adversary in the United States.

"Is that why you asked to meet me this morning?" Novikov asked. "To tell me about this woman's death?"

"I wanted to know—I want to know—what she was working on," Sechin said. "I thought you might be able to shed some light for me."

Novikov shook his head. "Sorry."

Sechin leaned in just a tiny bit.

"I want to know what she knew about my operation, my effort to recruit spies."

"What makes you think she knew anything at all?" Novikov asked.

Sechin straightened up, tried to smile but wound up looking sinister, like he was trying to frighten a roomful of children.

"I am just suspicious by nature, I guess," Sechin said. "It's kept me alive in this job."

"So far," Novikov said.

When Sechin's eyes darkened, Novikov said, "Sorry, that was a joke in poor taste. I am sure you will do quite well in this assignment. It certainly is critical to the postwar security of the motherland."

Sechin waited, perhaps considering whether Novikov was being sarcastic.

"You will let me know if you learn anything, Colonel," Sechin said after a moment. "In fact, if you have contacts, I'd like you to use them to learn what this woman had been working on."

"I will do my best," Novikov said.

Sechin turned, and Novikov watched his wide back amble away, cigarette smoke trailing him like the plume from a train.

Novikov turned and motioned to Gorodetsky, who waited on the nearby sidewalk out of earshot.

"You look spooked," Novikov said to the secretary as the young man approached.

"Colonel, I do not mind telling you, that man frightens me."

"I suspect that is part of his job, and he is good at it," Novikov said. "He wants people to be afraid of him."

Gorodetsky hardly looked reassured.

"You have something to hide, Lieutenant?" Novikov asked.

Gorodetsky turned to him quickly. "No sir! Not at all."

"Relax, Vladimir. I'm teasing you."

Gorodetsky licked his lips, put his hands in the pockets of his coat, then took them out.

"You know he has people watching us, don't you, Colonel?"

"To live as a Soviet citizen is to be under scrutiny always," Novikov said. It wasn't a dangerous statement to make, but it skirted the edge of being counter-revolutionary, and for that reason it did not reassure Gorodetsky.

"Of course the NKVD keeps tabs on what all embassy people are doing," Novikov said. "It is their job to make sure none of us has been so corrupted by our western friends that we become a danger to the state."

"Every time you meet with one of your American or British counterparts, I get called down to the basement for questioning," Gorodetsky said. "Sometimes I wonder if I will be allowed to leave."

"You have nothing to worry about, Vladimir," Novikov said, clapping the young man on the shoulder. "I will not do anything to put you at risk."

It was a lie, but Gorodetsky seemed momentarily relieved.

"Come, let us walk back and talk about your request for transfer. If you really think you're better off at the front than in the basement with Sechin's thugs."

7

When Eddie Harkins got back to OSS headquarters on Grosvenor Street, Tom Wickman was waiting. The captain stepped out into the hallway when he saw Harkins, then closed his office door.

"What did you say to Major Sinnott?" Wickman asked in a stage whisper.

"What are you talking about?"

"He was angry, said something about you holding back information."

Harkins hedged. "I'm keeping him updated on everything that's pertinent. I'm not sharing every thought I have."

A man in civilian clothes squeezed past them in the hall, cradling a huge, long-haired cat.

"Rats in the basement," he said when Harkins and Wickman stared.

When the man had passed, Harkins looked up at Wickman again. "Look," he said, keeping his voice low. "Sinnott is doing his best to keep CID away from this, and that's gonna bite us in the ass at some point. Until then, far as I'm concerned, I own this. Sinnott thinks we have our man just because Cushing was in the pub with Batcheller. But that's not enough to court-martial the guy; Cushing is just a suspect at this point. I've got to keep looking."

"Major Sinnott sure thinks he's guilty, and, as he pointed out, he's got more experience than both of us put together."

"He's got experience as a spy, or Resistance fighter, or secret agent, or whatever the hell he was before he got canned," Harkins said. "I don't want them sending a man to face a capital charge unless I'm convinced he's our guy. Getting that story right will be hard to do if I'm running to brief Sinnott a couple of times a day. Hell, he showed up at the Disciplinary Barracks with some lawyer who was ready to find a hanging tree."

"Captain Gefner," Wickman said. "That little prig Eighth Air Force sent over. I've been asking around, and I found out that Cushing is not well-loved with the brass over there."

"Why?"

"Cushing has been critical of the bombing campaigns. Apparently when he drinks—and he definitely has a drinking problem—he mouths off about how the bombing is a waste of men's lives with little to show for it."

"Hardly seems enough to want to railroad him," Harkins said. "Every GI I've ever met has something to say about idiotic army plans."

Wickman pulled himself up to his full height. The top of Harkins' head only came to the captain's chin.

"Let me help you," he said.

Harkins paused; Wickman was so eager it was hard to turn him down. "I don't think so."

"It'll be another set of eyes. Maybe I'll see something you missed."

"I prefer to work alone," Harkins said.

"I understand that. But I suspect Sinnott thinks that resolving this quickly will put him in good with the brass, maybe get him out of the doghouse. He might pull you from the investigation and let Gefner have his way, just so he can say it's solved. I can run interference, keep Sinnott happy, or at least keep him off your back."

"How?"

"Sinnott trusts me," Wickman said. "He already has doubts about you, but if I tell him what we're up to, he's more likely to buy it. Plus, he can't really get rid of me, which gives us some cover."

"What makes you think he can't get rid of you?" Harkins asked.

Wickman opened the door to his office, stepped to his left so Harkins could see inside without entering. There were neat stacks of money on the desk: American greenbacks, colorful British pounds, French francs. Thousands of dollars, maybe tens of thousands. All cash.

"What's all this for?" Harkins asked.

"We send it to our agents in the field," Wickman said. "They make requests and we stick the money in their supply bundles, drop it all in by parachute. But until I got here, nobody had control. No one knew how much we had on hand, how much was going out, to whom or for what. It's like OSS had a license to just leave money lying around. I'm on top of that now, and since it's more efficient, there's actually more money available for that pet project of Sinnott's."

"Which is?"

"He hasn't told me. Right now, I just turn the cash over to him. But I do know he doesn't want the tap turned off."

Harkins stood in silence.

"I don't want to spend the war doing this," Wickman said.

Harkins was about to say that was Wickman's problem, not his. But if it turned out that all the cash sloshing around the OSS had something to do with Batcheller's murder—and money and murder frequently went together—it might help to have someone with Wickman's skills take a look.

Harkins pulled the door shut and looked up at the captain. "He's never going to let you out of this office as long as you're the goose that's laying the golden eggs."

"Which is exactly why I need to plot my own course."

"He's going to want you to keep tabs on me. Spy on me."

"I can just feed him enough information—whatever you want—to keep him happy and off our case."

It was a risk, Harkins knew. Wickman might get in the way, might already be a spy for Sinnott. On the other hand, if he didn't toss Sinnott a bone now and then, the major might just shut him down completely.

"Please."

"Okay, we'll try it," Harkins said.

"Great," Wickman said, brightening. "What do we do first?"

Harkins, a bit leery of Wickman's enthusiasm, looked at his watch. "I want to look around Batcheller's place, maybe talk to her roommate, the one Sinnott notified this morning."

Wickman went into his tiny office, put the cash in cloth bank bags and shoved them in his safe. He came out with his hat and a folded piece of paper.

"I thought you'd want to talk to Batcheller's roommate, so I have her name and the address of the rented space."

"Okay, that's good. Thanks."

The two men walked downstairs and onto Grosvenor Street. It was still daylight, and Lowell leaned against the staff car reading a newspaper. She tucked it under her arm and saluted when the officers approached.

"Where to, sir?" she asked Harkins.

Wickman handed Lowell the address. "You know where this is?"

"Yes, sir. East End, or close to the East End," she said.

Harkins, lower-ranking, climbed in ahead of Wickman, as military courtesy dictated. "Okay," he said. "Let's go see what we can find at Batcheller's place."

Lowell drove them toward the Thames, then headed east, navigating around the worst bomb-damaged areas. Harkins was on the side of the car away from the river, but could still see boat and barge traffic. It had been another gray day, but still no rain to speak of. The drought, it seemed, continued. Soon he could see the dome of Saint Paul's.

"Was the cathedral damaged during the Blitz?" Harkins asked Lowell.

"The Jerries dropped a bomb through the roof," she said. "Destroyed the main altar, but other than that it came through in good shape. They attacked landmarks in other cities, though. Cathedrals, if you can believe that. Norwich, Exeter, Canterbury, and even the York Minster. I'm forgetting one."

"Bath," Harkins said. "Murrow talked about it in his broadcast."

"The Germans are animals," Lowell said. "They deserve everything they get and more."

Lowell turned left off East India Dock Road onto a small side street that wound mostly north and up a slight hill. One entire block had been razed, twenty or thirty homes turned into piles of broken brick, but on the next block north both sides of the street were lined with intact narrow-front homes, each two stories with a single gable.

"Here we are, gentlemen," Lowell said. She got out of the car and opened the rear door. Wickman didn't climb out as much as unfold himself, and still he banged his head on the doorjamb. "Number seventeen should be that one, with the dead flowers in the window box," Lowell said.

Harkins climbed the stoop to the front door, was about to knock when Wickman bumped into him. The big man had squeezed onto the same small step, so tall he could see right over Harkins' head.

"Do you mind?" Harkins said.

"Oh, sorry, sorry. I'm just a bit caught up, that's all."

Harkins knocked on the door and soon heard the shuffling of approaching slippers. The door opened and a white-haired woman, small as a bird, looked up at him, then craned her head to see Wickman.

"Ma'am," Harkins said, holding his cap. "Sorry to disturb you this evening. I'm Lieutenant Harkins, and this is Captain Wickman. We're investigating the murder of an American woman named Helen Batcheller. We understand she lived here. Is that right?"

"Yes, poor Helen," the woman said. "I heard all about it this morning when those nice Yank officers came 'round."

"Was one of them a Major Sinnott?" Harkins asked.

"That sounds right," the woman said. "I didn't hear the other man's name, but I think he was from your air forces."

"What made you think that?" Harkins asked.

"His hat. All the Yank airmen smash their hats down. Very dashing. Like our RAF boys."

Harkins looked at Wickman. It sounded like Gefner had been with Sinnott since the morning, a very rapid reaction to the murder.

"I'm Mrs. Peabody. Gail Peabody."

"Pleased to meet you," Harkins said. "What did these two officers do here?"

"They asked to see Helen's room. I told them Annie was probably in there, getting ready for work. Helen and Annie shared the front bedroom. It's the largest in the house. I shared it with my husband until he passed. Now I'm happy to lend it to the war effort. We all must do our part, right?"

"Absolutely," Harkins said. "Annie, that's her roommate. Miss Stowe. Is that correct?"

"Yes, Annie Stowe. She works at the embassy, too, I think. With Helen."

"Did the two officers speak to Miss Stowe?"

"The major was the one who had to tell her about Helen, I'm afraid, though I think he went into too much detail about the crime, which was brutal."

Peabody had been eavesdropping.

"But after a few minutes, Annie got up, thanked the men for coming, and went to work. Very English, that girl."

"What do you mean?" Harkins asked.

"It's a very English trait to keep one's emotions in check. None of this public blubbering or wailing that one sees in . . . some people."

She paused, weighing her next words. Harkins wondered if she'd been preparing to say "Americans."

"No melodrama is all I'm saying."

"How long have they been roommates?" Harkins asked.

"Seven months. They socialized, mostly at embassy functions. Oh, it was so lovely to have young people around. And Americans, they certainly brightened things up."

The old woman sniffled, pulled a pink handkerchief from the cuff of her housedress and dabbed at her tiny nose.

"Did they have guests here?" Harkins asked. "Entertain anyone?"

"No, Helen and Annie often left together of an evening or weekend, but no one called for them here."

"So no men came around?"

Peabody was not amused. "I'm not running a bordello, Lieutenant," she said. "I only ever allow nice girls to rent these rooms."

"Yes, ma'am," Harkins said. "I didn't mean to imply anything. Did the two officers who came this morning go through Helen's things?"

"No," Peabody said. "Annie was still getting ready when they came, and they left just ahead of her."

"May we see the room?"

"If you promise not to touch anything on Annie's side."

"Certainly," Harkins said. "Of course."

Mrs. Peabody walked them up a back staircase to a hallway that was poorly lit by a single bulb in an elaborate sconce. At the front of the house she led Harkins and Wickman into a bedroom with a couple of windows that looked out on the street. Wickman had to duck in the doorframe.

There were two single beds, close together, both of them neatly made.

"They always keep it this clean?" Harkins asked.

"They're lovely girls," Peabody said. "The bed on the left is Annie's, as well as that wardrobe. Please respect her privacy. I'll wait in the back parlor."

"Yes, ma'am," Harkins said.

When he could hear Mrs. Peabody going down the stairs, Harkins pointed to Batcheller's bed and nightstand and said to Wickman, "You take Batcheller's side. I'll take Stowe's."

"I was afraid you were going to do that," Wickman said. He stood still just inside the doorway.

"You want to investigate?" Harkins asked. "Then you've got to snoop a bit."

Wickman still didn't move, and Harkins was about to ask him to wait in the car when the captain nodded and said, "Okay, okay, what are we looking for?"

"Anything that tells us why Batcheller was meeting with a pilot who was not her boyfriend, or something that tells us what she was working on."

"Not a chance either of these women has anything work-related here," Wickman said. "OSS people are sticklers about that stuff."

"Yeah," Harkins said. "But people are always doing surprising things, aren't they?"

"Yeah. Me doing this, for instance."

There was a small armoire next to the foot of Annie Stowe's bed. Harkins opened it and started at the top, where three sweaters lay neatly folded, along with two small, threadbare bath towels. A mesh bag held a brush and comb, a small bottle of something called "Toneglints," which looked to be a British-brand shampoo, a toothbrush and tooth powder. Nothing remotely interesting.

Harkins checked the hanging clothes for inside pockets. In a drawer below, mixed in with undergarments, were a dozen or so letters bundled with string. The writing on each looked to be by the same hand, with return addresses all from the same house in Atlanta. Curiously there were no V-mail letters, the system the government had adopted to shrink letters to microfilm, thus saving precious cargo space on transatlantic shipping. Harkins wondered if embassy employees and OSS were exempt from that requirement.

Harkins looked through a couple of the letters. They were from Stowe's mother, written on lovely stationery and full of small news from home. Unlike the letters Harkins received from his sisters, there was no mention of siblings or a father or other family, no USO dances or neighborhood gossip or birth announcements; just a recitation of Atlanta society events: cotillions, debutante balls, and garden parties, all things Stowe's mother might have copied verbatim from the newspaper. The most recent one was dated December 1943; six months ago.

"Find anything interesting?"

Harkins looked up to see a young woman in the doorway; American, judging by the accent. Eyes a bit red, maybe from crying.

"Miss Stowe?" he asked.

"Oh, gosh, since you've already been through my underwear, I think we're close enough for you to call me Annie, don't you?" She was not smiling.

"I'm sorry, Miss Stowe. I'm investigating Helen Batcheller's death; I'm sure you can appreciate that I want to find out as much as I can about her time here. That includes the people close to her."

"And you are?"

"Lieutenant Eddie Harkins. This is Captain Wickman."

Wickman, embarrassed, looked like he was trying to shrink himself. An impossible task.

"Well, I feel so *privileged,* having my privacy trashed by high-ranking officers." Her mild southern accent was all moonlight, magnolia, and dripping sarcasm. "I presume you two are with the provost marshal."

"We're OSS, Miss Stowe," Wickman said.

"Well, that's unusual, isn't it?" she said. "Although hardly anything surprises me anymore about Wild Bill's gang. Mind if I come in?"

Since it was her bedroom, Harkins gestured with his open palm and said, "Sure."

Stowe sat on a bed while Harkins and Wickman stood in the small space near the window.

"I'm sorry about Miss Batcheller," Harkins said. "Helen."

"Which of you is the principal on this?" she asked. Wickman pointed at Harkins.

"Why a lieutenant and not the captain?"

"I was a cop," Harkins said. "Before the war. We both were, but I investigated a murder last summer. In Sicily."

"Catch your man, did you?" she asked.

"In a manner of speaking, yeah," Harkins said.

Stowe looked at him for a moment. He had not answered her question, and she knew it.

"That hardly inspires confidence," she said.

Annie Stowe looked to be about Harkins' age—twenty-seven or so—and was quite beautiful, with auburn hair, bright green eyes, and a tiny dimple on her chin. She wore a pearl choker, a navy-blue dress, and a cardigan that a demure teacher might wear to meet the parents of her students. If she was angry with Harkins and Wickman for going through her things, she seemed to be getting over it.

"Do you have any suspects?" she asked.

"We're making some progress," Harkins said. "Any chance we could go someplace else to talk? It's a little crowded in here. Close."

"Okay," Stowe said, standing.

Harkins and Wickman followed her down the stairs and out the front door. Lowell was waiting out front, standing by her staff car.

"We'll walk," Stowe said, buttoning her coat as she moved.

"Wait here," Harkins told Lowell.

Harkins and Wickman followed Stowe. It was dusk now, the streets fading in gray light, but Stowe knew the neighborhood and moved quickly. Harkins was happy he didn't walk into a sign or post in the blackout. When Stowe ducked into a doorway the two officers followed her into a small pub. Three older men stood at the bar; the few tables were empty.

"What'll it be, Annie?" the bartender called to Stowe as she sat and motioned for Harkins and Wickman to join her.

"Pint for me, Roger," she said. Wickman held up two fingers; Harkins shook his head.

Stowe slipped out of her coat, letting it slide onto the back of her chair. She crossed her legs and looked at Harkins, then Wickman, then Harkins again.

"Go ahead," she said.

Harkins produced his notebook. "Do you know of anyone who might want to hurt Helen?"

Her eyebrows moved closer together. "You mean 'might want to kill her,' don't you?"

"Yes," Harkins said.

The three men standing at the bar looked over, then turned back when Harkins met their gaze.

"I'm sorry," Stowe said. She moved her jaw side to side, as if to unclench it. "I guess it's just sinking in. What happened to her."

"Perfectly understandable," Harkins said.

"How long have you two shared a room?" Wickman asked.

"Six, seven months, I guess."

"And you were close?"

"I'd say so, yes. Lived in tight quarters, took a lot of our meals together."

"Did Helen get along with her colleagues?" Harkins asked.

"Not always, and not all of them. But nothing that would warrant this," she said, her voice catching.

Harkins waited a moment, let her compose herself. Stowe sat up straighter, shook her head, a tiny movement.

"Can you give me an example of a falling-out she might have had? Or a disagreement with a colleague?"

Stowe drew a deep breath. "Helen stood up for herself," she said. "Not everyone liked that."

"Meaning?" Harkins asked.

"Obviously, we work in a man's world. More often than you might think, a man will claim credit that doesn't really belong to him. When someone pulled that stunt with Helen, she called him on it. The trouble is that when a woman speaks up, even if she's sticking up for herself, she's a bitch. A man doing the same thing is strong."

Harkins made a note to find out how many women were on OSS staff.

"Did you do that, too? Stick up for yourself and your work?"

"I'm not as brave as Helen is. Was."

"She tussle with anyone in particular?"

"No," Stowe said, her face relaxing a bit. "But she'd *goddamn* one man as quick as the next."

"You ever hear her talk about a Major Cushing?" Harkins asked. "A pilot with the Eighth Air Force?"

"No."

Harkins figured Stowe would not tell him about her work, but he wanted to learn what he could.

"So you and Batcheller worked together?" Harkins asked.

"Only in the same way you and I work together, Lieutenant. We're both OSS."

"Of course, of course," Harkins said. "But you're an economist, too, right?"

"I was a mathematician," she said. "Once upon a time."

"Really?" Harkins said. "That's a field, a job? I mean, you can just do math all the time?"

Stowe allowed herself a smile, showing perfect teeth. Harkins noticed Wickman staring at her; he thought the other man's breathing had slowed.

"Let's just say Helen and I were both numbers girls."

And just like that, Stowe started to cry. Not a big, messy, snotty cry, but a lady-like and delicate sniffle, a bright tear on each cheek.

"I'm sorry," Harkins said.

Stowe forced a smile. "Not your fault. I was just thinking about her family, when they find out. What they'll be told. She was from California. Family had a big spread out there. Horses, sheep, goats, chickens, just all sorts of animals. A whole tribe of dogs. Her mother used to write about the dogs, especially. Once she even sent Helen a picture of some puppies."

"Funny, the things we miss," Wickman said. "You don't anticipate it, then it hits you."

Harkins thought Wickman was trying too hard to make an impression, but if it got Stowe talking, he'd let it ride.

"Did Helen have any friends from the Soviet Embassy?" Harkins asked. "Anybody she worked with, maybe?"

"We met some folks at various social events," Stowe said. "Cocktail hours, pub crawls. This was back when Maisky was the Soviet ambassador here; he was a big proponent of plain old friendship."

"He's not the ambassador anymore?" Harkins asked.

"No. He got sent back, maybe called back. Stalin was probably angry that the Allies didn't open a second front in the west last year. I hear he blamed Maisky."

"So Helen knew some of the Soviets?"

"Well, like I said, socially."

She seemed like she wanted to say more. When Wickman started to speak, Harkins silenced him with a glance.

"I think she had a falling-out with a couple of our colleagues who were, in her opinion, too close to the Soviets. I mean, we're ostensibly allies, but deep down, Helen didn't trust them. And she didn't think the Americans here should become too chummy."

"Was it a serious falling-out? Did she complain to your boss or the chain of command in the OSS?"

"I don't think so," Stowe said. "She did get drunk once and gave a few of the guys an earful."

"Who was that?" Harkins asked.

Stowe looked at Harkins, held his eyes.

"If I give you these names, you know it doesn't mean that they killed her, right?"

"Of course," Harkins said.

"I'd rather not have it come back to me that I gave the investigators some names over a little tiff."

"Was it a tiff?" Harkins asked. "Not a falling-out? Maybe an argument?"

"See?" Stowe said. "This is why people don't want to talk to cops. You share one confidence and suddenly they've constructed a motive and a crime scene and are lining up the hangman."

Harkins leaned back in his chair. It had been going well up to that point, but now Stowe seemed spooked.

"Are you afraid of repercussions? For talking to me?"

"Look, Lieutenant," she said uncrossing her legs and leaning toward him. Wickman, Harkins noticed, admired her legs for a few seconds before looking up again.

"I know you're just doing your job here," she said. "But you've got to understand, even the whiff of impropriety in the OSS or the embassy— that could mean the end of someone's career, get them shipped back home. I've seen it happen."

Harkins paused for a moment, returning her gaze.

"Well, I'm glad you appreciate that I have a job to do," he said.

After a moment, she said, "Lionel Kerr and Marty Adkin. She thought they were overly sympathetic toward the USSR. Apologetic for some of the stuff Stalin did to his own people."

"Did she have any reason to fear that these men would try to punish her? That they were angry with her?"

"Nah," Stowe said. "Helen told me she knew where the bodies are buried and didn't have anything to worry about from these guys."

"Do you know what she meant by that? About the bodies, I mean. Did she have incriminating evidence on them?"

"I don't know," Stowe said. "You'll talk to Kerr, I'm sure."

"I will. What about the other guy?" Harkins asked, reading his notes. "Adkin?"

"Oh, he's gone," Stowe said.

"Gone?"

She raised one hand, flipped her fingers as if brushing away an insect.

"To the continent, I presume. He spoke French, so that would be my guess."

"And Kerr?"

"Lionel will be around," she said. "I'm pretty sure he's allergic to the smell of gunpowder, so he'll be here in good old London until the end of the party."

8

By the time Harkins and Wickman had deposited Stowe back at her flat, it was approaching midnight.

"Calling it a day?" Wickman asked as they approached the staff car where Lowell waited, still on duty.

"Not yet," Harkins said to Wickman. "I want to go back at Cushing, see if he's sobered up. Why don't you have Lowell take you back to your quarters?"

"Well, I can keep going for a bit longer, but wouldn't it be better to question him in the morning after he's had a night's sleep?"

"I want to wake him up," Harkins said. "Keep him off balance."

The two men climbed into the back of the staff car.

"Where to, sir?" Lowell asked. She did not turn around to look at Harkins.

"Back to the drunk tank," Harkins said. Then, "You doing okay, Lowell? Need to get back and get some sleep?" It had been seventeen hours since she'd driven Harkins to the crime scene.

"I'm fine, sir," she said, pulling away from the curb and sounding not at all fine.

"'Cause chances are none of us is going to get much sleep while we're developing this case. If you need me to get another driver for a spell I will."

"No," Lowell said. "I mean, I'd prefer to keep driving. I'm doing well, Lieutenant. Really."

Harkins looked over at Wickman, who had jammed himself into the backseat. He couldn't see Wickman's face, so he couldn't tell if Wickman heard the same thing in Lowell's voice.

"What's eating you?" Harkins finally asked her.

He thought she was looking at him in the mirror. Maybe the phrase didn't translate. "Pardon, sir?" she said.

"Seems like something is bothering you."

Lowell was silent for a moment, maybe weighing how much to tell him.

"Vera Brittain," she said. She held up a folded newspaper from the seat next to her. Harkins couldn't read it in the dark, but it was the tabloid she'd been reading earlier.

"Who's that?" Harkins asked.

When Lowell didn't answer immediately, Wickman spoke up. "The pacifist."

"Some people are calling her a traitor," Lowell said.

When she didn't offer more, Harkins asked, "Are you going to tell me or should I guess?"

"Vera Brittain is a well-known author here," Wickman said. "Wrote a memoir about her time as a nurse in the last war. What was it called, Lowell?"

"*Testament of Youth*," Lowell said. She was driving slowly, following the barely visible glow of the car's blackout headlights.

"She lost her brother, her fiancé, and another friend, a young man, in the war," Wickman said. "Not to mention what she saw in service at the front."

Harkins watched the back of Lowell's head, her tense shoulders. Thought about what he had seen in just a few days at a field hospital in Sicily the previous summer. Mutilated bodies, platoons of corpses. One image that had visited him in dreams: an amputated lower leg, discarded in a metal trash can inside a surgical tent.

"Sounds like enough to make anyone a pacifist," Harkins said.

Wickman shrugged, and Harkins asked Lowell, "Brittain—that's her real name?"

"Yes, sir. Brittain, with two tees," Lowell said.

She handed Harkins the folded paper she'd been reading.

"What's this?"

"You can read it later, sir. It's a piece called 'Massacre by Bombing.' Supposed to be the facts about the British and American bombing of Germany. Brittain wrote it."

"So, what? You think it's bull?"

"I don't know. But she keeps writing these pamphlets and letters to the editor and making speeches about how we shouldn't bomb German cities. That we're killing innocent women and children. That it makes us no better than they are, no better than they were during the Blitz."

"Well, so far I'm with Brittain on this," Harkins said. "I'm no fan of the Germans, and I'd be happy if we pulverized every Kraut wearing a coal-bucket helmet. But these big bombing raids? Hell, even with the smaller bombing missions on Italian cities and towns we killed a bunch of people who had nothing to do with starting the war. We're probably doing the same thing in Germany, just on a bigger scale."

Even in the darkness Harkins could see Lowell glancing at him in the rearview mirror. Her grip on the wheel tightened.

"I take it you don't feel that way," Harkins said to the driver.

Wickman switched his gaze from Harkins to Lowell, his face unreadable in the dark.

"I don't know anymore, sir," Lowell said. "Mister Churchill says that we must wipe out their factories, all their capacity to make military supplies. And that they must pay for what they did to us during the Blitz."

"And what do you think of that line of reasoning?" Harkins asked.

"Well, it may be true that next time some madman wants to seize power, the people won't be such sheep. Maybe they'll speak up. Do something to prevent it."

"I don't know," Harkins said. "Seems to me your Mister Chamberlain was pretty sheepy at Munich. Handed over Czechoslovakia to the Nazis."

"He was not *my* Mister Chamberlain, sir," Lowell said. "I wasn't old enough to vote. I'm still not."

"That's kind of my point," Harkins said, not wanting to badger the kid but unwilling to swallow the sloppy logic of the politicians. "You had no more control over what Chamberlain did than some twenty-year-old German woman had over what Hitler did during the Blitz."

"A lot of people say we need to make them pay," Lowell said. "Punish them."

"Eye for an eye, right?"

Lowell didn't answer.

"My mother used to say that 'an eye for an eye' sounds great until everybody's blind," Harkins said.

Lowell was silent, but then she took one hand off the wheel and wiped the back of it across her face. She might have been crying. Harkins leaned forward, put his hands on the back of the driver's seat, an apology forming in his head. Here he was, getting all philosophical, when his homeland hadn't been bombed, his sisters didn't spend their sixteenth birthdays pulling bodies from the rubble.

"Look," he said to Lowell. "I don't know what I'm talking about, okay? You should just ignore me."

Before she could answer, the sirens began, drowning out everything else.

There must have been an air raid alarm on a pole right next to the car, because the sound felt like a physical assault, as if it might push the sedan off the road. Lowell yanked the car to the curb and jumped out with a torch—a flashlight—in her hand. There were people walking briskly along sidewalks that had been empty just a moment before.

The siren again. So loud Harkins could feel it in his chest.

"This way!" Lowell shouted over the din.

She led the men into a wide alley and behind an abandoned house. In an overgrown garden she found what she was looking for, an Anderson shelter, a half tube of corrugated steel about half the size of a small garage with an unprotected opening. The top was covered in dirt, the front a piece of sheet metal with a rectangular entrance cut through.

"In there," Lowell said, pointing with her light. Somehow she had taken charge of their little patrol.

Wickman went first, banged his head on the door. "Shit!" The big man stumbled inside; Harkins could hear splashing.

"It's flooded in here," Wickman yelled. Harkins plunged in next, tripping over a coaming and landing in the fetid water, his hands and knees sinking into mud. Lowell was behind him, her torch throwing crazy angled light.

"God, it stinks," Wickman said.

Lowell crouched in the low doorway and swept the small space with her light. There were no chairs or bunks or supplies, but Harkins saw a metal ring of some sort sticking just above the water.

"Well," Lowell said. "The good news is that the slop bucket is still upright, so maybe we haven't dived into a cesspool."

Harkins lifted his eyes to Lowell and the entrance, deliberately avoiding a few objects floating in the water. "I don't hear any bombs," he said. "Or ack-ack."

"Could be a false alert," Lowell said. "It happens."

Harkins heard voices nearby, maybe behind the house next door, others looking for shelter.

"Over here," Lowell called, backing out of the doorway and stepping into the darkness, dousing her light.

"Where?" A man's voice; Harkins thought the man was getting closer. Lowell, now in the garden, turned her torch on, then off again very quickly, signaling. Harkins could no longer see her in the undergrowth.

"This way," Lowell called.

Harkins stood in the small pit in front of the shelter entrance. Behind him, he could hear Wickman sloshing. Then, in between the siren wails, the voice of a second man called, "Ray, where are you?"

Harkins felt a tiny, electric jolt in his gut.

"Lowell," he yelled. "Come back here."

It was impossible to hear anything over the siren, so Harkins stepped out of the pit, willing his eyes to adjust to the darkness.

"Wickman," he yelled. "Come with me."

He saw Wickman—just a shadow—trip over the same coaming, then Harkins turned and put his hands in front of him, like a creature in a horror movie. When the siren pitched down again, he called. "Lowell!"

Just before the signal started its upswing, he heard voices from his left and lurched in that direction.

"Hello, love," a man said to Lowell. "Hiding out all by yourself, are you?"

"No," Lowell began. She switched on the lamp just as the man grabbed at it and called over his shoulder, "Here, Lenny. Look who's waiting on us."

The torch fell to the ground, but in its light Harkins could just make out Lowell and a man face-to-face.

"Ray?" a second man called from the weed-choked garden. He said something else, but the siren was climbing again.

Harkins pushed forward to get between Lowell and Ray, barking his shin on something solid. And it was only because of that second's delay that he missed getting kicked by Lowell, who brought her foot up into Ray's groin like she was auditioning for the Rockettes.

Wickman and Harkins reached her at the same time. Wickman grabbed the torch as Harkins turned Lowell away from the man, who had fallen into a fetal position, his hands on his gut.

The second man, still a few yards away, turned and ran back toward the street. The siren changed to a single long note: all clear.

"Jesus," Wickman shouted to Lowell. "You really laid him out."

Harkins looked at the young woman, whose breath was shallow and rapid. He helped her step around Ray and led her to the alley after he made sure the other man was gone. The siren dropped and Wickman called, "What do we do with this guy?"

"Leave that shitbird," Harkins said.

Lowell leaned over, backside to the wall and hands on her knees, trying to slow her breathing. Harkins stood beside her, one palm on her back.

"I'm sorry," Harkins said.

In the radio reports Americans heard at home, in the newsreels, in the papers and their editorial cartoons, the British were always portrayed as plucky, stiff-upper-lip types who helped each other into shelters and stuck it out together against the evil Nazis. In his years as a cop Harkins had seen too much of the seamy side of humanity to believe that was the whole story. Scumbags and thieves and rapists didn't take a break in a national emergency.

"It was terrible down there," Lowell said, still bent over but breathing regularly. "In the tube, during the Blitz. Most people were good, trying to be brave. But others—stealing, fighting over space, taking advantage of women." ·

She stood up, ran her fingers through her hair. Her hat was gone, her shirt pulled loose from her pants, her jacket twisted. She tugged at the woolen blouse, stood straighter.

"You said your father is a warden," Harkins said. "He must see a lot."

"My father *was* a warden," Lowell said. "He's dead."

"I'm sorry," Harkins said. "Did he . . . was it in a raid?"

"Best the police can figure is that he came upon some men rifling through the pockets of six or seven people who were killed when the bus they were on was hit. So, of course Dad tried to stop them. My father believed in law and order. In helping people."

Lowell reached down, tried using her dirty hands to brush muck from her dirty trousers. When she stood upright again she looked Harkins in the eye.

"Anyway, they stabbed him to death."

A few yards away Harkins heard people coming out onto the street again, talking in animated tones. He shifted his weight from one foot to the other, felt water leaking from his shoes.

Wickman walked by them. "I'm going to make sure that other asshole isn't trying to steal our car," he said.

"I'm sorry," Harkins said when he and Lowell were alone again.

"Yeah," Lowell said. "Me, too. My mother was heartbroken, but only for two weeks."

Harkins was quiet, anticipating the next turn in Lowell's terrible story.

"Then a bomb hit our house. Spot on. Mum and my little brother and sister were in a closet under the stairs; I was on my way home from my volunteer shift. When I reached my street, I could see our house and the one next door were gone; there was just a giant hole in the ground."

"All clear out here," Wickman called to them from the street.

Lowell gave the front of her blouse one more brush. A few yards away, the man called Ray had some of his wind back; he moaned softly.

"The Nazis started all this," Lowell said. "The Germans. That's twice in a quarter century. There are times, Jesus help me, that I hope we kill them all."

Wickman was asleep in the backseat and Harkins was nodding off by the time they got back to the jail near Finsbury Park. Harkins roused himself as Lowell pulled the car to the curb, rubbed his eyes with a thumb and forefinger. He'd left Scotland almost forty hours ago and had been traveling by train or staff car almost nonstop for the entire time, except for a forty-five-minute nap at his flat. He was at the point—as he'd been dozens of times since joining the army—where he'd take an hour's sleep over a steak dinner or a romp with a woman. Or both.

Lowell turned to the backseat after engaging the parking brake. "Here we are, Lieutenant."

These were the first words she'd said on the long drive. Harkins wondered where her head was after the incident near the Anderson shelter.

"Lowell," Harkins said. "You want to come inside with me? With us?"

"Yes, sir," she said. "I'd like that very much."

Harkins, Wickman, and Lowell went inside to find a different sergeant on duty. The noncom stood when Harkins approached the desk.

"I'm here to see my prisoner, Major Cushing," Harkins said. "Probably still in the drunk tank."

"Sorry, sir," the sergeant said. "That prisoner has been moved. Signed out."

"What are you talking about?" Harkins said, though he suspected he already knew the answer.

"Yes, sir," the sergeant said, picking up a clipboard and flipping to the second page. "A few hours ago. Some lawyer from Eighth Air Force."

"Goddammit," Harkins said. "Gefner."

"Yes, sir. That was him. Brought along a couple of big guys, like the prisoner was going to try to escape or something. Thing is, that major was not in any great shape to walk, much less run away."

"What do you mean?" Harkins asked. "Was he still drunk?"

"I don't think so, Lieutenant. I checked on him about an hour before the fly boys showed up, and he was shaking and sweating. Looked like the DTs to me."

"Where did they take him?"

The sergeant consulted his clipboard again. "Nothing here. But one of the goons was talking about being out in Norwich last night. So they gotta be near there, I guess."

Harkins walked outside, followed by Wickman and Lowell.

"I can't believe that son-of-a-bitch grabbed my prisoner," Harkins said.

"He probably has jurisdiction," Wickman said.

"Jurisdiction my ass," Harkins said. "He's got no case. Right now, I know more than anybody about what happened, and what I know ain't enough to bring him up on charges. Not on sound charges, anyway."

The three of them huddled on the blacked-out street. In a moment they heard a woman laughing, then the sounds of shoes hurrying across pavement toward the darkness of Finsbury Park. A man with an American accent said, "In the bushes?"

"The only people who'll see us," the woman answered, "are doing the same thing we're doing, love. Don't worry about it."

They listened to the retreating footsteps, then Harkins said, "Where's Norwich?"

"It's out in East Anglia," Lowell said. "That's where the RAF and the Yank air forces put their heavy bomber bases. Close to the continent. Norwich is a pretty good-sized town right in the middle of it all."

"How far?"

"Couple of hours by train," Lowell said. "I can get you on your way in the morning."

"Us," Harkins said. "You're coming along."

9

Harkins woke to a sharp rap on his door. He sat up too quickly and smacked his head on the ceiling, which was just above the top bunk, where he'd been dead to the world for four and a half hours.

"Sir?"

It was Lowell. He'd asked her to wake him at six to get on the road to Norwich, a trip that would take up most of the day.

"I'm awake," Harkins answered. He swung his legs over the sharp edge of the bunk, which had been slapped together out of packing crates. He lowered himself to the floor, found the uniform he'd worn yesterday in a wet pile. It smelled like the filthy water from the Anderson shelter.

"Give me a few minutes, okay?" he said.

"Of course, sir," Lowell answered. When he heard her walking down the stairs he found his shaving kit and a pair of fatigue pants for the trip to the WC and washroom. Ten minutes later he was back upstairs, rooting through the remaining uniforms in his duffel bag. He pulled out wrinkled olive trousers and a matching shirt, then dumped everything searching for the tan necktie, which the Army insisted on calling a kerchief. There was no mirror in the room, so he did his best, grabbed an overseas cap with his silver first lieutenant's bar and headed downstairs.

Harkins found Lowell sitting in the kitchen with Mrs. Ludington, his landlady, a dainty china teapot with pink roses between them. The two women were laughing quietly at something but stopped when he squeezed into the room. Lowell stood.

"Good morning," Ludington said. "Feeling better with a bit of sleep?"

"Much better, thank you," Harkins said, blanking on her first name.

"I've had a nice little chat with Pamela here," Ludington said. "I'd say you're in very good hands."

"That's good to hear," Harkins said. He looked at Lowell. "Are we ready?"

"Yes, sir," she said. She picked up a book from the table and squeezed by him. "I'll be right out front."

When she was in the narrow hallway, Lowell turned back.

"Thank you again for the tea and biscuit, Mrs. Ludington. I hope to see you again." She put on her cap—she'd changed out of her muddy uniform—and headed for the front door.

"Hope I didn't wake you last night when I came in," Harkins said.

"Oh, don't worry about that, Lieutenant," Ludington said, standing. "I like a bustling house." She reached for the teacups, managing to lift both in her right hand.

"Let me help you with that," Harkins said.

"Not at all," she said, scooping up cups and saucers and a tiny plate with a half biscuit on it. "I've learned to get along quite well, thank you."

As she busied herself at the sink, Harkins said, "Good-bye, then," and went out the front door. Lowell saluted as he approached the car, which was parked directly in front of the house. Before Harkins could speak, Lowell said, "Her first name is Beverly."

"What?"

"Her first name is Beverly. It just looked like you forgot for a moment."

Harkins wrote the name in his cop's notebook next to the street address of his lodgings.

"How did you know I forgot?"

"Just a hunch," Lowell said. "My dad owned a bookshop and I used to work there. He always had his nose in a book and frequently forgot the customers' names, so I got in the habit of prompting him. You just looked a bit lost, like he did at times."

Harkins paused with his hand on the car door handle.

"Okay, how about we turn that razor-sharp eye toward the investigation? What do you say?"

"Happy to help, sir. In *any* way I can."

Harkins thought she was smiling, but she turned her face away from him as she climbed into the driver's seat.

An hour later, Harkins and Lowell squeezed onto a crowded train at London's Liverpool Street Station, bound for Norwich. Sinnott had dumped a bunch of work on Wickman's desk the previous day, so the captain was staying behind.

The train was packed with GIs headed to East Anglia, a fertile and formerly quiet agricultural region that jutted into the North Sea like a fist aimed at the continent, with Nazi-occupied Netherlands across the cold stretch of water and, beyond that, Germany. Since 1940, scores of airfields had bloomed here at Britain's closest point to her enemy's homeland. GIs called England "the world's largest aircraft carrier."

Many of the men on the train were still drunk from liberty in London, so Harkins insisted that Lowell ride with him in the officers' car. When a conductor pointed out that she was supposed to be with the enlisted soldiers, Harkins said, "You want me to put this young woman on a car with seventy-five drunk Americans?" The old man nodded sagely, checked their tickets, and moved on.

Lowell did not look happy.

"I suppose you're going to tell me you can take care of yourself, right?" Harkins asked.

She took a moment to answer. "I appreciate that you're looking out for me, sir. I really do," she said. "It's just that it's hard to earn respect from the men if we're always being coddled."

"I'm not looking out for you, Lowell," Harkins answered, leaning back in his seat. "I'm looking out for myself. I've got a lot to do today and I don't want my driver getting shanghaied. Got it?"

"Yes, sir."

"What do you have there?" Harkins asked, pointing at the book Lowell had brought from Beverly's home.

"It's a medical textbook," she said, holding it so Harkins could read the book's spine. *Minor Surgery.*

"Beverly was a surgical nurse before the war. After she lost her arm she trained as a librarian."

"I have a friend who is a surgical nurse," Harkins said. "She wants to go to medical school after the war, become a surgeon."

"Are there many women doctors, women surgeons, in America?" Lowell asked.

"Oh, sure," Harkins said. "I'll bet there's as many as ten or twenty."

"In the whole country?"

Harkins sat back and studied his young driver. She was smart and, like his friend Kathleen Donnelly, no doubt frustrated at the limited options available to women.

"Let's just say she's going to have to fight her way through," Harkins said.

"Is she up to it?" Lowell asked.

Harkins looked out the window. He knew Kathleen from the old neighborhood, where he was a year behind her in school and he'd nursed a debilitating crush. The war had thrown them together in Sicily. The teenaged beauty of his memories had been worn down by the backbreaking work, too thin and too dirty and too tired. Harkins had been smitten all over again, as if meeting her for the first time. They had shared one night in a sweltering supply tent, bathing each other out of basins and lying together on a pile of clean hospital sheets. He had also seen her at work, caring for patients and mustering hospital resources to save lives. She was fierce and competent and, it turned out, fairly uninhibited for an Irish-Catholic girl.

Ten days later the war pulled them apart. He had written her a dozen mooning letters that he had not sent, and four chatty notes that he'd signed, "Yours, Eddie." He had not gotten a letter from her in two months.

"Yes, she's absolutely up to the challenge," Harkins said. "What about you? Is that your future? Nurse? Doctor?"

Lowell shrugged. "I'm not sure. I asked to borrow this because I'm interested and because I may be of more use if I know a bit of first aid."

"Ready to keep your favorite Yank alive in an emergency?"

"Exactly, sir," she said, opening the book and looking down. "As soon as I find a favorite."

A wheezing locomotive turned what should have been a two-hour trip into a four-hour test of stamina by the time they pulled into Norwich. Lowell, who was turning out to be very resourceful, had arranged for a staff car, and within ten minutes of disembarking they were squeezing along narrow country lanes, headed for the military police barracks at a crossroads village called Blofield. In the forty-minute drive Harkins did not see a single civilian vehicle. Almost all private cars and even the few pieces of mechanized farm equipment had been mothballed because of petrol rationing, Lowell explained.

Instead, the narrow lanes and unpaved roads were crowded with American military hardware of all shapes and sizes. For a while they crawled along behind a flatbed truck hauling the wing of an airplane. When they were finally able to pass, Harkins saw it up close; it looked brand new, as shiny as if it had just been delivered from a factory, someplace in California or Mississippi.

They found Major Frederick Cushing in the infirmary, alone in a small room off a larger ward. The hospital, which was just a series of connected wood frame buildings with walls of tarred paper, was heated only by a few tiny stoves. The staff had hung GI blankets over the windows to try to keep the heat in; Harkins wondered if spring would finally come in May.

Cushing was not asleep, but he was not quite awake, either. His face shiny with perspiration, he tossed and turned on a sweat-stained sheet, even though this room, too, was cold. Harkins told Lowell to wait outside while he went in. As he approached, he noticed Cushing's right wrist was handcuffed to the bed frame.

"Major Cushing?" Harkins stood over the bed. "Major Cushing?"

A moment later Cushing started shivering, and Harkins thought of the first driver he'd had in North Africa, a kid named Thomas who'd been laid out by malaria.

Harkins put his hand on Cushing's arm, then his shoulder, shaking him gently. He was wondering what his next steps might be when a captain in olive-drab trousers and a white lab coat came up beside him.

"Friend of yours?" he asked Harkins.

"No, sir. I'm an investigator," Harkins said.

The captain looked at him, waiting for an explanation of some sort, but Harkins didn't believe in sharing information unless it might help him make a case.

"How's he doing?" Harkins asked.

"Not well," the doctor said. He was young, twenty-four or -five tops, with a dark complexion and tired eyes.

"I don't know if he was a heavy drinker before the war, but he's showing all the signs of being an alcoholic now. He's been going through painful withdrawal for ten hours or so."

"I had an uncle who liked to pull a cork," Harkins said. "He looked like this some days."

"Did it kill him?"

"In a manner of speaking, I guess. He was drunk when he fell out a fifth-floor window."

Harkins' uncle Jimmy was a brawler, all hot temper and fast fists. Harkins' father and older brother sometimes called Harkins "Jimmy Junior" when his short fuse got him in trouble. He did not consider it a compliment, but he felt for people whose lives had fallen into a bottle, as Cushing's apparently had.

"Why is he handcuffed to the bed?"

"Some air force lawyer brought him here. They actually had him in a regular cell for about six hours, but the jailer saw that he was pretty sick and needed to be hospitalized. I heard the lawyer put up a fuss, didn't want him brought to the infirmary. Then the lawyer showed up here, making a stink, talking about bringing us all up on charges."

"So this was a Captain Gefner, right?" Harkins said.

"Yeah. What a loudmouth. I finally had to kick him out of here. Right before he left he put the cuffs on this poor guy, which is kind of a pain in the ass for the orderlies. I've got a couple of our guys looking for bolt cutters."

Harkins fished in his pocket and pulled out a set of keys. He unlocked the handcuffs and Cushing immediately pulled his arms across his chest, hugging himself through another round of shivering.

"So you're an MP, huh?" the doctor said, nodding at the keys. "You with that lawyer?"

"No," Harkins said. "This man was my prisoner and that lawyer pulled him out of custody."

"He a suspect in something?" the doctor asked.

"The lawyer?" Harkins asked. "Yeah, he's a suspected asshole."

The doctor grinned. "Actually, I meant this guy. He do something got him into trouble?"

Harkins looked at him. "Doc, you know what they say about curiosity and the cat, right?"

"Okay, okay," the doctor said. He put out his hand. "Name's Cipriotti."

"Eddie Harkins."

Cushing settled for a moment. Cipriotti pulled his stethoscope from his coat pocket, stuck the ends in his ears, and listened to the pilot's chest and back.

When he stood, he said, "These air force guys, they drink like it's their damned job. Like they can shorten the war by consuming all the liquor in Britain."

"Isn't that every GI?" Harkins asked. As an MP he'd seen up close how many GIs turned to alcohol to cure homesickness, fear, loneliness, loss.

"It's worse with the air crews. Not so much the ground guys, the mechanics and bomb-handlers, but the guys who have to keep going up, keep going back over Germany. A lot of them are just psychological wrecks."

"It's got to be pretty scary up there," Harkins said.

"I'm sure it is. Then you factor in the odds. I mean, there was a time when they were losing twenty percent of the bombers that went out on a mission."

"I heard twenty-five percent," Harkins said.

"Either way, you're not going to read that in *The Saturday Evening Post*. But I hear it from the operations officers. So that means you've got a one-in-four, one-in-five chance of getting shot down. Then they kept raising the number of required missions before a guy can rotate out. It started at twenty-five, then it was thirty, now it's thirty-five."

"That kind of thing might make a man cynical," Harkins said. While the two men looked down at him, Cushing grabbed his stomach and rolled onto his side. Cipriotti grabbed a bedpan from under the bunk and gently slid it under the pilot's cheek. Cushing promptly threw up. Cipriotti wiped the unconscious man's chin with a small towel that had been hanging on the bed frame.

"How long will he be like this?" Harkins asked.

"Could come around today. Could be another forty-eight hours. I never treated alcoholics before I got here. I was training to be a pediatrician, if you can believe that."

"Okay, I guess I'll come back later," Harkins said. "Do you know what outfit he's with? Or was with?"

Cipriotti walked to a table by the door and picked up a clipboard.

"Right now he's assigned to headquarters of the Eighth, but there's this note." He held out the clipboard so that Harkins could read it. "I don't recognize the handwriting. Might have been one of the nurses jotting down stuff he was saying when he was delirious."

"Why write that down?" Harkins asked.

"Eventually all these guys are going to need lots of help. I figure if we can gather a bit of information about their stories, the head-shrinkers might have a better idea about what treatment will work. I asked the staff to write notes about their conversations, their comments."

"May I?" Harkins asked, holding out his hand for the clipboard.

"Sure," Cipriotti said, handing it over.

There was a pitcher of water on a side table, a glass with a straw. Cipriotti tried to get Cushing to drink some water, but the aviator wasn't interested.

"I've got more rounds. If you can, try to get him to drink some water, okay? I'm worried about his fluid levels."

When Cipriotti left, Harkins studied the sheets on the clipboard, which were written in at least four different hands. The top page was a table with vital signs, the next a list of medications. Two of the sheets were notes about things Cushing had told his caretakers or mumbled while in some sort of painful daze.

One line said, "Patient alert and responsive. B-24. 787 Sqdrn. 35 msns."

Harkins took out his notebook and jotted down the information. It looked like Major Cushing, or at least the 787th Squadron, had flown thirty-five missions. He knew that the B-24 was a bomber, a big four-engine model called "the Liberator." He'd already seen scores of them from the window of his train.

Down the page, there was another note in neat cursive handwriting, a feminine script. The underlined letters, "delir."

Could that mean "delirious"?

There were a few lines about crew and weather. "Berlin" jumped out at him. Then, down in the corner of the page, squeezed in a space so small that he almost missed it, the tiny notation, "Russns."

Harkins looked at Cushing, who appeared to be sleeping fitfully.

"Well, Major," he said. "You certainly have a few things to say about our Soviet allies."

Harkins studied the pilot for another minute. The big man was sweating again. Harkins picked up the water glass and held the straw to Cushing's lips. When he didn't react, Harkins dipped the straw in the water, then closed the top end with a finger and used the straw to dribble water into Cushing's open mouth, like feeding a baby bird with an eyedropper.

"Don't die on me before we can have a decent conversation, okay?" Harkins said.

Even the intrepid Pamela Lowell had trouble finding the 787th Squadron. There were no signs on the roads, nothing indicating which units occupied which of the fifteen or so airfields they passed once they turned onto the paved two-lane toward Great Yarmouth, on the North Sea coast.

"No road signs out here, either," Lowell said as they pulled away from yet another headquarters that did not belong to the 787th. "Maybe they're still afraid the Germans will send a commando raid."

They passed a few farms that had not been paved over, and Harkins saw a group of military-age men knee-deep and swinging pickaxes in a roadside drainage ditch. They wore blue overalls with red circles painted on the back.

"Who are those guys?" he asked Lowell.

"Italian prisoners of war," she said. "They're given the option of working outdoors or sitting in a pen somewhere. A lot of them would rather be on a farm."

"The red circle looks like a target," Harkins said. "Is that in case they decide to run away? Somebody shoots them?"

"I don't know about that, sir. We're on an island, and it would be hard for a soldier who speaks Italian to fit in here in the countryside. Although," she said, dropping her voice, "from what I hear, some of the Land Army girls stuck out here would be happy to hide them."

Harkins laughed. "In the hay, you mean."

"You didn't hear it from me," Lowell said.

"In Sicily I spent a lot of time processing Italian POWs," Harkins said. "Most of them, the conscripts anyway, were thrilled to be out of the war. They used to smile and yell at my MPs. 'New York! Detroit! Chicago!'"

They drove for about forty-five minutes, the sky turning slate gray as they approached the coast. A flight of three fighters ripped overhead, loud and close enough to make Lowell and Harkins jump.

Eventually Lowell caught up to a convoy of American trucks and followed them onto an unmarked turn-off that gave way to an airfield. A Quonset hut sat close by the access road, smoke rising from a chimney made out of stacked ration cans. Harkins pointed to the building, and he and Lowell went in to find a lone sergeant sitting at a desk in a chilly orderly room, banging on a typewriter as if working out a grudge.

"We're looking for the 787th Squadron," Harkins told the man.

"I can take you there, Lieutenant," the sergeant said. He smiled, showing tobacco-stained teeth. "Glad to get away from all this dang paperwork."

The three of them piled into the staff car, the sergeant—he'd introduced himself as Curry—sitting up front with Lowell. He directed her onto a side road and past a few of the temporary huts, one big enough to be a mess hall. The land here was flat, with long vistas where the Americans had removed fences and hedges that had probably marked farmers' fields for centuries. They passed airmen on fat-tired bicycles.

Out the side window Harkins could see a long stretch of concrete airstrip. A half-mile on they passed some four-engine planes parked inside protective U-shaped berms of piled earth. Eventually they came to a line of tarpaper shacks, small groups of airmen loitering here and there in the chill.

"This is the 787th," Curry said, pointing. "That's the briefing room."

Lowell parked.

"You two kids stay here," Harkins said.

Inside the unheated hut, Harkins found three officers, a captain and two first lieutenants, studying a large wall map of Germany. There were rings drawn around the cities, concentric circles that Harkins figured had to do with antiaircraft fire or Luftwaffe defenses. When they noticed him, Harkins said, "I'm looking for anyone who knows a Major Frederick Cushing."

"Who are you?" one of the lieutenants asked. He and the other lieutenant were tall, well over six foot and plenty lanky; one was built like an athlete, the other scarecrow skinny. The captain was about Harkins' height, with a brushy, rust-colored mustache and an honest-to-God silk scarf around his neck.

"Name's Harkins. I'm doing an investigation that involves Major Cushing. Any of you guys know him?"

One of the lieutenants—the skinny one—glanced at the captain. It was clear they knew Cushing.

"Are you with that goddamn lawyer?" the captain asked. "What was his name?"

"Gefner," the athletic lieutenant said.

"No, I'm not with Gefner. In fact, I think Gefner may be part of the problem."

"How?"

"Is there any reason Gefner might be gunning for Cushing?" Harkins asked. "Anything between the two of them?"

The three men looked at him. Gefner had already come through, stirred things up.

"Look, there was a murder the night before last," Harkins said. "Cushing was seen with the victim, but that doesn't make him guilty. My job is to make sure we have all the facts and don't go off half-cocked."

"Which is what Gefner is doing, sounds like," the captain said. Then, after another three-beat delay, "Major Cushing is a good man and a cracker-jack pilot. I don't want to see him get screwed over."

The four of them stood there in a kind of standoff as the aviators tried to determine if they could trust Harkins. After what was probably thirty seconds but felt like five minutes, just to break the tension Harkins said, "Is it always this goddamn cold in these buildings?"

"The stoves aren't worth shit," the athletic lieutenant said. "And we only get the low-grade coal."

Finally, the captain said, "Come with me," and led them all outside. There was a mist drifting across the airfield, not quite rain but not just fog, either. Harkins had read somewhere that Eskimos had twenty different words for snow; he wondered if the British had twenty different words for precipitation.

"Should we ride?" Harkins asked. "I have a car."

"Nah," the captain said. "Just a few doors down."

Harkins jogged to the driver's side of his staff car and motioned for Lowell to roll down the window.

"Wait here," he said. Harkins was standing, so Curry, on the passenger side, couldn't see his face.

"See if you can learn anything," Harkins said, nodding toward Curry.

"Yes, sir."

When Harkins turned back around, the skinny lieutenant had mounted a beat-up bicycle that had been lying on its side in the wet gravel; he pedaled ahead. The captain and the other lieutenant led Harkins on a muddy path for about two hundred meters to a Quonset hut that looked exactly like scores of others. The captain went in, but the lieutenant held the flimsy door open for Harkins.

"Welcome to the palace," he said as Harkins went past.

The building's footprint was a rectangle, the ceiling the inverted half-moon shape of the roof. What looked like hundreds of pinups, Christmas and Valentine's cards, a few state maps, and a smattering of family photographs were tacked to the curved ceiling. There were fifteen or twenty iron bed-stands, three with mounded blankets that might or might not cover sleeping airmen; the whole place smelled like wet wool, tobacco, and body odor. Uniforms hung on pegs, government-issue footlockers sat on the floor between the bunks.

Some of the footlockers were set up like little shrines displaying framed pictures. There were some glamorous studio shots of young women; a sunlit candid of a man in uniform with his arm resting on the shoulders of a woman a head shorter. Another locker held a picture of a baby; next to it the same baby and a dark-haired mother.

"Don't touch anything," one of the lieutenants told him.

"Wouldn't dream of it," Harkins said.

A toy-sized stove in the center of the room was surrounded by a half-dozen chairs. Harkins thought it was colder inside than outside.

"Have a seat," the captain said, pulling out one of the chairs near the stove. When Harkins stepped up, the man held out his hand. "Jim Larson."

"Eddie Harkins."

"This is Strickland," Larson, said, indicating the athletic lieutenant.

"And that one over there is Holland. The navigator, not the country."

The four men sat on the mismatched chairs. Holland used a tool fashioned from a wire hanger to open the door to the stove.

"You bastards let this thing go out again," he said, apparently to the sleeping forms. No one responded.

"Is Major Cushing in trouble?" Larson asked.

"I'm still investigating," Harkins said. "But yeah, he's in trouble."

"They broke that man," Strickland said. He unzipped his coat, which was lined with sheepskin.

Harkins pulled out his notebook, wrote down the men's names.

"Did you all fly with Cushing at some point?" he asked.

"Yeah, he was our pilot," Larson answered. "On track to be a command pilot."

"What's that?" Harkins asked.

"Command pilot is on the lead airplane," Holland said. "He's responsible for getting the whole formation to the target. Everyone else follows, kind of like geese flying south for the winter. The command pilot also makes the call if we have to scrub or switch to an alternate."

"Sounds like a lot of responsibility," Harkins said. "He must have been good."

"One of the best," Larson said. "I mean, these days—not so much last year—but these days we're talking about formations of hundreds of bombers."

"Hundreds of planes on one raid?" Harkins asked.

"Doolittle wants to make thousand-plane raids the norm."

Harkins wrote "Doolittle" in his book. Figured that was Major General Jimmy Doolittle, who had become famous for launching a raid from a U.S. Navy carrier—using heavy bombers not designed to fly from a ship—to hit Tokyo and other Japanese targets just six months after the humiliation of Pearl Harbor. The attack did little real damage but was a huge propaganda coup and a boost for American morale. Doolittle now commanded the bomber forces based in England.

"Are there any targets in Germany still intact?" Harkins asked.

The three aviators looked at one another.

"Might as well be straight with him," Holland said to the captain. "All we do is sit around here bitching about this stuff all the time."

"What's he gonna do?" Strickland said to his comrades. "Get Doolittle to change the war plan?"

Strickland turned to Harkins. "Who do you work for, anyway?"

Harkins thought—hoped—they were on the verge of giving him some information that might prove useful. Telling them he was the newest member of the OSS would probably not encourage an open conversation.

"I'm a cop," Harkins said. "I'm investigating a murder."

"Shit," Larson said. "And you think that Gefner clown is trying to railroad Major Cushing?"

"That's one theory," Harkins said. "I'd like to know why Gefner might have an ax to grind with him. Also, Cushing is in bad shape. I'm trying to find out how he got that way."

Larson, the captain, looked at his hands for a long moment.

"You two take a hike," he said when he looked up. "If there's blowback, it can land on me."

The lieutenants got up and left the hut. Larson looked over at the sleeping forms on the bunks. No one had moved; he and Harkins were essentially alone.

"Cushing was totally dedicated to making his crew better, making the squadron better, to making himself a better pilot. But no matter how much he did, we kept losing planes. Lose enough guys and it's going to take a toll."

"I heard some raids had as many as twenty-five percent losses."

"Last year, yeah," Larson said. "And even into this year. We were losing hundreds, *thousands* of guys every goddamn month. And still the brass kept ordering bigger and bigger raids. Nobody expected the flak to be so heavy or so accurate. Hell, at the time I was shipping out of the states—this was January of '43—the goddamned generals were telling us that the Krauts couldn't touch the B-17. We were too high and too heavily armored. But once we started raids into Germany proper, shit, they were just slaughtering our guys. Then you'd come back here and get a day's rest and have to go back up again."

Larson leaned his elbows on his knees, took out a cigarette, offered one to Harkins, who declined.

When Larson flipped his Zippo lighter and held it to the end of the cigarette, his hand shook.

"Is it true that the Mustangs are making a difference?" Harkins asked. "You have fighter escorts all the way now?"

"Oh, they're making a huge difference," Larson said. "But we should have had them earlier."

He leaned back, one elbow on the back of an adjacent chair, blew a smoke ring into the fetid air.

"The first models had American-made engines, not enough power, so they didn't handle well is what I hear. The Brits got hold of a few and put in Rolls-Royce engines; they worked great. But fucking General Arnold, flying a fucking desk back in Washington, doesn't want *anything* British. No engines, no tactics, no cross-training. The sonofabitch slowed down procurement. Meanwhile, dozens of planes are getting shot out of the sky every goddamned day."

Larson took a breath, then pressed thumb and forefinger into his eye sockets.

"Sorry," he said.

Harkins waited a moment, then said, "A while ago I asked if there were any targets left in Germany. That's when you told the lieutenants to leave."

"Yeah," Larson said. "Because the answer is that Germany is the target. If the bombs hit the ground, the brass and the Eighth Air Force public relations weenies shovel some bullshit about precision bombing of vital war industries, especially aircraft factories. If we hit those targets it's only because we drop so many goddamned bombs."

"What about that fancy bombsight everyone is always talking about? I saw it in a newsreel."

"The Norden bombsight," Larson said. "Put a bomb in a pickle barrel, right?"

Harkins nodded.

"You know where they developed that? Tested it and trained the first bombardiers? Fucking Arizona. You know how much Arizona weather resembles the weather over Germany? Over northern Europe?"

Larson held up his hand, made a circle with his thumb and forefinger and looked through it at Harkins.

"Zero."

"And Major Cushing knew about all these problems with the targets and casualties?" Harkins asked. "Did he complain about it or something?"

"That's a good question," Larson said. "Some people think he talked to reporters—to one reporter in particular—that he spilled the beans about this whole fucked-up show."

"Who was the reporter?"

Larson sat still for a moment, watching Harkins through the smoke curling from his cigarette.

"Cushing has a cousin who writes for the *Chicago Tribune*."

"Oh," Harkins said.

The *Tribune,* owned by World War One veteran Robert McCormick, was a vocal—some would even say rabid—critic of everything that had to do with Franklin Roosevelt, starting in the 1930s with FDR's New Deal and continuing through the administration's wartime strategy.

"There's been a couple of articles attacking bomber command, especially all the horseshit about how we can win the war with air power alone. By the time the brass found out about Cushing's connection—he and his cousin have different last names—Fred had already been warned about shooting his mouth off, about being critical of the air campaign."

"Wow," Harkins said.

It was one thing for a dogface private to bitch to his congressman that he wasn't getting his mail. It was quite another for a decorated officer like Cushing to tell a major newspaper that the air force generals were lying when they said they were winning the war. That would be enough for the bigwigs to send their lawyers after Cushing.

"Did he do it, do you think?" Harkins asked. "Did he feed information to the *Tribune*?"

Larson shrugged. "Doesn't matter. They think he did, so they have it in for him."

The pilot took another long pull on his cigarette, then dropped the butt into a can of dirty water beside the stove. He held out his hand, palm down, fingers spread. It shook, just as it did when he held his lighter.

"See that? That's mild. Some guys get to where they can't button their fly. Tough to fly a plane when you shake like that."

"Cushing get to that stage?"

One of the men sleeping beneath a pile of blankets stirred, then shouted something unintelligible as he kicked the covers off. He sat up, looked at

Larson and Harkins, mumbled, "Shit," and fell back, pulling the blankets over his head again.

"Cushing was worse. The flight surgeon took him off status."

Outside, a siren wailed. Then the door to the hut banged open and Lieutenant Holland stepped inside. "Got some shot-up aircraft coming in," he said.

"On my way," Larson answered. He stood and slipped into the sleeves of his leather flight coat.

"Can I come along?" Harkins asked.

"Yeah," Larson said. "Sure. You might wind up carrying wounded."

"Wouldn't be my first time."

10

Lowell and Sergeant Curry watched from inside the staff car as a procession of tractors pulling wheeled racks of bombs rolled past them, headed for the flight line. The tractors moved slowly, ground crew walking along beside like shepherds.

"Just think," Curry said. "In about twelve hours those bombs will be ruining some Kraut's day."

The siren saved Lowell from responding. A tractor stopped on the road next to the staff car, its rack of two fat bombs just a few feet from Lowell's window.

"What's happening?" Lowell asked.

"Planes coming in with wounded," Curry said, checking the sky through the windshield. "They might be damaged, so we won't haul any more bombs up near the flight line just yet, in case there's a crash or something."

Lowell and Curry got out of the staff car. The three GIs escorting the closest batch of bombs all noticed her at once.

"Hello, gorgeous!" the GI atop the tractor said when Lowell stepped into view. "I see you brought your car for our date."

He was chubby, with the stripes of a staff sergeant, wireless spectacles that made his eyes look oversized, like an owl in uniform. The two other men, both privates, chuckled.

"Is it okay if I look?" Lowell asked. She had never seen a bomb up close, though she had certainly seen the effects of their explosions.

"Sure," the sergeant said, jumping down from his seat. "Sure, come right on up. They won't bite. They're not armed yet, so they can't hurt you."

He drew close to Lowell as she approached, then pulled a big wrench from his pocket and tapped one of the bombs on the nose. Lowell jumped at the sound of steel on steel.

"Don't worry, sweetheart," he said. "Ol' Sergeant Rickover ain't gonna let anything happen to you. Just wanted to show you they're harmless is all."

Lowell couldn't take her eyes off the bomb. Each was about four feet long, the cylinder domed at one end; the other end sprouted large fins that stabilized the bomb as it fell. Up close, the weapons were enormous—it would take two people to wrap their arms around the body.

"How much does this weigh?"

"This is a five hundred pounder," Sergeant Rickover said, standing too close beside her.

"Here you go, miss," one of the other ground crewman said, holding his hand out to Lowell.

When she reached toward him, he laid a big piece of chalk in her palm.

"Good idea," Rickover said. "Why don't you write a message on one of them bombs?"

"What would I write?" Lowell said, caught off guard. She held the chalk between her thumb and forefinger, as if it might be a smaller bomb.

"Anything at all. Here, let me show you."

Rickover took the chalk from her, squatted down and wrote in big block letters on the metal cylinder, "TO ADOLF FROM THE MIGHTY EIGHTH."

He stood, smiled at Lowell, and offered her the chalk. Another one of the privates came close. "Let me," he said.

In a sloppy script he wrote, "Kiss my ass, Krauts!"

Rickover took the chalk from the GI. "That's no way to talk in front of a lady," he scolded. He lifted Lowell's right hand by the wrist and used his other hand to lay the chalk on her palm, then he folded her fingers over it.

"Go ahead," Rickover said. "It's fun. Harmless fun."

Lowell took a step toward the bomb, reached out with the chalk, then drew back. She looked back at the fins, remembered a sequence from a newsreel that had been filmed through an empty bomb bay. The big canisters went out in a cluster, the bombs eventually sorting themselves out and pitching nose down. In that newsreel, she could just make out what looked like a river, then a geometric pattern that might have been a city. The short, which played in packed movie houses before the feature film, never named the target.

"I got something to write," the third soldier said, stepping up.

Yet another American accent, Lowell thought. His "write" sounded like "rat." He was very young, very handsome, with dark curly hair and a dimpled chin. When Lowell handed over the chalk, he squatted and wrote below Rickover's inscription, "rember pearl harbor!!"

"What the hell is that supposed to say?" Rickover asked.

The handsome soldier looked at Rickover, then at the bomb, as if he'd forgotten what he wrote.

"The fucking Germans didn't bomb Pearl Harbor," Curry said, laughing.

"Watch your language," Rickover said to Curry. Then, turning to the handsome soldier, he said, "And you spelled 'remember' wrong." He shook his head, a disappointed schoolmaster.

Lowell took the chalk back, stepped up and wrote, very slowly, "Arthur" on top of a bomb. She looked at her work, then quickly wrote, "Betty, Thomas, Joan."

She straightened up, tossed the chalk to Rickover, dusted off her hands and turned back toward the staff car, Curry following.

"Is that King Arthur?" Rickover asked her back.

"No," she said. "My dad."

There was a jeep, engine running, outside the Quonset hut, Strickland driving. Harkins squeezed under the canopy and into the back. Larson jumped into the front passenger seat just as Strickland pushed the accelerator and the vehicle lurched forward. They bounced along a muddy track and turned left through a gap in a tall hedge, an ambulance hard behind them. The control tower—three flimsy stories of white-painted wood—came into view after the turn, and in front of them a wide, muddy field, a long runway with steel matting and a windsock at either end. Trees around the edge were bare of leaves, like ink drawings on a gray canvas. The ambulance pulled even with the jeep and the two vehicles veered right until they were parallel to the runway. Harkins saw a white flare arc up from a deck atop the tower.

"What's that mean?"

Larson turned and yelled over the noise of the engine.

"Damaged aircraft coming in, wounded on board. Planes that aren't in distress will circle and wait."

Harkins heard the plane before he saw it, not the steady buzz-saw drone of healthy engines, but a choppy sound that reminded him of a car on its last few miles. Then, to their left, a B-17 skimmed the tops of the trees and came into view.

"Holy shit," Larson said.

The tail assembly looked as if it had been attacked by a machete-wielding giant, and Harkins could see pieces of the aircraft's aluminum skin flapping in the prop wash. A propeller on the left wing was barely turning, the engine trailing gray smoke. None of the landing gear was down. The plexiglass nose was shattered, just a gaping hole.

"Belly flop," Strickland said. "Jesus."

The wounded bomber came down to a hundred feet or so, then held steady at that altitude as it headed for the trees on the far end of the field.

"Is he going to land like that?" Harkins asked. "No wheels?"

Larson and Strickland looked at each other, then Larson got out of the jeep and trotted over to the base of the control tower, where a knot of officers had their heads together in some sort of heated exchange.

The wounded airplane did not land and barely cleared the trees at the end of the runway. Harkins watched, fascinated, as the ship banked in a slow turn.

"What's he doing?" Harkins asked Strickland.

"Coming around again," Strickland said. "They're probably trying to get the landing gear down using the hand controls."

By the time the bomber made its racetrack turn and was headed back to the field for another attempt, Larson had returned to the jeep.

"Hydraulics are out," he said to Strickland. "Landing gear mechanism shot up. Ball turret stuck."

"Shit," Strickland said as he turned to look through the windshield again.

"What does that mean?" Harkins asked.

"They can't get the landing gear down, which means they have to do a belly landing," Larson said. "But without hydraulics they can't move the ball turret either, and its tracks are jammed, probably hit by flak."

Harkins knew the ball turret was the plexiglass bubble that hung from the belly of the plane to engage enemy fighters attacking from below. A gunner, usually the smallest man in the crew, squeezed inside through a small hatch. The whole thing moved like a ball joint, the twin machine guns swinging toward targets.

"The gunner is still inside?" Harkins asked.

"He can only get out if the hatch is aligned, and they can't move the ball, so he's trapped."

"What happens when they do a belly landing?" Harkins asked.

"What the fuck you think happens?" Strickland said without turning around.

The bomber was aligned with the runway again, two engines now trailing smoke, the right wing dipping lower than the left, but clear of the trees and lowering itself to the English soil. The ball turret would hit first, the weight of the plane crushing it. Harkins forced himself to breathe.

"They radioed in," Larson said. "Said they had everybody in the crew back there at some point, trying to get the ball aligned."

The plane hit tail first, then bounced as it appeared to stumble, the propellers throwing sparks when they hit the steel matting, the blade ends bending back like wilting flower petals. The ball turret simply disappeared.

The ambulance dashed forward, and a fire truck appeared on the other side of the runway. Harkins could see two men in white overalls, maybe flame suits.

Strickland pulled the jeep closer to the aircraft, and Harkins got out when Larson did. Up close, the fuselage looked like it had been used for target practice. Jagged holes from machine-gun rounds stitched lines across the wings. Shrapnel from antiaircraft fire had torn long gashes in the aircraft. The nose of the plane, where the bombardier sat, had been destroyed by cannon fire, as best Harkins could guess.

He did not ask any more questions.

There were fifteen or twenty people around the wreck now, helping wounded crew members climb free, passing stretchers inside. Harkins caught a glimpse of a mechanic standing inside the belly of the plane where the waist gunners would be, holding a plasma bottle above his shoulder while, below him, a medic worked in the dark space, trying to save a man's life.

A few members of the ground crew had gathered around an opening in the fuselage where it had been sliced open, above where the ball turret had been.

"Get away from there!"

Harkins turned to see a captain in a thick jacket, his life vest still around his neck, hurrying from the front of the plane to where the little mob had gathered.

"Get away from there!" the pilot yelled again, tearing off his life vest and tossing it aside. His cap was gone, the sleeve of his coat torn open so that the lining hung out in clumps.

"What do you think you're doing? Get away!"

The men had been straining to see what had happened to the ball turret and its doomed gunner.

"You fucking ghouls! I said get out of there!"

The men closest to the pilot couldn't move fast enough, and the officer shoved one man, who stumbled into his comrades. Harkins heard someone say, "Sorry, sir."

They removed the wounded first, the men from the ground crews threading stretchers into the torn body of the aircraft, then passing them out gingerly, trying not to jostle the casualties. Harkins stood at a distance and watched, a little bit embarrassed. In comparison with these men, he had risked little in the war except discomfort, loneliness, and boredom.

The pilot checked on the wounded and said a few words to each man, grasping their hands before they were loaded onto ambulances.

Once the wounded were gone, they pulled out the dead, wrapping the bodies in blankets, several for each man, tucked in tightly around the feet, around the head. The dead went on the back of a cargo truck, headed for Graves Registration.

It took over an hour to get the remains of the ball turret gunner free of the mangled belly of the aircraft. All that time the pilot stood by, arms folded, occasionally looking into the wreckage, which was crawling with mechanics and noncoms. From inside the wounded machine, Harkins heard hammering and the back-and-forth singing of a hacksaw on metal.

Larson sent an enlisted man to the mess tent to get a thermos of coffee and a blanket for the pilot, who accepted both with a nod. Meanwhile, Larson and Strickland stood in silence, smoking and shifting their weight back and forth, one foot to the other. Harkins kept his hands in his pockets. He had nothing to add here and lots of other things he could be doing to further his investigation, but he didn't want to interrupt what was so clearly a mourning ritual.

When it started drizzling, the pilot pulled the blanket over his head and shoulders. Finally, the last stretcher cleared the airplane, passed through one of the giant holes in the fuselage. The pilot stepped up, lifted the blanket and, after a few seconds, leaned close to his crewman. Harkins was at least fifty yards away, but it looked to him like the officer said something to the dead man. Then they loaded the stretcher into another truck while the pilot climbed into the cab. He still had the wet blanket covering his head when the truck rolled past Harkins, who wondered if Major Cushing had ever stood by as wounded and dead were pulled from his airplane. No wonder the guy drank.

Larson got back into the jeep.

"Seen enough?" he asked Harkins.

"Yeah," Harkins said. "More than enough."

11

The trip back to London went faster than the trip to East Anglia, but the train was packed tightly with horny, giddy air force GIs going on liberty. Harkins and Lowell found a seat in the relative quiet of a second-class compartment. An elderly couple sat across from them, the woman with a death grip on her handbag, neither of them saying anything past "hello."

The compartment door did not latch and so squeaked open and closed, open and closed as the train made its multiple stops. Every time it opened, some already-drunk airman stumbled in from the noisy passageway and tried to chat up Lowell. When the older couple left, Lowell asked Harkins for his kerchief, which she used to tie the door closed. Harkins moved to the seat opposite.

"Now I feel like we're missing the party," he said.

Lowell pulled out the "Massacre by Bombing" essay by Vera Brittain and bent over it, making small check marks next to some passages with the stub of a pencil. A few lines got her muttering.

"Glutton for punishment, aren't you?" Harkins said.

Lowell looked up at him.

"Listen to this," she said, holding the paper up to the dim light from the window and reading. "According to the German Government Statistics Office in Berlin, one-point-two million German civilians were killed or reported missing and believed killed in air raids from the beginning of the war up to the first of October, 1943."

Lowell sat up and looked at Harkins. "Why would I believe anything the German government puts out?"

"If the Germans were going to lie about it," Harkins said, "don't you think they'd lowball the numbers for the sake of propaganda?"

"What are low balls?"

"Lowball. Deliberately under-report."

"What does that have to do with, you know, bollocks?"

Harkins laughed. "Not that kind of ball," he told her. "It's a baseball term."

Lowell shook her head. "It's like we're from different planets," she said, looking back down at the dog-eared paper. "Anyway, she also quotes British and American sources that corroborate that information."

"That's a big number," Harkins said.

Lowell shook out the paper and continued reading. "The number killed by German air raids on Britain from the beginning of the war to the thirty-first of October, 1943, is just over fifty thousand."

She looked up again. "A million-two versus fifty thousand."

She sat quietly for a moment. "It's just hard to buy the argument that they have to pay for what they did during the Blitz when the balance is tipped so far," she said. Harkins could feel the agitation coming off her like a fever.

"And listen to this," she said, flipping to an earlier page. "During the year from late 1940 to early 1941, the Luftwaffe dropped approximately thirty-five thousand tons of bombs on British cities."

She looked out the window. When she turned back to Harkins, he said, "Go on."

"On the eighteenth of November of last year," she read, "a force described by the *Daily Herald* as the greatest number of four-engine bombers ever to raid Germany dropped more than two thousand tons of bombs on Berlin. In that *one week* we dropped a total of five thousand tons of incendiaries and explosives on Berlin."

Lowell reminded Harkins so strongly of his little sister that he felt a wave of homesickness roll over him, as if someone had sat on his chest. Lowell eventually tucked the paper under her leg, folded her arms, and looked out the window. Outside, dusk settled over the farmlands and airfields. Harkins pulled the blackout curtain shut, blotting out their reflections in the windows.

"The incendiaries create a firestorm," Lowell said after a few minutes of silence. "The fire so big it pulls in all the air. The streets act like wind tunnels. Typhoon strength winds make it impossible for anyone to leave the shelter, impossible for the firefighters to do anything."

She leaned forward, elbows on her knees. "Eventually all the oxygen is pulled from the shelters and people who aren't cooked to death just suffocate."

She sat up again, looked right into Harkins. "I used to take my little brother and sister into the shelter near our home. That could have been us."

"Something happen to you out there?" Harkins asked. "On the airfield, I mean."

"A couple of the men encouraged me to write on a bomb. A message for the Germans."

"Did you?"

Lowell nodded, looking, Harkins thought, like the saddest woman in Britain.

By the time Harkins made it back to OSS headquarters most of the lights in the building were out, but Tom Wickman was still in his office. Harkins filled him in on what he'd learned in East Anglia, and Wickman recounted his conversation with Detective Sergeant Hoyle.

"He said they didn't find anything in their canvass, but he was glad you did," Wickman said. "Then he said his boss was probably going to pull them off the case, since an American has been arrested."

"What the hell?" Harkins said. "Did you tell him we have very little evidence on Cushing?"

Wickman shrugged his shoulders. "Yeah, but it wasn't Hoyle's call. His boss made the decision."

"Shit."

"You think Sinnott asked the Brits to back off?"

"Him or that lawyer," Harkins said. "Let's see if we can find Sinnott."

The two men were walking down the stairs to the ground floor when Harkins saw his landlady, Beverly Ludington, in the lobby with two other women.

"Oh, hello," Harkins said. His first thought was that she had come to see him, which made him happy.

"Lieutenant Harkins," she said, looking not at all flustered. She smiled at him but did not stop, and the three women kept up their pace across the lobby, finally disappearing into a ground floor conference room.

"Who was that?" Wickman asked.

"My landlady, if you can believe that."

"She works here, too?"

"She told me she was a librarian."

"Don't believe everything you hear," Wickman said as they walked outside to the blacked-out streets.

The two men tracked Sinnott down just before midnight at a party in the crowded back room of a pub off Leicester Square. Everyone was in civilian clothes, talking too loudly and laughing too hard and drinking too fast, as if this might be the last party before the war snuffed out all the fun. Sinnott was perched on a stool in a corner of the room talking to two young women, one of whom held a pint glass, the other a tumbler that might have been a whiskey and water. Sinnott had a large glass sitting on a shelf at his elbow.

"Well, if it isn't Laurel and Hardy," Sinnott said when Harkins and Wickman walked up. "How's the weather up there, Wickman?"

One of the women snorted. Sinnott looked pleased with himself. Harkins resisted the temptation to look at Wickman and mouth the word "drunk."

"Would you ladies give me a few minutes here?" Sinnott said to the two.

One woman put her hand on Sinnott's thigh to steady herself as she slid off her stool.

"How was your visit to Norwich?" Sinnott asked.

"I got a very different picture of our Major Cushing," Harkins said. "Turns out he was a good pilot who took care of his guys. Had their respect."

"Gefner said he's an eight ball," Sinnott said.

"Gefner was looking in the mirror when he came up with that," Harkins said. "Besides, I think Gefner is trying to railroad Cushing. Might be because Cushing has been critical of the bombing campaign. He's got a cousin works at the *Chicago Tribune,* and some people think Cushing has been talking out of school."

"Cushing's a drunk," Sinnott said. "Probably shoots his mouth off when he's had a few."

Harkins resisted, but just barely, saying something about the pot calling the kettle black.

"I think the stress got to Cushing," Harkins said, "and he fell apart. But he wasn't always like that."

"Did you talk to Cushing?"

"Not really," Harkins said. "Oh, and that asshole Gefner had him handcuffed to the bed."

"I heard about that kinky stuff," Sinnott said, smiling a lopsided grin at his own joke. Harkins wanted to punch him.

"I want to see that report Cushing was carrying when I picked him up," Harkins said.

"Why?"

"Because we have no motive for Cushing to kill Batcheller. It's all just circumstantial. I want to know if that report was why they were together."

"Do a man and a woman need a reason to get together?" Sinnott asked, leering again.

"They weren't a couple," Harkins said. "So there might have been another reason."

"You don't have a need-to-know what Batcheller was working on," Sinnott said.

"That report is evidence, so it will have to be introduced if this comes to trial," Harkins said.

Sinnott closed his eyes and shook his head.

"You forget that we're not back in Philadelphia," he said. "Different rules here, especially about classified materials. I doubt you'll ever see that report again, and there's certainly no guarantee that it will be produced for the trial.

"In fact, that's how I got CID off the case completely. I convinced some colonel at the provost that the investigation touched on too much classified stuff, too much secret OSS shit, for their guys to handle. So you're the lead, Harkins."

Sinnott stood, wobbled a bit, put his hand on the shelf holding his drink. He wore a suit, double-breasted, and he jammed a hand into one jacket pocket, then the other. "Where are my cigarettes?" he asked of no one in particular. "Either of you have a smoke?"

Both Harkins and Wickman shook their heads.

"By the way, Harkins," Sinnott said, still patting his jacket and pants. "It's not 'if' Cushing comes to trial. We have our man—you caught him. Why do you want to make this so hard?"

"I want to make sure we got the right guy," Harkins said. "Basic police work."

"Okay, okay," Sinnott said, holding up his hands in surrender. "I get it. You want to be thorough. But from where I sit it looks pretty clear."

"From where you sit in this pub, you mean?" Harkins said.

Sinnott narrowed his eyes. "Watch yourself, Lieutenant," he said. "You'll ruin my party mood."

"Did you contact the Brits, the detectives who were working on this? Tell them to stop looking for a suspect?"

"We don't need them, either," Sinnott said. "British detectives have an inferiority complex; did you know that? I learned that on my first visit, when I came for the Rhodes. It's all because they didn't catch Jack the Ripper, back in 1888."

Sinnott leaned toward Harkins, poked him in the chest with a forefinger.

"That makes you our ace detective."

He picked up his glass from the shelf, smoothed his necktie with one hand.

"Now run along, you two. Have a drink. Talk to a girl, relax a little bit."

Sinnott waded into the crowd, headed to the bar on the other side of the room.

Harkins turned to face Wickman. "Well?"

Wickman hesitated. "Well, he doesn't inspire a lot of confidence. But you have to admit that antagonizing him with comments like, 'from where you sit in a pub' isn't a good idea, either."

Wickman went to the bar. Harkins sat on the stool vacated by Sinnott and was looking at his notes when Annie Stowe came up to him.

"Well, if it isn't my favorite burglar," she said. "Come to rub elbows with the forgotten and powerless?"

"I doubt that describes you, Miss Stowe."

Harkins stood, offered her a stool. "I'm surprised to see you."

"I couldn't sit in my room alone," she said. "And I'm pretty sure I told you to call me Annie, or is it too informal?"

"I think I can swing it," Harkins said. "Can I get you a drink?"

"I think my friend is bringing me one," she said, glancing toward the bar. Her face looked drawn.

"So what have you been up to today? Go through any more underwear drawers?"

"I was out in East Anglia," Harkins said.

"Oh, where all the airfields are, right? I also heard you made an arrest. That was very quick."

"I made an arrest, but I'm still investigating," Harkins said.

"Why? Did you get the wrong person?" she asked. "You asked me earlier about a Major Cushing. Is that the guy you arrested?"

"You have a good memory," Harkins said. "I just like to tie up loose ends, and the case against this guy isn't very strong, so I need to do more digging."

"Very conscientious of you," she said.

Wickman appeared carrying two cocktail glasses. "Hello," he said, smiling at Stowe. "Would you like a whiskey and water?"

"Thanks," she said, taking one of the drinks. Wickman offered the other to Harkins, who waved him off.

Stowe took a sip. "Everything here is so watered down. I believe when I get back home and have my first real drink in years it will knock me on my bottom."

Wickman laughed, though it hadn't been much of a joke.

A tall man in a tailored suit stepped into their little circle. He also held two glasses.

"I see you already have a drink, Annie," he said.

"These gentlemen have been taking good care of me," Stowe said. She lifted her glass toward Wickman and said to her friend, "This is Captain Wickman." She pointed her glass at Harkins next. "And this is Lieutenant Harkins. Gentlemen, I'd like you to meet Lionel Kerr of the embassy staff."

Kerr put one of his drinks down and shook hands with Wickman, then Harkins. He looked a healthy thirty or so, a bit over six feet, with the wide shoulders of a swimmer and thick brown hair that he wore in an elaborate wave. He had soft hands and a clipped, not-quite-American accent that made Harkins wonder how long he'd been in Britain.

"Lieutenant Harkins is investigating Helen's . . . case," Stowe said.

"Such an awful thing," Kerr said, shaking his head. "Just unbelievable. You survive all that bombing and then someone turns on you."

"So you knew her?" Harkins asked.

"Just socially. I work in the embassy and she did whatever it is they do over there." He lifted his hand as if the OSS was on a foreign continent. Another man, who seemed to be tagging along with Kerr, laughed.

"Did you get along with her?" Harkins asked.

Kerr smiled, looked directly at Harkins. "We mostly got along," he said, nothing hesitant in his tone.

"But not always."

"Look, Lieutenant. I'm sure you've heard that Helen and I disagreed on some things." Kerr avoided looking at Stowe; he probably knew that Stowe had given this tidbit to the investigators.

"Anything in particular?"

Kerr took a dainty sip of his drink, thought about what he wanted to say. "In my opinion, Helen did not understand the importance of the alliance, that this war is being won alongside our allies. Because of our allies, in fact."

"The British?" Harkins asked.

"Don't be coy," Kerr said. "The Soviets are doing most of the heavy lifting. They've been keeping a few million Germans tied up along an enormous front for three years while we, the British and Americans, have been dithering around the periphery."

Harkins thought of the temporary American cemetery near Gela in Sicily. A field of wooden crosses rolling over a grassy hillside, a parade of dead men.

"Is that what we've been doing?" Harkins asked. "Dithering?"

"I'm sure that's what it looks like from Moscow," Kerr said.

"Do you work with the Soviets?" Harkins asked. "Is that a normal part of your duties?"

"I have in the past, but it's not part of my portfolio."

"Portfolio?" Harkins asked.

"My normal list of responsibilities."

"What is in your . . . portfolio?"

Two other men in suits drew closer to their little group, retainers hanging on Kerr's every word.

"Government policies of all sorts. I recently wrote a paper on what the British, maybe even we Americans, can learn from the Soviets about a centralized economy."

Kerr glanced around, smiling a little, enjoying the attention.

"Perhaps you've read it," he said. The line drew a few laughs. Harkins and Wickman were the only ones in uniform in the entire room. Apparently, no one assumed they were readers.

"I'm just a cop," Harkins said, smiling. "I mostly stick to the funny papers."

There was a little crowd now, Harkins, Wickman, and Stowe pressed into the corner.

"What's the short version?" Harkins asked.

"Well, the Communists clearly don't have everything figured out. But I'd say that the Great Depression was the death knell for the kind of free-market, all-out capitalism that's dominated the west since the Industrial Revolution."

One of the suits standing behind Kerr said, "Exactly!"

"Roosevelt himself has shown interest in Stalin's collectivization," Kerr went on. "Of course, FDR is a bit of a socialist himself, but he knows a good idea when he sees one."

"So you and Batcheller talked about some of these ideas? You thought the Soviets were . . . let me see here." Harkins made a show of looking at his notes, though he knew the exact phrase Kerr had used. "You said the

Soviets are doing most of the heavy lifting. I assume you mean in fighting the war. You two argued?"

"I wouldn't call it an argument," Kerr said.

"A fight, then?"

Kerr polished off his drink in one gulp. "Nothing quite that dramatic," he said. "And, I'm afraid, nothing pertinent to your investigation. Sorry I couldn't be of more assistance."

Kerr turned to Stowe. "Annie," he said. "Perhaps I'll see you later."

Kerr had already turned away when Harkins said, "So Gareth Jones had it all wrong?"

Kerr stopped, turned back around to face Harkins. His gaggle of followers bumped into one another, looking a little like Keystone Kops.

"I see that you read more than the funny papers," Kerr said.

Harkins shrugged.

"Jones has been sufficiently discredited. Every western journalist in Moscow all but called him a liar."

"Maybe we'll find out some day," Harkins said. "After the war, I mean, since we'll be all chummy with the Soviets."

Kerr smiled at Harkins. "I think I'll get another drink."

When Kerr had gone, Stowe said to Harkins, "I knew you two would hit it off right away."

"Who the hell is Gareth Jones?" Wickman asked.

"A journalist. He walked across Ukraine when Stalin was starving all the peasants. This is back in '32, '33. He saw the beginning of a famine. The Soviets were taking all their food, but no one was reporting on it. Jones had to wait until he was out of the country before he could write about it."

"And he was discredited?" Stowe asked.

Harkins turned to face her. "The whole foreign press corps in Moscow could only send out dispatches that were approved by the Soviets. Everything the journalists had or did—apartments, access to officials, cars, food, travel permits—all of it was in jeopardy if they criticized the regime, so they turned on Jones instead."

"Jesus," Wickman said. "They just took the food away from starving people? And these are our allies?"

Stowe studied Harkins for a long moment.

"Just like the British took food out of Ireland during the hunger, right?" she said.

Harkins nodded. "Something like that."

"That was pretty impressive," Stowe said. "How you pulled that name out of thin air."

"So you thought I was just another pretty face?" Harkins said, trying for levity. Stowe did not smile.

"You surprised, me, that's all. Lionel isn't a bad guy, just a know-it-all, maybe a bit of a dandy. He comes by it honestly. Went to one of those fancy New England prep schools. I think he grew up rich in Connecticut."

"Is there any other way to grow up in Connecticut?" Harkins said.

"Where are you from, Annie?" Wickman asked.

"Atlanta," she said, maybe leaning on her accent.

"Just like Scarlett," Wickman said. "Did you lose your plantation in that misunderstanding? I think they call it 'The War of Northern Aggression' down in Georgia, right?"

Stowe looked down, sipped her drink.

"Sorry," Wickman said. "Did I put my foot in my mouth?"

"My family was comfortable," she said. "We didn't live at Tara, but my father did very well. My sister and I—I'm a twin—we got horses for our twelfth birthday."

Harkins figured Stowe was about his age, and he turned twelve in 1929, the year the market crashed.

"By 1931 pretty much everything was gone. Daddy was desperate to make money, get us back the lifestyle we had. He eventually went to Argentina, some cattle-ranching scheme. He died of a fever down there. We didn't know for months."

She shook her head slightly as if to clear it.

"Sorry," she said. "It's been a rough two days. But what is it Scarlett says? Fiddle-dee-dee?"

"But you continued with your education?" Wickman asked. He looked like he wanted to hug her.

"Yes, yes. I was always the smart girl in school. My sister and I both. We came here to England, actually. Then I went back to Cambridge—to Boston—for my graduate work in mathematics."

"You went to Harvard?" Wickman asked, a little too surprised.

"Try not to look so shocked," Stowe said. "No, I went to MIT. Harvard only admitted women in the School of Education then."

"And now you do math for the OSS," Harkins said.

"Good try, Lieutenant."

"Please," he said. "Call me Eddie."

One corner of her mouth turned up in an almost-smile. Her glass was empty, so Wickman took it from her and scooted off to the bar for a refill.

"You're not a drinking man?" Stowe asked.

Harkins shrugged. "Another surprise, right? An Irish cop who reads *and* doesn't drink."

She smiled, let out a breath, maybe exhausted by grief.

"Was there more to Kerr and Batcheller than he let on?" Harkins asked.

"I don't know," Stowe said. "I think they had an actual argument, but I wasn't there. I only heard about it."

"Who was there?"

"There was a guy Helen dated for a while. A Navy guy. Lieutenant named Frank Payne. He might know something."

Harkins wrote the name in his book.

"Where can I find him?"

"Oh, he got moved. Portsmouth, I think. Or Southampton."

"Down on the channel, then," Harkins said. "Getting ready for the invasion."

Stowe put her index finger to her lips, a smile behind it. "Shhh."

"Right," Harkins said. "Loose lips and all that."

"Don't be upset, love," the woman said, propping herself on one elbow and pulling her other hand from beneath the sheet. "Happens to every fella now and again."

"Not to me," Sinnott lied.

"I'm sure you have a lot on your mind," she said. "People have started making plans *pending*."

"What do you mean?"

"Well, there was a handbill about a dance coming up, to be hosted by some regiment or other, and at the bottom of the page it said, 'pending.' I asked my girlfriend what it meant, and she said, 'pending the invasion.' The regiment might not be around for a dance. Since then I've seen it in a couple of places."

Sinnott put his hands behind his head and stared at the ceiling, where a water stain was shaped a bit like Lake Michigan.

"Shall we wait a few and try again?" the woman said. Her name was Elizabeth, but that had been Sinnott's grandmother's name, so he called this woman "darling" or nothing at all.

"What? No," he said, rolling over on his side and reaching for his trousers. He fished his money clip out of the pocket. It looked significantly depleted, which meant he'd gone through more than he'd planned for the night, no doubt buying drinks for everyone within earshot. He peeled off some bills, including enough for a generous tip. He wasn't sure this would encourage the woman to be discreet, but it might mean she'd give him another chance over the weekend. She was quite attractive, in a pouty-lipped, Greta Garbo kind of way, and she had her pick of overpaid Yanks. He held out the money.

"Thanks, love. Would you mind putting it on the chair?"

Sinnott had forgotten that she didn't like the money handed to her. Everybody had a favorite delusion. Hers was that she wasn't a prostitute.

She stood up and began to dress, Sinnott studying the small of her back, the lovely curve set off by a small birthmark.

"You must leave work at work," she said. "You've got to give yourself permission to unwind a bit."

Sinnott leaned back again. She was right, but it wasn't the invasion on his mind. It was goddamn Eddie Harkins, the persistent little bastard. He'd solved the case in half a day, but he wasn't happy with that.

"Have you heard the new ditty the Piccadilly Commandoes are singing?" the woman said.

"Piccadilly Commandoes" was the name the press had given the legions of streetwalkers who did business near Piccadilly Circus, sometimes servicing their soldier and airmen customers while standing upright in alleys or doorways.

"No," Sinnott said.

"It's called 'Into the Tube.' Isn't that naughty?"

"What a clever metaphor," Sinnott said, sounding more sarcastic than he'd intended.

"I only know bits of it," she said. She stood there in her camisole, held her hands in front of her, batted her eyelashes, and sang to him.

> "Bombs falling; it's Adolph a-calling.
> Slip *into* the Tube, my dear!
>
> "Where it's deep and it's warm,
> And you can ride out the storm,
> Far away from the chaos and fear.
>
> "No gin to be found anywhere.
> Meals are grim, and they're frightfully spare.
>
> "In the Tube you'll find bliss,
> It all starts with a kiss.
> And it only gets better from there.
>
> "You'll feel swell, I'll be flush,
> And if it ends in a rush,
> Please come back, the Tube will be here!"

Sinnott pulled his hands from behind his head and applauded. "You're too adorable," he said.

She curtsied, then slipped into her dress, which was much too fancy for the places he took her.

"And you drink too much, my love. You're a good customer and seem like a nice enough fellow, but our appointments would be more enjoyable if we could follow through."

Dressed now, she leaned over and kissed him on the forehead, like she was tucking him in for the night, and in the same motion palmed the money from the bedside chair. When she was gone, he got out of bed and went to the armoire, where he had a new bottle of real Kentucky bourbon. He'd paid an OSS courier a small fortune to bring it from the States.

He poured two fingers into a glass and tossed it back, feeling the heat spread through his chest. No sense getting sober if it just meant a massive headache before morning.

His demotion had started him on this spiral. For ten of the most exciting, terrifying, and fulfilling months of his life he'd been a field agent, building a network of Resistance members to smuggle downed Allied airmen across the border from occupied France to neutral Spain. Then he discovered that two of the people in his network—a married couple—had been turned by the Gestapo and had given up the names of at least four others in the cell. He got the news from a trustworthy source at dusk one evening. In the course of that single night Sinnott had gone from house to house to warn his people, bicycling, running, crawling, moving in the shadows, setting in motion the contingency plans he'd created to get them out of the area ahead of the Germans.

At every farmhouse he expected to see the Gestapo come tearing up in their black sedans. He visited the turncoats last, knocking on their door just as first light was breaking over the mountains. The husband had greeted him coolly, though middle-of-the-night visits were not unusual. But the wife knew immediately why Sinnott was there.

He didn't ask them any questions—they would have denied everything anyway. Instead, he picked up a pillow, turned on them, and fired his pistol through it, scattering feathers and muffling the report. He hit the husband in the left chest and the man went down instantly, his heart exploded. The wife turned, probably reaching for a gun, and Sinnott's first shot punched her in the hip, driving her to her knees, her upper body on the bed as if for nighttime prayers. Sinnott was on her in two steps and pushed the now smoldering pillow against the side of her head and fired again. He left the house through the kitchen, where the table was set for breakfast, two plates and a child's bowl.

The Gestapo made the rounds that morning, and the only two people they found were the dead informants. But the Germans turned the execution into a propaganda coup, putting pictures of the murdered couple and their unharmed infant in newspapers throughout France. One headline Sinnott saw read "The Resistance Kills Its Own."

Sinnott got his recall four weeks later, walking across the Pyrenees into Spain with a half-dozen American and British airmen who'd been shot down over France and Belgium.

Now, in his dingy rented room, he sat back on the bed, sipped his whiskey, and thought about the invasion. Everyone in Britain and on the continent knew it was coming. Certainly, the Resistance would play a part; the Allies had dropped tons of weapons and explosives by parachute to equip the cells for sabotage and direct attacks on Germans. They'd be screaming for trained and experienced OSS officers at the front once things really got rolling. The trick was landing a plum job. He didn't want to end up in some front-line division as an interpreter—he spoke both

German and French—interviewing civilians and prisoners. He wanted something bigger than that.

He poured himself another double. He thought it was only his second, but the bottle was almost half empty.

The problem was that no one at OSS headquarters wanted to take a chance on him, and no one owed him a favor. But when he contacted Eighth Air Force to let them know that Cushing was in custody, another possibility opened up. The air force brass had been itching to get rid of the pilot, and they had the perfect attack dog in the hyper-ambitious Gefner, who was sure that Cushing's downfall would lead to his—the lawyer's—promotion, maybe a cushy assignment in London. Gefner had been even more excited when Sinnott handed over the report Cushing had been carrying. Gefner was sure they could put Cushing away for good, and the lawyer hadn't flinched when Sinnott suggested a quid pro quo, maybe a job as the OSS liaison to Eighth Air Force. If Gefner could get a few air force generals to ask for Sinnott by name, Sinnott's boss would probably go along with it.

It would all work out if he could just get Harkins to play ball, to stop looking for ways to clear Cushing. The bastard's doggedness might eventually lead him to the Soviets, and that would not be good for Richard Sinnott.

He went back to the armoire, poured another two fingers of bourbon. One of his summer-weight uniforms was on a hanger inside. He'd been promoted to major in the fall and had not worn it since, so the right collar point still had the railroad-track silver bars of a captain. Harkins was still a first lieutenant.

Maybe, Sinnott thought, *I can buy him off with a promotion.*

It had worked before.

Impressed with his own ingenuity, he lifted his glass to toast the reflection in the armoire's small mirror, then drank the remaining bourbon in a single gulp.

He went to the bedside table, found his money clip, which held less cash than he expected. He rarely remembered where it went. More to the point, where would he get more?

"Fuck."

He rifled through the pockets of his trousers again, then his raincoat, then the uniform he'd worn earlier that day. He found a single, badly stained pound note. Payday was two and a half weeks away, and if the invasion happened before that, payday might be postponed.

"Fuck," he said again.

He'd have to go back to the Russians, the bastards.

12

When Harkins came downstairs in the morning, Beverly Ludington was already dressed, sitting with a pot of tea and a book.

"Good morning, Lieutenant. Care for some tea?"

"Yes, please. What are you reading?"

She closed the book so he could see the cover. Vera Brittain's *Testament of Youth*.

"Lowell mention that book to you?" Harkins asked.

"She did, though I read it before, years ago. Young Lowell has been quite upset by Brittain's latest writings about the bombings."

"I have a feeling we're all going to be astonished, once the war is over, to see what we've done."

Ludington looked at him for a long moment, gave him a gentle smile.

"Sorry," Harkins said. "Didn't mean to get all philosophical."

"Don't be sorry. I think you're right. Things we do in the moment, the expedient things, may look different when we have time to reflect."

Harkins sat at the small table, his knee bumping hers. She wore a dress more suited for warmer weather, and a tiny gold locket lay against the pale skin of her throat. Harkins admired how gently she managed the tea service with just one hand, and it must have showed.

"I count it a small blessing that I was right-handed before," she said. "It would have been a much tougher adjustment, otherwise."

After a few seconds Harkins said, "I can't even imagine."

She finished pouring and gently pushed a cup and saucer toward him. "It's all right to be curious," she said. "It's not like I haven't noticed that my arm is missing."

Harkins laughed, was relieved when she laughed, too.

"Did it happen in that raid you mentioned?"

"Yes. Tenth of September, 1940. Nothing heroic. I was running to a shelter and was hit by a piece of masonry. Knocked me down and crushed my arm."

"Who pulled you out?" Harkins asked.

"An ambulance team got me out. First, they had to do the surgery right there, me facedown in the road. The arm wasn't going anywhere."

"I'm sorry," Harkins said.

Beverly shrugged, sipped her tea. "A lot of people had worse things happen."

Harkins drained his cup. "I was surprised to see you yesterday when I got back to headquarters. You always work that late?"

"When there's a need, yes."

"You said you were a librarian."

"I am."

"Well," Harkins said. "I've only been assigned there since yesterday, but I've already figured out that people don't talk much about their jobs. Can't help but be curious, though."

"A few of us who used to work in the British Library helped our intelligence crowd early in the war. We've been asked to do the same for your American team."

"So, there's a library?"

"Yes, though it's not a room with books."

"Years ago I worked at a university library," Harkins said. "This was back in my short stint in college. Students were always coming up to the desk with their hair on fire, asking the most bizarre questions of the librarians."

He widened his eyes in imitation of every panicky undergrad he'd seen.

"What's the temperature on the surface of the moon? How deep is the Pacific? Was it raining when Keats died?"

Beverly laughed out loud, which made Harkins happy.

"I'll bet there are some real head-scratchers at an OSS library," he said.

"Head-scratchers?"

"You know," Harkins said, putting on a puzzled look and scratching the top of his head. "Like this."

"I imagine you are correct," she said. "But it's not just about information going out, of course."

"What do you mean?"

"Well, let's suppose that you're a German intelligence analyst. You're getting ready to invade the United States and you've got a hundred, make it a thousand agents in that country feeding you information that will be helpful for your offensive. What do you want to know?"

"Well, you want to know all about the defending forces."

"Sure. What else?"

"Oh, gosh," Harkins said. "I guess road networks, conditions of bridges and how much weight they can hold. You'd want to know all about the railroads, where the rolling stock is. You'd want to know about food supplies and gasoline and coal. Which mines are the most productive. Which factories are where."

"What about the people?"

"Well, you'll want the names of all the police. Government workers, especially utilities people who can keep the lights on."

"Let's say you're invading as a liberator," Beverly said.

She was talking about France. Both of them knew it, though neither said it out loud.

"Then you'd probably want to know who can provide you reliable information. Who can spy on enemy movement? Who can guide friendly forces in unfamiliar terrain?"

"So you've got a great deal of information coming in," she said. "Just pouring in, a veritable monsoon of disorganized data. You can't just stick it all in a drawer and hope you'll be able to retrieve what you need, right?"

"I get it," Harkins said. "Librarians organize information, categorize it so it can be found easily. Probably cross-reference everything, too."

"And if there's no system of categorization—because no one has ever done this before, not on this scale—librarians have to come up with a system that works."

"Wow," Harkins said. "I see a knighthood in your future."

"Silly, women can't become knights. And no one will ever know about this," Beverly said. "Maybe in fifty or sixty years they'll let some historian see the records."

"Doesn't seem right. I got a little medal for qualifying as an expert with my pistol, but you'll get no public recognition?"

"Women are used to working and not getting recognized," she said.

Harkins thought about the army nurses he'd met in Sicily. The second lieutenants among them got half the pay of a male second lieutenant.

"So you may see me from time to time over on Grosvenor Street," she said. "Probably best if we don't let on that we know each other. That would just make people curious."

"Did they send me here to board with you because of that connection? You and the OSS, I mean?"

"I doubt it. Just a coincidence, more likely."

Harkins looked at his watch. It was time to go.

"Well, I'm happy for it," he said.

"Me, too."

"I've got a question—hypothetical—about classified documents."

"Not my field, exactly, but I'll try my best."

"Suppose there's a document that figures in an investigation. It might bear on the testimony, but is not going to appear at any trial because it's classified."

"That sounds plausible."

"But the investigator thinks it was classified later for the express purpose of keeping it out of the trial, maybe because it will exonerate the accused."

"So this hypothetical investigator wants to determine when the document was actually classified?"

Harkins nodded.

"Well, it's easy enough to backdate a classification. There really is a big

rubber stamp that says 'Secret' or 'Top Secret,' and the date is just written in with ink. Someone could just write in an earlier date."

Harkins put his hands in his pockets.

"Is this germane to your investigation?"

"Maybe, maybe not. I might be grasping at straws."

"Sorry I couldn't help more."

"Not at all," Harkins said. "Listen, maybe if I'm back at a decent hour,
we could grab a bite to eat together."

"I'd like that," Beverly said. "Now, off you go. Be careful traveling
today."

Harkins pulled his cap from his pocket. "How did you know I was
traveling?"

"Just a guess," she said, giving him a mischievous smile. "Either that,
or I'm a super spy. But you'll never get anything out of me, Yank. Not
until you buy me dinner."

"So, no Captain Wickman again today," Pamela Lowell said to Harkins
as they drove south toward the channel coast. "You did tell him we were
headed out, didn't you?"

"Why, Private Lowell, I'm surprised you think I could be so devious as
to abandon my partner."

It had been Wickman's idea to let Harkins go to the coast alone to
interview Batcheller's friend, Lieutenant Payne. The captain said he was
working on something that would help them.

"So why are we driving and not taking the train?" Harkins asked.

"All the trains have been requisitioned," Lowell answered. "The clerk
told me she couldn't find a single seat on anything going toward the
coast."

"Is that right?" Harkins asked, looking sideways at Lowell, who kept
her hands at ten and two on the wheel.

"What do you mean?"

"Well it just seems odd, with gasoline—excuse me, petrol—so tightly
rationed, that we're motoring down to Southampton," Harkins said.
"You didn't pull this little stunt so you could stay involved in the investigation, did you?"

"It's not a little stunt, sir," Lowell said, glancing at him quickly. "But
I am glad to be out of the rotation at the motor pool. I would like very
much to be useful, but I'm also happy to be away from Corporal Moore."

"Is that your squad leader?"

"Team leader, yes, sir. If she gets wind of a good assignment, she often
pulls the girl off the job and takes it herself."

"Do you think I'd like her better?" Harkins asked, smiling. "Should I
trade up?"

"Well, she's quite pretty, but I'm sure you're better off with me."

"If you say so."

They drove south and west, the land unfolding around them in dozens of shades of green, low hills and ancient hedges close to the road. Since the highway signs had been removed, Lowell named the towns, a strange-sounding litany: Chertsey, Woking, Farnborough, Basingstoke, Sutton Scotney, Kings Worthy. The closer they got to the coast, the more military hardware they saw parked in fields and along roadsides, much of it under camouflage netting. They passed one great pile of crates—Harkins thought it was ammunition—with a footprint half as big as a football field, the wooden boxes stacked eight or ten high, all of it tucked below a giant overhang of corrugated metal. He counted six gleaming new locomotives parked on a railroad siding visible from the highway.

"Why did you become a police officer?" Lowell asked Harkins when they got past the jam.

"A girl told me that the blue uniform went well with my eyes."

Harkins turned to Lowell, certain that she'd look to confirm he had blue eyes, but she stared straight ahead.

"Okay," he said. "That's not true, but I did take typing in high school because there were lots of girls in the class."

Lowell didn't crack a smile at this tidbit, either. After a pause, she said, "So?"

Harkins looked out the windshield as they passed a horse-drawn cart hauling milk cans. An old man sitting on the bench seat lifted a hand when Harkins waved.

"I was in college for a year," Harkins said. "Catholic school called Villanova, near Philadelphia."

When he didn't go further, Lowell asked, "Then the war came long?"

"No. I was asked to take my talents elsewhere. There was this big guy on the rowing team, and he kept pushing around some other guy, a smaller guy who wore glasses. I asked the rower to lay off."

Harkins looked off to the right, and when the hedges parted he saw a man standing in a muddy field, examining a horse's hoof.

"So, what? The big guy didn't stop?"

"No, he stopped," Harkins said.

That part was true; the bully got the message, but only after Harkins had smacked him around in front of his teammates at the boat house. Harkins got expelled for fighting, but he suspected it was because he beat up a rich kid.

Lowell downshifted and braked, giving way to a shepherd moving thirty or so sheep across the road in front of them.

Harkins doubted he'd told a half-dozen GIs that he'd had a year of college, in part because he didn't want to get stuck with the nickname "college boy," which was not a compliment in the army, and in part because he was embarrassed at getting kicked out of school.

"But why a cop?" Lowell asked. "Why not something else?"

Patrick, his priest brother, had asked him the same question before he joined the force. Harkins had said something about law and order, about helping people, protecting the weak, and all that was true. But there was also some truth to the comparison Harkins' father made, that Eddie Harkins was like his uncle Jimmy, the brawler. He liked to mix it up. Sometimes Harkins was afraid it was darker than that.

"I told you," he said. "I look good in blue."

They passed through three different security stations before reaching Southampton, which sat on a triangle of land where the River Itchen met the River Test, thirty miles upriver from the English Channel. The address they'd been given took them to a cluster of temporary buildings set up in what had been, pre-war, a city park. All lawns had been turned to mud by tire tracks, and there was a latrine dug in one of the garden beds. A small sign beside the security gate said ROYAL NAVY LOGISTICS, SOUTHAMPTON.

"Is Payne a Brit, sir?" Lowell asked.

"No. Looks like he might be a liaison officer."

Harkins and Lowell got out of the car and approached a group of three American naval officers coming out of a large building. Harkins wasn't sure how to read naval rank, but there was a double handful of gold stripes among the men, so he threw up a hasty salute. Lowell followed suit, and Harkins heard her heels click together. He'd have to ask her to lighten up on the spit-and-polish so he didn't look so bad by comparison.

"Excuse me, gentlemen," he said. "I'm looking for a Lieutenant Frank Payne."

"Right over there," one of the men said, pointing back over his shoulder. "But you'd better hurry. He spends most of his time on the road between here and Bournemouth."

"What's at Bournemouth?" Harkins asked.

"Buddy, if you don't already know, I sure ain't gonna tell you."

When the three walked away, Lowell said, "I guess we're smack in the middle of the staging area for the you-know-what."

Harkins and Lowell went inside the building, and a clerk pointed out Lieutenant Frank Payne, who stood at a table covered with charts. He had a telephone in each hand and seemed to be yelling into them both at the same time.

"Yeah, well, that's not going to happen anytime soon," he shouted into the right handset. "So you better make do with what you got."

He jammed that phone onto its cradle and turned his attention to the other.

"Hello?" he said into the left handset. Then, louder, "Hello?"

Apparently there was no answer, so he dropped that one into its cradle and looked up at Harkins.

"He hung up on me," he said. "He called me for help and he hung up on me. Can you believe that?"

Payne was shorter than Harkins, maybe five eight, with a bald, bullet-shaped head that was, at the moment, shiny with sweat.

"Lieutenant Payne?" Harkins asked.

Payne looked at Harkins without saying anything, then at Lowell. His anger seemed to leak out of him.

"Annie called me," he said. "Told me you might be coming."

"I'm Lieutenant Eddie Harkins. Is there someplace we can speak privately?"

Payne took a deep breath. "I'm not sure I can help you. I'm really quite busy." He looked at his watch. "I've got to be somewhere in an hour. Less than an hour."

"This shouldn't take long," Harkins said.

"And it's a thirty-minute drive is what I'm saying," Payne said.

"Look, Frank," Harkins said. "May I call you Frank?"

"Sure."

"We can give you a ride, if that helps."

"I don't know," Payne said. "Like I said . . ."

"I know; you're not sure you can help," Harkins said. "I hear that a lot."

Harkins lowered his voice, leaned over the table a little so that he was closer to Payne. They were in an open space, all kinds of people in U.S. and Royal Navy uniforms bustling about carrying file folders and papers stuck to clipboards.

"So, you know this is a murder investigation, right? I'm the investigating officer, and I can detain people if I see the need, but I don't want to do that."

Harkins stood straight, tried a smile. "I hear there's a war on," he said. "So let's not waste any more time, okay?"

Payne picked up his hat and a canvas satchel. "Okay, let's go," he said.

Outside, Lowell opened the rear door to the staff car; the two officers got in the back.

"Where to, sir?" Lowell said when she was behind the wheel.

"Left out of the gate," Payne said. "Then keep left at the fork on the main road."

"Annie Stowe told me you and Helen dated," Harkins said, pivoting on the rear seat to face Payne.

Payne wiped his mouth with the back of his hand. Harkins had thought he was starting with an easy question. When Payne didn't answer, Harkins asked, "Is that true?"

"Yes," Payne said. "We were friends. I mean, we went around together, but we were mostly friends."

Payne was anxious, which made Harkins more curious.

"You married?" he asked.

"What?" Payne said, turning to Harkins. The question had hit a nerve of some sort. "No. Why do you ask?"

"Lots of married people, overseas for a couple of years, have other lives," Harkins said. "I'm not judging; you just seem nervous talking about Batcheller."

"No, I'm not married. Helen was great company."

"Okay," Harkins said. He sat back, looked out the windshield. "How long have you been here?"

"I got transferred last month, maybe five weeks ago," Payne said.

"Have you been back to London since then?" Harkins asked. He had not thought about Payne as a suspect, but the guy was clearly on edge.

"No."

"Did you request the transfer?"

Payne looked at Harkins. "I did."

Harkins wanted to ask him if he and Batcheller had a falling-out, but he needed to turn down the heat a little to get Payne talking, so he took another tack.

"More interesting work down here?"

"Well," Payne said. "Yes. I'm a supply officer, and this is the biggest buildup of supplies, maybe anywhere, anytime."

The road led north alongside the River Test and its giant docks stacked with everything from oil drums to jeeps. Lowell slowed to let a formation of marching men cross the road in front of them, two bagpipers in the lead.

"I love that music," Lowell said.

"Sounds like somebody's strangling a cat," Harkins said.

Every road and side street was jammed with military vehicles or men in uniform and on foot.

"I'm sure it's a puzzle, sorting out where all this stuff has to go," Harkins said, trying to draw Payne out. Lowell caught Harkins' attention in the rearview, lifted her eyebrows as if to say, *Tough one.*

"It's incredibly complex," Payne said at last. "Just thousands of moving parts, all kinds of commanders' egos getting in the way. I can't wait to see how it turns out, but I'm also afraid."

"Afraid of what?"

"It's possible the invasion could fail," Payne said. "Look what happened to the British at Gallipoli in the last war. For that matter, look what's happening at Monte Cassino. A few Kraut divisions are dug in deep as ticks in the mountains south of Rome. Can't scrape 'em out, can't bomb 'em out, can't pray 'em out."

Even the American newspapers most sympathetic to the war effort had howled when the Allies reduced to rubble the seventh-century Benedictine monastery south of Rome, ostensibly because German artillery spotters were using the high ground to hold up the Allied offensive.

Harkins thought about the thousands of tons of equipment and vehicles he'd seen just on this one drive to the coast. Hundreds of thousands of men geared up and ready to spring. Could the Germans really stop them on the beaches?

"What would it look like?" Harkins asked. "If it failed, I mean."

"An amphibious invasion is like an orchestra piece," Payne said. "All the parts have to work together just so. And don't forget, most of the people involved in this thing are amateurs. Me included. I'm Naval Reserve."

"You don't hear much about the possibility of failure," Harkins said.

"That scenario keeps a lot of us awake at night. Ships sunk, troops landed on the wrong beaches. Not enough ammunition where it's needed. Everything piling up at the water's edge."

Payne gave his head a quick shake, trying to clear the images of disaster.

"There's no contingency plan to get the troops off the beach if things go south. But a group of us have been tasked to look at the problems."

"A doomsday group," Harkins said.

"No, doomsday would be if the Germans found out where and when we were coming and were waiting for us. But I have to say, I've been impressed with how tight things are. I'm working on the logistics and I'm not even bigoted yet. Probably not until D-minus-ten or so."

"Bigoted?"

"Bigot is the name of a timetable for who learns the details, the big date, and the target area. Starts at the top, naturally, and at every level you only find out at the last minute, when you absolutely need to. Probably only a few dozen people already know. We refer to them as *bigoted*."

"I hope I live long enough to read about all this in the history books," Harkins said. "So I can make sense of it all someday."

Payne was quiet again, and Harkins did not have all the time in the world.

"What do you know about Batcheller having a falling-out with a guy named Kerr? Lionel Kerr, from the embassy."

"What did you hear?" Payne asked, still squirrelly.

Harkins looked at him. Maybe he just didn't like cops. Could be that he was feeling the pressure of trying to get all these supplies lined up in the right places for the cross-channel invasion.

Or it could be that he was hiding something.

"Lowell," Harkins said. "Pull over here."

They were on a long straight road, bordered by muddy fields, the only living things in sight a few cows.

"What are you doing?" Payne asked. "I've got work to do."

"And I want to get out of your way as quickly as possible," Harkins said. "I also want answers to my questions. Quicker you cooperate, quicker we get you where you need to go."

"So, what? You're holding me hostage?"

"I don't care if you call it a fucking kidnapping, Frank," Harkins said, not trying to hide his exasperation. "But you've been less than forthcoming, I'd say, and I'd be within my rights to haul you back to London. Let somebody else run the invasion."

He doubted he could actually lock up Payne, or even detain him, but Harkins was committed now, and he liked a good threat.

Payne grabbed the door handle, but he didn't have to look around to see that it was a long walk to Bournemouth. He sat back in the seat.

"Helen had a blow-up with Kerr," Payne said. Harkins could see, out of the corner of his eye, that Lowell was riveted, frozen in place so Harkins wouldn't be tempted to make her get out of the car.

"Over what?"

"Couple of things," Payne said. "Helen was a talented economist. Whenever Kerr started in with that horseshit about Soviet farm collectives, she shot holes in his arguments, which were mostly based on information the Soviets put out themselves."

"And they fought over that?"

"It was more that Kerr didn't like being upstaged by a woman. She also let him have it one time when he took credit for one of her ideas at some meeting. I don't know the details, but apparently he did that a lot, especially to the women."

"Okay," Harkins said.

When Payne didn't respond, Harkins said, "Is that all? Was that the big falling-out?"

"No," Payne said. "Kerr was the same arrogant ass he's always been, but a few months ago Helen started really attacking anyone who spoke up for the Soviets. She always called them our 'so-called' allies."

"And this was a change?"

"I don't think she was ever a fan of the Russians, but she became much more adamant, more strident in the last few weeks that I was up there."

"What happened?" Harkins asked.

"Something about Poland, or maybe the Polish government in exile in London," Payne said. "Maybe the Polish squadron in the RAF. I honestly don't know."

Cushing had said that the Russians were the source of whatever information Batcheller used to write the report Cushing had been carrying when Harkins arrested him, the report Sinnott would not let him see. But that seemed unlikely if she didn't trust the Russians.

"Is it possible that she worked with the Russians, or a Russian, on a report of some sort?" Harkins asked.

Payne chewed on the inside of his cheek. "Is it possible? I guess so. It just doesn't seem likely, you know?"

"Do you know the names of any of the Russians, anyone from the Soviet Embassy, that Helen knew personally?"

"She talked about a couple of women she liked, but I never met them and their names all sound the same to me. Sorry."

"How did Batcheller . . . ?" Harkins began. "How did Helen get along with Annie Stowe? Were they close?"

Payne looked at Harkins, like he expected there to be more to the question.

"I think so," he said. "Sure."

Harkins sat quietly, his notebook on his lap. In the front seat, Lowell had not moved. He could hear the ticking of the cooling engine, then a few drops of rain on the roof of the car.

"Do you think Lionel Kerr is capable of murder?" Harkins asked.

"No," Payne said. "I mean, I don't know. He's a vain little peacock and I can't stand the guy, but murder?"

"Okay," Harkins said to Lowell. "Let's get Lieutenant Payne to his destination."

Fifteen minutes later Lowell, following Payne's directions, pulled the car to the side of the road in Bournemouth, which was hard by the English Channel. A deserted beach curved alongside gray water, and a phalanx of houses stood shoulder-to-shoulder looking out over the sand. A hundred miles to their south was occupied France.

When they stopped, Payne opened his door, then turned back to Harkins. "I'm sorry I couldn't be more help," he said, sounding sincere. "Helen was a lovely woman, just a nice person, and I hate to think what happened to her."

Harkins thought Payne wanted to hear something encouraging, like Harkins saying, "I'll find her killer." But he couldn't promise such a tidy ending.

"Thanks, Frank," Harkins said.

Payne closed the door and started to walk away along the sidewalk.

"What do you think, Lowell?" Harkins asked.

"I think you should ask him where he and Batcheller stayed when they spent any free time together," she said. "Overnight, I mean."

"Why?"

"Because Batcheller's landlady didn't allow gentlemen to stay overnight. Isn't that what you told me she said?"

"Okay," Harkins said. "Pull up there."

Lowell moved the car forward and caught up with Payne. Harkins rolled the rear window down.

"Say, Frank. Where did you and Helen stay when you visited her? Your free time together. You must have had some nights off, right?"

"Why do you ask?"

Harkins tilted his head toward Lowell, so Payne would think Harkins was looking for a place to bed his driver.

"Oh, I see," Payne said. "We stayed in her room. Whenever Annie wasn't there, of course."

"Okay," Harkins said. "Thanks."

When Lowell pulled the car back into traffic, Harkins said, "So he's lying about that."

"It doesn't mean he's lying about everything," Lowell said. "It could be that he was hiding just a few specific things. Things he didn't want to discuss with a police officer."

"Not sure what you're getting at," Harkins said.

"Lieutenant Payne reminded me of my uncle Terrence. Uncle Terry."

"In what way?"

"Uncle Terry never married. He used to go to the continent once or twice a year on holiday. Paris. Berlin before the Nazis was quite libertine."

"Uncle Terry was a homosexual?"

"Maybe," Lowell said. "Didn't matter to us; we all loved him. But it had to be kept hidden, you see? It's a crime in this country and one can wind up in prison."

"Like Oscar Wilde," Harkins said.

"Exactly. He got two years at hard labor."

Sentences were much harsher in the American military. Harkins heard of a U.S. Marine convicted of sodomy who got ninety-nine years.

"So Batcheller pretended to date him as a favor? Help him hide his secret?"

"Maybe they were doing each other a favor," Lowell said.

13

Harkins and Lowell were back in London by late afternoon. She was able to park just a few blocks from OSS headquarters on Grosvenor.

"Will you need me this afternoon, sir?" Lowell asked as they got out of the car.

"You have someplace more important to be?" Harkins asked.

"No, sir," Lowell said. "I want to help in any way I can."

"Relax, Lowell. I'm only teasing. I'm not letting you back into the driver rotation at the motor pool, and you've already been helpful."

Lowell smiled and pulled her shoulders back, looking a little taller as they weaved through the heavy pedestrian traffic, almost all of it Americans in uniform.

"But if you start missing Corporal Moore, let me know," Harkins said.

"Funny you should mention Corporal Moore," Lowell said. "I've been thinking about her."

"She haunting your dreams?"

"Not yet. I was wondering, sir. And I hope I'm not being impertinent here, but you have so much more experience than I do."

"Spit it out, Lowell," Harkins said. He walked quickly, and she lengthened her stride to keep up.

"Well, I've noticed that you don't suffer fools, or bullies."

They stopped at a corner to let traffic go by, and Harkins remembered to look to his right before stepping into the street.

"What do you mean?"

"Well, when Lieutenant Payne was less than cooperative, you threatened him."

"So?"

"And you resist Major Sinnott, too. Some of your comments could be construed as insubordinate."

"You going to turn me over to the manners police?"

"No, not at all, sir," Lowell said. "I want to know how you judge how far you can go."

"I'm not sure I think about it very much, which is why I'll wind up in the stockade at some point. Or I'll be a lieutenant until the end of the war."

"Do you care?" she asked.

When they reached the far curb, Harkins stepped close to a building, a storefront with boarded-up windows, to get out of the crush of foot traffic. He stopped and faced Lowell. "Are you worried about me?"

"No, sir. I guess I wish I had a little more of your gumption."

"You're smart. You can use your wits to stand up for yourself, or to defuse a situation. I'm more likely—or I have been more likely, in the past—to use my fists. Not always a great idea."

When Lowell didn't respond, Harkins asked, "You getting pushed around?"

"Well, I'm a private and a woman, a young woman, so it's not surprising that I'm at the bottom of the pecking order. But I feel like there are times when I shouldn't put up with so much."

"Then don't," Harkins said. "Sometimes you just gotta say 'fuck it.'"

Lowell looked down at her feet, maybe embarrassed. Harkins knew his flippant remarks weren't helping.

"You read a lot in your dad's bookshop?"

"All the time," she said, looking into his eyes again. "We two were quite the bookworms."

"Ever run across e. e. cummings' poetry?"

"Some."

"He's got a phrase somewhere, 'there is some shit I will not eat.'"

"I remember that," Lowell said.

"Well, that implies that there is some shit you *will* eat."

"I never thought of it that way."

"But you have to draw a line somewhere. At some point you've got say, 'enough.'"

"Isn't that poem about a conshy who gets killed?"

"Conshy?"

"Conscientious objector."

"Oh," Harkins said. "Right. Yeah, I think he does die. You have to be ready to suffer the consequences."

"Are you?"

"I'm not doing anything that's going to put me in front of a firing squad," Harkins said. "Not yet, anyway. The most I've gotten is a few slaps on the wrist. To me, it's worth it to do what I think is right. I don't want to be sitting around twenty years from now—assuming I make it that far—trying to avoid thinking about the time I was a coward."

Lowell watched the traffic for a moment, a tiny crease between her eyebrows. "There's another private in the motor pool. Agnes Bercon. She follows Corporal Moore around like a puppy. Like a bodyguard. Bercon punched another girl in the face for making a rude comment. Broke her nose."

"So you're worried Corporal Moore is going to get Bercon to punch you, too?"

"It's crossed my mind," Lowell said. "It wouldn't be pleasant. Bercon is a big girl. Much heavier than I am."

"I'll let you in on a little secret," Harkins said. "The vast majority of people you run into have never been in a real fight and will go a long way to avoid one. When it comes to guys, most of the big ones have never had to mix it up because they intimidate people with their size. But if somebody thinks *you're* willing to go through with it, most of the time they'll back down."

"And what if you're wrong? What if they're willing to let it come to blows?"

"Then you might get your ass kicked."

Lowell did not look reassured.

"I'll share a couple of things my brother Patrick told me when I started boxing. First, getting punched in the nose probably isn't going to kill you. It's unpleasant, but you're not going to die."

"And second?" Lowell asked.

"You get knocked down, get back up again."

Lowell allowed herself a tiny smile. "A life lesson."

"I guess," Harkins said. "Look, I'm sorry if I'm not being much help here. And what applies to guys might not apply to girls."

When she didn't respond, Harkins looked at his watch. "How about this? Whichever one of us ends up in the stockade, the other will visit. Okay?"

"Or ends up in the hospital."

"Or the hospital."

"It's a deal, sir," she said.

On the second floor of OSS Headquarters, Harkins found Wickman and Sinnott in the hallway.

"So," Sinnott said. "How was your little jaunt down to the channel?"

Before Harkins could answer, Sinnott noticed Lowell and said, "Who's this?"

"Private Lowell is my driver, sir. She's been helping me."

"You have a private helping you investigate a murder?" Sinnott spoke as if Lowell wasn't there.

Harkins didn't want to get into a debate, so he just said, "Yes, sir."

"*Okaaay,*" Sinnott said, though he clearly found it odd. "Did you learn anything new about Batcheller? Anything useful?"

"It appears she had some sort of a falling-out with a guy at the embassy," Harkins said. "Lionel Kerr. Apparently, Kerr is a fan of the Soviets; Batcheller was not."

"That's it?" Sinnott asked.

"Those are the highlights," Harkins said.

"Not sure what that has to do with Major Cushing," Sinnott said. "I got the impression you were keen to find something that would exonerate him."

"I'm looking for anything that will help me understand why this woman was murdered," Harkins said. "And who did it. I am not looking to exonerate Cushing or frame him."

"Well, all of that will come out soon enough, I guess," Sinnott said. "Captain Gefner already has Cushing's trial scheduled. Could be as early as two weeks from now, first week in May."

"I haven't even filed a report yet," Harkins said. "Why is Gefner in such a goddamn hurry?"

"Look, I know you want to have everything tied up in a neat bow," Sinnott said. "But we don't have the luxury of all the time you'd like to take. Besides, Cushing is the Eighth Air Force's problem now. And when you're called to testify, don't bring up that damned report that you're so eager to see. It won't be part of the evidence."

"Things are moving too fast," Harkins said.

"You got your man," Sinnott said, a little exasperated. "You should be happy with that. At least this investigation cleared; that's better than you did last year in Sicily."

Harkins didn't take the bait. Sicily was ancient history.

"We're talking about a court-martial that could send a man to the gallows," Harkins said. "Certainly could send him to prison for life. I think we should be careful, take our time."

"All that will be up to the court-martial board," Sinnott said. "There'll be competent senior officers sitting in judgment. Unless you think you're the only one who is capable of finding out the truth."

Harkins' mind had already moved on to consider how he could derail the trial.

"I've got another bit of news for you, Harkins," Sinnott said. "I've put you in for promotion to captain."

Sinnott reached into his trouser pocket and pulled out the twin silver bars.

"Your work at OSS really calls for captain's rank. And you wrapped this case very quickly. You've impressed a lot of people."

Sinnott stepped closer and reached for the first lieutenant's bar on Harkins' right collar point. Harkins looked over Sinnott's shoulder, where Wickman drew his eyebrows in tight and shook his head just a tiny bit.

"There's a big jump in pay," Sinnott said as he unhooked the clasp on Harkins' insignia. "The paperwork will take a couple of weeks, but you can pin on the rank now. And it's time for you to move on to other things, let Eighth Air Force take over from here."

Harkins reached up and covered his single silver bar with his left hand.

"No thanks, sir," he said.

Sinnott stopped, surprised, standing so close Harkins could smell his aftershave, could smell the alcohol working its way through his pores. Harkins was careful not to look at Wickman, but held Sinnott's eyes instead. The promotion was a bribe, and Harkins wasn't on the take.

"What's this? Somebody getting promoted?" someone said.

Wickman popped to attention, and Harkins saw Colonel Haskell, the OSS station commander, over Sinnott's shoulder.

"Almost, sir," Harkins said, smiling. "I'm afraid my orders got a bit mixed up with my transfer from Italy. Turns out I'm not eligible yet. I jumped the gun a little bit."

"Well, that's okay," Haskell said. He clapped Sinnott on the shoulder. "We'll want to have a proper ceremony when the time comes, maybe a little celebration, right, Major?"

"Absolutely, sir," Sinnott said. He slipped the captain's bars back into his pocket.

"The tradition in the Regulars is that the officer getting promoted spends half of his first monthly pay raise on a party," Haskell said. "Of course, things are a little different these days, what with everyone running around hell-bent-for-leather. But I think it's worth preserving some of those customs, don't you, Harkins?"

"I'll be happy to host a party when the time comes, sir," Harkins said.

Haskell nodded to Wickman, then turned to Lowell.

"Who are you?" he asked, friendly.

Lowell, already at attention, drew herself up a bit taller.

"Private Lowell, sir. I've been helping Lieutenant Harkins get around while he conducts the investigation."

"Ah, yes, the murder investigation," Haskell said, turning back to Harkins. "How's that going?"

"Well, sir, Major Sinnott and I were just discussing that. We think that Eighth Air Force is being a little hasty, scheduling a court-martial before I've had a chance to really wrap things up."

Haskell turned to Sinnott. "Tell me more."

"Uh, yes, well," Sinnott said, stumbling. "Lieutenant Harkins is more familiar with the case, Colonel. I'll let him fill you in."

"I haven't yet filed a written report, sir, so I don't see where the court is going to get the pertinent information."

"Why are they in such a hurry?" Haskell asked.

Harkins wanted to say that he thought Gefner, the lawyer, was a hatchet man for somebody higher up in Eighth Air Force, but he knew that might make him sound like a nut job, like some private spinning conspiracy theories while peeling potatoes on KP.

"I couldn't say, sir," Harkins said. "I just need a bit more time to figure out the connection between Major Cushing and Helen Batcheller, some time to talk to a few people she didn't get along with."

"Well," Haskell said. "Cushing is locked up, right? He isn't going anywhere, so what's the hurry? We want to make sure we do a thorough job of investigating before we accuse him of this awful crime."

Haskell looked at Sinnott again. "Can you ask Eighth Air Force to tap the brakes a bit, Major? You and Harkins can tell them why, right?"

"Of course, sir," Sinnott said, the only answer available to him.

"If you need me to weigh in, let me know. I have a few West Point classmates over there I can call."

"Will do, sir," Sinnott said.

"Thank you, sir," Harkins said.

"Good," Haskell said. "Carry on, everyone."

The four of them—Sinnott, Wickman, Harkins, and Lowell—stood in the hallway for an awkward few seconds. Sinnott drew a sharp breath through his nose.

"Would you excuse us, please?" he said to Wickman. He pointed at Lowell and said, "And take this one with you."

When Harkins and Sinnott were alone, the major smiled and said, "One can be a bit too clever for one's own good, sometimes, *Lieutenant*."

When Harkins didn't respond, Sinnott said, "Did you tell your little driver to bring up the investigation because you knew Haskell would ask you about it? That you'd get the chance to make your case for more time?"

"No, sir, I did not," Harkins said. *But I'll certainly thank her.*

"Look, Harkins. I'm not the enemy here. I want you to do a thorough job investigating, but the fact is that we don't control the timeline. The folks over at Eighth Air Force are in charge of this court-martial. You seem to think that someone over there has it in for Major Cushing. But they're not making up the crime. Helen Batcheller was murdered; you saw the goddamn body. If Major Cushing didn't do it, we have to have some faith in the system. He'll be acquitted."

"No, sir," Harkins said. "That's not the way it works. You don't just throw someone into court to face a murder charge and hope that things get sorted out. First, the investigators have to persuade the prosecutor that we have the right guy. Then the prosecutor has to convince the commander. Then a board of officers hears the evidence, and they have to be convinced, too. All those steps act as safeguards. For some reason Captain Gefner, or someone higher up at Eighth Air Force, is ready to skip some critical parts."

"Okay, Harkins," Sinnott said. "So what's your next move?"

"I'm not sure yet, sir, but I'll be sure to keep you updated."

Sinnott looked at him for a long few seconds.

"Don't ever set me up like that again in front of my boss," Sinnott said. "Is that clear?"

"Crystal, sir."

Harkins thought the interview was finished, but Sinnott did not move, kept looking in Harkins' eyes.

"I know you think your little trouble-maker persona is cute, or brave, or will get you laid or give you some good war stories to tell when all this is over with," Sinnott said. "And you may be right. But maybe you heard what happened to the last people who fucked with me."

Sinnott was talking about the Resistance turncoats he shot. Harkins kept his mouth shut.

"Don't try my patience, Harkins," Sinnott said. "I want a daily briefing on what you've accomplished."

"And you're going to call over there to Eighth headquarters, get them to—what did Colonel Haskell call it?"

"Get them to tap the brakes," Sinnott said. "Yeah, I'll see what I can do."

"Thank you, sir. Thanks very much."

When Sinnott was gone, Wickman stuck his head around the corner at the end of the hall.

"All clear?"

"All clear," Harkins said.

"The promotion was fake," Wickman said as he approached.

"That's what I guessed," Harkins said. "Yours, too?"

"Mine, too. My pay raise hadn't come through, so I went over to the finance office this morning to ask about it. Sinnott never submitted any paperwork about a promotion. It was a sham."

"You're still wearing your bars," Harkins said, indicating the captain's insignia on Wickman's collar.

"Haven't figured out how to break the news. No telling what his reaction will be."

"I hear you. The more I learn about him the stranger he gets," Harkins said. "You figure he was trying to buy your loyalty?"

"I guess," Wickman said. "Pretty ham-handed, if you ask me. It's not like I was never going to notice that I didn't get a pay raise. Though I do feel like a bit of a dunce, falling for it like that."

"Don't beat yourself up," Harkins said.

"Maybe he doesn't want me looking too closely at what happens to the money I find for him."

"And it's pretty clear that he wants me to let that prick Gefner and the Eighth Air Force chew up Cushing."

"So there's no way he asks Eighth Air Force to back off."

"Right," Harkins said. "If we want them to tap the brakes, we're going to have to find someone else to help us."

"You got somebody in mind?"

"I do. A captain I worked with in Sicily. Guy named Adams. Pretty sure he's in London, but I have to find him."

"Well, in the meantime, you're quite in demand," Wickman said.

"How's that?"

"I ran into some paratroopers in Grosvenor Square this afternoon. Easy to pick them out with those fancy boots. I asked if any of them knew a chaplain named Harkins, and two of the guys were from his regiment. Said he rode the train into London with them this morning, a couple chaplains traveling together, maybe going on a tour of Saint Paul's."

"Today?" Harkins asked.

"Tomorrow afternoon, I think," Wickman said. "These guys were on a three-day pass, but he didn't know how long the chaplains would be around."

Harkins looked at his watch. It was almost half past six. He wanted to talk to a few more people in the embassy about Kerr and Batcheller, and he wanted to go back to Batcheller's boss to see what he might learn about the mysterious report that Cushing said had to get to Ike. He also knew he'd be going back out to East Anglia to talk to Cushing. Plus he'd just picked a fight with his boss by claiming that the investigation was urgent. And he'd suggested to Beverly that they have dinner together. There was no way he could make time tomorrow to look for Patrick.

"I have to try to find him," Harkins said.

"Don't you want to hear the other messages?" Wickman asked.

"Oh, right," Harkins said.

"Tomorrow night there's a little gathering, a little memorial for Batcheller at a pub near here. I heard there might be some of her friends from the Soviet mission."

"She didn't like the Soviets," Harkins said.

"It's probably just some low-level flunkies. Maybe she didn't burn all her bridges."

"Okay," Harkins said. "Might be worth going."

"One more thing," Wickman said, motioning him into the conference room, closing the door.

"A Soviet lieutenant named Gorodetsky approached me in Grosvenor Square. Said he worked for a Colonel Novikov, who has some information on Helen Batcheller."

"He used her name?"

"He knew her name and he knew your name, too."

"That's a little unnerving," Harkins said.

"Novikov wants to meet you. Tonight. Gorodetsky said you should be in front of the Royal Albert Hall at twenty-one hundred."

"What do you think?" Harkins asked.

"Now it sounds like some real spy stuff," Wickman said. "You told me Cushing thinks the data for the report he had, the one Batcheller wrote, came from the Soviets, or a Soviet, right? Maybe this is the guy."

"Or maybe this guy is looking for the other guy, the one who cooperated with Batcheller," Harkins said.

"You want me to come with you?" Wickman asked.

"Nah," Harkins said. "We're allies, right? What could go wrong?"

"You going to tell Sinnott?"

"Hell, no," Harkins said. "But if I wind up like Helen Batcheller, make sure you tell him it was my idea to go alone."

14

22 April 1944
2050 hours

Harkins crossed the bridge over the lake called the Serpentine seven minutes before nine o'clock. He'd changed his mind and had asked Wickman and Lowell to come along, though they'd hang back while he met with the Russian. He tried telephoning Beverly about dinner, but the lines in her neighborhood were out.

"Follow this to the intersection," Lowell said. "The Royal Albert Hall will be on your right."

Harkins turned to Wickman, who wore the single silver bar of a first lieutenant again.

"You demoted yourself?" Harkins asked.

"Just putting things in order."

"Okay. Give me an hour. If I'm not back, just take a stroll over there. Try not to make it too obvious that you're looking for someone."

"And if we don't find you?" Wickman asked.

"Go back to headquarters. I'll show up eventually."

"If you call for help, we'll come straight away," Lowell said.

Harkins couldn't help but smile.

"Yes," he said. "Please do."

He looked at his watch, an Army-issue model with a luminous dial. It was five minutes to nine. Just over fifty hours since he examined the crime scene, fifty hours in which the investigation had branched out in completely unexpected, seemingly random directions.

"Okay," Harkins said. "Here goes nothing."

"Wait," Lowell said. She reached out in the dark, shook his hand firmly.

"Be careful, sir," she said.

"Don't worry, Lowell," Harkins said. "I won't let anything happen to me that would put you out of a job."

He walked toward the dark hulks of buildings on the south side of Kensington Gardens, then trotted across the street. He passed the Royal Geographical Society, where some of the world's most famous explorers found supporters and told stories about their travels. The entrance to Albert Hall here on the north side was close to the road, under a wide arch that offered a bit of shelter. Even in the dark he could see the columns, two or three stories up, that flanked what was probably a window, now boarded up. A few figures hurried by, and only then he realized he had no prearranged signal for recognizing his contact.

Need to work on my field-craft, Harkins thought. He resisted the temptation to look at his watch again, and just leaned against the wall, arms folded.

A figure separated itself from the gloom and approached.

"Excuse me," the man said in heavily accented English. "Do you have the time?"

There were so many foreigners in London that Harkins wasn't sure he'd be able to tell a Russian accent from a Polish accent from another eastern European accent.

"Yeah," Harkins said. "It's straight up nine o'clock."

"Thank you," the man said before turning away, back toward Kensington Gardens.

Harkins was facing the park when someone came up behind him.

"Lieutenant Harkins," the figure said.

Startled, Harkins flinched. "Yes."

"I am Colonel Novikov, Sergei Novikov. Thank you for coming."

"You have information on Helen Batcheller's murder?" Harkins asked.

The colonel chuckled. "I heard you Americans like to get to the point," he said. "Let us walk a bit, shall we?"

Novikov headed west, toward Queen's Gate. No hurry. Harkins fell in step beside him.

"You have people with you?" Novikov asked.

"Sir?" Harkins said, stalling.

"You have people watching over our meeting? In case something goes wrong."

"I, uh, yes. I do."

"I expected so," Novikov said. "It is only prudent. We will travel just one block. They should be able to keep up."

Novikov turned to Harkins, and even though Harkins couldn't see his face in the darkness, he thought the other man was smiling.

Which is probably what they do right before they kill you, Harkins thought.

"Your English is very good," Harkins said.

"My mother was a professor of languages. I was fortunate to travel when I was a child."

The Soviet officer entered a narrow-front building and Harkins followed, pushing through the blackout curtain into a dimly lit front parlor.

"What's this place?"

"A house we rent for our staff," Novikov said. "You live in a rented flat, is that correct?"

"How did you know that?" Harkins asked.

Novikov laughed out loud this time. "I did not know; I guessed. Since there are thousands of American officers in London and there are no barracks, it stands to reason that you live in a rented room. Just logic, that is all."

Novikov was a bit taller than Harkins, maybe six feet, with dark hair and a patch over his left eye, like a comic book pirate. Square-jawed, broad shouldered, and relaxed, his right arm at his side, his empty left sleeve pinned to the front of his coat.

"I have not been spying on you," Novikov said. "Not yet."

He seemed to be joking, and Harkins managed to smile back.

"Let's sit, shall we?" Novikov said.

"Who else is here?" Harkins asked, looking around before taking a chair at a small table. A cheap glass ashtray held a dozen cigarette butts.

"No one. We will not be disturbed," Novikov said. "How is the investigation coming?"

"You first, Colonel," Harkins said. "What was your connection to Helen Batcheller?"

"Miss Batcheller was doing an analysis," Novikov said. "An ambitious project. Did you know she was an economist?"

"Yes."

"My father was an economist, too," Novikov said. "Miss Batcheller and I met at an embassy function at the end of last year. I asked what kind of work she did before the war, and about her schooling. She spoke quite a bit about California. Spoke quite lovingly of her home there. It sounded beautiful. Have you ever been?"

Harkins had spent the longest seven weeks of his life in the Mojave, training for North Africa's desert conditions. Both places had been miserable, fly-infested, dusty, and hot as hell. The only good thing about the California desert, compared to North Africa, is that there had been no one shooting at him.

"Yes, I have been to California. Sounds like Batcheller had a different experience," Harkins said. "What was she analyzing?"

Novikov smiled at him again. The colonel looked completely relaxed, as if he held clandestine meetings with Americans from OSS all the time. Harkins, who was decidedly not relaxed, wiped his sweaty palms on the legs of his trousers.

"Production numbers for German factories. Specifically, factories that produced military vehicles. Tanks, armored cars, trucks."

"Why was she doing that?" Harkins asked.

"Now it is my turn to ask a question, yes?"

Harkins nodded. "Okay."

"Did you find a copy of a report on her, or in her flat?" Novikov asked. "It would have had a list of German cities. Some columns of numbers."

"I did."

"Where is it?"

"That's two questions, Colonel."

Novikov chuckled, then gestured with his open palm. "Go ahead."

"Batcheller was with a man, a pilot named Cushing, on the night she was killed. I have detained Cushing. He was found with some papers. Sounds like it might be the report you're talking about. He implied that Batcheller's source for information was a Russian. That's the only reason I agreed to this meeting. Was that you?"

Novikov reached into a pocket inside his jacket and produced a silver cigarette case. He flipped it open and offered it to Harkins.

"No, thanks."

Novikov extracted a cigarette, put the case back, then pulled out an American lighter and, using his one hand, flipped the cover and struck a flame. When the cigarette was lit, he closed the lighter and put it back in his pocket. He took a leisurely pull on the smoke.

"That is an interesting question," Novikov said. "I could only be authorized to cooperate with Miss Batcheller—who worked for your American spy agency—by my ambassador."

"And he hasn't authorized you?"

"The ambassador is still learning his way around."

So that's a no, Harkins thought.

"Are you trying to cover up a connection with Batcheller?" Harkins asked.

"That is an indirect way of asking me if I killed her," Novikov said. "Or had her killed. The answer is no. In fact, I needed her."

"Needed her for what?"

"For the very thing that has everyone preoccupied these days," Novikov said.

"The opening of the second front."

"Precisely. It is difficult for Americans to understand—no, that is not the right word. It is *impossible* for Americans to understand how important this is, to really appreciate how the Soviet Union has suffered."

"So I've heard," Harkins said.

"In 1942, we battled the Germans across a front that stretched eighteen hundred kilometers from the Baltic to the Black Sea. An invasion of that scale in America would mean holding a line from Maine to Miami, in a battle space that went from the eastern seaboard to your state of Missouri."

"Jay-sus," Harkins said.

"We may never know how many of our citizens, or even our soldiers, have died. But certainly, it is in the millions."

Harkins thought about Kerr and his claim that the Soviets were bearing the brunt of the fight.

"So you need—we need—the second front to relieve some of the pressure in the east, right?" Harkins said.

"Exactly," Novikov said.

"Well, it's pretty clear that something is about to happen. This island is crawling with GIs, and more keep arriving every day. The big jump has to be soon."

"It would seem so," Novikov said. "If only because you and your fellow Americans are wearing out your welcome here."

Novikov balanced his cigarette on the edge of the ashtray and unbuttoned his coat. He wore an unadorned gray tunic underneath, plain brass buttons.

"Do you think this Major Cushing killed Miss Batcheller?"

"No, I don't," Harkins said, surprised at his candor with this stranger. "Or, at least I haven't found any reason he might want to. I am getting the feeling that someone is trying to railroad him."

"Railroad?" Novikov asked.

"Set him up to take the fall. Frame him. Get him convicted of a crime he did not commit."

"What makes you think that?"

"Eighth Air Force was very quick to file charges against him. They've already scheduled his court-martial for early May. It's like they want to get it over with as quickly as possible."

"And you want to conduct a responsible investigation?" Novikov said.

Harkins opened his mouth to speak but was cut off by an air raid siren.

"Shit," he said.

Novikov looked up at the ceiling, as if he could see the sky. "Our friends from the continent are back. This is becoming annoying."

"Might be a false alarm," Harkins said. "The other night I jumped into a shelter and there was no raid."

Then he heard the *crump, crump, crump* of distant exploding bombs.

"No false alarm this time," Novikov said.

Harkins stood, put his hands on the back of the chair and waited for Novikov to move. The colonel took another slow pull on his cigarette, then ground it in the ashtray on the table.

"Perhaps we should find a shelter," Novikov said. He stood slowly, buttoning his coat with one hand. Harkins wondered if it would be impolite to offer help. Outside, the sirens wailed, and Harkins could hear the distant hammering of antiaircraft fire.

"Doesn't sound like it's too close," Harkins said.

"Still, it pays to be careful, no?"

Harkins followed the colonel outside. There were several antiaircraft batteries scattered throughout Kensington Gardens, and the sky lit with bright wands of searchlights and curving streams of outgoing tracers. All around them, people were hurrying, presumably to shelters.

They crossed the road into the garden, following voices. Just beside an ornamental fountain they saw a knot of people backlit by the firing; a shelter had been cut into a low berm. When Harkins and Novikov reached the entrance, three men came out and trotted off, back toward the buildings south of the park.

"All full, gents," one of the men called.

"Let us see for ourselves," Novikov said. He had to raise his voice to be heard above the sirens, but he did not seem especially excited.

Harkins pulled open the steel door to the bunker. A man and a woman were crowded just inside; Harkins could see two small children behind them.

"It's quite full," the mother said. "I'm sorry. We cannot take the children elsewhere."

"Of course," Novikov said. He nodded, and Harkins pushed the door shut until it clanged into place.

"We will wait here," Novikov said.

More bombs farther away. Harkins could see the outline of St. Peter's dome as searchlights played around it.

"So," Novikov said. He spoke loudly, but his tone was friendly. "Have you served at the front? In a combat unit?"

"I was an MP," Harkins said.

I guess we're going to chat while the bombs fall, he thought.

"Military Police. In North Africa, then Sicily."

"So you are a detective?" Novikov said.

"I'm investigating this murder," Harkins said.

A string of five or six bombs crunched just on the other side of the river. Novikov looked up, calm as a birdwatcher.

"I think the German bombers just scatter about the city," he said. "They don't seem to be aiming at anything in particular."

Harkins took a deep breath. Novikov was testing him. He could hear something landing in the street just a few yards away, shrapnel coming back to earth. He shoved his hands in his pockets to keep them from shaking, wondered if Wickman and Lowell had found shelter.

Novikov shook out another cigarette, lit it with the same one-handed grace.

A warden hurrying by shouted, "You're not supposed to have a light out here, mate."

"I believe the enemy has already located London, your lordship," Novikov called. Then, just to Harkins, "I don't think my cigarette is giving us away. Do you?"

Another string of bombs fell in Hyde Park, somewhere north of where they stood. There were five big explosions, then a series of smaller ones, with tracers flying in every direction. Harkins squatted down quickly, pulling his shoulders up to his ears in a natural but probably futile gesture. When he saw that Novikov remained standing, Harkins got to his feet.

"It sounds like they hit one of the antiaircraft batteries," Novikov said. "Those are secondary explosions. The ammunition, I imagine."

Finally, the ack-ack slowed and a few minutes later the all-clear sounded, so that the city was left with just the clamor of fire engines racing to answer alarms. The shelter door opened and the young parents came out, each holding a crying child.

"You just stood outside the door?" the father asked Harkins. "You must be mad!"

Novikov and Harkins walked toward Royal Albert Hall, stopping at a bench.

"You were very calm back there, Lieutenant," Novikov said. He actually sounded sincere.

"Yeah, well, I may have crapped my pants."

Novikov settled on the bench, patted the seat next to him.

"London will be a dull place once the invasion takes place," Novikov said.

Harkins sat, thought about the desperate feel to last night's party, everyone wanting to get in a last good time.

"Have you ever thought about what would happen if the invasion failed?" Novikov asked.

"I have," Harkins said. "I visited some of the channel ports the other day and a naval officer who works in supply counted off all the things that can go wrong. Not a very cheerful conversation, to tell you the truth."

Harkins had spent part of the ride back to London thinking about how long the war might drag on. It might be years before he saw home again, if at all. And the Allies still had to push Japan out of the Pacific.

"Stalin knows the invasion will take place," Novikov said. "It is the only reason this giant American army is here."

He turned in his seat, put his arm on the back of the bench so he could face Harkins. "What frightens us is the possibility of failure. If the invasion force is thrown off the beach, if the push inland fails, especially if there are heavy casualties, Stalin is afraid Roosevelt and Churchill will not have the stomach or the political will to start a buildup all over again."

"What would happen?" Harkins asked.

"A separate peace."

"You mean negotiate with Hitler?"

"If Hitler defeats the Allied invasion," Novikov said, "he will propose a separate peace with the Americans and British so that he can finish the war against us, against the Bolsheviks."

"Holy shit," Harkins said.

"So you see why I want to do everything I can to make sure the Allied invasion succeeds."

"What does that have to do with Batcheller?"

Novikov ground his cigarette on the bottom of his shoe, scattered the tobacco, and rolled the paper into a ball, which he stuck in his pocket.

"Cushing was a bomber pilot, correct?"

"Yes," Harkins said.

"So, since you are a thorough investigator, I'm sure you spoke to some other fliers who knew him."

"I did."

"And what did they tell you about the effectiveness of the Allied strategic bombing campaign?"

"Well," Harkins said. "One pilot told me that if they actually hit any targets, it's only because they smother Germany with so many bombs."

"And yet the air force generals claim that they are winning the war through air power alone."

"I haven't heard it expressed that way," Harkins said. "But I do know the pilots think the stuff put out by Eighth Air Force is just public relations bullshit."

"But there has been no one to contradict them," Novikov said. "No hard proof."

"Okay."

"Since their claim that they are winning the war on their own is undisputed, they are using that to justify keeping all the air assets tied up in deep bombing raids."

Harkins thought about the scores of airfields he'd seen in East Anglia, the hundreds of airplanes, the thousand-plane raids, the tens of thousands of air force soldiers. He'd left there with the impression that the resources were endless, but now that he thought about it, that wasn't possible. There was always a limit.

And just like that he saw it clearly.

"So, air force assets used over Germany can't simultaneously support the invasion," he said. "Can't keep German reinforcements from attacking the beachheads. Too little air support over France and the invasion might fail. That's what's keeping Stalin up at night."

"Comrade Stalin and me," Novikov said. "And this brings us to Batcheller. I supplied Batcheller with the serial numbers of German war equipment—tanks and artillery, trucks, staff cars, ambulances—destroyed, abandoned, or captured on the Eastern Front. I sent teams around recording the information. And because the Germans are so famously organized and efficient, there was a pattern to the serial numbers; the equipment could be traced back to individual factories. Miss Batcheller's analysis showed that, in spite of two years of strategic bombing, German war production has actually *increased* in some categories."

"Which gives the lie to the air force and RAF claims," Harkins began.

"That they can win the war with bombing alone," Novikov finished.

"Cushing said something about getting this report to Ike's headquarters. To his planning staff."

"Yes," Novikov said. "Eisenhower wants command of *all* Allied assets, including the air forces, so that he can use those aircraft to isolate the beachhead, cut off German reinforcements. This invasion is the most important thing going on in any theater."

"Let me guess," Harkins said. "The air force generals don't want to give up the airplanes."

"Precisely," Novikov said. "Either because they believe their own propaganda, or they don't want to share credit, or they don't want to be subordinate to a commander of ground troops."

Novikov removed his cap and ran his fingers through his hair. He pulled out his cigarette case, then thought better of it and shoved it back in his coat pocket.

"There is a battle going on at the highest levels of Allied command right now," Novikov said. "Eisenhower wants to control the air assets, the bomber men want to keep flying over Germany. Eisenhower has, I understand, threatened to step down if he does not command everyone and everything, with no interference from the generals at Eighth Air Force."

"And Batcheller's report would help Eisenhower and his staff with their argument," Harkins said. "That Ike should command the air forces, as well as the ground forces."

Novikov nodded.

"Holy shit."

"You use that expression a great deal," Novikov said.

"Well, Colonel, when I came out here tonight I thought that, if I was lucky, I'd get some information to help me solve this murder. Instead I have a ringside seat to a fight at the four-star general level."

"Oh, it's bigger than that, my friend," Novikov said. "A failed invasion might mean a failed war against the Nazis."

"Well," Harkins said. "Thanks for pointing that out. Because I wasn't anxious enough."

"Holy shit, right?" Novikov said. He stood. "You have friends who will be in this invasion?"

"My brother is a paratrooper," Harkins said. "He'll be one of the first men in."

"And no way back out if the invasion fails." Novikov let the remark hang there, a sobering observation.

"Let us walk some more. Do you see your people anywhere? Or are you supposed to meet them?"

Harkins looked at his watch. It was nearly half past ten.

"I hope they got out of that park before the raid. I'll meet them later."

"So," Novikov said. "All of this brings me to your role."

"You're going to ask me where the report is," Harkins said. "My boss took it. Is there another copy?"

Novikov thought for a moment before answering.

"Perhaps. I will find out. The important thing is that I need your help in getting the original or a copy to Eisenhower's headquarters. To his planning staff. As soon as possible."

"Why can't you do it?"

"I would be suspect, and all Soviet officers here are watched over by our own NKVD. But if you brought it in, presented it as the legitimate work of an OSS analyst, you would be believed. You could claim igno-rance of her sources."

"Couldn't I just explain to Major Sinnott what the report is about and have him turn it over?"

"Can we be sure that he will do that?" Novikov asked. "Why did he take it from you in the first place?"

"He said it was classified."

Novikov smiled. "But it was not classified, because no one knew of its existence except me, Miss Batcheller, and your Major Cushing."

Harkins recalled his conversation with Beverly about classification. It was possible that Sinnott marked the report as classified after Harkins gave it to him.

"Why would Sinnott say it was classified?" Harkins asked.

"It is possible that someone at Eighth Air Force figured out what the report was about, figured out its conclusions, in which case they will want to bury it. Nevertheless, I'm not sure we should bring Major Sinnott into the conversation, in case he—like the air force people—wants to frame Major Cushing."

Harkins, who didn't trust Sinnott anyway, decided he could live with that.

"Is there anyone in the Soviet mission who would kill Batcheller to keep that report from surfacing?"

"I cannot imagine any Soviet citizen wanting to suppress that report—as long as they understood what it is. But as for someone killing Batcheller?" He shrugged his shoulders. "There are factions in the Soviet mission here," Novikov continued. "One does not always know what one's com-rades are doing."

"I still have a murder to solve," Harkins said. "If I agree to help you, I expect something in return."

"You would like me to learn if she was killed on the orders of someone in our mission."

"I'd *like* you to bring me the murderer in handcuffs," Harkins said. "Though I can see that would put you in an awkward position. I'd be grateful for enough information to clear Major Cushing, at least."

Novikov extended his hand. When Harkins shook it, the colonel said, "I am happy that you agreed to meet me, and since this is such an im-portant mission for our cause, I am happy that you are willing to trust me, to work with me to some extent."

"We're both sticking our necks out," Harkins said.

He left his next thoughts unsaid. At worst, Harkins might get sent back to a front-line MP unit for running a rogue investigation that in-cluded a Soviet officer. Novikov could wind up in the basement of his own embassy, a bullet in his skull.

15

Harkins did not see Beverly Ludington in the morning, did not hear her getting ready for work. He tore a page out of his notebook, wrote, "Sorry. Got caught up last night." He considered writing more, but left it alone, signed, "Eddie," and stuck it under a teacup on the table.

He caught a bus to headquarters, secured a thermos of coffee from the canteen. He carried it upstairs to Wickman's office, where the rangy accountant had managed to score a half-dozen stale donuts from a meeting the previous day. The two men drank the coffee and ate every crumb while Harkins filled Wickman in on his meeting with Novikov.

"Well, that's a turn of events I didn't see coming," Wickman said at last.

"Me, neither," Harkins said. He used his finger to blot the last bits of sugar from the paper napkin.

"I saw your landlady again this morning," Wickman said. "She works here?"

"Helping out," Harkins said. "Part-time, I think. She's from the British library. Sounds like they brought librarians on board to help organize all the raw data coming in from the continent."

"That makes sense. It's probably a mess when it arrives. Kind of like the accounts were when I got here."

"I also asked her about how stuff gets classified, like the report I found on Cushing. She said it's not really her area, but that it's not hard to do. Someone just stamps a document and records the date and time."

Wickman was quiet for a moment, staring at a point over Harkins' head. "I'll bet there's a log," he said. "Some record of what gets classified and by whom."

"What are you thinking?"

"Well, if Batcheller's report really was done outside of regular channels, like your Soviet friend suggests, then it won't be in any log, at least until after Sinnott got a hold of it."

"And if there's no record anywhere of it being classified until Sinnott had it," Harkins began.

"Then Sinnott—or Gefner—might be trying to squirrel it away."

"To make sure the report doesn't get introduced at Cushing's court-martial."

"My head is spinning a little bit," Wickman said. "Let me see what I can find out. What's your landlady's name?"

"Beverly Ludington."

"I'm on it," Wickman said.

"Don't get her into any trouble," Harkins said. "Or yourself, come to think of it."

"No one will even notice me," Wickman said, standing to his full height. "I can completely blend in to any crowd."

Harkins spent a frustrating day chasing down one uncooperative lead after another. He wasted nearly three hours at the headquarters of the Judge Advocate General, pinballing from office to office and lawyer to lawyer, posing hypothetical scenarios in which someone who was not a lawyer, not the accused's commander, or even a witness might derail an ill-advised court-martial. No one offered him an approach. He cooled his heels for another hour outside the office of Professor Reed, Batcheller's boss, before being turned away by some flunky. Harkins wondered if Reed had been warned by Major Sinnott not to discuss Batcheller's work with the cop.

It was seventeen hundred hours by the time he decided that it would be better for his mental health to look for his brother.

"When did you last see your brother, sir?" Lowell asked as they drove east toward the oldest part of this old city and Saint Paul's Cathedral.

"Last summer," Harkins said. "In Sicily. His unit jumped in ahead of the invasion. That was July. We spent some time together over a few days in August."

They'd been together shortly after they learned that their younger brother, Michael, was lost at sea. Then Patrick left Sicily to prepare for the next campaign, leaving Eddie Harkins to stew in his anger at the navy, at the Japanese, at the war, at himself.

In September Patrick's regiment made another combat jump onto the Italian mainland. Harkins did not hear from him for five weeks, plenty of time to imagine all the things that could have gone wrong. Finally, a letter from his sister saying that Patrick had written to the family; he had come through safely.

"Are you two close?" Lowell asked.

Patrick Harkins had left home at eighteen for seminary. Eddie Harkins, then sixteen, felt abandoned, as if he'd been competing with the Church for his brother's attention—and lost. He'd said something to that effect to his mother, who told him, "You can't lose to Jesus." That didn't make him feel any better, and he didn't bring up the subject again.

"Yeah, we were close," Harkins said. "He was my first boxing coach, and we used to go to the gym together all the time. He was a good fighter."

Lowell glanced at Harkins in the rearview mirror.

"Though he kept his fights inside the ring."

"And you?" she asked, smiling.

"I spread myself around."

"Your family must have been proud of him," Lowell said. "A son who is a priest. That's very important to a Catholic family, isn't it?"

"It's a big deal, yeah."

Harkins remembered Patrick's ordination, their mother beaming like a shined penny, all faith and happiness. He didn't know if it was because Mary Theresa Harkins felt all her prayers had paid off—her eldest now a respected man of the cloth—or because she felt secure that Patrick's soul was saved.

A bomb-cleared lot by the river offered a parking place for the sedan.

"May I come along, sir?" Lowell asked.

"Can I stop you?" Harkins said.

The two of them got out of the car and walked toward the iconic dome. As with every other place in central London, the streets were full of soldiers on pass, most of them American. Just inside the church the great aisle was clogged with GIs, heads tilted back to stare at the vaulted ceiling, some with their hats still on, a few chewing gum. Harkins stepped past the first group, removed his own cap. Lowell moved up beside him.

"Quite a sight, isn't it?" she said.

"You religious?" Harkins asked.

"I suppose so," she said. "We were regular churchgoers when I was a child."

"And now?"

"I struggle a bit, to be honest."

They were jostled by a gaggle of GIs who pushed past, making too much noise.

"Hey, men," Harkins said. "Try to keep it down to a low roar, would you? It's a church."

The little gang quieted for a moment, then started jawing again once they were past. As he watched them, Harkins got a glimpse along the entire length of the nave to the transept and another group, a half-dozen men in uniform, their dress trousers tucked into the tops of their distinctive brown boots.

"Paratroopers," he said, moving forward. He pushed past the noisy GIs and got a better look. Then he spotted the red, white, and blue shoulder patch of the Eighty-Second Airborne Division, Patrick's outfit. He felt a giddy rush of adrenaline, sensed Lowell hurrying along behind him.

Patrick wasn't in the group. These were all junior enlisted men, privates and privates first class, the little brass discs on their collar points showing the crossed rifles of the infantry. They listened as a tour guide, an elderly man with wispy white hair and a bow tie, explained that the King, in this constitutional monarchy, did not have complete power.

"That don't make no sense," a GI offered. "What good is it being king, then?"

"Any of you men from the 505?" Harkins interrupted.

"We're 507, Lieutenant," one of the men said.

"Do you know if anyone from the 505 is here? Did you see anyone on the train?"

A voice from behind him. "Does somebody from that outfit owe you money, bub?"

Harkins turned to see his older brother smiling at him. A bit overcome, he grabbed Patrick in a two-armed hug, pulling the bigger man close, hard enough to squeeze some of the breath from him.

"Well, well," Patrick said. "Good to see you, too, brother."

And suddenly Harkins felt the back of his throat close up. Beside them, the herd of paratroopers had gone silent at the spectacle of two officers in a fierce embrace.

Harkins grasped Patrick's arms, pushed back to get a good look at him.

"You look better than the last time I saw you," Harkins said. Patrick had put on some of the weight he'd lost in that first campaign. He was taller than Harkins, a bit over six one, with dark-haired good looks he got from his father's side of the family. Eddie Harkins, wiry, pale, and freckled, looked like his mother's brothers.

"Hello," Patrick said over Harkins' shoulder.

"Oh," Harkins said. "This is Lowell. Private Pamela Lowell. My driver."

"How do you do?" Patrick said, extending his hand to the young woman. "You're quite an improvement from the driver he had last year."

Lowell's cheeks flushed at the compliment. "Thank you, Reverend. Vicar. I mean, Father."

Harkins and his father used to joke about which women in their home parish had a touch of "Father Pat Fever."

"She's never even been in the stockade," Harkins said. "So that right there is an improvement."

Lowell gave him a quizzical look.

"In Sicily last summer, Patrick set me up with a paratrooper as a driver," Harkins said. "Turned out to be quite a character."

"Are you visiting London or working here?" Patrick asked.

"Working," Harkins said. "Been here three days."

"They keeping you busy?"

Harkins laughed. "Let's go outside, shall we?"

They stepped out into the garden behind the high altar. American deuce-and-a-half trucks were dropping off and picking up groups of GI tourists.

"So what are you doing in London?" Harkins asked.

"Well, today I'm taking in the sights," Patrick said. "Tomorrow I have a meeting with a bunch of the other chaplains."

"What do chaplains talk about in meetings? Whose God is better? No, wait. I'll bet you argue over who has the more arcane rituals. Catholic voodoo will win that every time."

Patrick looked at Lowell and said, "My brother likes to keep me grounded, so I don't get an outsized picture of my own importance."

The benches nearby were full, so they found a place to sit on a low wall near the base of the building. Lowell seemed hesitant to join them until Harkins motioned her to sit.

"What do you hear from home?" Harkins asked Patrick.

"You heard about Aileen's beau?"

Aileen was their youngest sister, same age as Lowell. Harkins had set her up with a young patrolman named Timothy Brady.

"Her beau?" Harkins said. "Tim Brady, you mean? Was that a serious relationship?"

"They weren't engaged or anything, but I know they'd talked about getting married," Patrick said.

"I heard he enlisted," Harkins said. "Wanted to be a pilot."

"Wound up as a gunner in a bomber," Patrick said. "Went missing a month or so ago, over Germany."

"Oh, shit," Harkins said. "Is he a prisoner?"

"Other crews reported seeing four chutes from the plane. It's possible that Tim was one of them."

"How's Aileen holding up?"

Patrick shrugged. "Hard to say. For a while there she went over to Tim's parents' place every day, to see if maybe a Red Cross postcard had come."

Sometimes a family got a confirmation from the International Red Cross that a son or brother or husband had been captured alive and was in a POW camp.

"I guess the visits got to be too much, maybe too painful a reminder," Patrick said. "Tim's mother asked Aileen to stop coming by."

Harkins thought about his parents, living in the home where they'd raised their kids, where they were surrounded by reminders that their youngest, Michael, was never coming back. Lost at sea. Not even a body to bury.

Harkins felt Patrick's hand on his shoulder, as if his older brother could read his thoughts. Eddie Harkins would always feel complicit in Michael's death. Patrick understood and forgave him.

"So what do they have you doing in London?" Patrick asked.

"Funny you should ask," Harkins said. He started with his arrival, just a few hours after the murder of Helen Batcheller.

Patrick had always been a sounding board and counselor to him, so Harkins shared the details and challenges of the case, hoping to get another perspective. He talked about Captain Gefner and the vendetta Eighth Air Force appeared to have against Major Cushing. He told him about the airfields and East Anglia and the ball-turret gunner. He talked about Lionel Kerr and Annie Stowe and Major Sinnott.

He told Lowell to take a walk and, when she was gone, he filled the priest in on Sinnott's drinking and the offer of a promotion that Harkins knew was a bribe. And then he told Patrick about Colonel Novikov.

"Holy cow," Patrick said at last. "If it's true that all these generals are battling it out—including Ike, for crying out loud—I mean, do you really want to get involved in that?"

"Not in a million years," Harkins said. "But look at it this way: Batcheller had some sort of bone to pick with the Soviets. If I believe Novikov and help him, maybe he can help me learn if somebody from their mission killed her. Besides, it's certainly in my best interest to have the invasion succeed."

"Mine too," Patrick said. "Why do you believe this Novikov?"

"He shared a lot of stuff with me that could get him into trouble. Hell, just meeting with him can probably get *me* in trouble. Anyway, I think he's got to be desperate, turning to some American lieutenant for help."

"Could he be trying to recruit you as a spy? A mole inside the OSS?"

Harkins was brought up short. "Damn," he said. "I didn't think of that."

"If he somehow gets you to compromise yourself by cooperating with him, then he has leverage over you. Maybe he gives you a copy of this report and then your boss catches you with it. What was his name?"

"Sinnott."

"And Sinnott already told you it was classified. You get nabbed with a copy, that's not going to look good. I'm not saying that's what's happening, but you sure as heck have to be careful."

Harkins leaned back against the wall. "I'm on the second case in my illustrious career as a detective; the first one was a bust and the second one looks even more complicated."

"You know," Patrick said after a pause. "Not to make this any more difficult, but why would this Novikov guy give up some other Russian?"

"Yeah, I thought of that, too. But he said something about factions in their embassy. They might not all be rowing in the same direction."

"So, if Novikov is all about helping the invasion succeed, even to the point of asking you for help, what's the other faction trying to do? I assume it isn't trying to make the invasion fail."

Harkins saw Lowell appear about twenty yards away. She stopped on the garden path, waiting for him to say it was okay to approach. He waved her over.

"I have no idea what else is going on over there, or who has another agenda," Harkins said. "But I know where I can ask a few questions."

16

23 April 1944
2200 hours

Captain Patrick Harkins' name was on the guest list for an informal dinner hosted by the chaplain of the U.S. First Army, of which the Eighty-Second Airborne Division would be a part when they reached the continent. His seat, between a rabbi from St. Louis and a Unitarian minister from New Jersey, remained empty, as Father Harkins accompanied his brother Eddie to a pub a few blocks north of Piccadilly.

"Tell me again what we're doing here," Patrick said when they threaded their way into the crowd inside a pub called John the Unicorn.

"Drinking and mingling," Harkins said. "This is a little memorial for Batcheller, and I want to learn anything I can about her connections with the Soviets. What they thought of her. What she thought of them."

"Stay together or separate?" Patrick asked.

Harkins looked at his brother's dress uniform, whose lapels were adorned with silver crosses. "What do you think?"

"The chaplain costume sometimes makes it easier to talk to people," Patrick said. "Of course, I might wind up hearing someone's drunken confession."

"If a drunk can make a good confession I might start taking the sacrament again."

Harkins got his brother a watered-down whiskey. By the time he waded through the crowd to hand Patrick his drink, three women had gathered around the priest and Patrick was sweating, though the room wasn't all that warm.

"I should get myself a Roman collar," Harkins said to no one in particular.

He chatted with a few of the Americans, listening to their stories about Batcheller. The words he heard most often were "smart," "tough," and "independent." No one mentioned an argument with Lionel Kerr.

It was easy to spot Wickman entering the pub, since his head floated far above everyone else in the room. Harkins waved at his partner, who was followed by a young woman in a dress with a modest neckline, a little clingy. Harkins was admiring the curve of her neck as she drew closer.

"Good evening, sir," Lowell said.

"Oh," Harkins said, flat-footed. "Hello, Lowell."

Wickman grinned. "I didn't recognize her, either!" he said, a little too loudly.

Lowell looked down at the floor.

"You look great, Lowell," Harkins said. It was Lowell's idea to join them for the memorial, and she had asked if she could wear civvies. Harkins was glad to have her. She was observant and patient and it might help to have another set of eyes and ears.

A man started banging a glass with a spoon to get everyone's attention. "May I have your attention?" he said. "May I have your attention, please?"

When the room quieted a bit he said, "Thank you all for coming. My name is Wade Foley, for those of you who don't know me. I worked with Helen. In fact, she was the first one to welcome me here to London. I'm glad you all could join us to hoist a glass in her honor, in her memory."

Wade Foley lifted his glass to shoulder height, but it seemed like everyone was waiting for him to say more. He took a big gulp, wiped his mouth with the back of his hand. Harkins thought it wasn't Foley's first drink of the evening.

"Yes, well. Helen was a hardworking girl with a brilliant mind. A true idealist who believed the world could be a better place if we were willing to sacrifice. She gave up a cushy job at Stanford to serve her country. Gave up all that California sunshine to come here to not-so-sunny England."

"You can say that again," Wickman chimed in, turning a few heads his way. Harkins looked over; it was possible his partner had started drinking earlier, too.

"We don't know why she was taken from us," Foley continued, his voice catching. Another man approached, whispered in Foley's ear.

"No, thank you. Thanks anyway. I'll be okay."

Foley climbed onto a chair, never a good idea for a drunk.

"This war has taken so many good people from us, and I suspect it will take many more before we hear church bells announcing victory."

Foley looked into his glass, searching for his train of thought. After a long few seconds he held his drink high and said, "To Helen!"

"To Helen," the crowd answered.

Harkins and Wickman made eye contact; Wickman made a *Can you believe it?* face.

"Mingle," Harkins said to his colleagues. Lowell walked away, but Wickman stayed in place.

"You okay?" Harkins asked.

"I'm not much good at parties," Wickman said, surveying the room from his vantage point. He looked at Harkins, swirled his drink. "That's why I needed a little pick-me-up."

"You can just listen," Harkins said. "Most people here will have something to say about Batcheller."

Wickman looked around, like a kid who wasn't sure how he'd wound up on the high dive. "You have a girl back home?" he asked.

Harkins thought about Kathleen Donnelly, who was somewhere in Italy, as far as he knew.

"Not really," he said.

"I was seeing a girl," Wickman said. "Met her right before I shipped out. Only had a few dates, so we weren't really a couple or anything. She wrote a couple of times, signed her letters 'fondly.'"

When Harkins looked at him, Wickman shrugged and smiled.

In the few letters Harkins had gotten from Kathleen, she drew a little heart above her name.

"It's passing strange," Wickman went on, reluctant to leave Harkins' side. "With everything that's going on, the ways our lives have been upended, I think we crave a little normalcy. Just a chat with a nice girl, or a drink at the bar."

Harkins often had the same feeling, a longing so powerful it was nearly a physical pain. He reached up and patted Wickman on the shoulder.

"Go on," he said. "Maybe you'll meet a nice girl."

Wickman lifted his glass in a mock toast, drained it in one swallow, squared his narrow shoulders, and waded into the crowd. When Harkins glanced around, Patrick stepped away from the knot of female admirers and picked his way through the room toward his brother.

"Lots of women here looking for spiritual counseling, I see," Harkins said.

"Aren't they all?" Patrick said. He looked at his watch. "I've got to get back to my gang. I already stood up my boss for dinner. I better be there at breakfast. I'm going to ask for a pass, see if I can't wiggle free for a few hours while we're in the same city."

"That would be great, Pat. You can always leave a message for me at Grosvenor Street."

The two men shook hands, then Harkins watched his brother make his way to the door.

"Excuse me."

A woman tapped Harkins on the shoulder. He figured it was one of his brother's admirers. "He's gone," he said.

She looked confused. "You are the police, yes?"

"I am," Harkins said.

"I am Elena Didenko. From the Soviet Embassy. I am friends with Helen for a time. Some months ago."

She was short and thin, brown hair pulled up in a tight bun, thick glasses. She couldn't weigh a hundred pounds, Harkins thought.

"So you weren't friends recently?" Harkins asked.

"Our relationship changes," Didenko said. "She becomes impatient with us, with the Soviets."

"Do you know why?" Harkins asked.

Didenko shrugged, then looked around the room. Anxious.

"I do not speak freely here," she said.

"Is someone watching you?"

She made eye contact with him again. "Someone is watching always."

"Can I meet you somewhere? Later on?"

"I will leave in fifteen minutes," she said. "You follow me. We will walk outside and talk."

She shook his hand, one quick pump, then turned back to the bar. Harkins did not see her speak to anyone else. He checked his watch, then looked up to see Lowell approaching.

"Learn anything?" Harkins asked her.

"I learned that your brother attracts a crowd," Lowell said. "Mostly women."

"Yeah. It figures the guy who looks like a movie star doesn't date."

"I think the women feel safe approaching him," Lowell said. "He's nice, but it's also because he doesn't pose a threat."

Harkins studied her for a few seconds. "How old did you say you were?"

Lowell laughed. "My mother used to say that I was an old soul when I was a little girl."

Her dress was plain but pretty, a tiny floral print. Her hair was past her shoulders, pulled back with a tortoise-shell clip; he wondered how she fit it all under her cap. He caught a whiff of something floral, maybe lavender.

"Anyway, I asked him if he'd read Vera Brittain."

"And?" Harkins asked.

"He has. I told him many of the things she writes about disturb me. He promised we could talk about it."

"Around your work schedule, you mean."

"Certainly sir," Lowell said. Then, "Who was that woman?"

"She was a friend of Batcheller's, at least until something changed."

"Will you be able to interview her at some point?"

"She's leaving in fifteen minutes," Harkins said. "Wants me to follow her outside."

"To go where?"

"To talk as we walk, I guess," Harkins said.

"You can't do that." When he looked again at her she added, "Sir."

"Now you're telling me what I can and cannot do?"

"I just mean it doesn't sound safe. You've never seen this woman before and you're ready to follow her out into blacked-out London streets."

"I never met you before I got in a car with you. I didn't even know if you could drive." He was smiling, but Lowell was clearly alarmed.

"We're allies," she said.

"And the Soviets? I thought they were allies, too."

"Sir, please don't tease me. This is serious."

Wickman approached them, definitely a little sloshy. "What's serious?" he asked.

"I thought we were going to move around the room and talk to people," Harkins said. "Not stand around like the shy kids at an eighth-grade dance."

"He's going to follow a woman outside to talk to her about Batcheller," Lowell tattled. "A woman he's never met."

Wickman looked around. "That short girl you were talking to? She doesn't look like much of a threat. I'll come with you."

"No one is coming with me," Harkins said. "I'm a grown man and can take care of myself. Besides, it's hard enough to get people to talk without convening an inquisition."

"Sinnott is not going to like you meeting with all these Soviet Embassy types," Wickman said.

"So we won't tell him," Harkins said. "I'm not going to stop digging."

Wickman looked worried. When it came to spontaneity, he talked a good game. Living that way would take a bit longer. Lowell also looked worried, but she was more concerned with Harkins' safety.

"I'll be fine," he said, patting Lowell on the upper arm.

Harkins turned away, checked his watch, and stepped out into the darkened street.

There was a crowd of four or five Americans a few steps from the doors of the pub. In the near blackness, their accents gave them away.

"You guys see a woman come out here a few minutes ago?" Harkins asked. "On the short side?"

"Yeah," one of the men said. "None too friendly."

Another man gestured, the lit cigarette in his hand a tiny beacon. "She went thataway."

In the little bit of ambient light, Harkins could just make out the fog-dampened sidewalk, lined on one side by the white-painted curb. He walked about half a block before hearing a woman's voice say, "Here."

"Elena?"

She stood in the doorway of a building, a disembodied voice more than something Harkins could see.

"Any persons followed with you?"

Harkins looked back toward the pub. He could hear the GIs laughing. "No."

"Walk with me."

A sliver of moon came out from behind a cloud, and Harkins could see her shape, head down, hands in the pockets of her long coat.

"You said you were friends with Helen Batcheller," Harkins said. "But then her attitude changed and she wasn't as friendly. Do you know why?"

Didenko looked over her shoulder once, twice, before stopping. She reached out and took Harkins' arm to pull him close.

"This is very dangerous for me," she said.

Harkins looked around, spooked by her anxiety.

She turned abruptly, walked to the next corner and onto a narrow street where the buildings blocked what little moonlight there was. He tried to keep track of their turns so he could find his way back to someplace familiar.

"Helen was friendly at first," Didenko said, still walking. "Then she was not."

"Where did you meet her?" Harkins asked.

"Come this way," Didenko said, turning right again, maybe heading back to where they'd started.

"Elena, stop."

She halted a few steps ahead of him. He could hear her breathing but could not see her expression.

"Where did you meet her?" Harkins asked again.

"At the embassy," Didenko said.

"Which one?"

"The Soviet Embassy, of course."

"Why was Helen at the Soviet Embassy?"

"I don't know," Didenko said. Then, "A party."

Harkins felt a tingling at the base of his skull, a warning. Didenko's story was shaky, but it could just be that she was nervous about talking to an American OSS officer.

"Please," she said. "We walk."

She didn't wait for an answer, but marched off, moving surprisingly quickly for someone with short legs. Harkins hurried to keep up.

"We have to stop somewhere," he said to her back when he got close.

They turned another corner and Harkins heard the same GIs laughing a few blocks away. He wasn't sure, but he thought they'd circled around and were on the same street, passing the same darkened buildings.

Didenko was covering the same ground.

Harkins lengthened his stride, caught up to her in a few steps, and pulled her arm. She'd talk to him here or he'd abandon her, stumble his way back toward the American voices and the pub.

"Stop!" he said in a stage whisper.

Then he heard footsteps. Someone, no, two people, coming up behind them. Harkins yanked Didenko into one of the dark doorways. Just for a second he considered putting his hand over her mouth, but she quieted on her own. Did she know who was coming?

Harkins waited as the footsteps drew closer. Then he heard a woman's laugh, and a man with an American accent saying something to keep her laughing.

"I could get used to warm beer faster than I could figure out the money," the man said when they were close.

The couple, just visible in the weak moonlight, passed from left to right in front of the doorway where Harkins and Didenko sheltered. Harkins could make out epaulets on the man's coat, some gold striping. A naval officer. He let a few seconds pass before he stepped back out onto the sidewalk behind the couple, holding Didenko's arm close by his side. He could see the other woman's pale legs under the hem of her coat as she moved away. The man was closer to the street, the light barely enough to catch the gold on his shoulders.

Then a shadow appeared from another doorway between Harkins and the couple. In quick succession, a gunshot flash, someone running, and a second of stunned silence before the woman up ahead screamed.

"Stay here," Harkins told Didenko before sprinting to where the woman, now on her knees, keened over the body. "No! No! No!"

There was just enough light to see that the victim was on his face, arms flung in a perfect T, the back of his head splashed open in a monstrous wound. Beside Harkins, the woman had fallen to a sitting position, her legs curled under her, her hands pressed to her face.

Harkins turned away from her and looked back. Didenko was gone.

17

"What the hell were you thinking?" Major Richard Sinnott yelled, slapping his palm on the desk. Harkins and Wickman stood at attention across from him, the closed door behind them doing nothing, Harkins was sure, to prevent staff in the adjacent rooms from hearing the tirade.

"You don't have goddamn free rein to go anywhere you want! Talk to anyone you want!" Sinnott said. He held up his hand, thumb, and forefinger close together. "We're this goddamn close to an international incident."

Harkins knew, from long experience of getting chewed out by authority figures, that he was supposed to stand there and take it in silence. He'd never been good at that approach.

"Sir, all we did was go to a memorial service," Harkins said. "That woman approached me and offered information on Batcheller. What was I supposed to do? Say, 'No, thanks' and let it drop?"

Harkins had spent most of the night with Scotland Yard detectives, then with U.S. Navy investigators, as the victim was an American naval officer. Everyone told him he wasn't a suspect, but he wasn't released until Wickman showed up to vouch for him. They arrived at Sinnott's office just after zero six hundred, fifteen minutes before Sinnott came back from what looked like a long night on the town.

"Who else did you talk to?" Sinnott asked. "Have you had contact with any other Soviets?"

Harkins sidestepped the direct question. "We tried to talk to people at that little memorial. Turned out to be mostly Americans. We weren't there that long when that woman approached me."

"That brings up a good goddamn point, Harkins," he said. His face was red, maybe from anger, maybe from alcohol.

The Soviet Embassy says they don't have a woman named Elena Prodenko on their staff."

"*Didenko,* sir," Harkins said. "Her name was Didenko, just like I wrote in my statement. Did they deny her, too, or just this Prodenko person?"

"Don't fucking get wise with me, Harkins," Sinnott said, pointing Harkins' own written statement at him.

"And you say here that you think you were the target," Sinnott said. "Or you and this woman."

"Me," Harkins said. "When she led me around the block the second time, I got suspicious, so I pulled her into a doorway. That's when this couple passed us. I think she was supposed to parade me in front of the shooter."

"All the more reason to stay away from the goddamn Soviets," Sinnott said. "You two are to go nowhere near their embassy. You're not to approach these people without my specific permission. *In advance.* I don't even want you talking to anyone with a goddamn accent, you hear me?"

"Loud and clear, sir," Wickman said.

"Where's your goddamn captain's bars?" Sinnott asked.

"The paperwork never came through, sir," Wickman said, managing to sound a bit surprised. "I didn't get my pay raise, so I looked into it. I can't imagine what happened."

"Goddamn paper shufflers, that's what happened," Sinnott said.

Sinnott looked at Harkins. "No talking to the fucking Soviets. Got it?"

"Got it, sir."

Sinnott left them at attention while he paced the small space behind his desk. He drew and let out a deep breath, then stood at the window. It would have made a good photo, Harkins thought—Sinnott looking out on war-ravaged London—except that the window was boarded up.

"Have you been asked to testify at Cushing's trial yet?" Sinnott asked, a bit calmer.

"Not yet."

Sinnott turned around. "You will be, I'm sure. Don't go bringing up all this wild conspiracy horseshit you think you've been uncovering."

Harkins did not respond.

The major studied Harkins for half a minute. "It's time for you to start getting ready for your follow-on assignment," he said.

"What's that, sir?"

"You'll be going over after the invasion. Maybe with the invasion."

"To do what?"

Instead of answering, Sinnott sat—Wickman and Harkins still at attention—and pulled a cigarette case from his desk drawer. He clicked it open, stuck a cigarette in his mouth, and produced a lighter from his jacket pocket. He studied Wickman and Harkins over the flame.

"At first you'll be a liaison with the Resistance. We're expecting the French to help us by delaying German reinforcements. Someone has to coordinate as the landing units roll inland. After that—if you're still alive—you can help us chase spies, maybe French collaborators. Colonel Meigs thought you were a good detective, apparently. He didn't tell me you were a goddamn cowboy."

Sinnott reached into his desk drawer and pulled out a heavy glass ashtray, PARK DRIVE CIGARETTES painted on the side.

"There's a landing exercise taking place in a few days. I'm going to make sure you're part of that."

"I'm in the middle of a murder investigation, sir."

"You're closer to the end of the investigation than you are to the middle," Sinnott said. "You've got your man."

"I'm not sure I do, sir."

"Well, that'll be up to the court now, won't it? Any other goddamn problems you want to bitch about?"

"I don't speak French," Harkins said.

"Now what?" Wickman said after he and Harkins were kicked out of Sinnott's office. "Let me guess: no way in hell you're going to stop."

"Well, I have to admit I'm a tiny bit curious as to who was trying to kill me," Harkins said. "I'd like to find out, if for no other reason than to make sure I don't give them another opportunity."

"Seems pretty obvious it was because of this investigation. Cushing, Batcheller, the Russians," Wickman said. They reached the bottom floor, where a sergeant and a private stood at the security desk, the sergeant showing the young GI how to break down an army shotgun. Outside, Lowell stood by the staff car, which was parked at the curb. Surprisingly, the sun was shining. In the harsh light, Harkins could see that Lowell's eyes were puffy. She'd been quite upset by the night's events.

"Look at this, gentlemen," Lowell said, saluting. "Your first sunny day in London."

"Somehow we've got to go back at the Soviets without Sinnott getting wind of it," Harkins said. He and Wickman stopped about fifteen feet from the car, Harkins facing his partner. "Wish I could tell you it will all work out. I can keep at it on my own."

"In for a penny," Wickman said, forcing a smile.

Harkins turned back to the street, where Lowell, looking tired but determined, had opened the back door of the sedan. "You, me, and the world's most energetic ATS driver. The Russians won't know what hit 'em."

Major Richard Sinnott stood, as instructed, on the south bank of the Thames. The Tower Bridge, an icon in this city of icons, stretched across the brown water just a few hundred yards upstream. Everywhere he went in this town he smelled ash: burned buildings, burned docks, charred history as far as one could see. On his first visit to London, when he'd come for his Rhodes in 1935, their guide talked about the Great Fire of 1666, the thousands of buildings destroyed, the desperate footrace for the river, the legions of homeless. The Germans had tried to do the same thing and had mostly failed. Now the allies were incinerating Berlin.

He pulled a silver flask from his jacket pocket and took a swig. A British couple passing by noticed, gave him an unfriendly look, probably because it was only nine in the morning.

"Cheers!" Sinnott said, raising the flask in salute when the couple looked back.

He took another pull. The flask was engraved with a gothic "CGZ," the initials of the medical officer with whom he'd shared a cabin on the crossing from New York in '43. He'd liked the doctor, right up until the officious little prig told him that drinking in the morning was not a good sign.

"How you gonna drink all day if you don't start in the morning?" Sinnott had joked. The doctor hadn't smiled, so Sinnott pocketed the flask while the man slept.

One more sip.

A man approached from behind, gestured at the bridge. "Something the Luftwaffe missed," he said.

"Their aim is not so good after all," Sinnott said, the second half of the recognition signal.

The man turned away and Sinnott followed him, down into a passageway that snaked below some warehouses, dark in spite of the bright daylight above ground. Sinnott stayed behind the man, scanning the sides of the walkway for alcoves, possible hiding places where an attacker might lurk. He looked over his shoulder once; there was no one behind them.

They emerged onto a mostly empty street and his guide pointed to an American-made staff car, this one with its markings removed. *Of course,* he thought, *the Soviets get all of their equipment from us.*

Sinnott got in the backseat, where he found Colonel Yury Sechin of the Soviet NKVD. If the Americans and Soviets had actually been cooperating, Sechin would be an ally in Sinnott's work tracking down spies. Instead, Sinnott feared for his life.

The driver glanced in the mirror, Sechin nodded, and the car slunk away from the curb. Sinnott resisted the urge to pull out the flask again.

"A little early for the drinking, is it not?" Sechin said. His English was stilted, like he was reading from a textbook, but he could hold a conversation.

"Or perhaps you need the liquor courage."

Sechin smiled at him, a frigid look he'd probably perfected torturing enemies of the state in Lubyanka prison.

"It's 'liquid courage,' Colonel," Sinnott said. He knew he shouldn't provoke the man; Sinnott was quite sure Sechin was capable of murdering someone right in his own car. The Soviet looked at him sideways with his small, black eyes.

"What do you want?" Sechin said.

"I want you to stop having people killed," Sinnott said. "Or attempting to have people killed. It's drawing too much attention."

"If you managed the situation better, there would be no need for these drastic measures."

"I already got our criminal investigators out of the way, and I have a plan for getting Harkins out of the way," Sinnott said. "One that doesn't involve piling up bodies. If he'd been killed, they just would have replaced him with another investigator. Maybe a whole team."

"And you are afraid they will investigate you, no?"

In the beginning, Sinnott had believed that he and the Soviets could work together; they were allies, after all. He had discussed with a few of his counterparts details of how the British captured German agents sent to Britain. Basic counterespionage that his bosses at OSS should have been willing to share. His handler, Sechin's predecessor, had not asked him for more than he was willing to give. He'd felt no pressure, had been excited, truth be told, at the idea of being an unofficial liaison between the OSS and the Soviets. The trouble wasn't ideology or information or spy-catching techniques.

The problem was money.

Sinnott was perpetually short on cash. He had requested an entertainment budget from his OSS bosses and been flatly refused, even though the agency was swimming in money, thanks to Wild Bill Donovan's friendship with FDR. As far as Sinnott knew, no one was counting what OSS spent. Not even the simplest bookkeeping rules were in place until Wickman started working for him. Thanks to the former L.A. cop, Sinnott got his hands under the spigot, but it wasn't enough and there was always the chance Wickman would start asking awkward questions. Sinnott still spent his own money to take OSS officers and newly arrived Americans out on the town, burning through his paychecks. He borrowed money from others in the agency, then borrowed from still others to pay off the first loans. He thought of himself as a gentleman—he was a goddamn Rhodes scholar—and was determined to cover his debts. It was simply a matter of timing. He spent money faster than he earned it, sure that he could convince his bosses that the rewards for his socializing, in terms of close relationships within the agency, were worth every penny. But so far, every official request for reimbursement had been turned down.

A friend at the Soviet Embassy picked up one bar tab for Sinnott. Now, looking back, he knew that had been his first misstep, though others followed quickly. Bar bills, then cash, then quid pro quo payments for information. Sinnott had been hooked, like some unsophisticated newcomer.

He needed Sechin—more to the point, he needed Sechin's purse—but he was also angry. Sechin's penchant for violence threatened to expose him. And of course there was always the threat that Sechin would decide that Sinnott was of no use to him any longer, at which point Sinnott would be revealed as a spy and jailed by his own people, or simply shot to death by some Russian on a dark London street.

Finally, he had nowhere else to turn.

"I need money," Sinnott said. The sentence left a copper taste in his mouth.

Sechin smiled. He held all the cards and he knew it. He would only give Sinnott more money if there was a chance the American OSS officer could be useful in the future.

"What will you do to stop this investigation?" Sechin asked.

"Send the investigator, this guy Harkins, to train for the invasion, then send him over to the continent."

Sinnott didn't want Harkins to uncover his connection to Sechin. Eighth Air Force, in the person of the lawyer Captain Gefner, didn't want Harkins interfering with their plan to get rid of Major Cushing.

"You're going to need me even more when things start moving quickly, after we reach the continent."

He hated the way his voice sounded. Pleading.

"Perhaps you are right," Sechin said. He reached into the pocket of his greatcoat and produced an envelope. Not a very fat one, Sinnott observed.

"This Harkins is a threat," Sechin said. "It will not be good for you or for me if he starts asking who has helped me."

"The court-martial is starting in a few days," Sinnott said.

"Major Cushing," Sechin said.

Sinnott couldn't help but admire Sechin's ability to gather information.

"Yes, Major Cushing. He was with Batcheller the night she was murdered. He's also a bit of a maverick in the air force, a real pain in the ass for his superiors. Once there is a conviction—and I'm sure there will be—Harkins will have no reason to investigate any further."

Sechin held the envelope, drawing out the moment and Sinnott's humiliation. Finally, he dropped it on the seat between them.

Sinnott waited until he had the cash in his pocket before he said, "And no more murders. They're more trouble than they're worth."

Sechin said something in Russian to the driver, who pulled over.

"I want to know what the OSS has planned for the first weeks after the invasion," Sechin said.

Sinnott paused with his hand on the door handle. "I can't tell you that before I know."

Sechin made no further comment, so Sinnott opened the door and swung his legs out.

"Major Sinnott," Sechin called. Sinnott, standing on the curb, leaned down to see into the backseat.

"Be careful. The Blitz is finished but London is still a very dangerous place."

18

Annie Stowe was waiting for Harkins in the crowded lobby of OSS head-quarters, sitting on a bench, legs crossed, her raised foot beating time on an invisible drum. She stood quickly when Harkins, bone tired after a sleepless night, made his way down the stairs.

"I'm glad to see you," she said. "I heard about what happened last night. How are you?" When Harkins stepped close, she put her hand on his shoulder. A few people hurrying by had to steer around them.

"Doing all right, I guess," he said. "Though I don't really have much to compare it to. It's been a while since someone tried to kill me."

Stowe, surprised, put her hand to her mouth. "So it's true."

Harkins, unsure about how much she knew or had heard, didn't want to discuss it in the teeming lobby.

"Let's go outside," he said, taking her arm.

Lowell was still parked at the curb. When Harkins drew close, he told the driver, "Let's go to my flat."

Lowell glanced at Stowe, whose arm Harkins held. It was the kind of look his sisters gave him if they ran into him when he was out with a date.

"To drop me off," Harkins said. "Then you can take Miss Stowe where she needs to go while I change clothes."

"Of course, sir," Lowell said.

When Harkins and Stowe were in the backseat, Stowe inclined her head toward Lowell. "Is it okay to talk?"

"It's okay to talk about me," Harkins said. "But if you're finally going to tell me about your job we should make Lowell jump out."

When Lowell looked at him in the rearview mirror, Harkins said, "You can jump from a moving car, right, Private Lowell?"

"Of course, sir," Lowell said. "I used to be in the circus. Got shot out of a cannon three times a night."

"Well, you two are pretty cheery, considering," Stowe said.

"What did you hear?" Harkins asked.

"The scuttlebutt is that you witnessed a murder. That you and a woman—I assume it was Lowell here—that you and a woman were walking by and saw the whole thing."

Harkins studied her face. It was possible that she knew more and was fishing for details, maybe out of a morbid curiosity, maybe out of genuine concern for him.

"Actually, I think I was the target," Harkins said.

"Oh, my God," Stowe said. She pivoted to face him on the seat. "What makes you think that?"

"It was a woman from the Soviet Embassy, or a woman who claimed to be from the Soviet Embassy, who took me out to where the shooter could see me. We crossed paths with another couple, and I think the shooter got the wrong guy."

"Oh, that's just awful!"

"Especially for the poor bastard who got shot."

Stowe sat upright, her back off the seat, ran her palms over her thighs, smoothing her skirt again and again. Anxious gestures.

"Any reason you can think of that the Soviets might want to kill me? Might want to stop this investigation into Helen's murder?"

"How would I know?" Stowe said.

"You were roommates," Harkins said. "Did she talk about her relationships with the Soviets? With anyone in particular?"

"No, no. I just know she soured on them."

"On a particular person or the whole alliance?"

Stowe looked out the window. They passed a small park where an antiaircraft battery snuggled behind a triple wall of sandbags. A truck was delivering cases of ammunition for the guns, male and female soldiers working side by side hefting the wooden crates.

"They're shitty allies," she said finally, meeting his eyes again.

"Well, they're certainly not my favorites right now," Harkins answered. He wasn't sure, but he thought Lowell had slowed the car, probably wanting to hear how this conversation played out.

"They want us to share information and techniques and don't want to reciprocate," Stowe said. "And now it seems their mission here is full of thugs. Murderers."

Harkins thought of Patrick speculating that Novikov might have been trying to compromise him by giving him classified documents.

"Are they trying to recruit spies?" Harkins asked. "Maybe moles inside the U.S. or British delegations?"

Stowe dropped her eyes to her lap. "I think Helen thought so."

"Helen thought the Soviets were trying to recruit spies?"

"I'm not one hundred percent sure," Stowe said. "But she had that blowup with a couple of people who were pro-Soviet."

"Lionel Kerr."

"He's one of them, I guess. Then she made that cryptic comment about knowing where the bodies are buried."

"And you think that means she knew who'd been compromised?"

"It's just a theory," she said. "She and I never talked about it in any great detail. No names or anything."

"Is that what turned her against the Soviets? She found out that they were recruiting people?"

"Maybe," Stowe said. "There was also an incident of some sort. In Poland. I feel like a dummy because I only just found out about this."

Lowell had stopped the car at an intersection. There was no cross traffic; she waited, hanging on every word.

"What was the incident?"

"This is all based on gossip," Stowe said, tugging at the cuffs of her jacket sleeves. "I mean, I guess some people saw some things in writing, some official reports. Anyway, it seems a bunch of Polish prisoners were murdered. Captured Polish officers. Thousands of them."

"By the Germans?" Harkins asked. Poland had been the testing ground for the German *blitzkrieg*, lightning war. In late 1939 Harkins had seen newsreel footage of Polish lancers on horseback riding out to meet German tanks.

"By the Soviets."

"Oh," Harkins said.

"This was back when the Nazis and Soviets were allies. The Soviets invaded Poland from the east, and Stalin wanted to get rid of their officer corps so they couldn't pose a threat later," Stowe said. "This was before the Germans betrayed their so-called allies and invaded Russia."

Harkins thought about the descriptions of Batcheller he'd heard at the memorial. An idealist. If she believed that America's ostensible allies were capable of mass murder, that might be enough to turn her against them.

And yet.

She was pragmatic enough to recognize that the Soviets, or at least Colonel Novikov, had information that could help the all-important invasion succeed. Information Batcheller used to generate a report that she and Cushing tried to put in Eisenhower's hands.

She hated them and had to work with them, Harkins thought. *What a position to be in.*

"Oh, Christ," Stowe said, the words catching in her throat. She gulped her breath like a swimmer going under for the last time, then leaned in to Harkins and pressed her face into his shoulder, sobbing. He patted her on the back, unsure of what to say.

"You can't let anything happen to you," she managed, her voice muffled against him. "You're the only one interested in any justice for poor Helen."

She leaned back, face splotchy, hair slipping loose from its pins.

"You have to promise me you'll be careful," she said, her gaze intense, her pretty face just inches from Harkins' own. "Promise me."

"Okay, I promise," Harkins said.

Stowe sat back in her seat, fanned herself, and took a deep breath, then another. "I'm okay," she managed. "Can you drop me at my flat first?"

She pulled herself together in the few minutes it took to get to her place.

"I'm sorry I lost it back there," she said. "It's all been a little much."

"I understand," Harkins said. "You've had a rough couple of days."

"Yes," she said. "We all have, I guess."

Stowe got out of the car curbside and shut the door. Before she walked away Harkins slid over and rolled down the window.

"Say, Annie," he called. When she turned around, he asked, "Did Helen ever have that Lieutenant Payne guy stay overnight? Maybe while you were away?"

"No," she said. "Our landlady didn't allow gentlemen callers. Why do you ask?"

"No reason," Harkins said. "Just wondering, that's all."

Harkins rolled the window back up and Lowell pulled away, leaving Stowe curbside, watching the sedan move into traffic.

"So," Harkins said to Lowell. "You were practically taking notes. What did you learn?"

Lowell downshifted as they pulled close behind a column of trucks.

"Well, Lieutenant Payne told us he did spend the night sometimes. If we believe Miss Stowe, either she's not very observant or he was lying. There's something else, too."

Lowell looked at him in the rearview.

"I'm not convinced the weeping was real."

"Oh?" Harkins said. "What makes you think that?"

"I'm not sure, exactly. It came and went very suddenly."

"So what reason would she have to fake a crying jag like that?" Harkins asked.

"Maybe she's hiding something."

"I guess that's possible," Harkins said.

He had come to the same conclusion: Annie Stowe's concern for his safety fell a little short of genuine.

"Or she's pushing something into plain view in the hopes I'll seize on that."

"A red herring," Lowell said.

"Exactly."

"So what could it be?"

"Don't know yet," Harkins said. "But I better figure it out quickly. Major Cushing could be on trial in a week."

19

Eddie Harkins spent the rest of the morning typing his report on the past seventy-two hours, laying out the timeline from his arrival at OSS Headquarters, to what he saw at the crime scene, to how he tracked down Major Frederick Cushing. Major Sinnott made him revise it. Twice.

"Too many theories in here," Sinnott said the first time. "You're writing like a defense attorney, for chrissakes. Just stick to the facts up to the arrest. Make sure you include that I confiscated the report—the *classified report*—that you found on him. And don't worry, you'll get a chance to shoot your mouth off in court, float all the strange theories you want."

In his third version, Harkins didn't mention that he'd found no murder weapon or motive, but made it clear Cushing's uniform had no traces of blood, that he'd identified no witnesses who'd seen Cushing and Batcheller together outside the pub. He left obvious gaps in the timeline big enough for a blind man—a blind defense counsel—to see.

Harkins signed the form, then waited until he was sure that Sinnott was out of his office before ducking inside to slip it onto the major's desk. He jogged downstairs and out the front door, where he found Patrick and Lowell side by side, leaning against the fender of the staff car.

"I hear you had an exciting night," Patrick said.

"A little more than I bargained for, yeah," Harkins said. "What are you doing here?"

"I wrangled that twenty-four-hour pass. I was hoping we could spend some time together, though I can't promise anything as interesting as what you just went through."

"You know I'm on this case, right?"

"That's okay," Patrick said. "I can tag along."

"How do you feel about a ride out to East Anglia?"

"What's out there?"

"Just the whole Eighth Air Force," Harkins said. "And the only suspect we have so far."

"The pilot you told me about?"

"Yeah. I need to talk to him now that he's had a chance to dry out, maybe become a little more coherent. Also, there are some things I need to corroborate, stuff that has to do with the air campaign."

"Well, doesn't sound like it'll be as much fun as what I had planned," Patrick said.

"Which was?"

"Touring another few cathedrals." He reached into a small canvas bag and pulled out a book. "I got this guide to churches. The stuff about how the architecture evolved to reflect the changing theology is fascinating."

"Be still my heart," Harkins said. "And get in the car."

"Why not the train?" Patrick said as he climbed in.

"We took the train last time. Too many drunk GIs. Too many guys trying to make time with young Lowell here."

Lowell climbed into the driver's seat, red-cheeked again. Harkins' sisters had learned to ignore his teasing, eventually gave it back to him in spades. He wondered if Lowell would get to that point.

"Let's go to the airfield outside Stratford, see if we can catch a ride," Patrick said.

"On an airplane?" Harkins asked.

"That's what you find at airfields," Patrick said. "Don't worry, we won't parachute out. I'll make sure we find one that will let us stay on board for the landing."

"You think you can get us a ride? Lowell, too?"

"I've never been in an airplane," Lowell said. "That would be *very* exciting."

"There's a group we train with, a troop transport outfit that drops paratroopers. I talked to some of the guys the other day and they were supposed to be down this way. They said if I needed a lift somewhere they'd see if they could oblige me."

"I hate airplanes," Harkins said. "Got sick flying from Ireland to Scotland, and that was on a clear day."

"Think of it as a training opportunity for Private Lowell," Patrick said.

Harkins rolled his eyes. "I never really liked you."

The ever-competent Lowell found the exact airfield and, true to his word, Patrick knew some of the pilots who were eating in the mess hall. There were two aircraft scheduled to fly out to the Eighth Air Force area, and space enough for the three of them among a cargo of repair parts to be delivered. Lowell could barely contain her excitement.

"This is turning out to be quite a day," she chirped as they climbed up the narrow aluminum ladder at the rear of the C-47 Dakota. Patrick went after her, then extended a hand back to his younger brother.

"Come on, Eddie, it's perfectly safe." An air force sergeant—the crew chief—stood near the bottom of the ladder, smirking at the back-and-forth. Harkins looked at the nose art: a woman in a skimpy bathing suit and high heels leaning over script lettering that said "Malibu Baby."

"Perfectly safe right up until it's not," Harkins said. "What if Hermann-goddamn-Goering makes a surprise appearance and shoots us down?"

"He's too fat to get in an airplane," Patrick said. "Let's go."

"I need a bag or something," Harkins said to the crew chief. The sergeant reached into a pocket and pulled out a folded, waxed paper bag.

"Don't throw up all over my airplane, Lieutenant, okay?"

Harkins nodded, and the sergeant said, "That big guy is a paratrooper, right?"

"Yeah. He's my brother."

"He going to recruit you?"

"Not in a million years," Harkins said, setting his foot on the ladder's bottom rung.

They found seats among the crates just before the engines turned over, shaking the fuselage, rattling the cargo, punching their eardrums. Harkins saw his brother pull a wad of cotton from his satchel. Patrick broke off two small pieces for Lowell, two for Harkins, and two for himself, which he stuffed into his ears. Lowell and Harkins did the same. It helped with the noise, but Harkins was still sure his teeth would come loose if the flight lasted more than thirty minutes.

The plane bumped down the muddy runway and Harkins grabbed the rail that formed the front edge of the canvas bench. Through a small window across from him, he could see the ground fall away and the houses shrink to the size of toys.

Patrick and the other paratroopers made this kind of trip at night, with antiaircraft fire slicing up at them, flak bursting all around. Crammed into the plane, the troopers could only hope that the pilot had found the drop zone, that he wasn't putting them out over the sea—as had happened in Sicily—or on top of some enemy formation. Harkins tried to imagine what that kind of courage felt like. He had never fired his weapon in battle, had never seen a German who was not dead or a prisoner. He'd been under artillery fire a few times but hadn't done anything brave, unless you counted running for cover as a courageous act.

"Hey!" Patrick yelled. When Harkins looked at his older brother, the priest said, "I'll bet I can get you to say a few prayers now, right?"

Harkins answered by opening the vomit bag.

He looked to his left at Lowell, who smiled and shot him a thumbs-up. Patrick sat between them, yelling and gesturing something about how the paratroopers prepared to jump. When the plane took a sudden dip, Harkins' stomach tried to maintain altitude, ending up somewhere in his chest cavity. He held the bag up to his mouth to catch his breakfast, now liberated. When he managed to look up again, both Lowell and Patrick were smiling at him.

"Come on!" Patrick shouted at Harkins. "Say it with me! Hail Mary, full of grace!"

It took Pamela Lowell only thirty minutes to sign for a staff car once they landed, and that was barely enough time for Harkins to feel human again.

"I'm sorry about the teasing," Patrick said.

"No, you're not," Harkins croaked.

"Did I get you to pray?"

"Yeah. I prayed that you'd lose your breakfast, too."

Harkins practically fell into the backseat when Lowell pulled the car up, and Patrick sat up front to give his younger brother room to stretch out. The flight seemed to have energized both priest and driver, and they chatted amiably. Finally, Harkins was able to sit up.

"Lazarus!" Patrick said. "Back from the dead!"

"You should tour with Bob Hope," Harkins said. "You're so god-damned funny."

Patrick spent the next ten minutes catching Harkins up on news from home: which men from the neighborhood were overseas, who'd become a colonel, who was in a stockade somewhere. After he'd exhausted the list of mutual friends, there was only one name he had not mentioned.

"We're coming up on the anniversary of Michael's death," Patrick said.

When Harkins didn't respond, Patrick addressed Lowell. "We lost our youngest brother last year, in the Pacific. His ship was torpedoed."

"I'm sorry to hear that, sir," Lowell said.

Harkins wanted to tell Patrick that he dreamed of Michael, that some nights he was stalked by panic and nightmare images of small spaces. But that would be putting himself at the center of the story, which seemed wrong and selfish.

"Lowell has lost family, too," Harkins said. Then, to his driver, "I hope it's okay I said that."

Lowell nodded but didn't answer, and they rode in silence. From time to time, great fleets of bombers passed low overhead, their engine noise filling the sedan. Lowell rested her forearms on the big steering wheel and looked up through the front windshield, keeping her thoughts to herself.

Colonel Montgomery Corland, whose official title was Chief of Information for the Eighth Air Force, had set himself up in an English country house outside Norwich. When Lowell turned the car onto the narrow lane from the town road, Harkins thought he was looking at a public building, a country hospital or school. The house—which Lowell referred to as a "cottage"—was a symmetrical pile of dun-colored brick, four stories, with a square tower on the southeast corner that climbed another two, at least. Large windows wrapped the upper floors all the way around, none of them boarded up. Harkins would not have been surprised to see a coach-and-four parked in the gravel driveway, instead of three jeeps and two other staff cars.

"Nice digs," Patrick said as they pulled up. "Where are the footmen?"

"I hope we'll be able to come inside, sir," Lowell offered. When Harkins looked at her and cocked an eyebrow, she added, "I mean, Father Harkins and me."

"I hope they'll let *me* in," Harkins said. "I got thrown out of a college whose buildings were smaller than this."

They climbed out of the car and approached the entrance, where a large dog slept on the top step near the main door. The dog looked up without lifting its gray muzzle, thumped its tail in greeting.

When no one answered Harkins' knock, he pushed open the heavy door, all thick wood and iron bands. They entered a large hall where hunting trophies—mostly small deer along with an elk head or two—hung on the walls to a height of at least twenty feet. A balcony wrapped around the mezzanine level, but the great space was mostly empty. The surfaces of two enormously long sideboard cabinets were covered in used drinking glasses, overflowing ashtrays, discarded napkins, and small plates of half-eaten hors d'oeuvres.

"Hello?" Harkins called. "Anyone here?"

"Look at this," Patrick said.

Harkins looked over to where his brother and Lowell were standing by five or six stacked crates, one of which was open. Patrick reached into the packing straw and lifted a bottle by the neck.

"Whiskey," Patrick said.

"Looks like it was a helluva party," Harkins said.

"Hey!"

Harkins looked up. A man in a dressing gown stood leaning over the railing of the mezzanine.

"You want to put that back, bud?"

Patrick lowered the bottle.

"We're looking for Colonel Corland," Harkins called out.

"I'm Corland," the man said. "Come on up."

Harkins found a wide staircase, the steps covered in threadbare oriental carpet, burned through in a couple of spots by discarded cigarette butts. He climbed past a nearly life-sized statue of a naked woman with a bow and arrow. Diana, goddess of the hunt.

Colonel Corland wore a dressing gown over silk pajamas, velvet slippers peeking out from the cuffs. His hair looked like it had been styled by a pillow. It was two o'clock in the afternoon.

"Are you the gang from OSS?" Corland asked. "One of our lawyers told me you might come by."

"Yes, sir. I'm Lieutenant Harkins."

"And those two?" Corland said, looking over the railing. He held a china cup in one hand, a cigarette in the other.

"My driver and my brother. He's on pass, so we're spending a little time together."

"Okay," Corland said. "Welcome to our little place in the country."

Corland took a sip from his cup, then ground his cigarette in an ashtray on a side table.

"I understand you arrested one of our fliers who murdered an analyst in London," Corland said.

"Allegedly murdered," Harkins said. "He's a suspect, but I'm not convinced we have the right guy, to tell you the truth."

"Well, I asked around about him. He was a troubled soul, poor guy. Cracked under pressure, is what I hear. Of course, you'll want to be sure about something like that," Corland said, holding out his hand. "Montgomery Corland."

"Eddie Harkins."

He looked to be in his late thirties, Harkins thought, with pale skin and dark, thinning hair. The belt on his dressing gown was cinched tight around a thick middle.

"This lawyer, Captain Gefner, said you might want to ask me a few questions about the strategic bombing campaign. You've come at the exact right time."

Corland led Harkins into a large dining room. All but a few of the curtains were closed, which made the room gloomy. The chairs had all been pushed back to the wall and the long table was an inch deep in aerial photographs in haphazard piles. Another dog of indeterminate breed trotted out from under the table to sniff Harkins' leg.

"What's all this?" Harkins asked, stepping up to the table.

"BDA," Corland said, lighting another cigarette with a gold lighter. "Bomb damage assessment."

Most of the photos were high level, but Harkins could clearly see the pockmarks of bomb craters, jagged shadows that might be toppled buildings. The photos showed what the American taxpayers were getting for the millions spent on high explosives. Showed what the Germans were reaping for what they had sown during the Blitz.

"Is this Germany?"

"The ones on this side are Germany," Corland said, waving his arm. "This corner of the table is France."

The difference was apparent even to Harkins. The photos from France showed damage to rail yards, some bridges. The pictures taken over Germany showed the destruction of entire towns, whole quarters of cities.

"What are all these for?"

"We're making a photo album for FDR," Corland said, smiling. "We want to show him what the Mighty Eighth is doing over here to win the war."

"A photo album? Like you'd make for vacation pictures?"

"A picture is worth a thousand words, my friend," Corland said, stabbing a finger onto a pile of images.

"And what is the bombing campaign accomplishing?"

Harkins thought Corland might ask what the question had to do with a murder investigation, but Corland became quite animated.

"We're tearing the heart out of German industry, for one thing. They'll have to go back to riding horses by the time we get finished with all their factories. And the Luftwaffe? Forget it. Between the pummeling of their aircraft facilities and our Mustangs sweeping the skies of fighters, pretty soon there'll be no enemy planes to attack our bomber formations."

"Wow," Harkins managed.

"The Brits are just carpet-bombing everything, going over at night to pile up bodies. Churchill wants revenge. But our missions are bombing with pinpoint accuracy to knock out factories, ball-bearing plants, oil production facilities. We're crippling the German war machine and destroying the will of the German people."

"Hard to believe they're still putting up a fight," Harkins said.

"We're sure that the Western Front will collapse very soon. The Krauts don't want the Soviets to gobble up Germany. They'd rather let the Brits and Americans roll through. I've seen some reports that ordinary German soldiers are making plans to surrender as soon as the Allies land. Better to be captured by the Americans than shot by the Russians."

"How can you tell from these pictures?" Harkins asked. "I mean, they're taken from so high up."

"We have experts who do the analysis. These guys can point to something that looks like a bunch of squiggly lines and explain it so that even a layman can understand what he's looking at. That's what we were doing last night. Until this morning, actually."

"What's that?"

"We had a party for about forty reporters. Mostly Americans, though we had a handful from Latin American newspapers, too. I had our guys give them a briefing in here last night, show them the progress we're making. That's why I'm dressed like this," he said, smiling. "I just kicked the last ones out about an hour ago."

"That must have been fascinating," Harkins said. There was a magnifying glass on four legs standing on a pile of photos. Harkins doubted it was powerful enough to show the mangled bodies. "To hear it explained like that."

Corland walked to a sideboard, where he poured a brown liquid into a crystal glass, tilted his head back, and drained it all at once.

"Hair of the dog," he said.

"Are you an aviator, Colonel?" Harkins asked.

"Me? No, no, no. I don't even like flying," Corland said. "I was a publicity agent before the war. Hollywood. I traveled to Washington on my own dime and got an audience with the man himself, Hap Arnold. Convinced him that he needed to mount a good public relations campaign— win over support from the American people, from Congress, from the president—if he was going to get all the assets he needed. And now it's paying off."

Harkins had some trouble picturing the famously gruff General Hap Arnold, commanding general of the two-million-man Army Air Forces, being swayed by a Hollywood press hack who wore a dressing gown and slippers until well into the afternoon.

"Truth is," Corland said, "the air force can win this war without the ground-pounders. It's only a matter of weeks, maybe a month or two, before Germany collapses, just like in the last war."

"I've only been at OSS for a couple of days," Harkins said. "But I hear there are people who disagree with that assessment."

"Who cares what those pencil pushers think? Bunch of people who won't even come out to debate this in the open."

Harkins considered pointing out that the OSS was mostly a spy agency, and that public pronouncements of any kind—much less debates—were hardly tools of the trade. Instead, he said, "I heard there was a study, or maybe some studies, about German war production."

"I heard some bullshit like that, too," Corland said. "But where are they getting their data for this so-called study? From a bunch of teenage Resistance fighters sending notes from the Continent by goddamn carrier pigeon? And who is doing this so-called analysis? No one who has flown over Germany, I can tell you that."

Corland slapped one hand on the photos from Germany, sending a few fluttering to the floor.

"We've got the damned *evidence* right here!"

The photos were not evidence, of course, at least not evidence of anything specific. Aerial photos of London in 1940 would have shown a city in flames, and yet the Brits went about their business and even turned the tide. But it was something else Corland said that intrigued Harkins.

"What did you hear?" Harkins asked.

"What?"

"You said you heard about a study, or some studies. What exactly did you hear, and from whom?"

"I don't remember," Corland said. He turned back to the sideboard, poured another two fingers from a decanter, and drank half of it.

Harkins moved closer to the table, bent over the photos in the France pile, then straightened and looked at Corland. "Let's say, hypothetically, that there was a credible report, an analysis that showed that all your claims about damage to German war industries were suspect."

Corland smirked.

"Let's say this report found that all your assessments were bullshit," Harkins said. "That's what some of your pilots are saying, by the way. Anyway, it would be in the best interest of the air force, of General Arnold, of you, for that matter, to keep that report from becoming common knowledge. Keep it under wraps."

Corland had one cigarette burning in an ashtray. He lit another.

"A report like that, if taken seriously, might threaten your cushy job here," Harkins said. "The question is: How far would the air force go to squash something like that?"

"I don't think I like your implication, Lieutenant," Corland said.

"I don't really fucking care, Colonel," Harkins said. "You ever hear of a woman named Helen Batcheller?"

"She was the murder victim, right? Captain Gefner told me."

"Yes," Harkins said. "Had you ever heard of her before that call from Gefner?"

The hesitation was so brief, Harkins would have missed it if he hadn't spent years watching liars up close.

"No," Corland said.

"You sure, Colonel?" Harkins pushed. "I'm not going to find someone who heard you talking about her? Some chatty journalist, maybe?"

"Journalists are liable to say anything," Corland said. He tried a smile, but he was a terrible actor.

"Yeah," Harkins said. "Sometimes it's hard to get a straight answer to a simple question. But me, I'm just a stubborn Mick, and I figure if I keep plugging away, something will give. Somebody will break."

Harkins tapped his leg with his folded cap.

"I hope your hangover goes away soon, Colonel," he said, then walked out of the shadowed room.

In the courtyard outside, Harkins, Patrick, and Lowell climbed into the sedan, Harkins up front.

"Who was the guy in the bathrobe?" Patrick asked from the backseat.

"Former Hollywood public relations man, if you can believe that," Harkins said. "Now, apparently, a colonel in the U.S. Army Air Forces."

"I knew I should have held out for more rank when I volunteered," Patrick said. "What did you learn?"

Harkins looked at Lowell, who glanced back at him before returning her eyes to the road.

"He said the RAF is just carpet-bombing Germany. Churchill's revenge, he called it. Said they're just trying to pile up bodies."

"What about targeting war industries?" Lowell asked.

Harkins shook his head. "The RAF goes over at night so they can hide from the fighters. But they're just dropping bombs. Not much aiming, other than to find the right city."

Lowell pressed her lips into a tight line.

"I'm sorry, Lowell," Harkins said.

She shook her head. "I hate them for what they did to my family, but we're doing the same thing. Some other mom and little ones getting crushed in their home."

Patrick patted Lowell on the shoulder and the three of them settled into silence.

Harkins knew that Lowell and his brother had discussed Vera Brittain and Lowell's concern about the morality of waging war on civilians whose chief crime was being born German and living in a city chosen off a list by some Allied planner. Harkins didn't like it any better than she did, but the final truth was that, as with so many aspects of his life since putting on a uniform, he was powerless. He'd been shoved around Africa, Sicily, Italy, and now Britain with little to no say over how he would spend his time and energy, where he would risk his life, and only a sometimes understanding of how his daily efforts contributed to anything. He wasn't winning the war; he was cleaning up after other people's messes.

Harkins looked out the window. He was getting better at shoving things to some unvisited corner of his mind. That's where he pushed memories of Kathleen Donnelly, where he abandoned daydreams about the future, where he directed Michael's ghost. He would deal with it all later, or his memories would deal with him.

"Drizzling again," Patrick said as a couple of drops splattered on the windshield. "Just enough to be annoying, and nothing like Ireland. I tell you, I got so sick of the rain there this past winter."

"Is it true that your California has sunshine all the time?" Lowell asked. "Somebody said that about the university where Miss Batcheller taught."

"Just like the movies, I guess," Patrick said. "Why, you thinking of chucking all this wonderful weather, moving to Hollywood?"

"What do you want to do after the war, Lowell?" Harkins asked.

Lowell chewed the inside of her lip, looked at Harkins, perhaps to see if he was teasing. "I'm not sure. I was intrigued by the story of your friend, the woman who wants to be a doctor."

"Kathleen?" Patrick asked. "She's tough, but that would be a hard road for a girl."

Harkins watched Lowell as she let the comment sit for a few seconds.

"Before the war, you never heard much about women flying planes, either," she said. "Except for Amelia Earhart."

"So?" Harkins asked.

"Who do you think ferries all those planes around Britain? Delivers them to the airfields after they're unloaded. Inside the States, too. Lots of women are shuttling aircraft around."

"I read about that in *LIFE* magazine," Patrick said.

"And you know that women are running those antiaircraft batteries we saw in London, right?"

"Yeah," Harkins said. "I saw them unloading ammo."

"Working in just about every factory back home, too," Patrick added.

"Well, we might just surprise you men someday," Lowell said. She smiled, and Harkins realized she was teasing him. "Aldous Huxley says it's a brave new world."

20

Harkins had Lowell drive him to the infirmary where Cushing had been a patient, but the prisoner had been moved the day before. After a few wrong turns they found the temporary stockade, a large garage standing next to the fire-blackened remains of some commercial shops.

"What happened over there?" Harkins asked the sergeant on duty inside.

"They think an antiaircraft shell set it all on fire," the sergeant said. He was a big, cheerful guy with blond hair and a mouth full of bright teeth, like something out of a magazine ad for milk. "That stuff's gotta come down someplace, right?"

The jail was solid, cavernous, and chilly, with narrow windows high up in the stone walls. The space had been subdivided by adding wooden partitions that looked to be about ten feet high. Clearly not a maximum-security holding pen; probably just someplace for drunken airmen. And one accused murderer.

"My name's Harkins. I think you have a prisoner of mine here."

"Oh, right," the desk sergeant said, suddenly a little anxious. "Major Cushing, just over from the infirmary."

"That's him."

"I'm real sorry, Lieutenant, but I got instructions this morning that you're not allowed to visit the prisoner."

Although he figured he knew the answer, Harkins asked anyway. "Who told you that?"

"Well, my captain told me. But there was some air force lawyer in here this morning. He's the one who put your name on this here list."

The sergeant held up a clipboard. Harkins' name was printed in block letters on an otherwise blank page, with a note beside that said "NO VISITING PRIVILEGES."

Harkins might have tried to bullshit his way in, but the sergeant looked genuinely upset, and Harkins had another idea.

"Okay," he said. "It wasn't critical that I see him. Just doing some double-checking, that's all."

"Like I said, sir. I'm real sorry, but I got my orders. You know how it is."

"I sure do, Sarge," Harkins said. "I surely goddamn do."

Two and a half hours later Harkins, Patrick, and Lowell were back in the sedan and parked just down the street from the stockade. Patrick and Lowell sat up front, watching the jailhouse door. Harkins lay on the backseat.

"Tall bloke, blond hair?" Lowell asked.

"Yeah," Harkins said. "A buck sergeant."

"I see him. He and a couple of others are coming out." She looked at her wristwatch. "Looks like shift just changed."

"Good," Harkins said. "Let's give them a few minutes to get out of the area, give the new guys a few minutes to settle in."

"We've actually done something like this before," Patrick said to Lowell. He was perfectly relaxed, his long left arm resting on the top of the front seat. "In Sicily."

"You went into a stockade?" Lowell asked.

"Didn't have to. My brother's girlfriend just waltzed in and walked out with our guy. She knew the commander or something. Just turned on the charm, I guess."

"We're not trying to get Cushing out," Harkins said. From his spot on the backseat he could see both of their faces.

"Not yet," Patrick said, winking at Lowell.

"Well, Lieutenant," Lowell said, glancing back at Harkins. "I'm learning so much about how officers operate."

They waited another ten minutes before getting out of the car. Patrick had ditched his jacket with the shoulder patch of the Eighty-Second Airborne Division and pulled his trouser cuffs over his paratrooper boots. He had taken the stiffening ring out of his cap in imitation of Air Force officers. If one didn't look too closely, he could pass for an air force chaplain. Harkins had gone through a bigger transformation. Lowell had chatted up an airman, selling him a story about having to sneak her GI boyfriend back onto base and could she please borrow a uniform blouse. When Harkins climbed out of the car to stand next to his brother, he wore the insignia of a corporal on his sleeve.

Patrick went in first. A little more than ten minutes later, a soldier came out of the stockade, looked around, spotted the sedan, and walked over.

"You the chaplain's assistant?" the GI asked Harkins.

"That's me."

"He wants you to bring his bag in. One of the prisoners wants to receive communion."

"I told him he should have carried it in there," Harkins complained. He pulled Patrick's canvas satchel from the seat. As far as he knew, it contained only some clean underwear, the book about cathedrals, and a sandwich; he hoped no overzealous guard would ask to see inside.

As Harkins expected, the big, blond desk sergeant was off duty. The man who'd come on shift—who'd never seen Harkins before—barely looked up as he waved him in. Harkins stepped into a long hallway formed by the temporary wooden walls. He followed Patrick's voice to the far end and found his brother sitting on a folding chair just inside an open cell door. Across from him, perched on the edge of a bunk that was the only other piece of furniture in the tiny space, was a sober Major Frederick Cushing.

"You look better than the last time I saw you, Major," Harkins said.

"I feel better, too." Cushing had some color in his cheeks, looked like he'd gotten some sleep. He was still thin, and his unwashed hair was long for a soldier. Harkins wondered how many times the prisoners were allowed to shower in a week.

"The chaplain here tells me we're both on Captain Gefner's shit list," Cushing said.

"He doesn't want me talking to you," Harkins said. "But as far as I'm concerned, I'm not finished investigating."

"So you believe me?" Cushing asked. "I didn't kill her, you know."

"What I believe doesn't matter as much as what the prosecutor can prove," Harkins said.

"It's important to me," Cushing said.

"Yeah," Harkins said. "I believe you. But I'm pretty sure Captain Gefner doesn't, and so I'm going to need your help."

"Is there a date for the court-martial?"

Harkins sucked in his breath, laid out the bad news. "Gefner is pushing for the beginning of May."

"So, a week."

"Maybe," Harkins said. "Let's concentrate on what we can control. I've been talking to some people about the report that you had on you the night Batcheller was killed," Harkins continued. "You said the Russians were the source of the information she used to write it. Said that it showed that the bombing campaign was not destroying German industry and that, in fact, production numbers for military equipment were going up."

"Production numbers *were* going up," Cushing said. "She proved it."

"And you were trying to get this report to Ike's headquarters because he needed it to make the strongest possible case for controlling all the air assets for the invasion."

"Exactly. The bomber boys don't want to give the aircraft to Ike," Cushing said. He looked down at something in his hands. When he ran it through his fingers, Harkins saw that it was a set of rosary beads. Patrick must have had them in his pocket.

"Eighth Air Force planners want to keep going deep into Germany; claim they can win the war without a massive ground assault. Ike wants to use as much air power as he can to isolate the beachheads in France,"

Cushing said. "Cut off German reinforcements and counterattacks after D-Day. Helen proved that the air force guys were wrong; that continuing to use every airplane deep in Germany wasn't as important as what Ike wants. Because if the invasion fails, we're fucked."

"I know I'll be," Patrick said.

When Cushing looked at him, Patrick said, "I'm a paratrooper. First ones to the party."

"I talked to a guy from the Soviet Embassy," Harkins said. "He more or less confirmed everything you told me."

"So where is the report?" Cushing asked.

"My boss confiscated it, but there might be another copy."

"Let me guess," Cushing said. "It's with the Soviets."

"I think so," Harkins said. "Did Batcheller say anything about being afraid of the Soviets? That they might be a threat to her?"

"Not exactly," Cushing said. "But I know she and her contact were being very careful. I guess they weren't supposed to be cooperating.

"Still," he continued, "it wouldn't make much sense for the Soviets to kill her. I mean, they'd be working against their own interests."

"It would seem that way," Harkins said.

The three men sat quietly for a moment; Harkins thought he heard something scratching inside the wall, maybe a rat.

"Patrick, you asked me if maybe they were trying to recruit me as a spy. Maybe somebody tried to recruit Batcheller."

"But why would they kill her?" Cushing asked.

"Because she turned them down?" Harkins said. "Maybe she could identify the recruiter."

"I don't know," Patrick said. "Murder seems kind of risky, you know, if they're trying to be secretive about it."

"They tried to murder me the other night. A Russian woman set me up, almost walked me into an ambush. I haven't figured out who's behind that yet."

"Jesus H. Christ," Cushing said. He looked at Patrick. "Sorry, Father."

"That was pretty much my reaction, too," Patrick said.

"I have another theory," Harkins said, turning to Cushing. "It seems pretty clear the air force has it in for you, Major. It's possible somebody in the air force might want to stop her, keep her from discrediting the air campaign."

"But would they stoop to murder?" Patrick said. "I can't see that."

"Anyone else in the Eighth know who she was or what she was working on?" Harkins asked.

Cushing shrugged. "I don't know." He looked down. "But I drink, you know? I can't say for sure I didn't talk about it when I was in my cups."

If Cushing had blabbed, that might explain how Gefner had gotten a whiff of the report.

"How did you meet Batcheller?" Harkins asked.

"She sought me out, ostensibly to interview me about the bombing campaign as part of the work she was doing for OSS. Turns out she knew about my reputation at the Eighth."

"That you were saying the bombing campaign was a bad idea?" Harkins asked.

"That's putting it mildly."

"Did you really feed information to the *Chicago Tribune*?"

"Do I have to answer that?" Cushing asked. "You're not my lawyer. Anything I tell you might wind up with the prosecutor, right?"

"Fair enough," Harkins said.

The pilot stood, walked the three paces to the outside wall, where a window was just above eye level.

"They used us as bait," he said to the wall, the window, the sky. He put his hands behind his back, and Harkins could see that he was worrying the beads, rolling them in his fingers.

"It was pretty clear to all of us right away that our Mustangs were far superior fighters. This past February and March the Eighth kept sending huge formations of bombers over Germany, and the Luftwaffe put up everything they had. The bombers were there to draw their fighters out into the open so the Mustangs could destroy them. Just knock them down right and left."

Cushing turned back to face the brothers. In the small cell, his legs brushed Patrick's knees.

"But our losses were huge, too. Thing is, we can replace our losses. More airplanes, more bomber crews, more fighter pilots. The Germans can't do that, especially the fighter pilots. Hell, you could see it in their tactics, that we were facing guys with less and less experience. It was a plain old war of attrition. Effective, I guess, but in the meantime, we lost hundreds of aircraft. Probably thousands of crew."

Cushing sat down heavily on the bunk, his head low between his shoulders.

"I ever tell you about my last mission? The end of my time as a pilot?"

Harkins shook his head.

"I stopped a mutiny," Cushing said, managing a sad little smile.

"A mutiny? On your airplane?"

"No. On the ground. We came back from a mission pretty shot up, two dead, three wounded, the plane barely limping in, probably headed for the junkyard. We were in debrief, and some lieutenant colonel up front said something about the sacrifices being necessary. How we were shortening the war with every mission, how our families would be proud of us. America would be proud of us."

Harkins had no trouble imagining how poorly that kind of talk would sit with the men who had to pay the butcher's bill.

"My navigator had his sidearm with him. He pulled it out and started up the aisle. Racked a round into the chamber and started shouting something unintelligible. He was going to shoot that colonel, no doubt about it. So I tackled him. We rolled around on the ground a bit, everybody just kind of stunned, and I clocked him on the jaw. Knocked him out. Broke my hand, in fact." Cushing studied and flexed the fingers of his right hand.

"And that was the end of the line for you?" Harkins said.

"Yeah. They'd been looking to get rid of me, I guess. My official letter of reprimand said I'd lost control of my crew and that I was a threat to good order and discipline because I was openly critical of the missions."

"They want to get rid of you badly enough to frame you for murder?" Harkins asked.

"I've been thinking about that," Cushing said. "And I don't know, to tell you the truth. Everything I thought I was sure of has kind of gone out the window this last year."

He looked down at the rosary beads again, pulled them across his palm.

"If they're going to get rid of me," Cushing said, "I'd rather go back up in a bomber, tell you the truth. Taking my chances up there has got to be better than swinging from a rope."

"I'm not going to let that happen," Harkins said, though he was not entirely sure he could stop it.

Patrick was not able to conjure up an aircraft for their return to London, so they wound up on the train again, one full of GIs on pass heading to London. Patrick fell asleep within minutes of their leaving the station. Harkins talked through what he knew so far with Lowell, both to fill her in and to turn the facts over in his mind, see if he could dig up something he'd missed thus far. He was staring out the window when Lowell spoke.

"Your air force is part of your army, isn't that right?" she asked.

"Yeah," Harkins said. Beside him Patrick snored, his arms folded across his chest, chin pointing to the floor.

"Our forces are separate," she said. "We have a Royal Air Force."

"I know," Harkins said.

"So if your air force wins the war by bombing, or at least has a credible claim to being very important, maybe they could win a separate status after the war."

Harkins looked at her. "A motive."

"Just a thought," Lowell said.

Harkins had read about the fierce battles over resources between the army and the navy in the Pacific, between the commanders in the European and Pacific theaters. As fast as stateside factories could roll out steel, the armed forces gobbled it up. The navy wanted more big ships; the army wanted more landing craft to get men to the beaches.

"If the prize is a separate service after the war and the big budgets to go with it," Harkins began.

"That might be enough to get a woman murdered," Lowell said.

"That's pretty good, Lowell," Harkins said, pulling out his notebook. He wrote "Air Force" at the top of a blank page.

He turned to another clean page and wrote, "Soviets."

"Maybe someone on the Soviet side didn't want her to cooperate with you Americans," Lowell said.

"Could be that this person or persons didn't know she was trying to help the Soviets, at least indirectly, by helping the invasion succeed with the right use of air power. Maybe they thought Novikov, her Soviet contact, had been turned and was giving her sensitive stuff."

Lowell yawned, used her hand to cover her mouth.

"It's been a long day," Harkins said. "Why don't you grab some shut-eye."

Lowell pulled her cap down over her eyes and leaned back while Harkins scribbled away. A few seconds later she pulled the hat away from one eye and looked at Harkins.

"Maybe she was doing something, or threatening to do something, to the Soviets," she said. "Something that scared them. You said she didn't like them."

Harkins smiled and held up the page he'd been writing on, which read "Batcheller vs. Soviets?"

Lowell smiled at him. "I think I'm getting a knack for this," she said.

"Yeah, well, writing stuff in a pocket notebook is a long way from slapping handcuffs on somebody. And you might just as easily be worried that you're thinking like me."

21

"What's it like?" Pamela Lowell asked Patrick Harkins. "Parachuting into battle like that?"

The two of them were side by side on a hard wooden bench in the lobby of OSS headquarters. Harkins had rustled up three ham sandwiches at the officers' mess, which they'd wolfed down. Then Harkins had run upstairs.

"Terrifying, exhilarating," the priest said. "Mostly terrifying."

"Do they have to force men onto the airplanes?"

Patrick looked at her. "What?"

"The Royal Navy used to send press gangs ashore to round up crewmen," she said. "They got sailors by kidnapping them because they couldn't get volunteers."

"It's the other way around, actually. Last September we had a guy cut a cast off his arm and hitchhike to the departure airfield because he didn't want his platoon going off without him."

Lowell tried to imagine having that kind of bond with the likes of Corporal Moore. Lieutenant Harkins, maybe, but not Moore.

"What about you?" she asked.

"Not easy for me to get a spot on board. There's a limited number of spaces, limited number of aircraft, so the commanders want as many fighting men on there as possible. I don't carry a weapon, so I'm not much help when the shooting starts."

"So how did you get included?"

"The first time, the jump into Sicily last summer, I stowed away on the airplane."

Lowell raised her eyebrows. "Really?"

"The pilot let me on board before the troopers showed up. I squeezed into the cockpit until they started taxiing. When I went into the back of the plane with the other guys, the jumpmaster was not happy with me, but at that point there was nothing he could do."

"I see you and your brother are cut from the same cloth when it comes to following rules, sir."

Patrick laughed, head thrown back.

"What's so funny?" Harkins asked, trotting down the stairs.

"Young Lowell here has my number," Patrick said. "Yours, too."

"Yeah, so does Major Sinnott," Harkins said, sitting between them on the bench. "I just got off the phone with Major Adams."

"The lawyer we worked with in Sicily?" Patrick said. "He was a captain then."

"I sent him the statement Sinnott had me write up for the court, the one he had me revise a couple of times. Not surprisingly, it's not going to help Cushing very much. Sinnott had me strip it pretty bare. And that's not the worst of it.

"My testifying at Cushing's court-martial is subject to my availability. And this message was waiting for me upstairs."

Harkins showed them a handwritten note, "Warning Order" scribbled across the top. "Be prepared morning of 25 April for field exercise. More to follow." Sinnott's initials were at the bottom.

"So if Major Sinnott sends you on some training exercise—and eventually sends you along on the real thing—you won't be available to testify at the court-martial," Lowell said.

"How will the prosecution make a case?" Patrick asked. "It doesn't sound like Cushing is about to confess to anyone."

"The classified documents," Lowell said.

Harkins nodded.

"I thought those weren't marked 'Secret' when you found them," Patrick said.

"They weren't," Harkins said. "But it might be hard to prove that."

"So even if the murder charge is fabricated, they might still get him for mishandling secrets," Lowell said. "I imagine he could go to prison for that alone."

"Adams said he could get a life sentence."

"Jesus wept," Lowell whispered.

"Adams said that they might use the murder charge and all the sordid details about Cushing being a drunk just to prejudice the court against him. By the time they drop the bullshit homicide allegation and get around to his mishandling secrets, they'll want to stick it to him good."

The three of them sat quietly for a moment, then Lowell said, "I have the original statements you wrote, sir. Before Major Sinnott made you change them."

"You do?" Harkins asked. Then, "Of course you do."

Lowell tried to suppress a smile. "They were in a canvas bag," she said. "A map case you left in the car. I could get them to this Major Adams tomorrow while you go off on this training exercise. Maybe he can do something with them."

"He can at least get them to the defense attorney," Patrick said.

"I can do that," Lowell said, trying not to sound too eager.

The two brothers sat in silence for a moment, and Lowell imagined Harkins was considering whether he could trust her with her own mission.

Don't push too hard, she told herself. But finally, she couldn't help it, and a moment later repeated, "I can do that, sir."

"What?" Harkins asked. "Oh, of course you can. Yeah, yeah, you do that. I was just thinking about something else."

Harkins looked at Patrick.

"Give us a minute, will you, Lowell?"

She got up from the bench and was walking away when she heard Patrick say his pass was up at midnight. They were about to say good-bye, and all she'd been thinking about was her little adventure.

"Jesus, Pamela," she whispered to herself.

She reached the far side of the lobby and turned around in time to see the brothers embrace. The whole war came down to this: people saying good-bye to those they loved.

When Patrick headed for the door she waved, started to call his name. He looked her way, smiled, and gave her a friendly salute. She watched his back, wondering if he would have to force his way onto a plane leading the way to France.

22

Beverly Ludington was in her front parlor with Tom Wickman when Harkins made it back.

"Didn't expect to see you here," Harkins said to his partner. "Where have you been all day?"

"Beverly and I have had quite an interesting afternoon," Wickman said. He sat in a wing-back chair that would have been too small for Harkins; on the big lieutenant it looked like dollhouse furniture. "We learned a great deal about classification of documents and reports."

"Sounds thrilling," Harkins said. "Can't wait to hear it."

Wickman, clearly excited, looked at Beverly; she said, "You go ahead."

"We found a log of classified materials," Wickman said. "Anything classified at OSS headquarters is recorded in it. Not descriptions of contents, just the date and names of who submitted the stuff."

"Things are *supposed* to be logged there," Beverly said. "It's a good, but not a perfect system."

"Right," Wickman said. He smiled brightly and seemed terribly pleased with himself. "Anyway, nothing from our Major Sinnott."

"Meaning what?" Harkins asked.

"The report he took from you, the one you found on Cushing, it wasn't marked as classified when you gave it to Sinnott, right?"

"Not that I saw."

"He could have had it classified after the fact, but he would have had to submit it for review and it would have been logged in; but it was never submitted, by him, by Batcheller, or by anyone else."

"So, it's not really classified?" Harkins asked.

"Not at OSS. And since it was the product of an OSS analyst, that's where it should be logged."

"So Sinnott is just bullshitting us? Won't he have to show it to someone eventually if they're going to accuse Cushing of mishandling secret stuff? Seems like someone will notice that it's not really classified."

"That's what I thought, too," Wickman said. "Beverly suggested something else."

Harkins looked at his landlady.

"Thomas told me that there is a lawyer at Eighth Air Force who seems intent on putting Cushing away," Beverly said. "It could be that he will try to get the report classified by the Eighth Air Force intelligence people, or that he has already done that."

"So we end up in the same place," Harkins said. "It will be classified when they bring it up at the court-martial. Sorry, I don't see how this helps us."

Wickman's grin widened, showing all his teeth. He was enjoying this immensely.

"Eighth Air Force can't classify it, since it's an OSS product. If Sinnott and Gefner put it in the Eighth's log—trying to make it look legitimate—there'll be a discrepancy, because it's not in the OSS log. It'll be obvious that they're playing fast and loose with the rules in order to screw Cushing."

"So we have to somehow get access to the Eighth Air Force log of classified materials," Harkins said. "Compare it to the OSS log. How do we do that?"

Wickman leaned back as far as his outsized frame would let him in the tiny chair.

"We haven't figured that out yet," he said.

"Okay," Harkins said. "We know what to look for, at least. That was good work. Thanks."

Wickman jumped up, banging his head on a chandelier. "Ouch," he said, rubbing his bald spot. "I've been this tall forever. You'd think I'd know to look by now."

Beverly smiled at Wickman. They'd obviously enjoyed their day together.

"Thomas has some ideas as to how to approach the next problem," she said.

"That's what I'll be doing tomorrow," Wickman said.

"I spoke to a lawyer I know," Harkins said. "I worked with him in Sicily last year. He said that the prosecution might have accused Cushing of murder as a smoke screen. Once the court sees there's not enough evidence to convict, they'll drop the murder charge but leave in place the charge of mishandling classified materials. By that point, the court will be prejudiced against Cushing."

"That's pretty low," Wickman said.

"Oh," Harkins said. "And I got a warning order to be ready to head out to some training exercise."

"Well, that seems like poor timing," Wickman said.

"Not from Sinnott's point of view," Harkins said.

"You think he's trying to get rid of you?" Beverly asked.

"Yep."

"I'm on it," Wickman said. He brought his hand up in a sharp salute, then turned to Beverly, bowed, and said, "It's been a real pleasure."

194 ★ ED RUGGERO

"I feel the same."

Wickman straightened, took a giant step toward the door before turning back. "Off to slay the Eighth Air Force dragon!"

When Wickman closed the door behind him, Beverly said, "He's quite an enthusiastic fellow."

"He is that."

"I take it he's desperate to get out from behind his accountant's ledgers. He's quite brilliant, you know. Just a little shy."

"I'm glad to have him pitching in," Harkins said.

"Are you in for the day, or just stopping in for a quick bath?"

"Hasn't been a week yet," he said. "What would the King say?"

"Oh," she said. "Sadly, I just had an image of the King, naked, climbing into a tub. I believe you may have ruined my evening."

"I'm sorry I didn't make it in time for dinner the other night."

"Sounds like it's been an exciting few days."

"Very much so," Harkins said. He noticed a framed picture on the side table, a man in uniform.

"My husband," Ludington said, when she saw him looking. "Tomorrow is the anniversary of his death, actually," she said. "Three years."

"I'm sorry."

She picked up the frame, held it in her lap, used the heel of her palm to wipe the glass.

"I have a hard time remembering what his voice sounded like," she said. "Isn't that terrible?"

"I'm sure it's not your fault," Harkins said. "It's probably to be expected when we lose someone."

"We had so many plans," she said.

And then here comes the war, Harkins thought. *And it all goes to shit.*

He wanted to hug her, comfort her in some small way, but instead he stood in her tiny, dimly lit parlor like an out-of-place statue. He felt completely useless.

The awkward moment was broken when a man in a dark blue uniform opened the front door and let himself in.

"Oh, my apologies," he said, glancing into the parlor. "I must get some things from my room."

"Ah," Beverly said, animated again. "Lieutenant Wronecki. I'm so glad to see you! This is your roommate, Lieutenant Harkins."

The Polish aviator, Harkins thought. He offered his hand.

"Eddie Harkins."

"Bartosz Wronecki. Very nice to meet you."

"You're a pilot," Harkins said.

"Yes. The 303 Squadron. You have heard of it?"

Harkins knew the story. Polish airmen who'd battled the Germans and then escaped after the occupation of their homeland, come to England to continue the fight. Harkins had heard several British pilots claim that the Poles were the best of the RAF, had tipped the scales in favor of the defenders in the Battle of Britain.

"Yes," Harkins said. "I have heard many great things about your squadron. It's an honor to meet you."

Wronecki looked skeptical, as if he expected the compliment to be qualified. After a few seconds' pause he said, "Thank you."

"May I ask you a question?" Harkins said.

"Yes, but come with me. I must hurry."

Wroencki took the stairs two at a time. Harkins, behind him, turned to Beverly and said, "Good night."

"Good night, then," she said.

He put a foot on the bottom step, then turned back again.

"What was his name?" he asked her, nodding at the picture.

"William," she said.

"William," he repeated.

By the time Harkins got to their room, Wronecki had stuffed his uniforms into a canvas bag. He grabbed a framed picture of a family from the windowsill. A mother and father, a young man—Wronecki as a teen, Harkins thought—and two younger girls.

"Your family?" Harkins asked.

Wronecki nodded. It was possible he had not seen or heard from them since the 1939 German invasion. Harkins did not ask. Wronecki glanced at the photo, brushed off some invisible dust, wrapped it in a wool sweater for padding before shoving it in the duffle.

"I'm a military police officer," Harkins said. "Now working with the OSS to investigate a murder."

Wronecki stopped for a moment. "The American woman?" he said. "What was her name?"

"Batcheller," Harkins said. "Helen Batcheller."

"I did not know her, so I doubt I can help."

"The victim had a falling-out, maybe an argument with some colleagues that seems to have had something to do with news out of Poland. Maybe some Polish captives were executed?"

"The Katyn Forest," Wronecki said. "Murdered by the Soviets."

"You've heard of this incident, too?"

"Every Pole knows of this. The Soviets invaded my country when they were still allies with Hitler. We were not even at war with them and our commanders told us not to resist. They captured tens of thousands of Poles, even rounded up civilians. The Germans handed over their prisoners, too. The Soviets and the Nazis worked together, you see; they dissolved our government, our state. They took the prisoners into Russia, near Smolensk. You have heard of it?"

"I have," Harkins said.

"This was in the spring, 1940. They killed them. Thousands of prisoners."

Wronecki had stopped moving, one hand still inside the duffel, his gaze fixed on Harkins.

"Last April, the Germans announced that they had found the mass burial site. Published photographs. They blamed the Soviets, hoping that this would drive a wedge between Stalin and the other western allies. But the Soviets just blamed the Germans."

The pilot looked around the room, checking to see if he'd left anything behind. He picked up a small towel that was hanging on the end of the bunk. "You can have this," he said, laying the towel on Harkins' mattress.

"But some people in the west," Harkins said. "Some people in the American Embassy, the OSS, believed that the Soviets were responsible."

"The Soviets *are* responsible," Wronecki said, his face reddening. He twisted the top of the duffel closed with more force than was necessary.

"And yet," Wronecki said, "the Soviets are our *allies*. Roosevelt and Churchill accepted their lies because we need them right now. Because they kill so many Germans."

He lifted the duffel by the strap, put it across his shoulder, and picked up his cap from the now-unmade bed.

"Now I go kill Germans, too."

"You coming back here?" Harkins asked.

The pilot gave him a sad smile. "This is a question you must never ask a combat pilot. We are a superstitious lot."

"Sorry," Harkins said. "Are you moving to another flat?"

"We are moving. Perhaps I will see you in France."

Wronecki squeezed past Harkins to the landing at the top of the stairs, then turned back.

"Stalin will never willingly leave our country," he said. "After the war. He will want to keep Poland as a buffer between him and the west. And by the time the war is over, by the time you are reading about all of this in your history books, the lie about Katyn will have become the truth."

He lifted one hand, tapped a finger on his chest, over his heart.

"But I know, Lieutenant. I know."

23

Lowell knocked on his door a few minutes before eight. Harkins, startled, fell off the top bunk and landed on all fours. He'd been dreaming of
Kathleen Donnelly, and it showed when he looked down at his skivvies.

"Who's there?" he asked the closed door.

"It's Lowell, sir. I have a message for you from Major Sinnott. He said
it's urgent."

Harkins looked at his watch. He'd slept for almost nine hours and felt
reborn.

"What's the message?"

"It's in a sealed envelope, sir."

Harkins hid himself and his erection behind the door, which he opened
only enough to show his face. Lowell smiled and handed an envelope
through. "Sorry to disturb, sir."

If you only knew, he thought.

Inside the envelope was a single typed sheet ordering him to report
to London Paddington Station at 0930 to board a troop train for Plymouth. He was to bring gear for a training exercise that would start with a
practice amphibious landing on the channel coast. Sinnott had scrawled
across the bottom, "Now we get you ready for the real thing!" His initials
were at the bottom of the page.

And with just a few sentences, Sinnott had removed the threat of Harkins derailing the court-martial. There were no dates mentioned for the
training exercise, but if Gefner got things going the first week in May,
Harkins would not be around.

"Goddammit," he said to the back of the closed door.

"Sir?"

"Give me a few minutes, okay, Lowell?"

"Certainly, sir."

Harkins dressed quickly and found the canvas duffel that contained
his field uniforms, which he had not touched since leaving North Africa
weeks earlier. A blast of odor and memory shot out of the bag when he
yanked it open: the desert smell of dust, burned fuel, spilled rations,
cordite. He dumped everything on the floor, dressed quickly, and picked
up his most badly mildewed gear, which he carried at arm's length to the

first floor, then to the rubbish cans in the dooryard. He touched the kettle as he passed through the kitchen. It was cold. Beverly had probably been gone for an hour.

Lowell stood by the car outside, looking parade-ground sharp. She saluted. "Good morning, sir. I put a flask of coffee in the back for you. A few biscuits, though I'm afraid they're left over from yesterday."

"Lowell, you're a saint."

Harkins poured himself half a cup, burned his lip a little as he gulped. He handed the order from Sinnott over the seat to show Lowell the destination and time.

"Very good, sir. But there's someone I think you should talk to first."

"Well, unless you have this person stashed in the trunk, I won't have time. Major Sinnott ordered me to get on this train, and if I don't, I'll be missing movement, a court-martial offense."

"It won't take long," Lowell said. She pulled out onto one of the larger streets and accelerated. Harkins had to hang on to the door handle.

"So now you're a race car driver?"

"I promise to get you to the station, sir."

"Who is this person?"

"I met a girl at the canteen. British girl. She's a typist at the American Embassy."

Lowell downshifted as they crawled up the back of a bus filled with GIs. She hit the horn, then pulled out into oncoming traffic to go around. A jeep swerved out of their way, the driver wide-eyed at the near miss.

"Jesus, Lowell! Major Sinnott tell you to get me killed?"

"This girl—the typist—told me that this Kerr fellow and Miss Batcheller had a rather loud argument a while back," she said. She rattled on without taking a breath, excited by the prospect of having found useful information, or by the threat of sudden death in an automobile accident. "It was after hours, and they didn't know she was still in the building."

"She hear what the fight was about?"

Lowell looked at him in the rearview.

"You'll want to hear this straight from her, I think. I told her I'd try to get you to come by at half-eight, before you caught your train south."

Harkins looked at his watch. He was already cutting it close, but it seemed pretty clear that Sinnott was trying to get him away from the investigation, from London, from the court-martial. His natural inclination, when pushed, was to push back.

"Goddamn Sinnott," Harkins said, mostly to himself. Then, to Lowell, "How did the subject of Batcheller and Kerr come up when you met this girl?"

"She told me she worked for the American Embassy, and I asked if she knew Kerr, or at least knew of him. She told me she had a little crush on him, a schoolgirl thing, really. That is, until she heard him arguing with a woman this one evening. Apparently, he said some unkind things."

"What makes her think it was Batcheller?" Harkins asked. "I hope you're not going around blabbing about everything you've seen and heard these last few days. I'll send you back to the motor pool and Corporal Moore."

"Oh, no, sir! I would never do that. I'm the soul of discretion."

Lowell sounded hurt. Harkins thought she was probably constitutionally incapable of lying.

"Okay, okay," he said. "I just needed to give you a warning."

"This typist didn't know Batcheller by name," Lowell said. "She only knew who Kerr is. But she mentioned that she thought the woman was the one who was murdered later."

Lowell, still driving too fast, made a sharp turn. Outside his window Harkins saw a crew unspooling a cable attached to a barrage balloon. A half mile later, Lowell braked alongside a small café and turned to Harkins. "She's a chatty one, so when you've heard enough, we'll just drop her off."

Lowell jumped out of the driver's seat, but before she could even step onto the sidewalk a young woman came out of the café and approached the car. Lowell, standing with one foot on the driver's side running board, told her, "Get in the back."

She looked to be no more than eighteen or nineteen, wearing an elaborate hat and too much lipstick. Her spring coat smelled like mothballs.

"This is my boss, Lieutenant Harkins," Lowell said, turning to face them. "Sir, this is Lisolette."

Harkins put his hand out. "Eddie Harkins."

"Oh, my, this is very exciting, isn't it?" Lisolette said, shaking hands. "Very exciting indeed!"

"Private Lowell here tells me you might have some information on Lionel Kerr of the U.S. Embassy."

Lisolette turned to face him, close enough that their knees touched, and began talking rapid-fire. Harkins pulled out his notebook and scribbled as fast as he could to keep up with the stories that came rolling out.

Lisolette was still going fifteen minutes later when Harkins interrupted her. He leaned across the seat to open her door, and said, "Thank you very much." He thought she was still talking when she got out, maybe even as they pulled away.

Harkins finished making notes, then closed the little book and shoved it into a canvas bag along with another notebook he'd filled up in the course of the investigation.

"I want you to hang on to this stuff for me," he said, handing the satchel over the seat back to Lowell. "My investigator's notes so far. I don't want to take them with me on this exercise."

"Why me, sir? Why not Lieutenant Wickman?"

"Because Sinnott would expect me to give my notes to Wickman. He might even search Wickman's stuff, but he wouldn't expect me to give them to you."

"Very clever, sir."

"How much of what Lisolette told us do you believe?" Harkins asked as Lowell made a three-point turn to head to the train station.

"Most of it, I think," Lowell said.

Harkins tapped his knuckles against the inside of the window. "Let's go find Kerr," he said.

"Yes, sir," she said, her face breaking out in a grin. "I'm sure there'll be another convoy."

"Yeah, a one-car convoy to the stockade. Except I'll be the one in cuffs this time."

Harkins had Lowell park in an alley just down the street from the embassy on Grosvenor Square, then he sent her inside with a message asking Lionel Kerr to come out. He wanted to meet Kerr on neutral ground, poke him a little bit, surprise him, see if he got rattled. But it was Harkins' turn to be surprised when Kerr emerged accompanied by Annie Stowe.

"I didn't expect to see you here, Miss Stowe," Harkins said.

"Lionel has invited me to have coffee," she said. She put one hand in the crook of Kerr's arm, but did not smile.

Harkins leaned against the front of the staff car. He knew Lowell was just over his shoulder, standing by the driver's door, listening.

"Well, that sounds like so much fun," Harkins said. Kerr gave him a blank look.

"I'm still curious, Lionel, about this falling-out between you and Helen Batcheller."

"I didn't call it a falling-out, Lieutenant. That's your choice of words."

"Po-ta-to, pah-tah-toe," Harkins said, grinning. "Whatever you call it, did it happen around the time that everyone learned about what happened in the Katyn Forest?"

Something passed over Kerr's face. Not surprise, exactly, more like he'd hoped Harkins wouldn't get this far. He shifted his gaze toward Stowe for just a second, then looked back at Harkins.

"I already told you, Harkins," Kerr said. "We disagreed about how much we should be cooperating with the Soviets. I argued for more cooperation; Helen was overly suspicious of them."

"But did it come to a head when you learned about the murdered Poles?"

"It came to a head, you could say, when we heard the competing German and Soviet versions of what happened there. Nazis blamed it on the Bolsheviks, tried to turn it into some sort of propaganda coup, drive a wedge between the Soviets and us, the Soviets and the British. Helen chose to believe the German story that the Soviets did it. I trusted the Soviets and found their story—that the Nazis were guilty—much more plausible."

"You're a believer in the Soviet system?"

"As I said, they are our allies. What I believe or do not believe doesn't matter very much."

"You work for the Soviets?" Harkins asked.

Kerr blinked, wrinkled his brow. "Excuse me?"

"You heard me. Do you work for the Soviets? Do they pay you to pass along information you shouldn't be sharing?"

"That's a ridiculous accusation and I won't dignify it with an answer."

"So that's a 'yes,' then."

"No!" Kerr yelled. He caught himself, looked around to see who might have heard his outburst. Harkins smiled, just enough to infuriate Kerr further. Edgy, off balance people often gave up more information than they planned.

"Helen said she wasn't afraid of anyone at the embassy because she knew where the bodies are buried," Harkins said. "What do you think she meant by that?"

Kerr hesitated, and it seemed to Harkins that he wanted to look at Stowe, that he knew Stowe was the source of this bit of gossip.

"I have no idea," Kerr said.

"I was thinking that maybe Helen knew of some people at the American mission who were in bed with our allies, and that she threatened to expose those people."

"I wouldn't know," Kerr said. "And I resent the implication."

"You can resent whatever the fuck you want," Harkins said, an edge in his voice. "Did you kill Helen Batcheller?"

"I don't have to listen to this," Kerr said. He stepped forward, squeezing in between Stowe and Harkins, who grabbed his arm. Kerr was a big man, a good three inches taller and thirty pounds heavier than Harkins. He probably wasn't used to people putting their hands on him.

"I'll tell you when we're finished," Harkins said.

Kerr yanked his arm free of Harkins' grasp, a move Harkins expected. He did not anticipate Kerr's next move, which was to throw a sloppy left-handed punch aimed in the general direction of Harkins' head. Harkins slipped the punch, slid his hand down to Kerr's wrist and bent the man's index finger almost to the back of his hand. Kerr dropped to his knees in a vain effort to relieve the pressure.

"Oh, Jesus!" Kerr yelped.

Harkins leaned close to Kerr's ear and whispered. "I could lock you up for taking a swing at a cop. At an MP," he said. "But I'll tell you what I'm going to do. I'm going to let you up if you promise to be a good boy." He bent the threatened finger back another tiny fraction of an inch; Kerr twisted his body, cursed.

"Do you promise?" Harkins asked. Kerr managed a nod, grinding his teeth.

Harkins released him. Annie Stowe looked at the ground, either embarrassed for Kerr or angry at Harkins. Possibly both.

Kerr stood, turned halfway from Harkins as if to run, flexed his hand.

"Well?" Harkins asked.

"Yes, we had a falling-out around the time that news reached us of the Katyn Massacre."

"I heard you called her a naïve little bitch," Harkins said.

"Where the hell did you hear such a thing?" Kerr asked. He drew up to his full height, but Harkins reached for Kerr's hand, which the diplomat yanked back.

"Yes, okay. I might have said a few things in anger. But I valued Helen's advice. She was a brilliant colleague."

"So who do you think killed her?" Harkins asked. "And why?"

"You're the one who arrested that pilot," Kerr said. He was still rubbing his hand, but he allowed a tiny bit of indignation back into his voice. "Aren't you supposed to know who killed her?"

"I'll get there eventually," Harkins said.

24

Pamela Lowell dropped Harkins off at the station a few minutes past the scheduled departure of his train for the coast; fortunately for the American, the train was late and he was able to get on board after running the length of the platform. The last thing he'd said to her before jumping out of the sedan was, "Make sure you get those statements to Major Adams."

Her first independent mission in support of the investigation, and all she had to do was get past Corporal Moore.

The papers she was to deliver to Adams were in her locker inside the motor pool. Her first problem was that as soon as she showed her face, Moore was likely to pounce on her, as she'd been cut loose from her detail for Harkins for however long it took him to get back to London. Her second problem was that Moore had a tendency to rifle through the drivers' lockers; she claimed to be looking for contraband and black-market goodies, but Lowell and the other women knew Moore wasn't above pinching American cigarettes or chocolates a driver had stashed.

Lowell had to get to her locker, retrieve the satchel with Harkins' original statements—assuming it was still there—make up an excuse as to why she should be leaving again, and get to the American lawyer's office before Moore found something else for her to do.

Lowell pulled the sedan into one of the service bays for the checks she was required to perform at the end of a mission. She slipped out of the car, looked around for Moore, then ducked into the orderly room, where she dropped a memo envelope into a box marked INCOMING MESSAGES. She had almost made it back to the bay and her car when Moore spotted her.

"Well, this must be our lucky day," Moore shouted across the maintenance shed. "Look who's visiting!"

Lowell stopped. "Good morning, Corporal," she said.

"So, your boyfriend got tired of you?" Moore said, holding up a clipboard with a few sheets attached. "He didn't renew the request for his very special driver today."

"He's not my boyfriend," Lowell said.

"I was being sarcastic," Moore said. "I'm sure you're not sleeping with him or anybody else. Are you done with that mission, that investigation or whatever it was that made you so indispensable?"

"Lieutenant Harkins got called away on a training mission. He'll be gone a few days, at least. I believe he'll request me again when he gets back."

"You sure are good-and-goddamn chummy with our American cousins."

Lowell kept her mouth shut, and Moore eyed her up and down.

"Check the fluid levels on that car," Moore said. "And make sure it's clean, too."

Lowell opened the engine compartment, then used the propped-open bonnet to hide her movements as she stepped to the back wall of the shop, where the drivers' lockers were stacked. She scanned the room again for Moore, then pulled the door open. Her overalls hung on a hook; hidden beneath them was the canvas map case. She peeked inside, relieved to find the two folders she'd stashed were still there and, as far as she could see, still intact.

Lowell stepped into her mechanic's overalls to save her uniform from oil and grease stains, then shut the locker again just as Moore came storming up behind her.

"Lowell, what the hell is this?"

She turned to see the corporal waving a typewritten sheet. In her other hand was the interoffice envelope Lowell had just dropped in the orderly room.

"Is this Major Adams another one of your Americans?"

"I don't know what you mean, Corporal."

Moore narrowed her eyes and Lowell—who was not a good liar—wondered if she was blushing. The corporal waited a few long seconds, but Lowell stuck to her plan and played ignorant.

"Some Yank Major sent a note saying he needs to see you. *Now.* Does this have to do with that investigation?"

"I don't know any Americans named Adams, so I can't think what else it might be."

"Well, he can kiss my skinny arse. I'm tired of these blighters dictating to us. If he needs a driver, he can put in a bloody request just like everybody else."

Lowell opened her mouth, was about to speak.

"What?" Moore said.

"I'm just curious, that's all, Corporal. I mean, if this American officer asked for me personally, he must have a good reason."

Moore leaned closer, forcing Lowell to take a half step backward.

"You know something, Lowell? I don't trust you. I think you've been joyriding around with your Yank friends and now you think you're better than the rest of us who get stuck with shit details."

"Yes, Corporal."

"Now get that car ready. I'm sending you out in an hour to pick up some Great War veterans who are due at some ceremony for old codgers. You should have lost your virginity to one of your young passengers when you had the chance. These old bastards will probably smell like piss."

Moore laughed at her own joke, then turned on her heel and walked away.

Lowell pressed her lips together. She had anticipated that Moore might simply ignore a request from an Allied officer.

It was probably forty minutes on foot to Adams' office at the headquarters of the American Judge Advocate General. She could not take a car out of the motor pool without a dispatch ticket, which she did not have, and there was no way to walk there and back in time. If she wasn't present for duty in an hour, Moore would report her absent, and that would be the end of her detail with Harkins.

Harkins made jokes about his winding up in the stockade, or his being a lieutenant for the duration of the war, comments that were funny when it was all theoretical. Now, not so much.

She conjured up an image of Major Cushing, the terrible shape he was in when they found him in the back of that pub. She thought about Lieutenant Harkins, who would probably just do what he thought was right, consequences be damned. Finally, she considered Corporal Moore, who relished being mean.

Lowell drew in a deep breath and decided there was, after all, some shit she would not eat.

She left the sedan's bonnet open to shield her as she stripped off her overalls, then fished Harkins' bag out of her locker. She looped the strap across her body, squared her shoulders, and after one more sweep looking for Corporal Moore, stepped off for the gate, a scofflaw at last. At twenty years old and in the middle of a war, finally breaking a rule.

Lowell walked for nearly fifteen minutes before another ATS driver spotted her and gave her a lift. She was twenty minutes into the hour Moore had allowed her when she reached the lobby of the building where the American lawyer had his office, and she still had to find a way back. An English woman who could play a sweet granny in a West End theater greeted her from behind a reception desk.

"Can I help you, my dear?" the woman said, smiling behind bifocals.

Before Lowell could answer, a voice came from behind her. "Oh, she's looking for a Major Adams, I expect," Corporal Moore said.

Lowell spun around, and although she had considered the possibility Moore would jump in a car and come looking for her, she was still surprised.

"I didn't give you permission to come here, Lowell," Moore said. "So you're in a fix right there."

It may have been Moore's loud voice, or her tone, or the fact that a young woman was getting chewed out by another young woman, but a few of the American men walking through the lobby slowed to enjoy the spectacle.

"And chances are good you'll be late for your next detail," Moore went on, making a show of looking at her watch. "So I'll get you there, too, you little pisser."

Lowell saw the granny get up from her desk and disappear down a nearby hallway.

"But here's the thing that I'm wondering about," Moore said, waving a paper under Lowell's nose. "I never told you where this Major Adams wanted to meet you; I never showed you this goddamn message with the address. And you claimed you didn't even know who he is."

Moore stepped closer; her uniform smelled of cigarette smoke and wet wool.

"So how did you know to come to this address?"

Lowell hesitated, and that's when Moore snatched the map case from her hand.

"What's this?" Moore said, looking inside. She pulled out one of the folders; Lowell could read Harkins' handwriting on it.

"Corporal," Lowell began.

"Shut your trap and come with me," Moore said. She shoved the folder back inside the case, grabbed Lowell by the arm.

"Somebody looking for me?"

Lowell turned to see a Yank major, bald and pudgy, with gold-rimmed glasses and a tired look around his eyes.

"I'm Adams," he said. He consulted a piece of paper in his hand. "Is one of you Corporal Moore?"

Moore and Lowell came to attention and Moore, obviously flummoxed, finally managed, "I am, sir. Corporal Moore."

"Wonderful!" Adams said. If he was faking enthusiasm, Lowell thought, he was doing a good job of it.

"Are those my statements?" Adams asked, holding his hand toward the map case Moore had taken from Lowell.

"Uh . . . I don't know, sir," Moore said.

"Let me see."

Adams pulled out the typed papers, flipped through the pages.

"These are great," he said. "Just great. Exactly what I need."

Adams reached out and took Moore's right hand in his.

"Thanks very much, Corporal. I wasn't sure you guys could get these to me right away. You really came through."

"Uh, you're very welcome, sir," Moore said.

Adams turned to Lowell, said nothing.

"Okay," Adams said, tucking the case and statements under his arm. "Thanks again."

The drive back to the motor pool was quiet, Lowell at the wheel, Moore looking out the side window.

"So this American lieutenant you've been carting around; what's his name?"

"Harkins," Lowell said. She glanced at Moore, whose arms were folded across her chest, brow knit as she tried to figure out what had just happened.

"What were those papers? The ones in the bag."

"They were statements bearing on the case that Lieutenant Harkins has been working; that lawyer needed them."

"And you had them?"

'Yes, Corporal. They were in my locker."

"And this Adams fellow knew you had them, because he sent for you, asked for you by name in that note I got."

Lowell was content to let Moore think that; the truth was that she had written the memo, had made it look like it came from Adams.

"But you knew where to go even though I never showed you the note," Moore said. "Never showed you the address."

"I guess Lieutenant Harkins must have mentioned that place, and I just forgot."

"Come on, Lowell, don't bullshit me. Then this Adams fellow comes down the stairs with another note and asks for *me* by name? How do you explain that?"

Lowell pulled the sedan up to the fuel pump, got out, and stood by the rear fender. Moore got out of the car and came round to Lowell's side, stood nearly toe-to-toe with the driver. "You wrote both of those notes, didn't you? The first one—the one in the distro box that asked for you personally—you made it look like Adams wrote it. And the second one, the one that told Adams I'd have the papers?"

Lowell made eye contact briefly. "I sent it to Adams, signed Lieutenant Harkins' name."

"Why mention me?"

"Lieutenant Harkins' statements were in my locker a few days, and I knew there was a chance you would remove them, because you sometimes go through our things. Or that you'd grab them from me before I could get them to Adams. I needed him to come looking for you if I didn't have the papers."

Moore thought about the scheme for a bit. "You devious little bitch," she said. "I ought to knock your teeth out."

She lifted a fist, but, Lowell noticed, her thumb was sticking out. It would break if she actually threw a punch that way.

Lowell couldn't help herself; she smiled.

Then, a phrase she was pretty sure she had never heard anyone utter—but which sounded like something Eddie Harkins would say—Lowell whispered to Moore, "Take your best shot."

25

"Mind if I climb in?" Harkins asked a staff sergeant who sat in the front right seat of a jeep. It was one of the few vehicles on the deck of the LST—Landing Ship, Tank—that had its canvas cover in place.

"Sure, Lieutenant. Be my guest."

Harkins pushed into the back, where the seat had been removed and replaced with two large wooden crates. By taking his life preserver from around his waist he managed to squeeze between the boxes and get his butt down on the cold steel floor of the jeep. It was cramped, but he escaped the spray that had been blowing off the channel since they left port three hours earlier. Harkins could just see, when the sliver of moon came out from behind the clouds, the dark shapes of other ships in the convoy.

"What outfit are you guys with?" Harkins asked.

"Five-five-seven Quartermaster," the sergeant said without turning around. He had drawn his shoulders up almost to his ears, arms crossed, neck wrapped in a pair of field trousers he was using as a scarf. Harkins couldn't see the man's face, could not immediately place his accent.

"You?" the man asked, turning partway around. From Harkins' perch low in the back the sergeant looked like a pile of blankets.

"I'm with SHAEF," Harkins lied. He'd spent the last two days near Portsmouth waiting for the exercise to begin, and everyone who asked seemed satisfied with that answer. SHAEF was so big that it was like saying, "I'm in the army."

"Name's Harkins."

"Jesus Cortizo."

Harkins heard it now. The accent of someone whose first language was Spanish. When Harkins was in California for training in '42, he'd spent two of his precious weekend liberties flirting with a black-haired Mexican American barmaid named Louisa. She let him hold her hand one night. When he shipped out, he asked for her address so he could write, but he lost the slip of paper on the train back east.

"What do you guys do?" Harkins asked. "On the beach, I mean."

"Ammo and rations. Track what's coming in, what we need more of, what's going out."

"Will you do all that for this exercise?" Harkins asked.

They were headed for a stretch of the Devon coast that was similar, the planners thought, to what they would find on the still-secret invasion beaches. Operation Tiger was a giant dress rehearsal: scores of ships, thousands of men, hundreds of vehicles, and tons of supplies and equipment.

"We'll do most of it," Cortizo said. "We'll set up, but I don't think they'll push all the beans and bullets to us. Not for this practice run, anyway."

A wave slapped the side of the ship, spraying the deck, the steady wind from the south driving the water like birdshot. Harkins noticed that Cortizo's legs were wrapped in a waterproof poncho.

"I think it's a bit warmer down below," Harkins said. He tried pulling his shoulders higher, felt a rivulet of cold seawater tracing his spine. "Certainly drier."

"Nah, I was down there before."

"Did you see that poker game?" Harkins asked. "That was a big pile of cash."

When he'd first come on board, Harkins had been shunted below to the tank deck, just at the waterline. Because this ship carried mostly troops of the First Engineer Brigade, the heavy vehicles were not battle tanks but bulldozers and trucks loaded with stacks of steel matting that could be used to manufacture an instant airstrip. The cavernous space stretched nearly the entire length of the ship, which Harkins guessed was longer than a football field, and it was jammed with vehicles parked bumper to bumper, wheel hub to wheel hub. Seasick men lay about, draped over hoods and mechanics' boxes and machine-gun mounts, heads down, vomit running across the deck. Harkins watched as gangs of sailors, the ship's crew, hurried back and forth, checking the chained-down cargo. The navy men wore blue dungarees, wet weather jackets, and helmets stenciled USN. The sailors wore their life belts a little loose, low on their hips, like gunslingers in some movie Western. He did not see anyone showing the army guys how to wear the belts, so most of the soldiers kept them snug around the waist.

A navy lieutenant told him the LSTs had flat bottoms so they could run up on the beach to discharge their loads through big doors in the bow, but the hull's shape meant they rode poorly in even the smallest swells. Harkins felt the vessel's rolls deep in his gut as soon as the ship left the harbor's protection and hit the channel proper.

"I was in that poker game," Cortizo said. "I was up eleven hundred dollars."

Harkins figured the man's use of the past tense meant he didn't walk away with his winnings.

"Should have cashed out then," Cortizo said. "But there was this first sergeant, one of those goddamned know-it-all types, you know?"

Harkins nodded, even though Cortizo was still facing the front of the jeep and couldn't see him.

"I just didn't like the guy," Cortizo said. "The way he looked at me. He made a crack about Mexicans."

Every one of the dozens of card games Harkins had been in during his twenty-eight months in the army had featured some sort of comment like that. He'd been called every possible combination of "mick," "drunk," and "Paddy," often by other Irish Americans.

"Anyway, this guy had about forty bucks left, and I figured I'd quit after I took that money from him."

The ship took a sickening heave, and Harkins jumped as somebody dropped something heavy that clanged on the deck.

"So, did you get his forty bucks?" he asked.

"No," Cortizo said. "But that bastard got my eleven hundred."

The noncom laughed suddenly, kept chuckling as he lifted his helmet off, wiped his bald head with a sleeve. He turned around fully and Harkins could just see the bottom half of his face in the starlight. He was smiling.

"Maybe he was right," Cortizo laughed. "Maybe I *am* a dumb beaner!"

He slapped his thigh, and for an instant Harkins thought that was what caused the explosion.

The world went white and all sound disappeared. Harkins was thrown hard against the wooden crate to his left, while Cortizo shot across the driver's seat and out onto the deck, legs in the air, head down.

Harkins, moving in a silent world, scrambled to get out of the jeep, using both hands to hoist himself toward the front. His head felt like it had been spiked and there was a high whine as his hearing returned. The first sound he heard was a low groan, fear mixed with pain. It was coming from his own chest.

Harkins pushed himself clear of the jeep and landed on Cortizo. He clambered to his knees, lifted Cortizo by one arm.

"Can you move?" Harkins shouted.

Cortizo's face was orange and red, lit by a nearby fire. The ship was ablaze, flames leaping above the starboard rail, flames crawling out of the hatches in the deck. The truck to their right was already engulfed, its canvas top fluttering like burning laundry on a windy day. A giant wall of black smoke leaped from the flames; for the moment, the wind off the channel was pushing it off the deck.

"Come on, we've gotta get off the ship!" Harkins screamed.

"I can't swim!" Cortizo said.

"Inflate your life preserver," Harkins said. He clawed at Cortizo's jacket, pulled away the poncho he'd been huddled under.

"I don't know how," Cortizo said. He wasn't looking at the belt; his eyes were locked on Harkins.

"Nobody showed you?"

Cortizo shook his head. "They just handed them out."

They were crouched on the deck, the heat on their backs already tremendous. The jeep shielded them for the moment, but they had to move or they'd be roasted alive. Harkins grabbed Cortizo by the collar and yanked him to his feet. They had to get to the port rail, just a few feet away.

Harkins took a step, then was knocked down by a man who stumbled into him. It was a sailor, his clothing on fire, his hair a torch. He didn't make a sound, just raised his burning arms to heaven before falling to his knees, then onto his face.

Harkins tugged Cortizo, pushed the sergeant up against the port-side safety line. He grabbed the tubes on Cortizo's life preserver, pulling them free.

"Push this down," he yelled, showing the sergeant how to open the valve. "Blow into the tube. Fast."

As Cortizo started inflating his preserver, Harkins looked over the noncom's shoulder at the spreading fire. It was hard to tell, but the ship seemed to be slowing and turning. The dense plume of smoke was no longer being pushed completely over the rail. If the wind shifted or the ship turned into it at a different angle, they'd be enveloped, probably blinded, certainly in danger of choking to death.

Harkins looked at Cortizo, cheeks swollen as he tried to inflate the life belt. Harkins reached for his own.

It wasn't there.

He'd removed it to squeeze into the jeep, which was now burning just a few feet away.

"Shit!"

Harkins looked left and right. Many of the vehicles on the main deck were on fire, and there was a blanket of flame spreading across the water on the starboard side.

The fuel oil on the water is burning.

He looked over the port rail, where the water was definitely farther away than it had been before; the vessel was listing to starboard. An explosion of some sort had set the tank deck on fire and probably blew a hole in the hull. The ship was dying.

"I got it!" Cortizo shouted. He'd managed to inflate the life belt, though the top chamber was not as full as the bottom. Harkins thought there might be a leak, but he didn't want to add to Cortizo's panic.

"We have to go over the side," Harkins said.

He could see Cortizo's mouth move but could not hear him over the rush of the flames and the crash of vehicles tearing loose from their bindings and tumbling toward the starboard rail. A few feet away there was a tremendous burst of wind from one of the gratings as water filled the belowdecks and forced out the air.

"What?"

"It's a big jump," Cortizo said.

"It's only going to get higher," Harkins screamed, just an inch from the man's face. He pointed to his right, where the channel water was already moving across the deck, spilled oil showing blue and silver in the firelight. As he watched, the water found the open ventilation hatches in the deck and sluiced in. The cavernous tank deck would flood quickly. God help the men down there.

"I'll go first!" Harkins said.

Cortizo, eyes wide with terror, nodded, crossed himself. Then everything went black as smoke from the fuel oil fire found them. Mercifully, the wind shifted a tiny bit, driving the smoke back, but not before Harkins had sucked in enough to bend him over in a coughing fit, his lungs rebelling, as if suddenly filled with broken glass. Cortizo had his hands over his face.

Harkins forced himself upright, lifted one foot to the rail, and that's when he saw the trapped men.

He was facing aft, toward the superstructure. Near the base and on the starboard side there was a hatch, one of those small ship's doors you had to duck to go through. It was open only a few inches, but in the firelight Harkins could see that there was a man, no, two men, maybe three, pushing against the door from the inside, trying to force it open. One man had stuck his leg through, the door pinching him.

Harkins put his foot back on the deck. "You go first," he said to Cortizo.

The sergeant shook his head, mouth open. His face was bathed in sweat and soot where the smoke had curled around them.

"You have to help me when we get to the water!"

Harkins did not want to tell Cortizo that he was going alone.

"You go first, then I can dive in beside you to help. Your life belt will keep you afloat." To reinforce his point he tugged at the inflated belt, pulling it snug around Cortizo's waist.

The sergeant's face was contorted with pain, with indecision. Another tendril of smoke snaked out from the cliff face of black behind them. A wind shift would kill them before they had a chance to drown.

"Get over the fucking side!" Harkins shouted. "Or I'll throw you over!"

Cortizo pulled himself up onto the rail. The side of the ship was no longer vertical, but was on a steep angle toward the water. The smoke backed off a few yards, but the volcano sound of the fire was only getting louder.

"You have to go!" Harkins screamed. Cortizo gave his head a violent shake, said something in Spanish. Maybe a prayer.

Harkins looked back to where the men were trapped by the jammed hatch. They had not made any progress, and it looked like they were losing their footing as the angle of the list increased.

Harkins turned back toward Cortizo, put his mouth up against the man's ear. "Just paddle away from the ship any way you can," he said. Then he pried Cortizo's fingers from the rail and the man rolled down the side of the hull and into the black water.

Harkins hugged the port rail as he moved aft toward the superstructure and the trapped men. There were safety handholds welded to the front of the tower, and he held on as he let himself slip down the tilting deck toward the starboard side and the rising water. The closer he got to the jammed hatch, the more heat he felt from the fire. The ship had to be listing thirty degrees or more. Harkins slipped on some spilled fuel and only kept from sliding down the deck by hanging on with one hand, before getting his feet under him again.

He reached the corner of the superstructure and peered around. The jammed hatch was only a few feet away. The heat here was massive, like backing into a furnace.

Harkins made it to the door, which was now facing the water as the ship leaned over. The man who'd stuck his leg through wasn't visible. There had to be another hatch, a way out of the bridge area, maybe on the port side. He put his face close to the narrow opening. "Can you get to the other side?"

"No!"

A sailor pushed his face into the gap. He was just a kid, maybe eighteen. "You gotta help us!"

Another face appeared below the first, a soldier bleeding from an ugly gash at his hairline.

Harkins grabbed the edge of the door, which was hot to the touch, and pulled backward. When it didn't budge, he used all of his weight, hoping that it wouldn't give way so suddenly that he'd fall into the water behind him.

Nothing.

He did a quick look around the edge of the hatch. It looked like one or two of the dogs—the large wrench-like handles that held the hatch shut and kept it watertight—had been jammed by the explosion. If he could move them half an inch, he might free the men.

"I'll be right back," Harkins yelled.

"Don't you leave us!" the young sailor screamed, hysterical with panic. "Don't leave us!"

Harkins didn't turn back, as there was no time to argue. He moved up the deck, some part of his mind weirdly focused, trying to calculate the slant. An explosion below deck knocked him to his knees; the steel plates were griddle hot.

On his first pass by the superstructure he'd seen a long-handled wrench secured in a binding at the base of the bridge. It was one of the tools the sailors used to tighten the chains locking cargo to the deck. He unhooked the clasp and pulled it free, nearly dropping the wrench into the water.

He slid down the deck toward the trapped men, and when he reached the hatch and stood, he was in water up to his calves. It was possible the ship would settle—that is, sink more or less evenly—but it could also capsize. Flip over in a sickening instant, in which case Harkins would not escape.

Harkins heard a man inside the hatch yell, "He's back! He's back!"

He struggled to get his footing, braced himself on the lip of a locker, and started banging away at the bent dogs. Three hard swings and the first handle snapped off. He shifted his weight to have a go at the second, but slipped and dropped the wrench.

"Fuck!"

"Come on, come on!" the men inside shouted.

Harkins looked down, saw the wrench and some other detritus in a foot of water and oil that now covered the deck; the stench of the fuel stung his nose and lungs. If the fire reached the oil, he was a dead man. He reached for the wrench but did not look up to see how far away the flames were.

He took a big swing at the last bent dog, which popped off and hit him on the side of his face. Harkins staggered, shook it off, moved out of the way. The men inside pushed and the hatch swung open, spilling them like tossed trash. At least one of them tumbled full body in the water.

The young sailor and the GI with the head wound did not look at Harkins, but clawed their way up the slanting deck to the port rail.

The next sailor out offered his hand to pull Harkins up, shouted, "Thanks!"

Another man, a navy ensign, was still in the opening.

"Come on!" Harkins yelled.

"I need help," the officer said.

The ensign, one hand on either side of the hatch, leaned back so that Harkins could see inside the companionway. Another sailor lay on the deck, one leg braced on the bulkhead to keep him from sliding, the other leg gone at the knee and tied off with a crude tourniquet.

It was the man who'd forced his leg through the hatch. Harkins looked down into the water again, toward where he'd found the wrench. The man's leg was in the tangled mess of spilled equipment.

Harkins climbed inside, and—though he would never remember how they did it—he and the ensign got the wounded sailor out onto the deck, up and over the port rail.

The navy men had life belts, and Harkins found one floating in the water, already inflated. He held it as they paddled about a hundred yards, towing the wounded man, who was now unconscious. They stopped and, as Harkins struggled to wrap the life belt around himself, the ensign shouted, "Under your armpits!"

"What?"

"If you put it around your waist it'll flip you over and you'll drown!"

Harkins got the belt around his chest and had only a second to enjoy the relief before he thought of Staff Sergeant Jesus Cortizo, non-swimmer, going over the side, life belt snug around his waist, where Harkins had so helpfully tightened it.

26

28 April 1944
0500 hours

Harkins and the two navy men were in the water only a few minutes before they were rescued by some U.S. Coast Guardsmen in a thirty-foot
launch. The boat already held about eight survivors, and Harkins could
see what looked like two or three bodies under a tarp behind the small
wheelhouse. The coasties were kind enough to keep the dead out of sight.
One of their rescuers, a chief of some sort, examined the sailor with the
severed leg, testing the tourniquet with his fingers.

"Is this your necktie, sir?" he asked the ensign Harkins had freed.

The exhausted junior officer nodded.

"Good job," the chief said.

Eventually they unloaded onto a small pier, where some navy corps-
men and an older officer, probably a doctor, checked the survivors and
directed them to a nearby street, where a warming tent had been set up.
The most seriously injured men went directly into waiting ambulances.
Harkins, shivering but not badly hurt, stripped off his clothing, then used
bandages to wipe away the fuel oil before putting on a navy enlisted man's
uniform that someone handed him. He had lost his shoes in the water.

"What's your name?" the ensign asked. He was a small man, couldn't
weigh more than a hundred and twenty pounds. Improbably, his eyeglasses were still in place.

"Harkins. Eddie Harkins."

The ensign clasped Harkins' right hand in both of his own, which
dripped fuel. His uniform was black with the stuff, his neck and chest
smeared, but a corpsman had helped him wipe the oil from around his
eyes and mouth.

"I'm Guy Cedrick," the ensign said. "You saved us."

Harkins wasn't sure what to say to that.

"You could have left us," Cedrick said. "But you decided to stay behind."

Harkins, who was quite sure he'd made no such decision consciously,
said, "Yeah, okay."

When the sun came up, Harkins, still wearing a sailor's uniform and
wrapped in a blanket, sat on a stretcher in the same street where he'd

been triaged. He'd found some discarded cloth to wrap his feet, like a time-traveling soldier from Valley Forge. Someone handed out coffee and a loaf of bread, which he shared with three other survivors. None of them knew what to do or where to go. They gave their names to a sailor who came around with a clipboard and asked what unit they were in.

"SHAEF Headquarters," Harkins answered.

"You army?" the clerk asked.

"Yeah."

"The uniform threw me," the man said. "I'm going to have someone pick you up, soon as I can. Bring you to the right collection point."

No one knew exactly what had happened out in the channel, though there were already some fantastic rumors: the Luftwaffe had bombed them, the RAF had bombed them, the stricken ships had hit mines, there were saboteurs in the fleet. Harkins had heard blame heaped on the Soviets, the Free French, even British Communists.

He mostly sat quietly, though he got sick twice, either from swallowed fuel or adrenaline released by the ordeal. Throughout the morning he watched as other launches and bigger ships brought in stunned victims and more bodies. A detail of sailors set up a canvas screen to hide the door of a warehouse near the pier. A makeshift morgue. He watched for an hour before he could steel himself to walk through, looking for Staff Sergeant Cortizo, who had shared his jeep with Harkins. When he did not find the man, he allowed himself a tiny bit of hope. Thirty minutes later, a three-quarter-ton truck pulled up to take the GIs to a barn that had been turned into a collection point for army survivors. That's where Sinnott and Wickman found him.

"Harkins!" Wickman called.

Harkins was in the middle of changing into an army uniform when Wickman reached him.

"Thank God you're okay," Wickman said.

"I guess," Harkins said, pulling on the trousers, which came only to his calves.

"You guess you're okay or you guess we should thank God?" Wickman asked, trying humor.

Harkins shrugged.

Major Sinnott pushed his way through the crowd at the door of the barn, spotted Harkins and said, apparently to Wickman, "See! I told you he was a tough bastard and would make it!"

Sinnott and Wickman were both dressed in field uniforms. Sinnott wore a pistol belt and holster, but Harkins could see the holster was empty.

"You injured?" Sinnott asked.

Harkins touched his fingers to the lump on the side of his head, where the dog handle had hit him. "Just a bump on the head, I think. Banged-up ribs."

"You're a lucky son-of-a-bitch," Sinnott said.

"What happened out there?" Wickman asked.

"I don't know," Harkins said. "One second I was talking to this sergeant who let me sit in his jeep, out of the weather. And the next second there was a giant explosion and the ship was on fire and sinking."

Sinnott took off his helmet and ran his fingers through his hair. Harkins noticed that he was not wearing Brylcreem today. Ready for war.

"It's still preliminary, but it looks like some German E-boats out of Cherbourg found the convoy."

"What's an E-boat?" Harkins asked.

"A fast torpedo boat," Sinnott said. "They probably got in and out in a few minutes."

"Doesn't the navy guard these convoys?" Harkins asked.

"Who knows what happened?" Sinnott said. "I'm sure there'll be an inquiry. Somebody will hang or someone will get a slap on the wrist for a major fuck-up. Right now, we have another problem."

He produced a sheaf of papers from a map case slung over one shoulder.

"All the guys on this list were bigoted and part of the exercise. You know what bigoted means?"

"Means they know details about the invasion," Harkins said.

"We have to account for them," Sinnott said. "Find them alive or dead so we can figure out if the Krauts scooped up one or two as prisoners. That could be a disaster. I said we'd help look. You up to it?"

"I think so," Harkins said. "As soon as I find some shoes."

Sinnott left Harkins and Wickman while he went looking for whoever was keeping track of the identification of recovered remains. It was close to sixteen hundred when a Graves Registration unit took over the handling of the corpses, and Harkins was impressed with both their efficiency and sense of propriety, the dignity with which they treated the dead.

Wickman, following one of the teams, found a lieutenant colonel of engineers—dead—who was bigoted. Harkins found no one on the list, nor did he find Staff Sergeant Cortizo. After they'd checked every recovered corpse in this morgue—there were over one hundred and fifty—Harkins and Wickman stepped outside. A private noticed Harkins' bare feet and found him a pair of shoes. They were not broken-in and not his size, but he was grateful.

"You got a message from a Major Adams while you were gone," Wickman said. "He got the court-martial pushed back at least until mid-May, and Lowell got those original statements to him."

"Good. That's good."

"Also, Sinnott heard you had a dust-up with that guy Kerr from the embassy."

Harkins, who had not thought about the investigation for twenty-four hours, studied his partner.

"It's all he talked about on the way down here this morning," Wickman said.

"Did Kerr tattle on me?"

"Somebody did. Anyway, Sinnott now wants to know all about how chummy Kerr is with the Soviets."

"I'd like to know that myself," Harkins said.

"Got any theories?"

Harkins rolled his head on his shoulders, touched the knot on his skull. He was beginning to hurt now that the ordeal was over. His ribs were sore where he'd rolled down the side of the ship, and he'd aggravated an old shoulder injury while towing the unconscious sailor who'd lost a leg.

"That's all I got," Harkins said. "Theories."

Wickman shoved his hands in his pockets, looked at the ground, and said, "I'm really glad you're okay."

"Thanks. Me, too."

Another truck pulled up to the morgue. Two privates jumped out of the back and lifted big bundles of what looked like folded cloth out of the back.

"Body bags," Wickman said. "There are probably body bags stashed all over Britain, just waiting for the invasion."

"I almost ended up in one this morning."

"Beverly found the Eighth Air Force logs," Wickman said. He looked around for Sinnott. "The ones we talked about, for classified stuff. She's really sharp, you know."

"So I gathered," Harkins said. "She's a big fan of yours, too."

Wickman didn't say anything, but he was clearly delighted with this bit of gossip.

A jeep pulled up on the other side of the street. The two men inside set up a chow line, pulling insulated cans from a trailer, probably getting ready to feed the Graves Registration soldiers. Harkins was suddenly famished. Except for a few pieces of the shared loaf of bread, he hadn't eaten for twenty-four hours.

"What did she find?" Harkins asked as the two officers moved toward the chow line. If there was food left over when the enlisted men had eaten, maybe they'd get a meal.

"Our friend Captain Gefner submitted a report for classification the day after you found Cushing with those papers."

"I think I love Beverly," Harkins said.

"I definitely love Beverly," Wickman said. When Harkins looked at him, he wore a silly grin, an embarrassed schoolboy who'd just admitted a crush.

"Anyway, there's more. The Eighth's logs of reports waiting to be classified also list titles and authors, where appropriate. The title was something like, 'Bombing Campaign Effects on Manufacture of War Materiel.' And the author was listed as 'H. Batcheller.' There was a space in the log for the author's agency, but that was left blank."

"Adams was right. They know they'll never make the murder charge stick, so they're planting evidence about mishandling secret documents. They'll get Cushing on that."

"You think Sinnott is helping them?" Wickman asked.

"Looks that way."

"What's his next move?"

"Good question," Harkins said. "Seems like things will be easier for him and Gefner if I'm not around."

"You almost weren't."

Harkins looked at the taller man.

"Around, I mean."

"Right."

The news about Harkins' dust-up with Kerr made Major Richard Sinnott think his luck was improving, although it had been a terrible day for the First Engineer Brigade and the U.S. Navy.

"We're up to about four hundred or so bodies," an army captain with a harried look told him. Sinnott found the clearing center for victim identification inside a village chapel on the road to Plymouth. The team had set up some field tables in the sanctuary, where a dozen clerks banged away at typewriters. Not for the first time, Sinnott wondered what would happen, after the war, to all the millions of pages of reports, the endless lists, the duty rosters and charge sheets and court-martial transcripts.

"Jesus," Sinnott said. "How big was this exercise?"

"Looks like three LSTs were hit. One burned for a good long time before sinking, one capsized within a few minutes, and one had its rear end shot off—a torpedo, the navy guys say—but managed to make it to the beach under its own power, if you can believe that."

It was no small miracle that Harkins had survived when so many others didn't.

Sinnott went back outside and found a jeep with no one in it. He climbed in, pushed the starter, and drove off, heading back toward the coast, toward where he left Harkins and Wickman.

"Goddamn Harkins almost got himself killed," he said aloud as he drove. "Just when I figured out I need him."

After his meeting with Sechin—the cheap bastard had given him all of one hundred thirty British pounds—he realized that his biggest problem wasn't the threat of being unmasked by the OSS as some sort of collaborator; the biggest danger lay in Sechin deciding he was no longer useful, or—worse—that Sechin and his spy-recruiting operation would be safer if Sinnott could never speak to anyone, ever, about the Soviets' flimsy network of moles and spies.

Sinnott needed leverage to stay alive, and Harkins had found it for him.

Lionel Kerr.

It made sense for Sechin to recruit someone like Kerr to be a spy. He was ambitious, well-placed, and probably had a bright future ahead of him as a diplomat. He had that Ivy League background the State Department drooled over, and he was checking all the right boxes in London. He'd go over to the continent at the ass end of the fighting, just to get a little mud splashed on him, enough so that he could say he'd done something more than drink at Grosvenor House.

It was that snotty, stuck-up Annie Stowe who'd come to Sinnott about Harkins harassing Kerr. She'd been in quite a lather, which made Sinnott wonder if she was sleeping with Kerr.

That'd be a waste of some prime tail, he'd thought.

According to Stowe, Harkins had all but accused Kerr of being a Soviet agent. If that were true, Sechin would not want Kerr exposed. If Sinnott knew for sure that Kerr had been turned, he could use the threat of revealing him to save his own skin. Life insurance.

But it was a dangerous game. It was possible that Helen Batcheller was dead because she threatened to uncover one of Sechin's people, maybe more than one, so Sinnott wasn't about to do any digging himself. Harkins would do it for him. Sinnott had tried to direct him away from the murder—there were lots of reasons to let Cushing take the fall—including dreaming up this little sojourn to the coast. But now Sinnott *needed* Kerr's hide, and he needed it before Sechin made a move, and he needed Harkins to deliver it.

Sinnott found his way back to the temporary morgue, found Harkins and Wickman at the end of a chow line where the enlisted men from the Graves Registration company were being served a hot meal. He parked the jeep and joined them.

Harkins looked at the bumper markings on Sinnott's ride. Some infantry regiment in the First Division was now short one jeep.

"Nice wheels, sir," Harkins said as he and Wickman saluted.

It's like he just can't help himself, Sinnott thought.

"You expect me to walk?" Sinnott said.

By the time the officers got to the front of the line, they were out of chow. Wickman used one of the big aluminum serving spoons to scrape the insulated containers. Two sergeants brought their mess kits over and gave each of the officers a slice of bread and a bit of gravy, a few chunks of meatloaf.

"Millions of tons of American supplies stacked in all these fucking depots across the whole goddamned country, and we can't get a meal," Sinnott said.

He laughed, which seemed to surprise Harkins and Wickman, and that amused him even more. He had a plan to get one up on that bastard Sechin, and Harkins—who was going to do the work and take all the risk—hadn't spoiled it by getting himself killed.

"Fuck this," Sinnott said. "We've got work to do, then we're going back to London."

"Me too?" Harkins asked. He looked exhausted, still had fuel oil in his hair and on his chest and arms.

"Of course," Sinnott answered. "You're going to investigate Lionel Kerr. See what crawls out when you pick up that rock."

27

It took two more days of looking, but search parties eventually accounted for all ten missing officers who'd been bigoted. Once they were released, Sinnott got seats on a train back to London for himself, Wickman, and Harkins, who was still walking gingerly and had to hold his ribs when he coughed up oil.

"So they recovered all of the missing guys?" Wickman asked. They were in a private compartment, but whispered anyway.

"Yeah," Sinnott said. "Ike slapped a cover on all this, so don't breathe a word about anything that happened once we're back in London."

On his last day as part of the search team, Harkins had found Staff Sergeant Jesus Cortizo's name on a list of recovered remains. He had immediately stepped outside to vomit.

"Still gagging up that fuel oil, huh?" Wickman had said.

Harkins had nodded, afraid to say aloud that, in his ignorance, he'd helped kill a man.

"What about the families?" Harkins asked Sinnott. He sat at the window, head against the cool glass, arm pressed to sore ribs. The swelling above his right ear had gone down, but an area the size of a child's hand was a deep purple.

"What about them?"

"What'll they tell the families?"

"I don't know," Sinnott said. "Just be happy your family isn't getting a telegram."

Harkins wondered if his mother had hung a gold star in the window for his little brother. His sister Mary had written him two months earlier about seeing the telegram delivery boy turn onto their street ahead of them as they walked back from church. The four women—Harkins' mother and three sisters—had ducked into a soda fountain while their father went ahead to see if another telegram, another terse death notice, had come to their house. He returned a few minutes later to report that the kid had pedaled out of the neighborhood without stopping.

"Tell me about your discussion with Lionel Kerr the other night," Sinnott said to Harkins.

Harkins recounted the conversation as best he could remember.

"I want you to find out if he's been turned," Sinnott said.

"Into what?" Harkins asked.

"The Soviets are recruiting spies and moles in the American mission," Sinnott said. "Stalin thinks the postwar period will be a struggle between the U.S.S.R. and the U.S. to be the world's most powerful nation. He's using this time to get ready, plant the seeds for his postwar intelligence apparatus. Kerr is exactly the kind of guy they'd like to recruit. Plus, he's already sympathetic to their system."

They rode in silence for a while, and soon the rhythm of the cars made Harkins sleepy. He folded his arms across his chest, pulled his hat down over his eyes, and leaned back. He was vaguely aware of Sinnott leaving the car and opened his eyes once to see Wickman sitting across from him, face hidden behind a newspaper. He let himself be pulled down again, eyelids and limbs heavy.

And then he was back on the LST, but this time he was trapped inside the stuck hatch with Ensign Cedrick and the one-legged sailor, and his brother Michael was outside, swinging at the bent dogs with Beverly Ludington's teapot, trying to free them. Harkins kept calling Michael's name, but his little brother was beyond hearing. Harkins yelled to Cedrick, "He can't hear me!"

Cedrick peered around the edge of the hatch, then leaned back inside and said, "He's dead!"

Michael took a few more heroic swings, then just walked away, arm in arm with Staff Sergeant Cortizo. Somehow Harkins, though still inside the flooding compartment, could see the pier with its temporary morgue and a line of telegram delivery boys standing beside their bicycles, dark uniforms buttoned tight, messenger bags slung over one shoulder. One of them, a cheerful, freckle-faced kid of no more than sixteen, assured Harkins that he could ride clear across the ocean to Philadelphia.

"I've done it before," the boy said.

Harkins startled himself awake, slipping off the bench seat and getting his legs tangled with Wickman's.

"You okay?" Wickman asked.

"Great," Harkins said. He shook his head to clear it. "Why the sudden interest in Kerr?"

"What?"

Harkins climbed back onto the bench. "First he wanted me to stop investigating Batcheller's murder, then he got me out of London completely. Now he wants me back. What the hell has changed?"

"Well, we are supposed to be spy-catchers. The OSS, I mean. Counterespionage. If Kerr has been turned, it's our job to find out. Especially if he had something to do with Batcheller's murder."

"But why does he need me?" Harkins asked. "Getting me trained for the invasion was important enough so that I had to drop everything and hurry out to the coast; now it's not so important, or not as important as playing detective back in London."

"Maybe he thinks you're a good investigator," Wickman said. "Or maybe you're being paranoid."

"I may be paranoid, but you've got to admit that an unusual number of people have been trying to kill me lately."

Wickman chuckled, though Harkins hadn't meant it as a joke. He looked past his reflection in the window. Soon it would be dusk and they'd cover everything with blackout curtains, but for the moment the Devon countryside looked like the very definition of peace.

"I've got some other questions about our Major Sinnott, too," Harkins said.

"He's a puzzle, that's for sure."

"You ever figure out what he does with the money you've been giving him? For his so-called special project?"

"No," Wickman said. "What does that have to do with Kerr?"

"Maybe nothing," Harkins said. "Maybe something."

Harkins and Wickman met Lowell outside OSS headquarters on Grosvenor at twenty-one hundred; both men wore civilian clothes.

"I'm so very happy to see you, sir," Lowell said to Harkins. She was wringing her hands, worried about him.

Harkins thought about giving her a hug. Instead, he just said, "Thanks, Lowell. I'm happy to be seen."

The driver took a deep breath, shook her hands as if flinging water from her fingers.

"Right, then," she said. "A night on the town is it? Are you sure that's a good idea, Lieutenant Harkins, after what you've been through the last couple of days?"

Harkins had a story ready to explain his bruised ribs and other injuries, but the rumor mill hadn't been affected by Eisenhower's order to keep the disaster secret. Lowell knew about the sinking by the time Harkins called her. She had the same stock of fantastic rumors that Harkins had heard in the first twelve hours, plus an additional one: that there had been a mutiny on a U.S. Navy ship.

"I appreciate your concern, Lowell," Harkins said.

"We're working," Wickman said. "Sort of."

Wickman and Harkins had agreed to divide their efforts, spending part of their time looking at Lionel Kerr—whose questionable loyalties had sparked Sinnott's sudden interest—and part of their time looking at their boss. Their ace-in-the-hole for protecting Cushing was the questionable provenance of the so-called "secret" report Gefner had filed at Eighth Air Force. Harkins wasn't sure that was enough to save the pilot, and he was determined to keep digging until he had something better.

When he climbed into the backseat, Harkins found the notebooks he'd entrusted to Lowell.

"Did you read my notes?" he asked.

"Of course, sir," she said.

"Solve the crime yet?"

"I'm this close," she said, holding her thumb and forefinger a fraction of an inch apart.

"Well done," Harkins said. "Can you find a pub called the Lamb and Flag?" Sinnott had mentioned the place a number of times.

"The one in Marylebone, you mean?" Lowell asked. "Major Sinnott's pub?"

In the backseat, Harkins and Wickman exchanged a look.

"Why do you call it that?" Harkins asked.

"Oh, it's just one of the places the drivers take him pretty regularly. Or, I should say a place where we pick him up in the mornings."

Harkins sat back, looked out the window at the blacked-out London streets and said to Wickman, "It might be worse than we thought."

The Lamb and Flag turned out to be a narrow-front building set back from the street a good forty or fifty feet. A crowd of men in uniform and women in wool skirts spilled onto the sidewalk, where a rectangle of light from the doorway lit up the alley.

"Hope this isn't the night the Krauts decide to go after blackout violators," Harkins said as they approached.

"May I come along, sir?" Lowell asked. "After I park the car?"

"I don't know, Lowell," Harkins said, studying the crowd. "You might stick out. I don't see any other women in uniform."

"Oh, I'll bet I can find a chap to escort me in, sir," she said.

Wickman was already out of the car when he stopped, leaned back in, and addressed Harkins. "She can keep an eye on the door for us," he said. "Warn us if Sinnott shows up, which is a distinct possibility."

Harkins looked at Wickman, then at Lowell.

"Okay," he said. "You can be the lookout."

"The lookout! Yes, sir," she said, smiling again. "It will be just like one of your American gangster movies."

"Let's make it one where everyone gets away," Harkins said. "Not the kind where we all get machine-gunned in the back alley."

Harkins and Wickman headed inside and straight to the bar while Lowell parked. Wickman asked for a pint; Harkins shook his head and asked the bartender, "You know Major Richard Sinnott?"

"I do indeed. Comes in here all the time."

The bartender looked to be in his fifties, bald on top, with wild tufts of gray hair spreading out like wings from the sides of his head. He wore a dingy white shirt under a dark vest, a row of three medals on his chest.

"You served in the last one?" Harkins asked.

"Highland Light Infantry," the man said, pulling his shoulders back. He was missing three bottom teeth. "Name's Starkey. Richard Starkey."

Wickman and Harkins introduced themselves, then Wickman asked, "You seen Sinnott around lately?"

"No, but he might be down on the Devon coast. Been hearing rumors they stopped a German invasion down there. People have been talking about fires out on the channel and shooting everywhere. I didn't hear anything on the BBC, but I'm not sure they'd tell us anyway."

So much for the big secret, Harkins thought.

"How often does Major Sinnott come in here?"

"Seems like two, three nights a week. I think he starts here most nights, though some nights he ends up here. We've a couple of rooms upstairs where he's been known to sleep it off."

"He ran a tab here, right?" Harkins asked.

Starkey cocked his head, and the angle along with jutting wings of gray hair made him look like a too-large terrier.

"Kind of a personal question, isn't it?"

Harkins had anticipated this. "It would be," he said. "Except that I lost a good bit to him in poker, and he said I should come around and pay off his bar bill. I tell you, he was a lucky bastard that night."

"Uncanny," Wickman agreed.

Harkins pulled three one-pound notes from his shirt pocket and laid them on the bar. Starkey reached for a worn ledger next to the cash box.

"You're going to need more than that, mate," he said. He opened the book, licked the tip of a finger, and flipped through the pages. "He owes sixteen pounds."

"Wow," Harkins said. Then, recovering, "He's a pretty good customer, then."

"He'll be a good customer after he pays his bill."

Harkins did the calculation. Sixteen pounds was sixty-four American dollars, or a quarter of Sinnott's monthly pay.

"Well, I don't owe him that much," Harkins said.

"Just out of curiosity," Wickman said. "Just so we don't get in another card game with this guy, were there any bar tabs he paid before this one?"

"You gents investigators of some sort?" Starkey asked.

Harkins pushed the three one-pound notes across the bar. Starkey looked down, then pulled them toward him and put an empty glass on top. He licked his finger again, flipped pages back and forth a few times.

"He paid a thirty-pound debt in mid-March," Starkey said.

One hundred and twenty dollars, Harkins thought. Almost half of a major's monthly pay.

"And twenty-five pounds at the end of January."

"Was he entertaining groups of people?" Harkins asked.

"Sometimes he had a friend or two with him," Starkey said. "Not so many Yanks, but some local women."

"Girlfriends?"

"Of a sort, I'd venture."

"You said he stayed here some nights, ended here on other nights," Harkins asked. "Any idea what other places he frequented?"

"No idea," Starkey said, holding up the ledger. "But I'll bet this isn't the only debt he owes."

Harkins thanked the man and walked toward the door. Lowell was standing just inside, an American sergeant on either side of her. Harkins caught her eye and motioned for her to come to him. She excused herself from her admirers.

"Any idea where else Sinnott might go?" Harkins asked.

"I never drove him at night," Lowell said. "And this is the only place I remember any of the girls mentioning."

"We could walk the neighborhood, just check in at various pubs," Wickman said.

"The war will be over by the time we visit all the pubs just in this area," Harkins said.

"I have an idea," Lowell said. She pushed between them and headed for the bar, where she tapped an attractive, well-dressed woman on the shoulder. They were too far away for Harkins to hear anything, but he could see Lowell clearly. She stood with her hands in the small of her back, her feet shoulder width apart, as if on parade. At one point the woman laughed at something Lowell said, tossing her hair and reaching out to touch Lowell on the shoulder. After a few minutes of earnest conversation, Lowell appeared to thank the woman, then returned to Harkins and Wickman.

"Friend of yours?" Harkins asked.

"I asked her if she knew Major Sinnott, and if so, where else he might frequent. She gave me two more pub names."

"How did you know to ask her?" Harkins said.

Lowell smiled at him, looked back at the woman, then at Harkins. "Intuition."

While Harkins watched, a short colonel approached the same woman, chasing off the two unlucky sergeants who'd struck out with Lowell. The woman shook hands with the American.

Harkins chuckled. "She a working girl?"

"I don't know that expression," Lowell said. The woman and the colonel squeezed past Harkins to get to the door. The woman flashed a pretty smile at Lowell.

"She just seemed like a friendly sort, so I thought she might know some of the regulars."

The information Lowell had uncovered turned out to be accurate, and by midnight they had identified two other pubs where Sinnott owed substantial amounts. Harkins kept a tally in his notebook, Wickman kept a running total in his head, updating it as they moved from one establishment to the next. At the last pub, the Coach Maker's Arms, they grabbed a table. Wickman, who looked uneasy, wanted a whiskey and soda, Lowell a pint of ale. Harkins went to the bar to get the drinks, ordered himself a water.

"If you'd rather a Coke, we have some," the bartender offered.

"Where did you get Coke?" Harkins asked.

The man smirked. "It fell off a truck, Yank. Where do you think we got it?"

"Okay," Harkins said. "I'll take one off your hands." Harkins' Coke turned out to be the most expensive of the three drinks.

When he got back to the table, Harkins said, "How much of the stuff shipped over from the States winds up on the black market?"

"A third, easily," Wickman said. "Why? You thinking of switching over to chasing good old-fashioned thieves?"

"It would be a lot easier to make sense out of that than what we're dealing with," Harkins said. "So, what are the totals from the three pubs for our Major Sinnott?"

"Fifty-seven pounds," Wickman said. "And in February and March combined, he paid a total of seventy-two pounds."

Lowell held Harkins' notebook open, ran her finger down the page with the list of bar tabs. When she looked up, she said, "My goodness."

"It can't all be the 'special project' money I handed over to him," Wickman said. "That didn't start until I got here."

He didn't look relieved and gulped a bit of his drink. "I might be screwed if he implicates me for the funds that came later, claims I knew what was going on."

"We don't know that, yet," Harkins said. "There might be other explanations."

Wickman was still not consoled.

"A major makes about two hundred and fifty dollars a month, maybe a bit more if he's been in uniform for a while. So that's—what?—two months' pay, a bit more, that he's spent in pubs since the beginning of the year."

"Not to mention any payments in January, or last December," Lowell said.

"Shit," Wickman said.

"Is he independently wealthy?" Harkins asked.

"I don't think so," Wickman said. "He told me he had to scrape together cab fare to get to his interviews for that scholarship, the Rhodes. He likes talking about how he pulled himself up by his bootstraps."

"Is he on an expense account?"

"Please," Wickman said, shaking his head. "I would have uncovered that in the first few minutes of tidying up the books."

"Maybe he has a rich friend," Lowell said.

"Sort of," Wickman said. "But I'm afraid it's me, and it was never my money to give away."

"He could have more than one rich friend," Harkins said.

28

Major Richard Sinnott sat in the darkened front parlor of a formerly elegant townhouse near Charing Cross Hospital, a short-barreled pistol on the cushion beside him, a nearly full hip flask of whiskey between his legs, waiting for Lieutenant Eddie Harkins.

Because Harkins would definitely come for him.

When Sinnott learned of Harkins' background as a cop and a boxer, he thought he'd be just the right guy for the team, the kind who would persist through all the boring details of counterespionage. Harkins turned out to be all that and more. The problem was that Sinnott had assumed—mistakenly, as it turned out—he'd be able to control this mere first lieutenant, have him do a quick murder investigation before Sinnott trained him to be a spy-catcher.

Something rattled the rubbish cans in the alley behind the dooryard, most likely his landlady's enormous cat, Beelzebub, chasing the rats that lived in the piles of rubble punctuating every street. Sinnott loosened the cap of the flask, then thought better of it. He would need all his wits for this showdown.

The evening had started well enough, some folding money in his pocket and at least a half-baked plan for solving his problems. But as soon as Starkey, the bartender at the Lamb and Flag, described the men who'd been asking about him, Sinnott knew things were going south. He paid part of his tab, then hurried to the Running Horse, which Harkins and Wickman had also found. He ended his evening at the Coach Maker's Arms, arriving just thirty minutes or so after his two subordinates left. They'd found his three biggest bar tabs, maybe more. Harkins, who was supposed to be investigating Lionel Kerr, was following the messy, convoluted trail of Sinnott's money problems.

Since arriving home around one, Sinnott had been sitting in the dark, still dressed in his rumpled uniform, scheming and waiting for dawn. The funny thing was that he'd thought the enormous bills he'd run up all over London were the least of his problems. Once he left for the continent after the invasion to chase German agents and French collaborators, well, that would be that. Let them come and try to collect from him at the front. He certainly didn't think anyone besides the pub owners would care about his debts.

A bigger problem was the homicidal Sechin, who just might decide that Sinnott was too much trouble. He doubted Sechin would rat him out to the OSS; he was more of a brass verdict kind of guy: one shot to the back of the head.

Then there was the problem of how to get back into the action. Since his return from France and the propaganda coup he'd handed the Nazis, he'd been relegated to minor roles, like standing up a counterespionage unit that might or might not get sent to the continent and, at any rate, consisted of only one man so far, and that man—Harkins—had turned on him. Sinnott was smart enough to know he also had a drinking problem, but figured he could get a handle on that at any time.

He could almost see a way out of his various dilemmas, except for this pain-in-the-ass former beat cop on his trail.

He checked the pistol again, worked the action, made sure the safety was engaged. He doubted he would use it here, but—as one of his OSS trainers in Virginia had told him—it was better to have it and not need it than need it and not have it.

Sinnott jumped at the loud knock on the door, sending his flask clattering to the floor.

"Major Sinnott?"

It was Harkins.

Sinnott picked up the flask and set it on the tiny table, shoved the pistol down into the cushions of the settee beside him. He pulled the blackout curtain aside; there was just enough light to see Wickman standing on the sidewalk out front. Harkins was out of view on the top step. Sinnott went to the door and opened it. "Good morning, gentlemen," he said.

"May we come in, sir?" Harkins asked.

"Sure, sure." Sinnott stepped aside. "This is an early call," he said. "Is there an emergency?"

"Just some things that need attention," Harkins said.

The two junior officers squeezed into the tiny parlor. Harkins looked eager, Wickman uncomfortable.

"Get you some coffee?" Sinnott asked. "I have some from the officers' mess. Real coffee from back home."

"Sounds great," Wickman said. Harkins did not answer.

Sinnott stepped into the kitchen, struck a match to light the gas. A few minutes later he emerged, three china mugs of coffee on a tray.

"How are you feeling this morning, sir?" Harkins asked. He held Sinnott's flask in his hand. Shook it to see how full it was.

Sinnott took a sip of the coffee. "I'm great, thanks." He sat on the small couch, left the two junior officers standing.

"Because it looks like you had a long night," Harkins said. "Like maybe you slept in your uniform. If you slept, that is. Or were you out?"

This was the boxer come to call, and he would be relentless. *Probably thinks he has me on the ropes.*

"You giving out fashion advice now, Lieutenant?"

Harkins squeezed next to him on the crowded seat, practically forcing Sinnott to move. When Harkins leaned back, he felt the pistol; he reached behind him, pulled it out of the cushion.

"Do you always keep a loaded weapon in the sofa cushions?" Harkins asked.

"Not always."

"We found three pubs where your tabs add up to more than a month's pay," Harkins said, reading from a notebook. "Even more interesting, we learned that in these pubs—and there may be more, for all we know—you paid off even bigger bills over the last six months."

"So?" Sinnott said, trying nonchalant, trying to buy time to think. "You worried I'm not buying enough war bonds?"

"I'm just wondering where you're getting all this money, that's all," Harkins said.

"Is this part of your investigation of Lionel Kerr?" Sinnott asked.

"In a manner of speaking, yes, sir," Harkins said.

"I don't see where my finances are any of your business."

Harkins actually smiled. He pulled a folded pamphlet from his back pocket, smoothed it out on his thigh.

"This is one of the things Lieutenant Wickman here gave me to read when I came on board," Harkins said. "It's a—what did you call it, Tom?"

"A draft handbook for the counterespionage section," Wickman said.

"That's it," Harkins said. "Imagine, we're fighting this whole war using doctrine that's still in draft form. Pretty amazing, if you ask me."

Sinnott knew what section Harkins was going to read. He looked up at Wickman, who wore a glossy sheen of sweat across his forehead. In contrast, Harkins was nearly gleeful as he flipped the pages.

"Says right here in part two, paragraph seven, that—quote—indebtedness makes a person vulnerable to being recruited by a foreign agent."

Sinnott did not respond. He wanted Harkins to put all his cards on the table.

"You told us that the Soviets were probably trying to recruit people in the U.S. mission," Harkins continued. "So, you can see how all this cash caught our interest."

Sinnott studied Harkins. Did he know about Sechin?

"Lieutenant Wickman very helpfully supplied me with some of those monies."

"Oh, Christ," Wickman said.

"Don't be so dramatic," Sinnott said. "It's not like we tried to assassinate the king. Just a little misuse of government funds."

"I didn't know anything about what you were doing with that money."

"Perhaps. But who's to say, really, what you knew, or for that matter, what Colonel Haskell will make of it?"

"The timing doesn't work," Harkins said. "Lieutenant Wickman wasn't here when you paid those big bills over the winter."

Harkins was right, of course, and Sinnott knew the cop was smart enough to note the discrepancy. Sinnott had even anticipated the self-satisfied look Harkins would wear when he thought he had Sinnott backed into a corner. Harkins was proud; Sinnott couldn't wait to squash that ego.

Sinnott stood. "Let's go out back," he said. "There's a place to sit."

He led them through the kitchen and into a tiny garden, where two chairs and a wooden stool were clustered around a small table that held a single candle. A small roof above them kept the light hidden. When the three men sat down, their knees were practically touching. Harkins laid his notebook and the pamphlet in front of him.

"Either of you ever been to France?" Sinnott asked.

"No," Harkins said.

"I was in Calais once," Wickman said. "Before the war, on a trip with my family."

"How sweet," Sinnott said. "How old were you?"

"Twelve."

"And did Mommy and Daddy buy you ice cream? Let you pick out a special treat at *la pâtisserie*?"

"Major," Harkins interrupted, "what does this have to do with anything?"

Sinnott leaned in, lowered his voice. "Because I fucking *parachuted* into France last year. By myself. Set up a Resistance cell to move downed Allied airmen into Spain, then Portugal. Either of you do anything like that?"

Neither junior officer answered.

"Ever have a price on your head? Had the Gestapo breathing down your neck? Shit your pants every time there was an unexpected knock at the door?"

"We know all about your record, Major," Harkins said. "We're not disputing that you've done some good work."

"And I've got a lot more to do," Sinnott said. "For one thing, I've got to teach you two enough to keep you alive."

Sinnott leaned back, slowed down his breathing.

"So indulge me, Lieutenant," Sinnott said.

Harkins made a palms-up gesture; the floor was Sinnott's.

"Some of the *maquis* thought I could work magic. We'd talk about what we needed—small arms, some *plastique*—and a few days later we'd get a parachute drop. Like manna."

Harkins folded his arms across his chest.

Arrogant prick, Sinnott thought.

"The money, sir," Harkins said, stone-faced. "Where did the money come from?"

Sinnott drew the moment out, smiled at his visitors. "I stole it from a captured agent," he said.

Harkins and Wickman exchanged glances. "What?" Harkins said.

"We caught some German agents who'd been put ashore by submarine near the end of last year. It was almost laughable, how inept these bastards were. Thin cover stories, the wrong clothes, documents that were obviously forged. You almost felt sorry for them. Probably trained for a year only to get arrested on the beach by some seventy-five-year-old Home Guard sentries. The Brits did most of the work, but they let me in on it, let me help with the interrogations."

Sinnott paused, took a sip of the fast-cooling coffee. He had to keep track of the lies so that he didn't contradict himself later.

"Anyway, a couple of these guys got caught carrying cash. Operating funds. I managed to get my hands on some of it."

Harkins leaned back. Sinnott might have imagined it, but he thought Harkins looked disappointed.

"You know you can get court-martialed for that," Wickman said. "On top of the other charge, you could pull twenty-five years."

"I know, I know," Sinnott said, trying to sound contrite, an attitude that did not come easily to him. "And I know I have a drinking problem. Have since I came back from France. All that shit over there really knocked me for a loop."

Wickman looked like he could drum up a half cup of sympathy; not so much Harkins.

"How much did you get?" Harkins asked.

"Three hundred and fifty pounds," Sinnott said.

"What was the alias of the spy who carried it?"

Sinnott anticipated Harkins' approach: he'd ask a bunch of questions rapid-fire, then circle back to see if Sinnott could remember the details. But Sinnott had survived months in occupied France with the Gestapo chasing him; he had some skills, too.

"Geert van der Laan. His story was that he was Dutch, a merchant seaman who'd been pressed into service by the Germans. Claimed he jumped ship in Portugal. Signed onto another ship bound for Dublin, then crossed into Northern Ireland on foot."

"Where was he apprehended?"

"South of Liverpool. Walking by himself early on a Sunday morning."

"With a suitcase full of cash?"

"Right."

"And you say it was three hundred pounds?" Harkins asked, looking down at his notebook.

"I said three-fifty."

Harkins stared into Sinnott's eyes. Sinnott held his gaze, did not blink.

"How do you know I won't turn you in?" Harkins asked.

"I don't," Sinnott said. He waited a beat, then another before pivoting. "But I still have a lot to contribute. Maybe some things to put right."

"Your redemption is not my concern, Major."

"We still have to find out about Kerr."

"We still have to find Batcheller's killer," Harkins said.

"Kerr is the thread we're going to pull for now," Sinnott said.

Harkins didn't answer, but picked up his notebook and stuck it in his shirt pocket.

"The trick is to find out as much about Kerr as you can without alerting him," Sinnott said. "If we catch him out and the Soviets don't know we're on to him, it's possible we can turn him into a double agent. The OSS brass is practically slobbering over the prospect. We'll have him feed the Soviets whatever information *we* want them to have, and they'll think it's from a trusted source."

Sinnott stood, surprised to find his knees were a bit shaky.

"Obviously I'd appreciate your keeping this conversation about my spending to yourselves," Sinnott said. "I won't forget your loyalty."

He opened a gate in the garden fence to let the two men out.

"I'll be in the office around six thirty," Sinnott said. "I'm looking forward to hearing how you're going to find out if Kerr is compromised."

Wickman went out first, then Harkins began to step through. Sinnott reached out and touched him on the arm.

"I'm glad you came through that fiasco down on the coast," he said. "Now let's keep our eye on the ball, okay, Lieutenant?"

"You mean this sideshow with Lionel Kerr?"

"You don't see it yet, but the murder investigation is already a feather in your cap," Sinnott said. "I trust you'll know everything we need to know about Kerr soon enough. Then you can concentrate on getting ready for your next job, over on the continent somewhere."

"I can't wait, sir," Harkins said. He walked away without saluting.

"So you're saying it's a diversion?" Wickman asked when they were back on the street.

"I don't know. Maybe. This sudden fascination with Kerr—it all just looks fishy to me."

Lowell was asleep in the car when they left Sinnott's house. Harkins startled her when he knocked on the window, but she was instantly awake and had them back at headquarters in just a few minutes. Harkins told her to take a few hours to get some sleep and a change of clothes.

"So what now?" Wickman asked when they were in the building.

"Look," Harkins said. "Kerr isn't going anywhere, and Sinnott is stonewalling us. Since Cushing is definitely getting court-martialed, let's try to clear him before we spend any more time worrying about Kerr, and before Sinnott ships me off to invade France, or Holland, or fucking Timbuktu."

"Sinnott was pretty adamant," Wickman said. "He wants us looking at Kerr."

"To hell with him."

"I've only known you for a few days, but it sure seems you spend a lot of time and energy doing things you've been told not to do."

"Gives me a certain charm, don't you think?" Harkins said.

"He's got me by the balls with this money thing."

"I'm not sure he does," Harkins said. "You weren't here to give him any OSS money when he was paying those big bills a few months ago. And that story about stealing money from a captured agent was total bullshit."

"So what do you propose we do now?"

"Novikov," Harkins said. "He wanted me to do something for him, and I said I'd consider it if he found out if someone from the Soviet mission had Batcheller killed."

"You think he'd rat out somebody from his own side?"

"I don't know," Harkins said. "It seems unlikely, until you weigh it against the possibility of a failed invasion. It's worth a try."

"And what if it was Kerr? If he's an asset they're not going to give him up."

"I'll tell him that Kerr's career as a diplomat is over because he's come under suspicion. He's of no use to them anyway."

"Is that true? Is it over for him?"

"Probably," Harkins said. "I don't know for sure, but if you get painted with that brush—a suspected foreign agent—I imagine it's tough to be considered trustworthy."

"So you're going to meet this Novikov again? Aren't you a little worried, since it looks like they tried to kill you after the first meeting?"

"I've got a plan," Harkins said. "Half a plan, anyway."

29

Eddie Harkins got just three hours of sleep before he heard Beverly talking to someone in the kitchen on the first floor. He took his time getting out of bed, careful of his bruised ribs, dressed, and went downstairs to find Wickman chatting with his landlady. They sat at her tiny table, Wickman's long legs jammed below.

"Good morning!" Wickman said, unfolding himself gingerly from the too-small chair.

"Sorry if we woke you, Eddie," Beverly said. She checked her watch, then stood, slinging her bag over her left shoulder. "Off to the salt mines."

"Don't break up the party on account of me," Harkins said. Beverly smiled; Wickman's face got bright red.

When she was gone, Wickman said, "She's great, isn't she?"

"Yes, she is," Harkins said.

"Smart, too."

"Yep."

Harkins went to the WC, shaved and brushed his teeth. When he was finished he strapped on his pistol belt with his holstered forty-five—Wickman was also wearing his sidearm—and the two men set off by bus for the orderly room of the 371st MP Company, where Harkins was to meet Colonel Sergei Novikov.

"You have any way of knowing if he got the message?" Wickman asked. "Or if he's even willing to come out here?"

"Lowell told me she could get the word to him," Harkins said. "Some back-channel thing through a woman she knows over there, and Lowell hasn't let me down yet."

When they arrived, they found two squads of military policemen, twenty men in all, in formation outside their Quonset hut barracks, waiting to march to a pistol range to practice marksmanship. Harkins had gotten permission from the commander to tag along, but it wasn't marksmanship that concerned him.

Harkins was nervous about meeting Novikov—not because he was disobeying a direct order from Sinnott that he was not to meet with any Russians, but because of the attempt on his life after the memorial service. He figured a broad daylight meeting more or less in the company of twenty armed American MPs was as safe a place as he was likely to find in all of Britain.

The pistol range was carved into a natural berm at the southern edge of Richmond Park, southeast of London. The MPs were part of the security force for nearby Bushy Park, where SHAEF headquarters was located. Eisenhower had disappointed a lot of Allied officers and soldiers by moving his giant staff out of London and away from its distracting nightlife to the more remote area that was almost halfway to the channel coast. Fewer distractions, Ike figured, more work getting done.

Harkins and Wickman followed as the two squads marched a mile to the range. Harkins moved slowly—his ribs hurt with each deep breath—and fell behind by a hundred yards or more by the time they reached the training area. There was no sign of Lowell or Novikov.

"Let's wait out here," Harkins said as they reached the gate; the soldiers were already inside, putting up their paper targets.

"You want me here with you?" Wickman asked. "Because I'm not sure that's a great idea."

"Why?"

"Well, if all this back-and-forth and cooperation with us hasn't been approved by his boss, the fewer Americans who know his name and have seen his face, the less he's likely to worry."

Just then Harkins saw the staff car, Lowell behind the wheel, turn onto the dirt track toward the range. Glare on the windshield hid whatever and whoever was in the backseat.

"Good thinking," Harkins said. "Just don't go too far."

Lowell pulled the staff car off the track near the gate, saluted Harkins when she got out.

"Mission accomplished, sir," she said as she held the rear door open for Colonel Sergei Novikov. He wore knee-high leather boots and blue trousers, a khaki jacket and what Americans called a Sam Browne belt: a wide waist belt with an over-the-shoulder strap. He was not carrying a pistol.

Harkins came to attention and saluted, bringing his right hand up slowly to minimize the pain in his ribs. "Glad you could come, Colonel."

Novikov returned the salute, then looked around. On the range behind Harkins, a noncom used a parade-ground voice to command, "The range is now active! Weapons up and pointed downrange! Find your target and fire at will!"

When the shooting started—a continuous popping—Novikov smiled, then laughed out loud.

"Lieutenant Harkins," he said. "I see you are not taking chances on your safety." He held out his hand, which Harkins shook, wincing a bit.

"I'm sure you can understand my concern."

"Of course," Novikov said. "You are injured?"

"I got a little banged up in a training exercise."

Novikov paused, perhaps waiting for more information. Harkins wondered how much the Soviets knew about the disaster of Operation Tiger. When Harkins offered nothing else, the Russian turned halfway toward Lowell, who was behind him, standing beside the sedan. "Private Lowell here was a wonderful tour guide. Told me this was a royal hunting ground for centuries."

"Yes, sir, I heard that, too," Harkins said.

"And today we will also talk about hunting, yes?"

"Yes, sir," Harkins said, relaxing a bit. "You could call it that, I guess. Why don't we walk a little bit?"

The two officers strolled along a path about fifteen yards behind the firing line, where the military policemen were using various stances— standing, kneeling—as they popped away at targets with their forty-fives. The range sergeant nodded at the two officers, then ran up to a soldier who'd let the muzzle of his weapon drift to his right, so that it was nearly pointing at the other shooters.

"Bennett! What in the fucking name of all that is fucking holy do you fucking think you're doing? You want to shoot your buddies here? 'Cause you're going to need them; you're going to need your whole squad to pull your ass out of the fire about ten times a week, you fucking colossal eight-ball!"

"Sergeants are the same in every army," Novikov said.

"God bless 'em," Harkins said. Then, "When we last spoke, you asked if I would deliver a report to a certain headquarters not too far from here."

"I did."

"Have you found another copy?"

"I have. It turns out Miss Batcheller mailed me a copy in case I needed to prove that we were working on something together and not passing state secrets. It arrived after she was killed."

Harkins felt his pulse trip, like a stutter-step; he pressed his elbow against the bandage around his ribs.

"I asked for help solving the murder of Helen Batcheller."

"Actually, you asked me if anyone from the Soviet mission was respon-sible," Novikov said. "If I knew such a thing and told you so, some might see it as a betrayal of my comrades."

They reached the end of the firing line. Wickman was the last man, shooting at targets alongside the MPs. He only glanced at Harkins.

"So you would excuse a murderer?" Harkins asked.

"I am not in a position to excuse anyone or hold anyone accountable," Novikov said. "At the same time, such an act—murder—would be det-rimental to our relationship as allies. If someone from my mission was behind this crime, I would have to notify the proper authorities in my own embassy. Let them handle it."

It was possible, Harkins thought, that a murderer in the Soviet Em-bassy might have diplomatic immunity. If he could not bring a killer to justice, maybe he could keep an innocent man from prison.

"What if you determined that someone in your embassy was responsible, and that person got called back to Moscow before being identified to American authorities? That might keep Major Cushing out of prison and allow you to protect whatever it is that you're protecting."

"That might be acceptable," Novikov said. "But bear in mind that I do not know who killed this Helen Batcheller."

"Not yet," Harkins said. "But you're a resourceful man. And you need a messenger."

"And you will help me?" Novikov asked.

"Yes, sir."

"I will get the document to you, and I will look for evidence that exculpates this Major Cushing."

They reached the gate, where Lowell waited with the staff car.

"I admire your passion for justice in this case, Lieutenant," Novikov said. "It seems that everyone is telling you to forget about this Major Cushing, but you won't."

"I don't think he's guilty, and I hate to see a guy get screwed by some big shots."

"And you are willing to take risks to prove this."

Harkins watched the MPs on the line. Wickman had stepped away from his firing point and was having his pistol checked by the range sergeant, who made sure it was clear, the magazine ejected.

"You're talking about the risk of my getting caught with a classified document?" Harkins said. "Or the risk I'm taking here talking to you after I've been told to stay away?"

"We both share in the second," Novikov said. "I have not been authorized by the ambassador to deal with the American OSS. But, yes, carrying a document that you have been warned is classified presents a risk for you, too."

"Cushing is facing a more immediate threat," Harkins said. "I figure I'll deal with one crisis at a time."

When Harkins and Wickman arrived at headquarters on Grosvenor Street, Annie Stowe was waiting for them in the lobby, sitting on the edge of a bench in the waiting area. She stood when she saw them.

"Shit," Harkins said under his breath.

Wickman raised his hand and waved. "Hello, Annie."

"Major Sinnott told me you guys are investigating my colleague," she said.

"Let's take this upstairs," Harkins said. "Someplace a little more private."

When they were settled in the conference room with the painted-over windows, Stowe continued, "As I was saying, Major Sinnott told me you guys are investigating Lionel Kerr."

"Really?" Harkins said. "Because I heard you went running to Sinnott because I was too hard on Kerr." He hated a tattletale.

"We spoke about that," was all Stowe would say. She and Harkins looked at each other for a few awkward seconds. Wickman crossed his long legs, a model of patience.

"I just gave Sinnott my impressions of that conversation," she said. "At the time I thought you were a bit hard on Kerr; now I've come to see why."

Harkins was skeptical. "Why did you come here?" he asked.

"Look, I've been through a great deal recently. My roommate—my friend—was brutally murdered, and now there's talk that another colleague might be involved, or at least knows something about the crime. It's like everything I thought I knew turns out to be built on sand."

"You've had a tough few days," Wickman said. "That's for sure."

"Lionel said something to me that might be germane," Stowe said, looking at Harkins. When he didn't respond, she continued.

"He said that Helen had threatened to identify people she thought were Soviet agents, and he thought that got her killed."

This was one of Harkins' theories, but it was interesting to hear that Kerr had shared it with Stowe.

"Is Kerr one of those agents?" Harkins asked.

"Well, I thought that was unlikely, since he brought it up. You'd think he wouldn't want to draw attention to himself, you know? But now I'm not so sure."

"Why would he tell you something like that?"

"I think he just wanted to impress me." She crossed her legs at the ankles, sat back in her chair. "He's asked me out a couple of times. On dates, I mean. I told him I'm not ready."

There was a knock at the door. Harkins said, "Come in."

Lowell stuck her head in the room. She didn't hide her surprise at seeing Stowe. "Oh, pardon," she said. "I, uh, I just wanted to let you know I'm here, sir. Car is parked nearby, in case you need me."

"Okay, thanks," Harkins said. Lowell looked at Stowe and smiled, then closed the door as she left.

"Why is Kerr's faltering love life important to us?" Harkins asked.

"The dates were just a front, I think. I believe he wants to talk to me about something else."

Stowe looked down at her hands. There was a tiny gold signet ring on her right hand, which she twisted around and around. Harkins looked at Wickman, who nodded. Stowe was ready to talk.

"What else?" Harkins asked.

"I think he might try to recruit me."

"What makes you think that?"

"He asked too many questions about my work. I made up some stuff to kind of string him along, see where he went with it."

"Did you tell him about your actual work?" Harkins asked.

"No, of course not. I made up a fictional project, something that doesn't exist anywhere in the OSS, as far as I know. He told me he thought we could all benefit if we shared that kind of stuff with our allies. I didn't disagree with him, but I changed the subject and promised to think about what he said."

"So now he's waiting for—what? For you to get back to him? To show further interest?"

"Yes. At least, I think so. But I wanted to let you guys know about it, once I found out you were looking at him. I thought this could help."

Harkins leaned back in his chair, wondered if she had an angle or if her offer of help was sincere.

"This must all be very difficult for you," Wickman said to Stowe.

She took out a pink handkerchief and blotted the corners of her eyes, though Harkins had not seen any tears.

"How did you leave it with him?" Harkins asked. "I mean, what's your next move?"

"Well, I imagine he's waiting for me to tell him I want to talk further."

"Okay," Harkins said. "Let it ride for a bit. Be patient. If he approaches you again, let me know before you go anywhere with him."

"Do you think you're in danger?" Wickman asked Stowe, who shook her head.

"I appreciate your coming by, Annie," Harkins said. He stood, and Wickman and Stowe stood as well.

"Major Sinnott said they're moving pretty quickly on the court-martial for that pilot," she said. "I guess that means the case against him is pretty strong."

"Maybe," Harkins said.

"All this stuff with Lionel is a sideshow to the investigation of Helen's murder, but I think it's important, don't you?"

"Major Sinnott certainly thinks so," Harkins said. "Which makes it important for us, I guess."

Stowe shook hands with Harkins and Wickman, who took her hand in both of his.

When Stowe left the room, Lowell stuck her head in again. "Have a minute, gentlemen?" she asked.

"Sure," Harkins said. The driver came in and closed the door gently behind her.

"I found out some things about Miss Batcheller and Miss Stowe that might bear on the investigation."

"Oh?" Harkins said. "And where did you get this intelligence?"

"Two of the women in the motor pool," she said. "They told me these things in separate conversations. Unprompted."

She looked at Harkins, then at Wickman, hesitant to begin.

"Well, spit it out," Harkins said.

"Batcheller and Stowe were actually a couple. Lovers. Had quite a committed relationship, apparently."

"Come on," Wickman said. "That sounds like gossip."

"How sure are you about this?" Harkins asked.

"Well, as sure as one can be about such private matters," Lowell said. "Private matters that the parties want to remain private."

"That's kind of a surprise," Wickman said. He looked at the chair where Stowe had been sitting. "Beautiful, wholesome girl like that. Such a waste."

Lowell said something that Harkins didn't catch. "What's that?" he asked.

She looked up at Harkins, then at Wickman. "I said it's not a waste if they were happy. If they really loved each other."

Wickman shook his head, unconvinced, but Harkins smiled at his driver and said, "You're right, Lowell. Thanks."

"I need some air," Wickman said. He got up and left.

When they were alone, Lowell said to Harkins, "There's something that seems, I don't know, a little off, knowing what we know now."

"Go on."

"I can't put my finger on it, exactly."

"Let me see if I can help you," Harkins said. "Her lover is murdered, but Stowe is focused on an adjacent case."

"Did she ask about the murder trial?" Lowell asked.

"Nope. She's bought into the whole story that Major Cushing is responsible. She came here today to talk about Lionel Kerr."

"To accuse him?"

"Pretty darn close," Harkins said. "Looks like there's more to Kerr's story, and she made it clear she's willing to help."

"Kind of makes you wonder about her motivation, doesn't it?"

"Maybe she's just a patriotic American," Harkins said. "Wants to protect us from the Communists. Maybe there's something else."

"Think we'll find out?" Lowell asked.

"Well, depends on how fast Major Sinnott ships me out of here once the shooting starts on the continent."

"No time to waste, then, right, sir?"

"No time to waste," Harkins said.

30

When he got the message to report to Colonel Haskell's office, Major Richard Sinnott changed out of his service uniform, with its jacket and tie, and into the kind of rough civilian clothes he wore in field training at the OSS camp in Manassas, Virginia, and in the mountains of southern France: wide-legged woolen trousers, a long cotton shirt, heavy well-used brogans. He traded his army-issue holster and forty-five for a Spanish-made revolver.

Sinnott had heard the scuttlebutt: Haskell was preparing the next cadre of operatives to parachute into France. Now Sinnott, the most experienced field agent at OSS London Station, was being called up to the major leagues. The long wait was over; he was back in the game in time for what might prove to be the biggest event of the war.

He hurried to the latrine on his floor to brush his hair and teeth. Studying himself in the mirror, he could still see red rims around his eyes.

"Don't stand close enough for him to see," he told his mirror self.

He topped off the costume with a wide-brimmed hat that dated from his first visit to Paris during his time at Oxford. Its worn look, Sinnott thought, made him look like Hemingway's Robert Jordan. He smiled at his reflection, then hustled up the stairs to the fourth floor of OSS headquarters. The hallway outside Haskell's office was lined with a dozen or so men and women, also in civilian clothes and seated on chairs along the wall. Sinnott walked past them to the door with the hand-lettered sign that said "Haskell."

"The line starts back there, pal," one man said, pointing with his thumb to the others.

"Not for me, it doesn't," Sinnott said. He knocked twice and entered.

Haskell had taken a small conference room for his office, but instead of a desk he had long tables along three of the walls. Two stand-alone easels held large boards, each with a black cloth draped over whatever was displayed beneath.

"Good morning, sir," Sinnott said. Haskell was bent over a table, writing something with a pencil. He stood and turned around, removed another pencil he'd been holding in his mouth.

"Sinnott. Good to see you."

Haskell looked beat. Pasty complexion, dark circles under his eyes. He was also in civvies, and Sinnott noticed he was wearing carpet slippers instead of shoes. One ankle was wrapped in a bandage.

"What happened to your foot, sir?" Sinnott asked.

"Ankle. Twisted it getting off a goddamn horse, if you can believe that."

"Is it serious?"

"It'll keep me out of the field for six weeks or so, which is probably going to turn out to be really bad timing."

Suddenly Sinnott could picture himself serving as some kind of stand-in for the colonel during the next few weeks of training, maybe even a replacement for the big jump, if that came soon enough. The move would probably come with a promotion, and Sinnott had already purchased the silver oak leaves of a lieutenant colonel. He could certainly use the bump in pay.

"We're really ramping things up over in France," Haskell said. "We have to get a lot of people in over the next six to eight weeks, and I know you have a lot of experience over there."

Sinnott had a vivid memory of his first jump into France in 1943. He was terrified, but also felt more alive than he ever had before or since. He couldn't wait to get back.

"All those people out in the hallway are candidates, and I have another fifteen coming in later today."

"I ran an operation that size out of Toulouse, sir," Sinnott said. "And I've been giving a lot of thought to what kind of direct action we should take once the invasion starts. I'd like to share my ideas."

Haskell, who'd been reading something in his hand, looked up.

"Is that why—I mean, why are you dressed like that?"

"I'm ready to get back to work, sir. Back to the field. Getting those newcomers out in the hallway trained up, if that's what you need."

"No, that's not it. I just need someone to *interview* these people. Weed out the certifiable crazies from the ones who are just crazy enough."

"What about going over?" Sinnott asked. "I'd like very much to get back there."

"And I'd like eight uninterrupted hours of sleep," Haskell said. "But that ain't working out, either."

Sinnott's disappointment must have showed on his face.

"Look, I'm sorry, Sinnott. I'd love to send you back into the action; I really would. But you're still on the shit list with the brass hats because of what happened last time. I can bring your name up again, but for now I need help doing this. Interviewing the new folks."

"Sir, there were extenuating circumstances around that business in France."

"I'm sure there were," Haskell said, maybe losing a little of his patience. "I read your report. It's just that right now you're not in the lineup, and I can make good use of your knowledge right here."

Sinnott felt like a fool, standing there with his weathered cap in his hands, his pistol tucked into a shoulder harness, like some leftover from the Spanish civil war. Still, he tried to sound sincere when he said, "Yes, sir. Certainly, sir. Happy to serve where I'm needed."

"That's the spirit," Haskell said. "Let's go over what we're looking for in these new people before you bring them in."

Sinnott spent the afternoon and evening in another small conference room, talking to twelve field officers newly arrived from the States. He interviewed them in French and crossed two off the list immediately because they sounded like C students from some high school French club. Another one who claimed to have a cold probably had pneumonia, and Sinnott packed him off to the infirmary. Of the remaining nine, the most impressive were two women, one of whom had grown up on a ranch in Montana and the other in Manhattan society circles. They were about as different as they could be, except for their raw intelligence and a certain physical energy. Sinnott asked each of them, in turn, to meet him for a drink that evening. They both turned him down.

"Well, if that ain't the cherry on the cake of my fucking day," he muttered after the last woman left the room. He tidied his notes and left them for Colonel Haskell, secured his pistol in his office safe, and left the building. He had not eaten all day and was hungry, but in no mood for the collegial chitchat he'd have to endure if he ate in the officers' mess. All it would take to set him off would be for one person to ask what he'd been up to lately. Instead he walked south, crossing Piccadilly above St. James Palace. He kept glancing down the side alleys, looking for a pub he'd visited a few weeks earlier, a place where he didn't owe any money.

He first noticed the tail when he turned around to get his bearings. A man in a short jacket, dirty black pants, a hat pulled low across his brow. He was thirty or forty yards back, and when Sinnott stopped the man didn't react, didn't break stride, but crossed the street as if it had been his plan all along. If it was a tail, the guy was a pro.

Sinnott waited for thirty seconds to see if the guy would emerge from the same alley. When he didn't show, Sinnott turned back toward the river. He found the pub—The Footman's Holiday—after another few minutes of searching. He pulled the door handle and, just as he was stepping inside, he saw the tail again, about a block away.

Sinnott stepped inside, felt his pulse hammering his ears. He scanned the narrow room quickly; there were just a few patrons and what looked like a single exit out to an alley. If the tail was any good, he would not follow Sinnott into the front; that was too obvious. He'd use the back door.

Sinnott hurried down a tiny hallway and squeezed by stacked boxes, the space barely wider than his shoulders. He turned the dead bolt to unlock the back door, then flattened himself against the wall. He wrapped one hand in his handkerchief to unscrew the single light bulb above the entryway, then leaned back into shadow. He reached into a pocket he'd had sewn along the seam of his trousers and found his straight razor, his weapon of choice for close quarters fighting.

He did not have to wait long.

The guy he'd made as a tail pushed the door in slowly. When he had a foot and his head across the threshold Sinnott threw all of his weight into the door, slamming the man's skull. He pulled the door back, then smashed it again, three times rapidly. The man tried to get his leg free but fell backward, and Sinnott followed him out into the alley, swiping with the razor as the man held his arm up in defense. Sinnott felt the give as the blade bit through cloth and, he was sure, the man's right arm, even though his attacker did not make a sound.

Sinnott jumped and swung the razor at the face below him, but the man caught Sinnott's wrist and bucked his hips, nearly sending Sinnott flying. The guy was bigger than Sinnott first thought, and in a flash he held a long knife, pulled from a sheath on his left arm. He stabbed the point through the back of Sinnott's hand.

"*Gavno, blyad,*" the man spat, cursing in Russian.

Sinnott was not going to win on the ground; the man was too strong, too heavy, too quick. He scrambled to his feet, backed up into some trash cans. The Russian stood, grabbed a length of board from the ground and swung it like a cop's nightstick. Sinnott jumped backward, but the board stung his arm as if he'd been shocked. The razor clattered to the ground.

And at that moment, just when Sinnott thought he'd be London's next stabbing victim, a policeman appeared just behind the Russian.

"What's this now?" he said. "Break it up or I'll have both of you hauled off."

The police officer grabbed the Russian by the collar, but the big man kicked backward, catching the cop just below the knee. Sinnott heard a loud crack; the policeman said, "Ohhh," as he crumpled. Instead of letting the copper alone and facing Sinnott again, the Russian took a second to make sure the threat had been neutralized, and that's when Sinnott jumped on his back, grabbed the man's face with his left hand, and jammed his right thumb deep into the Russian's eye socket. He made a hook with his thumb and pushed his hand forward, felt the eyeball give. The Russian stabbed wildly with the long knife, but he was already going down. When his enemy hit the ground, Sinnott snatched the man's knife and stabbed him in the neck once, twice, three times. Blood geysered onto the policeman, who lay on his side, his right leg below the knee bent at a terrible angle.

Sinnott got to his feet, chest heaving. He picked up his straight razor and said to the policeman, "*Vse u tebya budet khorosho,*" before walking out of the alley.

31

"You have made great sacrifices, comrade," Colonel Yury Sechin said, nodding toward the mangled stump of Novikov's left arm. The two men were in a sauna in the basement of a boarding house for Soviet embassy staffers. Sechin sprawled naked on a wooden bench, his great, hairy belly resting on his lap.

"Others have made greater sacrifices," Novikov said. "I am alive, at least."

"I was thinking of your family."

Novikov's wife and two young sons died in the siege of Leningrad, probably in April 1942. Novikov had feared but could not confirm their deaths until January 1943, when the Red Army finally established a corridor to the encircled city. His loved ones—these pieces of his very heart—were just three out of the million Soviet citizens who perished there.

Novikov's soldiers thought him a brave commander, but the truth was that he fought like a man who was already dead.

Sechin did not try to hide the fact that he was studying Novikov's face, the missing left eye usually covered by a patch. "We cannot hide anything in here, right?" Sechin said.

Perhaps his idea of a joke, Novikov thought.

"So this is a metaphor for the openness you want to promote?" Novikov said. "Two naked colonels?"

"You and I can be open with each other," Sechin said. "We must be guarded with everyone else."

"Where shall we start?"

"Why are you meeting with this American investigator?"

"I will use him to deliver some intelligence to the American and British planners, something that will help the invasion succeed."

Novikov gave his NKVD colleague the briefest of summaries of the failures of the Allied bombing command.

"This came out of your work with that American woman, the one who got killed?"

Novikov nodded. "Her death set back my timetable," he said.

"She was a threat to my recruiting," Sechin said. "Though I am sorry she had to die."

Novikov doubted that was true. "Are your efforts bearing fruit?"

Sechin used a snow-white towel to mop his face. "Not as much as I'd like," he said. "I have one asset in place. Very weak. A second who has outlived his usefulness and is now a threat. There is a third, much more valuable asset that I know only by a code name, but I am working on making contact. In the meantime, there is the problem of this investigator sticking his nose into every corner."

"He is really only interested in the murder," Novikov said. "I think if he could solve that, he would stop looking for these other problems."

"Suppose I was in a position to deliver the killer?"

Novikov waited a beat before answering, running through a list of the many things Sechin might want in return—the things he might ask for outright, the things that would remain hidden until the bill came due.

"Then he might be satisfied. Even to the point where he stops looking for our friends in the British and American missions."

Sechin grunted. He rang a hand bell and a female attendant brought in a tray with a bottle of water and two glasses. She poured the water and left without looking up. Sechin had not bothered to cover himself.

"We are in the same business, you and I," Sechin said. He leaned back on the wood slat wall, his shoulders and the back of his head leaving a large wet mark.

"Oh?"

"You are working for the short-term success of the Allied invasion, which will help our country, and I am focused on the long term, getting us ready for the postwar struggle with the capitalists."

"We have slightly different methods," Novikov said. He resented the comparison, but knew that at some level Sechin was right.

"We are both loyal Soviet officers," Sechin said, turning his head slowly. He moved, Novikov thought, like a lizard.

"I will help you preserve your network to the extent that I can, of course," Novikov said.

Sechin turned his gaze to the front, took a long drink of water from one of the glasses, offered the second to Novikov, who drank it down.

"An American major named Sinnott killed the woman, killed the Batcheller woman, on my orders."

"I see," Novikov said.

Novikov wanted to protest that it was a terrible idea to use violence against one's allies, but he just said, "And this was because she threatened to identify some of your assets?"

"That was the report that reached me," Sechin said. "I had to be careful, you see."

"And you no longer need this Sinnott?"

Sechin shrugged, just a tiny movement of his shoulders.

"And if I identify him as the killer and Harkins—that's the investigator's name—if Harkins can make the case, then all you want in return is for them to stop looking for other assets."

"Exactly."

32

Annie Stowe found Harkins and Wickman walking back from the officers' mess.

"I've been looking for you," she said as she approached them on the
street. "I think tonight might be the night."

"Kerr?" Harkins asked.

"He's taking me to some school outside the city. Said we're going to
meet people there who will clear up some things about the real nature of
our relationship with our allies."

"Is that what he said?" Harkins asked. "Allies? Not Soviets?"

"He said allies, but if we were talking about the Brits there'd be no
need for sneaking around outside the city. I think you should come and
see who's there."

"If he shows up with a contact from the Soviet mission," Harkins said,
"that would certainly be enough reason to bring him in for questioning.
It would be even better if you let the meeting go on for a while, see exactly
what Kerr wants from you. See who else shows up."

"You want her to meet with these people?" Wickman asked. "We don't
even know who's going to be there. This could be dangerous."

"You guys can position yourself nearby," Stowe said. "If I get into
trouble I'll find you." She handed Harkins a slip of paper with the name
of the school.

"What time are you meeting Kerr?"

"We're meeting at Grosvenor House at nine. He and I are going out
together."

"Okay," Harkins said. "No heroics. You're just along to gather information, enough so that we understand how badly Kerr has been compromised."

"We need to leave a message for Major Sinnott," Wickman said. "Let
him know where we're going."

"I'd rather not," Harkins said.

"I know you'd rather not," Wickman said. "But this time we're not just
nosing around. There's a chance we'll run into someone from the Soviet
mission; there's a chance we might haul an American diplomat—low

ranking, but a diplomat—in for questioning. I don't think we should do this cowboy style."

Harkins watched Wickman for a moment, then said, "Okay. We'll let Sinnott know where we're going and why."

"Should we get Lowell back here?"

"No," Harkins said. "Too dangerous. In fact, I want to take some MPs with us for extra firepower."

"You think there's going to be a shootout?"

"I think that having four or five guns along makes it less likely that there'll be a shootout, which would be fine with me," Harkins said.

"Lowell is going to be pissed," Wickman said.

"She can get pissed all she wants," Harkins said. "As long as she doesn't get shot."

Major Richard Sinnott wrapped his wounded right hand in a kerchief and stuck it in his jacket pocket when he entered OSS headquarters on Grosvenor Street.

"You're Major Sinnott, aren't you?" the duty sergeant called when he stepped into the lobby.

Sinnott glanced around. The big space was unnerving; there were too many places for someone to hide. "I am," he answered.

"Message here for you, sir." The sergeant offered an envelope with a time and date written in the corner. The staff tracked incoming messages.

"Can you sign here?" The GI held up a clipboard. "For the message."

Sinnott, who was right-handed, considered using his left to sign, but instead he pulled out the bandaged hand. The kerchief was soaked through with blood, but it looked like it had dried, which meant the bleeding had stopped.

"Jesus," the sergeant said. "What the hell happened? You need me to call a medic or something?"

"No," Sinnott said, a little too sharply. The man pulled back a bit.

"No. I mean, it's just a normal Monday in the OSS." He tried to smile. "I'll be fine, thanks." He took the pen the sergeant offered and signed his name, leaving behind a bloody spot on the paper.

He went upstairs and into the supply closet, where he pulled out two large burn bags, used for the controlled destruction of classified material. In the latrine—where he'd been so full of hope about a promotion just that morning—he stripped off the civilian clothes and stuffed them in the bags, then washed himself at one of the big utility sinks. Once his hand was clean he saw that it was a puncture wound, rather than a slash. He'd been stabbed in the palm, the point of the man's knife going all the way through. Looking at the wound, now washed free of blood, he felt a bit dizzy. He steadied himself for a moment, then dressed in his service uniform and considered how everything was unraveling.

He was sure Sechin was behind the attempt on his life; apparently the Soviet spymaster had decided that he was no longer useful, maybe even a threat. His key to survival was to gain some leverage, which he planned to do by identifying Kerr as a Soviet asset. Sinnott would threaten to expose him unless Sechin backed off. Better yet, backed off and provided a regular stipend.

Sinnott opened his safe and removed his forty-five, checked the load and action. He would need more than a sidearm to protect himself, and he wondered if he could arrange some sort of MP escort for when he left the building. He could always sleep here, maybe figure out a way to have meals brought over from the officers' mess. There was a large planning and map room in the basement, and the staff downstairs was nearly quarantined. As the invasion got closer and they learned more details, their movements would be further curtailed. No one who knew anything worthwhile would be allowed to leave the building until after the fighting started. Sinnott could become just another vampire who didn't go outside, maybe for a month or two, then he'd skedaddle to the continent. Colonel Haskell could find something for him to do.

By now Sechin probably knew the assassination attempt had failed. Thanks to a few phrases he'd learned, London police were most likely looking for a Russian speaker who left the murder scene. That ought to keep them busy for a while.

What would Sechin's next move be?

There was a bottle of bourbon in the safe, one-third full. Sinnott yanked the cork and took a long drink, which made his eyes water. When he cleared his vision with the back of his left hand, he saw the envelope on the desk, where he'd dropped it. He opened it and pulled out a single folded sheet of typing paper. At the top, the time and date indicated the note was written at 1915 hours.

According to Stowe, Kerr is meeting with possible Soviet contact at Berkhamsted School. If that's true, we'll bring Kerr in. Otherwise we'll keep you posted. Harkins.

He sat down at his desk and took another hit of bourbon.

"Shit," he said to himself. If Harkins and Wickman arrested Kerr in front of some Soviet, Sechin would know that Kerr was exposed and Sinnott's leverage would be gone. He wanted Harkins to find evidence; he didn't want him to arrest Kerr.

"God*damn* it."

He looked at the note again.

"Where the fuck is the Berkhamsted School?"

Pamela Lowell sat in the driver's seat of the sedan, quite sure she'd never been this angry before. A half hour earlier Harkins had appeared in a jeep driven by an American MP, followed by a second jeep with Wickman in the front, an MP driving and another in the back. At least two of the GIs carried Thompson submachine guns. Harkins had asked for directions to the Berkhamsted School, then told her she was staying behind.

"I think you would agree that I've been a help to you," she said. "A big help, even. And now you're just going to leave me behind?"

"You *have* been a big help," Harkins said. "But for this part I need gunfighters, and that's not you."

Angry tears clouded her vision; she swiped at them with the back of a hand, determined not to cry. "I'm not one of your little sisters, you know," she said, surprised to hear her own raised voice.

Harkins had not even answered her; he just climbed into the front passenger seat of the jeep, spread a map on his knees, and said to the driver, "Let's roll."

Lowell sat like that for thirty minutes, breathing deeply and slowly and trying to ride herd on her rage. She'd been told she was part of the team, that she was making a contribution. Her twenty-eight months in the ATS had been the most trying, the most exciting and rewarding of her life thus far. But now she realized that it would all come to an end soon, when all the boys came back and shoved the women back into the homes and nurseries. She'd probably wind up as a schoolteacher. She was so angry she pounded the steering wheel and very nearly said, "Fuck!"

She was still sitting there, parked on Grosvenor Street, when she saw Major Sinnott come out of OSS headquarters carrying a large insulated bottle and a long weapon of some sort. She considered getting out and talking to him, but she didn't want to give Sinnott a chance to quiz her, since Harkins told her more than he was supposed to. Angry as she was, she still didn't want to get Harkins in trouble. Sinnott turned in the opposite direction and so did not pass her car. She was sitting there, watching him hurry toward the square when a man knocked on her passenger side window, startling her. It didn't help that when she looked over, the man had a black patch over one eye. Colonel Novikov.

"Oh, sweet Jesus," she said.

She got out of the car, saluted.

"Sorry to frighten you like that," he said. "It's Lowell, right? Are you waiting for Lieutenant Harkins?"

"No, sir. He left in another vehicle thirty, forty minutes ago."

The colonel looked over Lowell's shoulder at the front of the OSS headquarters. Lowell noticed the holster, the butt of a large handgun sticking out. She had never seen a high-ranking officer carrying a weapon.

"Have you seen Major Sinnott?"

"He came out of the headquarters after Lieutenant Harkins left."

"Do you know if they spoke to one another?"

"I don't think so. Lieutenants Harkins and Wickman weren't in the headquarters, at least as far as I saw. They came from the direction of the square, but I didn't see them go inside."

"Do you know where Harkins went?"

"Yes, sir."

"Can you take me to him?"

Lowell stood perfectly still, looking over the roof of the staff car at this one-eyed Soviet with the big pistol at his waist, who might or might not have a legitimate reason to want to track down Harkins. She desperately wanted an excuse to head out to the Berkhamsted School, but she had also been ordered to stay behind.

"Sometimes you just gotta say, 'fuck it.'"

"What's that?" the colonel asked, putting a hand to his ear. "My hearing is not what it used to be."

"Oh, it's just an expression that Lieutenant Harkins uses, that he told me I should use more often."

"Does that say sixteen forty-two?"

This from the MP who had been Harkins' driver, a nineteen-year-old from Oklahoma named Tallent. They were on foot, doing a reconnaissance to determine the layout of the school, and Tallent had spotted a plaque on one of the gateposts.

"They sure do have some old stuff over here," the private said.

It had turned out to be a fifty-minute ride north and west from London to the banks of the Bulbourne River, but after a few wrong turns and two stops for directions they found themselves parked in a wood on a rise above the school. To their left, about a hundred meters away, was the open gate. Below them, in a shallow bowl of lawns and muddy playing fields, Harkins could see a circular driveway and three large buildings arranged at right angles to one another, forming three sides of a quadrangle. The building on the far left was dark—he took that to be an academic hall. The three-story brick structure in the middle, with its ranks of symmetrical windows, looked more like a dormitory. On the right was a large white house he figured for an administration building or the headmaster's cottage. Beyond those lay dark woods, though he could just make out a slash of dull silver that he took to be the river.

Harkins and Tallent waited fifteen minutes for Wickman and the other two MPs to complete their look around and rejoin the group. The two jeeps were stashed amid the trees, parked in a small ravine that should hide them from view, in case anyone came out of the school looking for them.

"River is over there," Wickman said, pointing north. "About five hundred yards or so. There's another road—more of a trail, really—that runs from behind that big house. There's a car parked behind, then a couple smaller houses behind the big house; you can't see them from here, maybe faculty houses. Then the trail heads east. It's another approach to the campus, or another way out."

"When we stopped for directions that last time," Harkins said, "the pub owner told me this was a fancy boarding school before the Depression, then it went tits up. In 1940 they moved a bunch of kids out here from London, to get away from the Blitz. He said a lot of kids moved back to the city."

"Anybody left?" Wickman asked.

"Orphans," Harkins said. "And some kids who survived the Blitz but were so traumatized they kept them out here."

"Jesus," Wickman said. "Makes you think about how lucky we are back in the States."

"I'm going to position myself near the gate, see if I can spot Stowe coming in with Kerr," Harkins said.

"Then what?" Wickman asked.

"If we see her, or at least see a car, we'll watch where she goes. I'm thinking that they might meet in that building on the left, the one that's dark right now, or possibly in that house on the right. Then we'll want to get closer, see if we can figure out who's in there with her."

Harkins and Tallent got to within about twenty yards of the gate, where they could stay hidden among some undergrowth but still had a clear view of whatever drove onto school grounds. The woods here were dark, so Harkins was not optimistic about being able to see inside any vehicles. He and Tallent lay on the pine needles, just a foot or so apart.

"What are we looking for, sir?"

"There's supposed to be a meeting here. Couple of Americans from the mission in London, maybe somebody from the Soviet mission."

"Are we talking about spies and stuff?"

Harkins looked at the soldier. He probably should have brought along an OSS agent or two instead of young GIs.

"I won't know until later," Harkins said. "You're here to provide backup to me and Lieutenant Wickman."

"Holy crap," Tallent said. "You think there's going to be shooting?"

"It's possible. For now, just watch the road."

Tallent was quiet for a moment. Then, in a low voice, "I only shot paper targets before."

Harkins looked over and—because it was what the kid needed to hear—said, "You'll be okay."

A few minutes later it began to rain, a cold, light drizzle.

"The weather in this country is just awful," Tallent said. He reached around to where he had rolled a raincoat on the back of his pistol belt. "You got a raincoat, Lieutenant?"

"No."

Tallent scooted closer so they were lying side by side, then threw the raincoat over his own and Harkins' shoulders.

"You an MP, sir?"

"Yeah," Harkins said.

"I was thinking of volunteering for one of the divisional MP units," Tallent said. "Get closer to the action. I don't want to spend the whole war parading around in a white helmet and locking up drunk GIs."

"It can be pretty boring in a divisional unit, too," Harkins said. "You spend a lot of time breaking up traffic jams and guarding prisoners."

"Did you see any fighting? I mean, actual combat?"

"I saw the results," Harkins said. He looked over at the kid, just barely visible in the darkness. "Be careful what you wish for."

"That's what my older brother told me. He's in the First Division. Already fought in North Africa and Sicily. Too bad I can't take his place and let him go home."

Harkins thought of Patrick and his paratrooper comrades, getting ready for their third major campaign, and all the aviators out in East Anglia, who went to war night after night.

"How long you reckon we'll be out here, sir?" Tallent asked just as Harkins thought he heard something.

Harkins held up his hand. "Shhh."

A black car rolled slowly through the gate. As it was about to pass Harkins and Tallent, someone in the front passenger seat used a cigarette lighter. Harkins thought he saw Stowe in profile, leaning into the flame. When the car passed onto school grounds, Harkins stood and tapped Tallent on the shoulder. "Let's go."

He walked back to where Wickman and the other two MPs waited. All three MPs had raincoats, which probably meant their sergeant checked on them before they left the barracks. Wickman, who—like Harkins— did not have a raincoat, huddled with his shoulders pressed up to his ears.

"See anything?" Wickman asked.

"A sedan went in. American-made, driver on the left side of the car. I think Stowe was in the passenger seat."

"That last car parked in front of that cottage," one of the MPs said.

"What do we do now?" Wickman asked.

"What indeed?" Major Sinnott said as he appeared from the woods behind them, holding a rifle by the balance point. Two of the startled MPs reached for their pistols.

"Hold on," Harkins directed, raising his hand.

"How did you find us?" Wickman asked.

"A blind man could have found you, all the noise you're making out here," Sinnott said. He wore a stylish trench coat. "You two geniuses didn't bring raincoats? It's fucking England in May."

Out of the corner of his eye, Harkins saw Wickman glance at him. Probably thinking the same thing. Sinnott had been drinking. Maybe drunk, maybe not, but juiced.

"We have a lot of work to do on your fieldcraft if you're going to avoid getting hauled in by the Gestapo," Sinnott said.

Harkins studied the rifle, which was a bolt action. There was a removable canvas cover over the center of the weapon.

"Is that a sniper rifle?"

Sinnott cocked his ear toward Harkins. "What's that, Lieutenant?"

"Is that a sniper rifle, sir?"

Sinnott stood for a long two or three seconds. It was too dark to see his eyes, but Harkins felt his stare. Then he lifted the weapon, pulled off the canvas cover, revealing a scope.

"Springfield '03, sniper configuration."

"Plan on doing some shooting out here?" Harkins asked.

"You never know," Sinnott said. "Hey, I brought you guys some coffee. Warm you up a bit."

Sinnott had an insulated metal bottle slung on a strap over his shoulder. "You men have canteen cups?" he asked the MPs. They pulled their cups out and Sinnott poured some coffee in each. Then he poured some into the thermos cap and offered it to Harkins. "You're all wet," he said.

Harkins took a few sips, then handed the cap to Wickman. When everyone had been served, Sinnott turned to Harkins.

"So what's your big tactical plan?"

Sinnott and Wickman set off to watch the trail that led from the back of the headmaster's cottage and through the faculty houses, while Harkins and the MPs kept an eye on the gate. Wickman, who had scouted the area earlier, took the lead when they started walking, Sinnott just behind. They used the wood line to cover their approach, emerging behind a storage shed at the edge of an athletic field. They hugged the little building, and by leaning out slightly they had a clear view of the main house, one room brightly lit, a door on the back wall.

"We don't actually know who is in there," Wickman whispered. "I'm worried we put Annie into a dangerous situation."

Sinnott pulled out a small telescope and trained it on the window. There were curtains, but he thought they were fairly sheer; if someone moved around in there, he'd see.

He heard a low rumble next to him, turned to see Wickman leaning forward, hands on his knees.

"I don't feel so good," he said.

"Come around back," Sinnott said, holding Wickman under one arm and moving him to the side of the shed away from the house. "Just sit here. I'll let you know what's going on."

Suddenly Wickman leaned over and vomited onto his shoes. His left leg buckled and he pitched forward, landing on hands and knees.

"Ohhhh."

Sinnott helped him to an upright sitting position, pushed his shoulders back to the wall.

"Don't lie on your back," he said. "You'll choke."

Wickman locked eyes with him, grabbed Sinnott's arm in a weak grip. "You did this."

"Shut the fuck up," Sinnott said. He stood and moved closer to the shed's corner so he could watch the house.

33

2 May 1944
2145 hours

Harkins had no sooner put the two MPs in position to watch the gate when one of them—he thought the kid's name was Grant—leaned over suddenly and vomited.

"Jesus," Tallent said.

"You going to be okay?" Harkins asked.

By way of an answer Grant fell to his knees, took off his helmet, and threw up again, an entire meal, maybe two, hurtling from his belly and splashing on the pine needles. Tallent moved next to Grant and put his hand on his friend's shoulder, careful to stay clear of whatever was going to come out next.

"I feel like shit," Grant said, then promptly threw up again.

"Did you drink any of the major's coffee?" Harkins asked Tallent.

"Nah. Smelled like horse piss, so I tossed it. You think that's what's making him sick?"

By way of an answer Harkins stuck three fingers down his own throat, a trick that had the desired effect. He hadn't eaten since breakfast, so the result wasn't as spectacular as Grant's effort and he only vomited up a dark liquid.

"Take him back to the vehicle and check on the guy with the jeeps," Harkins said. "If he had any of that coffee, tell him to vomit it up. Anyone who's sick, make sure he sits upright."

"Yes, sir," Tallent said. He helped Grant to his feet, draped one of the sick man's arms over his own shoulder, then started shuffling back toward the jeeps.

"Tallent," Harkins said. The GI looked over his shoulder.

"If Major Sinnott comes back to your location, keep an eye on him. He's dangerous."

"Dangerous how?" Tallent asked.

"He did this—poisoned us—to take the five of us out of the picture, so I'm not sure what he has in mind. Just be careful."

"Okay, Lieutenant," Tallent said. When he turned away, Harkins heard the private say, "Fucking officers."

Sinnott left the incapacitated Wickman by the shed and made his way to the back of the headmaster's cottage, crawling the last few yards until he reached the deep shadows of the shrubs that were hard against the wall. When he stood, he could see into the kitchen. It was empty.

He crouched back down, crawled to a corner by the south side yard. There were two windows in this wall, but no shrubs; if Harkins or any of the others were still upright and watching from the hill it was possible they would see him silhouetted against the whitewashed cottage. He trusted the ipecac he put in the coffee to do its work; what he couldn't be sure of was how much any of the men had drunk.

He made his way to the back wall again, crossed under the kitchen window to the north side of the house, nearest the dormitory and away from the hill where Harkins had positioned the MPs. No shrubs, but it was a bit darker here, the only light a rectangle shining from one of the cottage windows and some weak illumination from a few dorm windows about twenty yards away. Apparently the blackout wasn't enforced out here in the country.

Sinnott duckwalked along the side of the house until he was beside the window and could look in without any of the light spilling onto his face. Inside, crammed into a tight parlor, were Sechin and Stowe, and another man seated next to Stowe on a settee.

That must be Kerr, he thought. He vaguely remembered seeing him in a pub, talking to Harkins.

A movement close to the window startled him and he dropped quickly. When he chanced another look he saw a fourth person, a big man in a dark coat, much younger than Sechin, probably his bodyguard and driver. He, at least, would be armed.

Sinnott slumped to the ground, his back against the cottage wall.

His plan to use Kerr as leverage was, he realized, now too far-fetched. Stowe was cooperating with Harkins, and soon the bastard cop would be able to confirm that Kerr was turned. Sinnott couldn't use the knowledge about Kerr as leverage unless he was the only one who knew, or unless Harkins agreed to cooperate with him.

"Fat fucking chance of that," he whispered.

And then a new plan came to him. It wasn't Kerr who held Sinnott's life in his bloody hands; it was Sechin. The Soviet was the threat; he was the one who had to be taken out.

Major Richard Sinnott swiped his hand over his forehead. It had stopped raining, but his face was damp with sweat. He wished he had his flask, but he'd left it in his jeep, hidden in the woods off the main road.

A short distance away he could see the lights slowly winking out in the dormitory windows as the students ended a day, probably with some good Church of England prayers. Just a few yards away, tucked in the trees, he could see the outline of a sedan, probably the car Sechin used to come from London. Then he spied something else, a pole maybe, about halfway between the headmaster's cottage and the nearest corner of the dormitory building. There was something on top, but it was hidden in the darkness. He moved his head and line of sight to see the pole backlit by one of the windows. He had to get on his hands and knees to get a good angle, but finally it became clear what he was looking at.

It was a bell.

Eddie Harkins was a little woozy, but he managed to make it back to the gate. From there, he could look down on the headmaster's cottage and the dormitory, now almost completely dark.

Why did Sinnott want him, Wickman, and the MPs out of the picture? Sinnott would get part of the credit if they arrested Kerr.

Why go to the trouble of poisoning us?

Harkins had just decided to move to the cottage when he heard a car crunching up the gravel road. He stepped into the woodline, where he could see without being seen, watched the tiny slits of blackout lights approach. When the sedan moved up to the gate he recognized a long scrape on the rear side door.

It was Lowell's car. There was a passenger in the front seat, a man, judging by size.

Harkins stepped into the clearing and waved. Lowell put the car in park and she and Colonel Sergei Novikov got out.

"What the hell are you two doing here?" Harkins asked, trying to keep his voice low. He had no idea where Sinnott was, but he had a sharp mental picture of that sniper rifle.

"Lowell, I told you specifically to stay away. I *ordered* you."

"I must take responsibility, Lieutenant," Novikov said. "I needed to warn you, and Lowell was the only one who knew where you were."

"If you came to warn me that Major Sinnott has gone crazy, you're a little late. I think he slipped some kind of poison into the coffee he served us. Made us all sick."

"Where is he now?"

"He and Wickman went around behind that house," Harkins said, pointing. "We're pretty sure that one or two people from the American mission are in there, most likely meeting with one of your colleagues from the Soviet mission."

"Is Major Sinnott armed?"

"He's got a sniper rifle. Why would he bring a sniper rifle to make a straightforward arrest?"

Novikov took a few steps forward of the car so that he could see the entire bowl of the school grounds.

"I suspect he wants to kill my colleague, who is in that meeting. Colonel Sechin."

"Has this Sechin fellow been paying Sinnott? Because Sinnott is ripe for being recruited. He owes huge tabs at pubs all over central London."

"Major Sinnott is trying to cover his tracks; his connection to our embassy," Novikov said. "He killed Helen Batcheller."

"Jesus Christ!" Harkins said. It took him a dizzying moment to process what Novikov had just told him.

"How do you know that?" Harkins managed.

"Colonel Sechin told me. Sinnott killed her on Sechin's orders."

Harkins stood quietly for a moment, taking it all in.

"Now Sinnott wants to get rid of everyone who knows that," Harkins said.

"Possibly," Novikov said.

Harkins looked at Novikov. It was too dark to make out his features, except for the eye patch set against his pale skin.

"Why should I believe you?" he asked. "Why would you tell me that?"

"I do not want you to walk into an ambush, for one thing."

"And you need me to fulfill my end of the bargain. Get that report to Ike."

"We are soldiers," Novikov said. "We must put the mission first."

Harkins looked down at the headmaster's cottage, which was still peaceful.

"So Kerr *is* one of your assets."

"I do not know who is inside that building," Novikov said. "It's possible that the Americans in there have been turned. There is one asset Sechin described as very valuable. I don't know if this person is American or British, in the cottage or not, and Sechin only knows a code name, not the identity."

"Let's just drive down to the cottage, sir," Lowell said, stepping around to the passenger side of the car. "Make everyone come out. We can sort things out on the lawn."

Harkins looked at her. "Are you holding a pistol, Lowell?"

Lowell raised a big Webley revolver, which looked gigantic in her hand, and which was secured—as per regulation—by a cord clipped to her belt. Just so. "Yes, sir," she said. "In my induction training I qualified as an expert, too."

"You'll need to rest that thing on the hood of the car to hold it steady."

"What are you thinking, Lieutenant?" Novikov asked.

"Well, I came here to catch Kerr in a compromising position with one of your colleagues, and I thought Major Sinnott did, too. But now I'm thinking that Sinnott has something else in mind. Now that I know he's a murderer, well, things just got a little more sporty out here. And I have to get Annie Stowe out of there. She volunteered to help us catch Kerr, but she didn't bargain for this. Oh, and Wickman is out there somewhere with Sinnott."

"And Major Sinnott might take a shot at you, too," Lowell added.

Harkins looked at her.

"Well, he's bound to figure that everything is going to come out in the open," she said. "And you already have your suspicions about him."

"Thanks," he said.

"Just considering all the possibilities, sir."

Harkins looked out on the scene, wondered how his MPs were doing over by the vehicles. Tallent was young, but he seemed a competent sort. He could protect his buddies for a while longer.

Lowell stepped up beside Harkins. "Colonel Novikov is armed, too, sir. The three of us could drive right up to the cottage door. It would be like a raid. It would *be* a raid."

Harkins looked at her, her eyes reflecting what little light reached them from the valley below. She was egging him on.

"Quick's the word and sharp's the action," Lowell said.

"What the hell does that mean?"

"Well, I'm not really sure," she said, a little sheepish. "I read it in a story about Royal Navy boarding parties and I've always wanted to say it."

"Lowell," Harkins began.

And that's when the bell started ringing.

Sinnott gave six or seven sharp pulls on the bell cord, watched as lights came on in the dormitory. A small fire he'd set in the neat pile of kindling and firewood alongside one wall of the dorm was catching. Finally, it wasn't so much the bell or even visible flames that caused panic; it was the fact that the kids in this country retreat had already been traumatized by the bombings they'd endured in London, by their separation from home and family, by the turmoil that—for the younger ones at least—had been part of their entire lives.

They raced out in pajamas, in robes, wrapped in blankets, many of them barefoot and every single one of them screaming as if sheer volume could make them safe, could save them from this latest peril.

"Fucking perfect," Sinnott told himself. He unslung the sniper rifle and moved into the woodline in the gap between the headmaster's cottage and Sechin's sedan, a spot that allowed him to see both the front and back doors of the house where the Soviet was meeting. He stretched out on the wet grass, laid the crosshairs of the sight on the front door, and used the bolt action to put a round in the chamber.

The bodyguard came out first, pistol in his right hand. He took one look at the big lawn filling rapidly with screaming children, then disappeared around the far side of the house.

Sweeping the area, Sinnott thought.

As expected, the bodyguard appeared again behind the house, where he opened the back door, which was closest to their car. The man made

COMES THE WAR ★ 267

a *come here* motion with his hand, then turned to scan the area. Sechin came out next and the bodyguard took him by the arm, pulling the older man along, dodging running children, and headed straight at Sinnott.

Sinnott took a breath, exhaled halfway, squeezed the trigger.

The bodyguard's head snapped back; a spray of blood and brains caught the light spilling from the open door.

Sinnott pulled the bolt back and shoved it forward, pressed his eye to the scope. Sechin was on his hands and knees, looking around, trying to determine where the shot had come from. The panic in his herky-jerky movements was almost comical, like a Charlie Chaplin movie. Sinnott laughed deep in his throat and aimed for Sechin's head. Then the Soviet surprised him, leaping from a crouch and grabbing a child, a black-haired little girl whose legs kept moving even as the big man wrapped her in his arms, a squirming human shield.

"Stupid piece of shit," Sinnott muttered. The bullet would pass right through her and into Sechin. He took a breath, let it halfway out, squeezed the trigger again.

Harkins was running toward the cottage when he heard the first shot. He ducked, yanked his pistol from its holster. He made it to the circular drive where a dozen or so children milled about, most of them crying.

Where are the goddamn adults?

"Move up toward the gate, kids," he called, trying to sound reassuring, like he knew what he was doing.

He spotted a flickering light on the wall of the dormitory; there was a fire nearby. He ran to the corner of the headmaster's cottage, stepped around and saw flames along the wall of the dormitory. It looked like a woodpile; the building was not on fire yet. He looked back over his shoulder and saw some kids heading toward the gate, a few taller ones helping little ones.

Then the second shot, very close. Definitely a rifle.

Harkins pivoted, crouched, his weapon held in a two-handed grip in front of him. There was movement in the nearby woods.

He took a step forward. "Sinnott!" he yelled.

Harkins took another step, and that's when the girl crashed into him. She bounced off and hit the ground in a tangle of white nightgown and skinny legs, black hair loose and nearly covering her face. She was beyond terror, not making a sound other than her breathing. Harkins reached down to help her up, but she scrambled away from him, headed toward the other children who were making their way to the gate area.

"Harkins! Over here!"

Annie Stowe was crouched over a figure writhing on the ground. Harkins ran to her, squatted down. They were completely exposed here, lit by the flames from the nearby woodpile, and someone was out there beyond the light with a rifle. Sinnott, most likely.

"Stowe! Are you okay?" Harkins asked. He did a quick sweep of the area. Another figure crouched in the shrubs on the back wall of the house.

"That's Kerr over there," she said. "This is his contact. Name's Sechin."

"Who's that?" Harkins asked, pointing at another figure sprawled nearby.

"Bodyguard."

Harkins stayed low as he moved to check the bodyguard, who'd been shot in the forehead, a single neat entrance wound almost perfectly centered above his eyes. He picked up the man's pistol, an unfamiliar automatic, and shoved it in his belt.

"He's dead," Harkins told Stowe when he moved back. Sechin had been shot in the neck, and Stowe held a kitchen towel over the gash. There was a lot of blood, but it didn't look to be an arterial wound.

"Did you see the shooter?"

"No. Came from over there, though," she said, tilting her head toward the nearby woodline. Her eyes were wide—adrenaline—but otherwise she was perfectly calm. "Whoever he is, he's gone."

Harkins heard footsteps behind him, spun around and raised his pistol.

"Don't shoot! It's me, Tallent."

The MP ran up, pistol drawn. "I came down when I heard shooting."

Good man, Harkins thought. "Where are the others?"

"They're sick," Tallent said, squatting beside Harkins. "Afraid I'm your only backup."

"We're going after him," Harkins said. "After the shooter. We'll stick together, head back to the main road, see if we can flush him out."

"How do you know he came from the main road?" Stowe asked. "Couldn't he have come the other way?"

"His vehicle is up on the road," Harkins said. He looked at Stowe. "It's Major Sinnott."

"Oh," Stowe said. She looked down at Sechin. "He was working for them, then. For the Soviets. For this guy."

She looked up at Harkins, her voice leaden. "Did Sinnott kill Helen?"

"Yeah," Harkins said. "Looks that way."

A few yards away two teenage boys beat at the woodpile fire with shovels, pulling the burning logs loose, throwing dirt on the flames.

"Ready, Tallent?" Harkins asked. The GI nodded.

Harkins stood in a low crouch and started jogging for the woodline. He heard Stowe call after him, but he was already a few steps into the trees when he realized she was saying, "Leave me a gun!"

Sinnott backed away from the firelight, furious with himself. He had eluded dozens of Gestapo agents for months, had managed to escape even after the treachery of the turncoats, and now here he was, on the run from a goddamned street cop who should have been satisfied days ago when he arrested Cushing. A goddamn street cop that Sinnott had brought on board, a self-inflicted wound.

He backed up, his rifle held low in two hands, finger on the trigger guard. Harkins and that big MP were on their feet. They hadn't spotted him, but would begin a search any second. He wondered if the other MPs had also recovered, if they were waiting for him at his jeep. His brain flashed with only one imperative: he had to get away.

Off to his left he saw the Soviet staff car, parked in the wood line behind the headmaster's cottage. He ran to it, yanked open the door, shoved his rifle inside, and climbed in. The interior reeked of cigarettes and body odor. The black sedan was one of those built in a Ford-designed plant east of Moscow, and Sinnott recognized the controls. He searched with his foot for a starter switch; when he found it, the engine turned over, though it sounded tiny and ran rough.

Sechin and his driver had come in by a back road, but Sinnott figured that Harkins' MPs had closed that off, so he steered the car between two of the small houses and headed for the circular driveway that ran in front of all the buildings. The gravel path that climbed toward the gate was filled with dozens of children, some moving away, some heading back toward the dorm, many just standing around, unsure of what to do. Sinnott pressed the horn, scattering some of the kids. He rolled down the driver's window and leaned out.

"Clear out of the way, please! Watch out, now. Clear out."

He climbed the slight grade toward the gate and passed between the stone pillars that marked the entrance to the grounds. He was about to accelerate when he saw at least a half-dozen children sitting in the middle of the drive. He put the car in park and opened his door, one leg on the ground, the other still inside the car.

"I need you kids to move," he said, trying for stern but not threatening.

A couple of the kids, the bigger ones, began to stand.

"That's it," Sinnott said. "Good. Help the little ones there."

They're so fucking slow.

Two children, maybe a boy and a girl, sat in the roadway, crying and resisting the help from the older kids. The little boy sucked his thumb and yanked his shoulder away every time one of the bigger ones tried to get him to stand.

Sinnott looked behind him. He could now see a couple of adults in front of the headmaster's cottage. He couldn't tell if Harkins was among them, but he knew the cop was looking for him. Harkins had even called his name when he approached the cottage.

"Get out of the goddamn road!" Sinnott shouted. He reached into the car and leaned on the horn.

That's when he saw the staff car, a big Dodge sedan with a white star on the side.

It was off to his left, about thirty yards away, tucked among the trees, pointing toward him. It was too dark to see inside the sedan, but Sinnott heard the other car's engine start up.

"Get out of the way!" he shouted again, then jumped into the driver's seat. He put it in gear and began rolling forward. The little boy who'd been sucking his thumb was still in the road, legs splayed in front of him, his pajama pants dirty, one foot bare, the other wrapped in a sock. He turned his little moon face toward Sinnott and the dim blackout lights of the car. The road here was too narrow to go around, ditches on either side. Sinnott pressed the accelerator and told himself the car had enough ground clearance to roll over the boy.

The boy's face was just about to disappear below the car's hood when another kid snatched the little one out of his path. Sinnott looked to his right as he rolled past, saw the bigger boy—who was no more than ten—and the little guy stumble backward away from the road.

"That's the way to do it, kid!" Sinnott shouted, suddenly elated. He stomped the accelerator. "That's the way to move!"

Then the big Dodge staff car smashed into the driver's side door, sending Sinnott flying across the front seat, bouncing his head on the passenger side window hard enough to break the glass. The sedan had tumbled into the roadside ditch, rested there at a steep angle.

"What the *fuck*?"

Still conscious, Sinnott scrambled to get clear of the car through the passenger door, pulling his rifle out behind him. He stood, swiped at a veil of blood running over his eyes, shouldered his weapon and began firing, working the bolt action rapidly and putting three rounds into the driver's side door of the other car, which was open.

Sinnott squatted down to reload, pulling a five-round stripper clip from his breast pocket. He shoved the ammunition into the rifle and pushed the bolt forward, then crawled on elbows and knees toward the back of his car. He wanted to get an angle on whoever had rammed him. He was low to the ground when someone started shooting; he heard the bullets plinking into his smashed vehicle.

He rolled to his left—they thought he was cowering behind his car—and got a glimpse under the other vehicle, spotted someone's feet, and started shooting. The big .30-06 rounds would, he knew, punch through even the heavy steel body of the American sedan. He thought he saw someone fall, then realized there was a second shooter on the far side of the staff car. Two rounds sang over his head, much too high. He emptied the magazine, reloaded. Waited in sudden quiet.

Sinnott looked over his shoulder, toward the school. The children had all scattered and he could no longer see any adults in front of the headmaster's cottage, but he heard someone, possibly two people, hurrying through the woods toward him. He would take the staff car that had rammed him.

He lifted the rifle to his shoulder and walked around the Dodge. The back end was riddled with bullet holes, but he was sure it would still run. On the far side he found Harkins' driver crouching over a man sprawled on his back, both her hands pressing an ugly wound in the man's gut. As Sinnott drew closer, he realized the man was dressed in the uniform of a Soviet colonel. The man's one good eye rolled toward Sinnott, who said, "Who the fuck are you?"

The straight-line distance from the headmaster's cottage to the gate was less than a hundred yards, but Harkins and Tallent kept to the trees as they moved toward the sound of the gunfight. At one point, Harkins patted his belt for the Russian pistol, but it was gone.

"Shit!"

Tallent ran into him, the two of them stumbled. He turned to see the kid picking himself up, lip bloody where he'd broken his fall with his face. The MP's eyes were big as dinner plates. "You with me?" Harkins asked.

"Yes, sir!"

Up ahead, the shooting had stopped. Harkins slowed, trying to see through the trees, get a picture of what was happening. He moved in a crouch, spotted Lowell's staff car, its front end buried in the side of a smaller black sedan. He slid to his left, behind Lowell's car, looking for an angle that would let him see the other side, and that's when Sinnott, visible for just a second over the hood of the sedan, shot him.

Harkins felt something pluck at his shirt, then the worst bee sting of his life along his right shoulder blade where the bullet grazed him. He dove forward and rolled to his left, came up with his pistol leveled at the car, but no target.

"Sinnott!" he yelled. "There's no getting out of here. I know about Batcheller. I know about you and the Soviets. It's time to give up."

Harkins looked left and right. There was no sign of Tallent. He looked at the sedan over his gunsight, maybe fifty feet away.

"Sinnott!" he yelled again.

Harkins shot at the rear wheels of the sedan, kept shooting until he saw the car list to the right where he'd hit at least one of the tires.

"We disabled your jeep, too," Harkins called. "There's no way out."

Harkins had lost count of how many rounds he had fired. There was still a bullet in the chamber, because the slide was in place. But was it his last round? He reached to his belt and the canvas ammunition pouch there. It was empty. His spare magazine had fallen out somewhere.

"Shit!"

He rolled onto his back, his wounded right shoulder feeling like he'd landed on hot coals.

He ejected the magazine from the pistol. It was empty. He had one shot.

"Harkins!" Sinnott called.

Harkins turned onto his stomach. Incredibly, Sinnott came out from behind the cover of the sedan, walking toward him. Harkins' first thought was that he was going to surrender, but he still carried the rifle, butt tucked into his shoulder in a firing position. He was smiling.

"Is that your magazine in your hand?" he asked, still advancing. "You're out of ammo? You dumb mick!"

Sinnott raised the rifle to his shoulder and Harkins lifted his weapon, with its last round. It was a long shot for a pistol, but Harkins—out of options—aimed for center of Sinnott's chest, and that's when the right side of Sinnott's head ballooned outward in a wet spray. Private First Class Tallent moved toward his target, pistol steady, but Sinnott was dead.

Harkins lowered his face into the dirt.

"You okay, Lieutenant?" Tallent called, voice high pitched.

"Yeah," Harkins said. "I'm okay."

"I had to shoot him, didn't I? I mean, he was coming right at you with that rifle in a firing position. You saw it, right?"

Harkins pushed himself up to all fours. He felt strangely calm, though he had pissed himself at some point.

"It was a clean shoot, Tallent. You saved my life," Harkins said.

Tallent pulled Sinnott's rifle away from the corpse as Harkins circled the sedan. He found Colonel Novikov on the far side, bleeding from a massive wound in his stomach. Pamela Lowell knelt beside him, her car's tiny first-aid kit open beside her. Her hands were shaking as she unwrapped a gauze that was much too small to do anything for the Soviet officer, who was clearly dying.

"I'm sorry, sir. I ran out of ammunition," she said. Her voice was steady, though tears cut tracks through forest-floor dirt on her face.

"I did, too," Harkins said.

Tallent came up beside them, Sinnott's rifle in his hand, his own pistol holstered again.

Harkins knelt beside Novikov, whose one eye was glassy.

"Batcheller threatened to reveal the names of Sechin's assets," Novikov whispered.

"I figured," Harkins said. "Thanks for coming out to warn me."

He took Novikov's hand.

"The pilot you arrested is innocent."

"I'll see that he's cleared," Harkins said.

Novikov seemed to relax. Lowell pressed the tiny gauze into the bloody mess of his midsection. She was still crying, but her hands had stopped shaking.

Harkins leaned close to Novikov. "Who are the other assets in the U.S. mission?" he asked.

Harkins couldn't be sure, since they sat in only the dim, reflected light from the buildings below, but he thought Novikov smiled.

"Oh, Lieutenant," he said. "I am still a patriot."

Then he died.

Harkins stood, helped Lowell to her feet.

"Harkins!"

It was Annie Stowe, walking up the hill, one hand under the right arm of the wounded Soviet spymaster, Sechin. The older man held a blood-soaked rag to his neck with his left hand. His shirt front was a dark blotch.

"I have a first-aid kit here," Lowell said.

"I told you to leave me a gun!" Stowe, clearly angry, shouted at Harkins.

"I think we're okay now," Harkins answered.

"Almost," Stowe said. She pushed Sechin hard, and the big man, weak from blood loss, stumbled, landing in a sitting position. Stowe snatched the rifle from Tallent, yanked the bolt back and shoved it forward, then aimed it at Sechin's forehead from a foot away.

The colonel leaned back, and in a tone that sounded part statement, part question, he said, "Rodya," just before she pulled the trigger.

34

4 May 1944
1300 hours

Eddie Harkins brought Stowe back to OSS headquarters in handcuffs and under arrest for the murder of a Soviet colonel. When he saw her again a day later, heading into a conference room with Colonel Haskell, she was decidedly not anyone's prisoner. In fact, Harkins, who was waiting in the hallway for a chance to talk to Haskell, heard the head of OSS London greet her by her first name. She was in there for almost an hour while Harkins sat outside, flipping through his well-worn notebooks.

He had found Wickman dazed but finally unharmed, right where Sinnott had abandoned him on the school grounds. The doc said he and the poisoned MPs would be fine with some rest.

It had taken a little longer to find Kerr, who was walking at dawn along one of the country roads near the Berkhamsted School when Tallent and another MP picked him up. Exhausted, wet, and hungry from an unaccustomed night outdoors, he had, Tallent said, climbed into the jeep happily, like he'd been rescued from a shipwreck. Harkins got the diplomat some breakfast and dry clothes, then questioned him for several hours about the meeting with Sechin.

Stowe, on the other hand, had been hustled off by Haskell to some unknown location, until Harkins was summoned to Haskell's office and his first meeting with Annie since the shooting.

"Harkins."

Harkins looked up from his notes to see the young colonel. He stood. "Sir."

Haskell looked like he hadn't slept since the last time Harkins saw him, which made Harkins wonder how many other officers—especially the planning staffs—would go into the invasion already worn out.

"You've done some good work here," Haskell said, shaking Harkins' hand. The motion made Harkins' wounded right shoulder bark in pain.

"I appreciate all your efforts, and I can see why Colonel Meigs was so keen to recommend you to us."

"Thank you, sir," Harkins said, not at all grateful.

"I'm afraid that, from here on out, this case isn't going to be as straightforward as you might expect."

Harkins had no idea what that meant, so he simply said, "Okay."

"I'm going to give you thirty minutes with her," Haskell said. "But I wanted to let you know, before you go in, that I'm completely satisfied with her explanations and with the outcome of this case."

"Okay, sir."

"Now, what's happening with this Major Cushing?"

"Major Adams, he's with SHAEF JAG, got the charges dropped. Even the ridiculous one about mishandling secret documents."

"Good," Haskell said. "I'm glad to hear it. That poor guy has been through a lot. I hope he comes out all right in the end."

Harkins thought about Cushing, about the airmen he'd met out in East Anglia. Who among them would ever be all right again?

"Anyway," Haskell said, motioning with his hand to the open office door. "Thirty minutes. Then I need her." He turned as if to walk away, then thought of something and turned back.

"By the way, the navy put you in for an award. A Silver Star, actually. They wrote up a nice citation about you rescuing a bunch of sailors who were trapped when that LST started to go down. Sounded like things got pretty lively out there."

Harkins pictured the ensign named Cedrick, who abandoned ship and never lost his eyeglasses. He thought about the sailor who now had a stump where his leg had been, about the men he'd helped save and all those bodies lined up in the morgue. He thought about Staff Sergeant Jesus Cortizo, whom Harkins had helped drown. He wondered if, some-day, he'd be able to look back on this and think it was all worth it, but he was not hopeful.

"Yes, sir."

"Trouble is, that whole fiasco is hush-hush. No reports on it are going out, at least not yet. So, obviously, we can't give you a medal for something that never happened. I'll make sure you get the write-up they did. The sensitive stuff will be redacted, but you might like it for your scrapbook. Too bad, really. A Silver Star would have gotten you home quicker after the war, I imagine."

"Somebody told me it's bad luck to think too much about what hap-pens after the war."

Haskell grunted. "Hunh." Then he turned and walked away, stooped as an old man.

Harkins pushed the door open and stepped into the big room. Stowe sat in a chair, an elbow resting on one of the conference tables arranged along the walls. There was a chair just in front of her, which she pushed toward him with her foot. "Have a seat."

"How you doing, Annie?"

"Pretty good, all things considered."

Harkins sat in the offered chair.

"This is not how I saw this interview going," Harkins said.

"I imagine your chat with Kerr was a little more—what's the word? Adversarial?"

At least the dynamics were out in the open. He had no power, no leverage. Harkins was here, he surmised, because Haskell thought he should be allowed to satisfy his curiosity.

"Kerr told me that he didn't set up that meeting with Sechin," Harkins said. "You did."

Stowe's tiny smile reminded Harkins of the Mona Lisa. She offered nothing.

"He was just your stooge. You were behind almost everything that happened. In fact, everything you did was to point us at Kerr and away from you. You sent me out to meet that navy lieutenant, Payne, because you knew he didn't like Kerr and would most likely talk bad about him."

Stowe leaned forward, reached for an ashtray on the table and dragged it toward her. She pulled a cigarette from a pack on the table, held the package out to Harkins.

"No, thanks."

She took her time lighting it, then inhaled a long drag and let blue smoke drift from her mouth.

"I suppose I should thank you," she said. "If it wasn't for you, I never would have found out who killed my Helen."

Harkins sat, completely still.

"I loved her, you know."

He nodded. After a few seconds of silence, he said, "It was never about that report, was it?"

"Never," she said. "Helen was an idealist at heart. All that stuff with the Katyn Forest, all the other shit the Soviets did, it really made her angry."

"So she threatened to expose Soviet moles in the embassy, in the OSS?" Harkins asked.

"Only once, when she was in her cups," Stowe said. "Trouble is, the only one she knew of for sure was Kerr. She didn't know about Sinnott."

"She didn't know about you," Harkins said. "That you were Rodya."

Stowe nodded. "She had no idea, but once word got back to Sechin that she was a threat to his operation, to this mysterious Rodya whose real identity he didn't know, well, that's when he put things in motion. Had her killed."

The door opened, and an American sergeant and a woman in civilian clothes stepped inside, kissing and giggling until they saw Harkins and Stowe. The man hid his face, but the woman said, "Sorry." A British accent. Then the pair scooted back into the hallway.

"Kind of ironic, isn't it?" Stowe said. "If Rodya—if I—hadn't been Sechin's most important asset, nothing would have happened to Helen."

"Kerr wasn't important enough for him to worry about?"

She shook her head. "Not even close."

"What happens now?" Harkins asked.

Stowe was staring at the burning end of the cigarette held in her fingers.

"It's up to Haskell," she said. She looked up, met Harkins' eyes. "I have some ideas, but finally it's up to him."

35

Harkins found Wickman in Sinnott's former office. He had moved out of his broom closet and into the bigger space without asking anyone's permission, and he now wore the silver bars of a captain.

"Your promotion came through?"

"The real McCoy this time," Wickman said.

"Feel like a walk?" Harkins asked. "It's finally a sunny day."

"Sure," Wickman said. The two officers left Grosvenor Street, headed east and a bit south toward Trafalgar Square. The sidewalks were full of men and women in uniform, drawn outside by the spring temperatures and the unfamiliar golden disc in the sky.

"Funny," Wickman said, "but I miss L.A. more on these rare sunny days than on the rainy ones."

They paused where Pall Mall reached the National Gallery, which had been emptied of its most valuable pieces years before when a German invasion seemed imminent. The four giant lions reclined in their places, unperturbed, while the base of Nelson's column was wrapped in a banner exhorting Londoners to BUY NATIONAL WAR BONDS.

They found a bench in a sunny spot on the side of the museum, and Harkins filled Wickman in on his interviews with Stowe and Haskell.

"What do you think she meant by that?" Wickman asked. "That it's up to Haskell?"

"Looks to me like she's back at her old job."

"So she got a pass on all that crap with the Soviets? No charges for working with them as Rodya? For whatever favors she did for them before all this blew up? No charges for killing that Soviet colonel?"

"Doesn't look like it," Harkins said. "If I had to guess, I'd say she's become even more valuable to the Allies. I think she's a double agent. The new Soviet spymaster is already in London, and as far as anyone can tell, he trusts the information she—Rodya—passes along. Which is, of course, only what the OSS wants her to pass along. The Soviets think she's helping them break American and British codes."

"I figured her for a code-breaker, given the math background," Wickman said. He shook his head in disbelief. "How about that, huh?"

"The Soviet Embassy made some inquiries about their two missing colonels and the bodyguard, but Haskell made sure all evidence of them being at the Berkhamsted School just disappeared."

"He looks like a stand-up guy, like a boy scout with a little bit of gray hair," Wickman said. "Turns out he's a sneaky SOB."

"Speaking of Haskell," Harkins said, "the CID finally came around, two investigators in civvies. None too happy that their agency had been cut out from the beginning. Haskell blamed it all on Sinnott."

"Who is—conveniently—dead."

The two men started back toward Grosvenor Street and OSS head-quarters, stopping in St. James Square to buy chips from a street vendor. The man handed each of them a cone made from newspaper, the grease staining the headlines. Harkins read as he ate.

"Look at this," he said to Wickman. "De Gaulle is forming a new government-in-exile, and he's invited the Communists to participate."

"I thought that's why Churchill didn't trust de Gaulle, because he was going to welcome Communists to join his so-called Free French."

Harkins ate another handful of chips. "Hard to know who we should trust these days, huh?"

"That's for sure," Wickman said. "I heard that lawyer, Gefner, is getting hauled in front of some sort of ethics board."

"Good," Harkins said. "That'll save me from having to track him down to beat his ass."

Wickman finished his chips and wiped his fingers on a handkerchief. "Did you ever get the second copy of Batcheller's report from Novikov?" he asked.

"Yeah. He brought it to that school; it was in the car. Lowell handed it to me. Next afternoon I took it down to Bushy Park, where the main planning cells are. Told my story to a lieutenant, then a captain, then a major; then they had me sit there for another couple of hours until this lieutenant colonel came out to give it a quick read. Then I waited around for some civilian intelligence guy to talk to me."

"So were they amazed?"

Harkins laughed. "Hardly. Guy says Batcheller came up with a pretty clever approach—analyzing the serial numbers—but that the situation with the air assets had already been resolved. I asked him how it came out and he just gave me a funny look."

"Like he wasn't going to tell you anything."

"Exactly," Harkins said. "I told him that people died getting that report put together and delivered."

"What did he say to that?"

"He said, 'What can I tell you, Lieutenant? Lot of people get killed every day. Maybe it'll all be over soon.'"

"That's it?" Wickman asked. "Maybe it'll all be over soon? What the hell kind of answer is that?"

"SNAFU," Harkins said.

They crossed Piccadilly, into the neighborhood by the Royal Academy of Arts. One entire block sat empty, whatever building that had been there before removed as if erased, every bit of rubble swept away.

"I'm seeing Beverly tonight," Wickman said.

"Good for you! You got up the nerve to ask her out, huh?"

"She asked me, actually," Wickman said, looking both pleased and more than a bit surprised. "And I'm really glad she did. No telling how long it would have taken me.

"Oh," Wickman said, reaching into a pocket inside his jacket for a folded sheet of paper. "The navy wrote you up for an award. Pretty impressive, too. You really did all this stuff on that LST?"

"If I had stopped to think about what was happening, I would have been the first one off the ship."

If I'd been in the water, Harkins thought, *maybe I could have saved Cortizo, instead of shoving him in to drown. Alone.*

"Haskell told you they can't actually go through with the award, since—officially—Operation Tiger never happened."

"Yeah, he told me. The ultimate irony," Harkins said. "Maybe the only straightforward, selfless thing I've done in the whole friggin' war so far."

"Well, you get to keep this swell-looking piece of paper to show your grandkids," Wickman said, handing over the printed citation.

When they turned onto Grosvenor Street, Wickman saw the staff car first.

"Looks like young Lowell has a new set of wheels."

The driver stood by a new car in front of the headquarters building. Lowell saluted as the two officers approached.

"Good afternoon, gentlemen," she said.

"Lowell, I'm surprised you're willing to be anywhere near the two of us," Wickman said. "We haven't exactly been your good luck charms lately."

"Oh, I just came by to tell you that I'll be moving on," she said.

"I see," Wickman said. "Can't say I blame you."

He turned to Harkins. "You should take a pass for the next seventy-two hours," Wickman said. "Come and see me when you're back and we'll talk about what's next for you."

"Great," Harkins said, saluting. "Appreciate the pass."

Wickman returned the salute, started up the stairs, then stopped and turned around.

"You've done a helluva job, Lowell," he said. "It's been a pleasure working with you."

"Thank you, sir," she said. When Wickman went inside, she turned to Harkins. "So where will you go on your pass?"

"I was thinking of a nice cruise on the English Channel."

Lowell laughed with her head thrown back, which made her look even more like Harkins' kid sister. Homesickness sat inside his chest like an empty jar.

"Are you staying here with the ATS and good ol' Corporal Moore?"

"Corporal Moore has been keeping her distance from me lately."

"Oh?"

"One could say we came to an understanding. But I still put in for a transfer. Just got the approval this morning."

"Where you headed?" Harkins asked.

"Alexandria, if you can believe that."

"Egypt! That's quite a ways from London. What will you do there?"

"I volunteered for a program in which I'll be trained as a nurse. I'll start in a hospital for prisoners. Germans."

"Looking to assuage your conscience?" Harkins asked.

"Something like that, I suppose, though I found out I am definitely not a pacifist."

"Oh?"

"I only stopped firing at Major Sinnott when I ran out of ammunition."

"Nothing like having someone shoot at you to test your commitment as a conscientious objector."

"Besides," Lowell said. "I think that after all this is over there'll be plenty of us with things weighing on our consciences."

An MP in a white helmet approached, saluted Harkins.

"This your car, Lieutenant?"

"Not anymore," Harkins said.

"I was just getting ready to move," Lowell answered, stepping to the driver's side door.

The MP walked away, and Lowell said, "If we each write to Beverly, send her updates on our addresses, we'll be able to track one another down. Stay in touch."

"That's a good idea," Harkins said. "I'd like that."

"Well," Lowell said.

"Would it be okay if I gave you a hug?" Harkins asked.

Lowell didn't answer, but took a strong step forward and wrapped her arms tightly around Harkins' chest, squeezing his battered ribs and the bandaged wound on his shoulder. He grunted in pain.

Lowell jumped back. "I'm so sorry!" she said. "I forgot about your injuries."

"It's okay," Harkins said, his jaw clenched.

She stepped close again, raised up on her toes, and kissed him on the cheek.

"Thank you for everything, sir. I hope I'm not being presumptuous when I say I feel good about whatever contribution I was able to make."

"You were a big help, Lowell, and I enjoyed working with you," Harkins said. "Promise you'll be careful in your next assignment. And don't let any bullying corporals push you around."

"Oh, that part of my life is over."

She pulled away from the curb and Harkins waved, but she had her eyes on the traffic and did not see his gesture.

Harkins walked to the Grosvenor Hotel and its massive American mess, where he'd eaten with Wickman in his first few hours in London. Since he was on pass and not in any hurry, he struck up a conversation with two other lieutenants who shared his table. When he mentioned that he was from Philadelphia, one of the men—Harkins thought his name was Durbinski—mentioned that he'd gone to school nearby.

"Where was that?" Harkins asked.

"Princeton," Durbinski said, mopping his plate with a slice of bread.

"What'd you study?"

Durbinski shoved the bread into his mouth, used the first two fingers of his right hand to wipe gravy from his bottom lip.

"Russian literature," Durbinski said when he'd finished chewing.

"You working with the Soviets?" Harkins asked.

Durbinski just raised his eyebrows. He wasn't about to say.

"Sorry," Harkins said. "I was a cop; I have a habit of asking questions like that. Should probably shake it around here."

"Probably."

"I do have another question you might help me with. You ever hear the name Rodya?"

"Raskolnikov," Durbinski said.

"No, I think it's Rodya."

"I heard you. Rodya is the pet name of a character named Raskolnikov, from Dostoyevsky's *Crime and Punishment*. His mother calls him Rodya. Any Russian school student would know that."

"What's he like?" Harkins asked. "The character, I mean."

"Well, completely amoral, for one thing. Thinks he's exceptional, above the law. Why do you ask?"

"Oh, the name just came up, that's all."

Durbinski stood, picked up his tray of dirty dishes. "Well, if you run into anyone with that name, I'd say you should keep your distance."

"Thanks for the tip," Harkins said.

He watched Durbinski wade through the crowd to the exit, then he followed. When he left the hotel, it was raining hard, a proper downpour. Maybe a drought breaker instead of an annoying drizzle or omnipresent fog. He picked up a *Stars and Stripes* from the hotel lobby and held it over his head as he jogged back to OSS headquarters. By the time he got there both the newspaper and his uniform were soaked.

He stood on the top step and looked out over sidewalks crowded with men and women in uniform, hurrying on their varied missions. The whole city, probably the whole island, hummed with a palpable energy, and soon all that energy would transform into movement and violence, a comet burning toward France. He would get dragged along with it, of course, which was all right with him. He would have a role to play, even though he wasn't sure, at this moment, what that would be. He only hoped his path eventually led back home.

SUPREME HEADQUARTERS, ALLIED EXPEDITIONARY FORCES

CITATION

For conspicuous gallantry in action with the enemy off the coast of southern England, on ▮▮▮▮▮▮▮▮▮ *, the SILVER STAR is hereby awarded to First Lieutenant Bernard Edward Harkins, Army of the United States, who, at great personal risk to himself, rescued five men from a burning and sinking ship.*

LST ▮▮ *part of Operation* ▮▮▮▮ *was on fire and in imminent danger of sudden capsizing after being struck by* ▮▮▮▮▮▮▮▮▮ *when Lieutenant Harkins spotted a group of sailors and a soldier trapped behind a bent watertight door. Refusing an opportunity to save himself by abandoning ship, Lieutenant Harkins made his way toward the men across the slanting deck, moving closer to the flames and into seawater covered in highly combustible fuel oil. When he could not get the hatch open, he climbed back up the deck to secure a tool, which he used to shatter the stuck dogs, thus freeing at least five men inside from certain death. Presented with another opportunity to save himself, Lieutenant Harkins instead entered the compartment, which was rapidly filling with water, and helped another junior officer extricate a sailor whose leg had been severed. Lieutenant Harkins and the ensign got the unconscious wounded man overboard, swimming and towing him to safety until they were rescued by a U.S. Coast Guard craft.*

Lieutenant Harkins' quick thinking and resolute behavior in the face of grave danger resulted in the rescue of five men who most certainly would have been lost with the ship. His actions reflect great credit upon himself, the Military Police Corps and the armed forces of the United States.

AUTHOR'S NOTE
AND ACKNOWLEDGMENTS

"All fiction arises from conflict," a professor once told me. That has stuck with me because I find it to be true.

The conflict that formed the original center of this story for me was the tension between the claims of the U.S. Eighth Air Force "bomber boys" that they could win the war singlehandedly through strategic bombing of Germany and Eisenhower's demands that he control all air assets for the invasion of the continent. There really were arguments at the general officer level and Eisenhower did threaten to "go home" if he didn't get the resources he thought essential to the success of Operation Overlord. (See Lynne Olson's brilliant *Citizens of London* and *Last Hope Island* for more, as well as Stephen Ambrose's *D-Day*.)

During the time this debate was going on, there was no hard proof that the bombers were reducing German war production, just the oft-stated claims of air force commanders. After the war, the U.S. Strategic Bombing Survey, which measured the effects of the air campaign, found that although bombing did hamper the German war effort, it achieved nowhere near the results claimed by the Eighth Air Force. Then, in my research, I ran across this fascinating tidbit: an economist with the OSS did a postwar analysis of the serial numbers of German war equipment destroyed or captured on the western front and found that vehicle production, in particular, had *increased* during the period that the U.S. Army Air Forces claimed that Germany was on the brink of collapse.

From there it was only a short leap to the question, "What if that information had been available before D-Day? Who would have an agenda around its use or suppression?" Soon my doodling was swirling with interested and competing parties, from Soviet spymasters to American turncoats to my overworked protagonist.

There are other places in the novel where fiction intersects with history. Colonel Joseph F. Haskell, West Point Class of 1930, ran the Jedburgh program—which put Allied operatives on the ground in occupied France—out of the London office of the OSS. Haskell's father had served with OSS chief "Wild Bill" Donovan in the First World War, and Haskell's older brother John also served in the OSS. By all accounts Joe, a former cavalry officer, was both efficient and likable, and he did have contacts that helped the OSS secure air assets.

The 787th Squadron of the Eighth Air Force flew B-24 Liberators, not the B-17 Flying Fortress. Both bombers had gunners whose job was to engage enemy fighters that approached from below the aircraft, but it was the peculiar design of the B-17 ball turret that sometimes left gunners trapped when the mechanism to raise and lower the plexiglass ball was damaged. An aircraft that lost control of its landing gear was forced to do a belly landing; I combined the two circumstances.

The characters use terms that were common, especially among American GIs, in describing the confusion and inefficiency of the vast military bureaucracy that had grown up over just a few years and consisted mostly of amateurs. FUBAR meant "Fucked Up Beyond All Recognition"; SNAFU meant "Situation Normal: All Fucked Up."

I used that state of confusion to justify a bit of poetic license: the U.S. Army's Criminal Investigation Division, CID, would likely have investigated the murder of an American civilian and would have worked alongside London police. It is true, however, that CID only became operational in January 1944; I thought it plausible that pushy OSS agents could have taken a role. I confess to playing fast and loose with rules governing courts-martial.

The spring of 1944 did see an increase in Luftwaffe air raids, though the final attack of the so-called Baby Blitz occurred on the night of 18–19 April 1944, about thirty hours before the beginning of this story.

Operation Tiger was a large-scale rehearsal conducted by the Allies along the Devon coast on beaches where the landing conditions were similar to those the invaders would find in Normandy. In a cascading series of errors, Royal Navy ships protecting the landing craft were off station or monitoring the wrong radio frequencies. A few fast-moving German *schnellboot* (literally: fast boat) armed with torpedoes found the fleet in the early morning darkness of 28 April 1944 and attacked. Three LSTs were hit, two of them sank quickly and one, its stern heavily damaged, limped to shore. Many soldiers and sailors were killed outright; others would die of hypothermia in the chilly waters. Some GIs who had been issued life belts were not trained in their use; some of those men drowned because they wore the belts incorrectly. In all, more than seven hundred soldiers and sailors lost their lives.

The Operation Tiger disaster, also called Slapton Sands for the stretch of beach, was kept secret until after the successful invasion of the continent. Unfortunately, there have been a few ill-considered reports (one by the usually reliable NPR) that the secret was kept for decades after the war. In fact, articles about the disaster appeared later in the summer of 1944. Families were told that their loved ones died in a training accident. There is a memorial on the beach, consisting of a U.S. Sherman tank dredged from the Channel by a British civilian.

The Polish 303 Squadron was made up of aviators who, after the collapse of their country, made their way to England to join the fight against the Nazis. They amassed a remarkable fighting record; the Royal Air

Force gave them credit for helping save Britain in those critical 1940 air battles, at a time when Great Britain was the last holdout against Hitler. After the war, these Polish aviators were excluded from official victory celebrations by the same people they had helped save. Churchill's government slighted them so as not to offend Stalin, who had no intention of returning Poland to the Poles.

The massacre of Polish soldiers and civilians by the Soviets at the Katyn Forest took place just as the fictional Lieutenant Wronecki maintains. German propaganda blamed the Soviets in order to drive a wedge between Stalin and the other allies; their efforts failed, but for once the Nazis were telling the truth.

I owe special thanks to my friend Jeff Holland, native of Manchester, England, whose suggestions on dialogue helped ensure that the British characters spoke English, not American English; or worse, an American writer's idea of how British people sound.

Thanks, too, to Rob Cannon, U.S. Naval Academy Class of 1990, whose navy training included firefighting and damage control, and who later served twenty-two years in the Charlotte, North Carolina, Fire Department. Rob helped me understand and imagine the terror of a shipboard fire.

Thanks to Elena Stokes and Brianna Robinson of Wunderkind PR, who helped me come to grips with marketing in the digital age.

Thanks to Robin Michener Nathan, who, in spite of evidence to the contrary, still has faith that I can handle social media.

Thanks to Kristin Sevick and the indefatigable team at Forge, who have built a community with their writers and who are living proof that work can be fun.

Thanks to Matt Bialer of Sanford J. Greenburger Associates, for his patience, guidance, and grit in the face of personal adversity.

And, as always, thanks to my wife, Marcia Noa. As I finished chapters I read them to her at our kitchen island. She always made great suggestions, confessed her love for various characters, her skepticism at some plot points (which did not survive revision), and who asked the most important, encouraging question, "What happens next?"

Ed Ruggero
Lewes, Delaware
March 2020